Sense and Second-Degree Murder

A JANE AUSTEN MURDER MYSTERY

Also by Tirzah Price

Pride and Premeditation

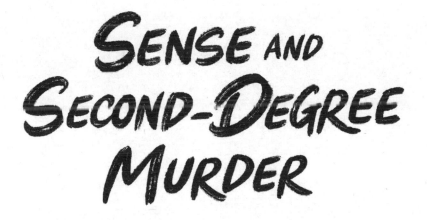

SENSE AND SECOND-DEGREE MURDER

A JANE AUSTEN MURDER MYSTERY

TIRZAH PRICE

HARPER TEEN
An Imprint of HarperCollinsPublishers

HarperTeen is an imprint of HarperCollins Publishers.

Sense and Second-Degree Murder
Copyright © 2022 by HarperCollins Publishers
All rights reserved. Printed in the United States of America.
No part of this book may be used or reproduced in any manner whatsoever without written permission except in the case of brief quotations embodied in critical articles and reviews. For information address HarperCollins Children's Books, a division of HarperCollins Publishers, 195 Broadway, New York, NY 10007.
www.epicreads.com

ISBN 978-0-06-288983-6

Typography by Corina Lupp
22 23 24 25 26   PC/LSCH   10 9 8 7 6 5 4 3 2 1
❖
First Edition

To all of the friends
who taught me the meaning of sisterhood.

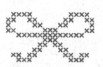

"I wish, as well as everybody else, to be perfectly happy; but, like everybody else, it must be in my own way."

—*Sense and Sensibility*
by Jane Austen

"Crime is terribly revealing. Try and vary your methods as you will, your tastes, your habits, your attitude of mind, and your soul is revealed by your actions."

—*And Then There Were None*
by Agatha Christie

ONE

*In Which the Dashwood Sisters' Lives
Are Forever Changed*

ON THE DAY THAT her life was to change forever, Elinor Dashwood awoke late with a wild hope fluttering in her rib cage. But, being the sensible sort, she kept it hidden as she rose, dressed, and joined her family for breakfast, stifling a yawn as she sat down at the table. It was a sunlit, cheerful morning, but her mind was still tucked between the pages of the book she'd stayed up far too late reading, so she didn't notice her younger sister's arched brow.

"You look as though you've been trampled by a horse," Marianne announced with her usual upbeat honesty.

"Marianne!" their mother admonished as Margaret, the youngest Dashwood, giggled. "That's hardly kind. Although, Elinor dear, you do look a little . . . peaked."

"I feel quite well," Elinor assured her mother and sisters, and attempted to look more alert by sitting up even straighter. "I was reading the most riveting study about oxygen. Did you know that a French chemist discovered that in order for combustion to occur, oxygen is essential?"

Mrs. Dashwood gave an uncertain smile, as she always did when Elinor began speaking of the sciences. But Margaret drew in an excited gasp. "Is combustion related to the smoke bombs you promised you'd make me?"

"In a way," Elinor said, helping herself to a piece of toast. "For smoke bombs to work properly, something needs to be lit with fire, and fire can't occur without oxygen, which is in the air all around us."

Marianne looked around, as if she could spot the oxygen lurking in the corner of the room, like dust motes. Not that there would be dust motes in the Dashwoods' breakfast room— the staff kept the place in impeccable order.

"You can't see it, Marianne," Elinor said with a little laugh. "It's invisible air—gas."

"It sounds unpleasant," Marianne said as assuredly as if she were proclaiming a new recipe wasn't to her taste.

"That's quite enough talk of gas and combustion at the breakfast table, girls," Mrs. Dashwood said. She knew from experience that when Elinor began speaking of science, and Margaret took an interest in various uses for gunpowder, Marianne was surely just a moment away from adding her thoughts about crime, and then a perfectly nice breakfast would take a darker turn. "Where's your father? I'm of half a mind to have Stewart fetch him."

The butler hovered by the door, ready to do Mrs. Dashwood's bidding.

"I think Father has a new case," Marianne informed the table. As the Dashwood sister most interested in the family business—Mr. Dashwood was the proprietor and chief investigator of Norland and Co.—she was privy to such knowledge. "He probably fell asleep at his desk again."

Mrs. Dashwood tsked. "That man will work himself to death, and he already has a cold."

Before Stewart could be dispensed for the task, Elinor leapt up. "I'll fetch him. He won't be able to say no or ask Stewart to bring in a breakfast tray if I tell him he's missing a perfectly nice meal with his family."

"I'll go," Marianne said, also standing. "You've hardly eaten a thing, and I was going to ask him about the case—"

"I'm already up," Elinor said, waving a carefree hand at her younger sister. It was a gesture that she knew for a fact infuriated Marianne, and yet what was the point of being the oldest if Elinor couldn't pull rank at times?

Besides, she knew that Father would be curious to know what she thought of Antoine Lavoisier's scientific discoveries, and he would not be shocked to learn that Lavoisier had met his fate at the guillotine in the French Revolution—and such talk was hardly acceptable in Mother's perspective.

And then there was the matter of Elinor's secret hope: she wanted to attend a scientific lecture, one of the ones given by the Royal Institute. Mrs. Dashwood was permissive when it came to her daughters' unconventional interests, but it was difficult enough for their family to gain the respect of their peers in society, given that Mr. Dashwood engaged in an occupation. The fact that he was so successful at it, and had solved a good number of mysteries that were regularly reported in the papers, earned the Dashwood family a modicum of popularity, if not respect. But Elinor didn't just want to attend a single scientific lecture—she wanted to study chemistry. Her mother would probably prefer that Elinor spend more time finding a husband than discovering a new element or compound, but Elinor was only eighteen! She wasn't inclined in the slightest to think about marriage. And she was certain Mother could be convinced . . . if Elinor could convince Father first.

She walked down the hallway to Father's study, which sat rather unconventionally at the front of the house. She practiced what she would say until she stopped in front of the closed doors—what might normally have been a formal parlor in any other house was where her father received clients. The only sound as she approached had been the soft echo of her footsteps on the marble floor, and now she pressed her ear to the crack between the doors, listening for sound. Nothing.

She knocked, brisk but light, and opened the door before waiting for a response.

The morning sunlight slid through the half-drawn drapes, and a slight chill clung to the room. Elinor looked to the fireplace, which was cold and empty—not surprising, as Father didn't allow even the maids to clean his sanctum without overseeing to ensure that nothing was disturbed. They wouldn't build a fire unless summoned.

Elinor looked next to the chaise longue in the corner, where her father sometimes slept while working a case, when he deemed it too late to ring for his valet to prepare for bed. But it too was empty, and she realized with a strange stirring in the pit of her stomach that the window behind the chaise longue wasn't latched.

Elinor's gaze flitted across the study as goose bumps raised on her arms and the back of her neck, her eyes skipping over stacks of books, piles of papers, and cabinets bursting full of disguises that Father relied on in his trade—clothing, fake mustaches, spectacles, and various other items that allowed him to transform into a slightly different person. Finally, her eyes settled on the great desk in the center of the room, and the chair behind it where Father sat, slumped over so that his head rested on the paper-strewn surface.

"Father?" Elinor asked, shocked by the waver in her voice.

A surge of fire rushed through her veins, and even though

she knew that something was very wrong, she walked over to the unlatched window and closed it before facing Father. Even as she drew close enough to see the gray pallor to his skin and the way his eyes were almost—but not quite—closed, she knew.

She knew that her beloved father was dead.

Still, she forced her hand to reach out and touch not his face—no, she couldn't bear that—but his arm, still covered in his jacket. It was cold, and not chilled from the open window. This was lifelessness.

Elinor wasn't certain how long she stood there, hand resting on her father's arm, mind churning with senseless thoughts that she couldn't grasp. This could not be—how could this be? Finally, she knew that she had to do something, and the one thought that surfaced with any clarity was that she didn't want her mother or sisters walking into Father's study to this shocking sight. Somehow, thinking of them allowed her to withdraw her hand and step away.

She left the study and shut the door gently behind her but was startled by Stewart. She saw a flash of concern and wariness before he masked it with a cool professional air. "I've come to see if Mr. Dashwood requires anything," he said.

"A doctor," Elinor replied, surprised by the words that sprang from her lips. "Please ring for a doctor."

"Miss?" Stewart asked, his professionalism slipping altogether.

Steady, Elinor told herself. She had to remain composed.

So much had to be done, and she could not, would not, dissolve into tears. Not now. Not yet.

"Can you please ring for a doctor?" she asked, holding Stewart's gaze. "Please watch for him and then show him to my father's study immediately. I must go inform my mother and sisters."

Elinor saw the understanding dawn on Stewart's face, and the shock. She nearly broke apart in that moment, but she had to be strong.

"Of course, miss," Stewart said, looking at the closed door behind her. "But . . . I mean, that is to say—miss?"

Stewart had been with the Dashwoods since before Elinor was born, and never once had she seen him so ruffled. Another small piece of her heart broke and she nodded once, sharply. "He's gone. I must inform my mother and sisters," she repeated, and took two faltering steps, then turned back to Stewart, who hadn't yet moved from where he stood, immobile with shock. "Once you've called for the doctor, could you please send Mrs. Matthews to the breakfast room? I think . . . that is, my mother might . . . there will be arrangements to make."

"Yes, miss," Stewart said, emotion thick in his voice.

Elinor blinked back tears and turned to leave the butler behind. Seeing Stewart affected, when it was his job to be unaffected by anything, started to unravel something inside her. She quickly retraced her steps down the grand hall, not allowing herself to pause outside of the breakfast room, because if she did, she might not be able to force herself to go in, and if she stood out in the hall, she might fall apart.

She opened the door, then paused at the sight of her sisters and mother. Marianne was in the middle of telling their mother a tale, her arms spread wide to illustrate her point, a look of seriousness on her face as she tried to convince Mother of something. Margaret was laughing, and she had raspberry jam smeared in the corner of her mouth. Mother wore a look of patience and fondness, which lingered when she turned to Elinor and said, "Oh, there you are. You were gone so long I sent Stewart to find you. . . ."

The room grew quiet as they took in her stricken expression. Elinor blinked against the cheery brightness of the room and then steeled herself to share the terrible news that had crushed that fluttering hope inside her.

TWO

In Which the Dashwood Sisters
Receive Shocking News

MARIANNE DASHWOOD WAS BORN to an extraordinary fate.

She knew it from the moment she learned how to read, when she clambered into her father's lap as he sat at his desk, pointed to a word scrawled in his notebook, and pronounced, "Ar-son! Papa, what's arson?"

Mr. Dashwood gaped at her in startled delight. "Arson is when you set fire to something on purpose," he finally said. "Because you want it to burn down."

"Oh. That's bad," little Marianne said after a moment's thought.

Her father nodded gravely. "Very bad. Which is why your papa will find out who would do such a thing."

Marianne looked at him and said, "And I'll help, Papa."

From that moment on, investigating cases with her father was all Marianne wanted to do. Although her mother fretted about propriety and safety, she never barred Marianne from spending hours in her father's office or accompanying him around the city on perfectly safe and (if Marianne was being honest) somewhat boring reconnaissance missions. Father had understood that there were certain things young ladies could do or ask that a middle-aged man could not, and even though he was careful to keep her away from the more dangerous elements of his work, Marianne had been his confidante. His protégée. His secret weapon.

And now he was gone.

And Marianne didn't even get to say goodbye.

By the time the horrific news had set in that morning around the breakfast table, the doctor had already arrived and inspected their father's body. He then came upstairs, where the Dashwood sisters and their housekeeper, Mrs. Matthews, had gotten their inconsolable mother into bed. The doctor prescribed a dose of laudanum to help her sleep, and Marianne had stayed and held her hand until she'd drifted off, with Margaret curled next to her in bed, face streaked with tears. Marianne hadn't even noticed that Elinor followed the doctor out into the hall, and by the time she'd left Mother's side and found her older sister, Elinor was standing in the threshold of the front door, watching as the undertaker's wagon rolled away, rattling like an omen.

Marianne felt as if the moment she'd learned of her father's death were replaying once more, only this was somehow worse, because he was truly *gone*. No longer in the house, no longer within Marianne's grasp.

"Why . . . you sent him away," she said, a hint of accusation in her tone.

Elinor turned, looking older than her eighteen years. Marianne felt older than sixteen, so it made sense. "The doctor said it was a heart attack," she said, answering the question that was next on Marianne's lips. "They'll prepare him for burial."

"How could you?" Marianne asked. "Before I could see him?"

She thought she saw a flicker of regret in her sister's face, and Marianne was ready to forgive her then. If Elinor had offered an apology, or simply hugged her, Marianne would have forgiven her.

But they were disturbed by a clatter of horseshoes and a shout. The sisters looked up to see their older brother, John, dismounting from a horse. The poor animal's sides were heaving and its coat was wet with sweat. A groom rushed forward to take the horse and Elinor whispered quickly, "We'll see him once more at the funeral," and turned to face their brother.

John rushed forward, his ruddy face nearly purple with

exertion and alarm. "Where is he?"

"The undertaker fetched him," Elinor said, drawing him inside. Stewart appeared to take John's coat.

"I came as soon as I heard—we were at Fanny's family's estate. What happened?"

Elinor explained in a patient, tired tone. How she'd found him, how the doctor had proclaimed the death a heart attack, the arrangements, and Marianne stood in wretched silence, wishing that she could say or do something that might help.

John stared at their father's study door, which was shut. Marianne noticed that John hadn't asked about their mother or how they were holding up. This wasn't entirely surprising— Mrs. Dashwood was their father's second wife after all, and although she and John had always gotten along tolerably well, there was no closeness between them.

"This is miserable," John finally proclaimed.

Marianne shook her head, but Elinor merely murmured, "I know."

"Who will pay for it?"

It took Marianne a moment to realize that he meant the funeral, and she had no idea how to begin to answer him. What did it matter who paid for their father's burial? Elinor's mouth tightened ever so slightly as they exchanged puzzled looks, but neither spoke. John was the son, the eldest, and, more important, the one with the most money.

John had grown up in his uncle's house after his mother's untimely death, when he was just an infant. Father hadn't the means to care for him—or to hire a staff to do so. This was a good year before Father had started Norland and Co. and another year before he'd become a financial and professional success and was in a position to remarry and take back his son.

But by then, John's aunt and uncle had come to think of him as their own. Mr. Dashwood rarely spoke about the decision to allow his son to remain with his first wife's family, but it seemed reasonable when their mother had explained it to Marianne and Elinor when they were little. John would live with his aunt and uncle and become their heir because they had no children of their own. John was still their brother, and Father loved him very much.

Yet it had always felt as though John were a distant cousin they ought to be nice to, not a brother. And from where Marianne stood, it didn't seem John was inclined to take on the responsibilities of a son.

"Well," Elinor said carefully, after a lengthy pause. "I had hoped that you might see to the expense?"

John stopped pacing and considered Elinor's suggestion while Marianne watched him closely. He seemed to gaze off into the distance, and then his head tilted slightly to the side. His blond curls were sweat soaked and had been flattened by his hat and swift journey. Finally, he shook his head, as if his

13

mental calculations pained him. "Fine. Send the bills to me." Then, in a murmur, he added, "It'll all shake out anyway."

And at that moment, Marianne became suspicious.

꒷꒷

The reading of the will occurred three days later, the afternoon of the funeral. The day had threatened rain all morning, and it finally gave way to a downpour just as everyone made a dash from their carriages into the Dashwoods' town house after the graveside service. As a result, everyone was rather damp and irritable as well as sad, although some were notably more irritable than sad.

"It's only my second-best mourning gown, and yet I'm afraid my maid will never get the mud from the hem," John's wife, Fanny, could be heard saying to a mourner. "If one must attend the graveside, then a proper day must be chosen for it."

"I hardly think there's a proper day to bury anyone," Marianne said to Elinor, just a touch louder than a whisper in the hope that Fanny would hear. "But next time we bury our father we'll wait for some sunshine."

"Shh," Elinor whispered, eyes darting around the room.

"*She* ought to be shushed." Marianne stared at Fanny and relished in her dislike of the woman—it was a welcome distraction from the sharp stab of grief that never ebbed, buoyed by her suspicions. She hadn't told her sister of them yet, even though she longed to confide in her.

Instinct will put you on a case, Father used to say, *but it won't close it.*

Instinct told her that her brother's first thought of money was suspicious. That the way Fanny flitted about the room with an appraising gaze while John kept his glass full of their father's best whiskey spoke of something other than genuine grief. That proved nothing, of course, but if there was something to prove, then Marianne would find it. Preferably sooner rather than later, given that Fanny was getting on Marianne's last nerve.

Fanny sat at the center of a cluster of guests, which included their father's solicitor, Mr. Morgan, a handful of past associates and clients, and a young man with curly brown hair. Marianne vaguely recognized the young man but couldn't recall where she had seen him before or what his connection to their family might be. The Dashwood sisters sat on the periphery of the small group as Fanny announced, "Our father died five years ago, you know."

"Oh, I'm sorry to hear that," Mr. Morgan murmured, looking into his tea.

"It was gout that did him in, in the end," Fanny continued, but the young man with curly hair interrupted her.

"Fanny, I hardly think—"

"Now, Edward, let me finish! I was just going to say, it was a dreadful thing but he was no longer in pain. And our dear mother—Mrs. Farrows, you know of her?—made sure to tell

15

everyone who came to pay their respects, 'Don't grieve, for he is at peace!'"

Fanny smiled, as if she'd bestowed a gem of wisdom upon the assembled group, and Marianne suddenly remembered Edward Farrows now. He was Fanny's younger brother and he'd been a lanky boy of fourteen or fifteen at John and Fanny's wedding five years earlier. He was taller now, and his lankiness had grown into a lean physique. His curly brown hair was slightly longer than the fashion, and his skin was tanned, as if he spent a lot of time outdoors. He was probably a great horseback rider, Marianne deduced. She also noticed that he appeared to be thoroughly scandalized by his sister's cavalier attitude.

"Sister," he began, but whatever he was about to say next was cut off by Margaret, who'd been very quiet all afternoon.

"Our papa didn't have gout."

Margaret's tone was all petulance and defiance, and she could get away with such rudeness because she was only eleven.

"Oh, I know, dear," Fanny said, smiling still. "But this is the way of the world. One day, you are going about your business and then the next, you catch a cold and it quite does you in. It isn't fair, but there's no use lingering over it. Life must go on."

"It wasn't a cold, it was—" *A heart attack.* That's what Marianne wanted to say, but she was interrupted by Elinor.

"Mr. Morgan, when should we proceed with the reading of the will?"

"Oh, whenever you like, Miss Dashwood," he said, looking

up. "But surely not in front of your guests?"

"I think it's time we see to business," Elinor said firmly, and stood.

The remaining guests took their leave and Marianne gathered Margaret while Elinor went over to their mother and began whispering to her. Mrs. Dashwood had refused to take laudanum today, wanting to be fully present for the funeral, but she looked as though she desperately wished for bed even as she nodded at the departing guests.

The only person who remained in the room that was not family was Edward Farrows, who hovered off to the side as if he weren't quite sure if he should stay or go. Marianne leveled a sharp look at him and said, "The solicitor will read the will for the family now."

He opened his mouth to say something, but Fanny cut in. "Oh, Edward came with us. He must stay!"

Mr. Farrows looked as though he'd like to disappear into the drapes, but Marianne took no pity on him. "All the same, the will reading is for beneficiaries only. Unless I am mistaken and Mr. Farrows is somehow named in my father's will?" *First John and Fanny don't act properly bereft when Father dies, and now Fanny's brother is lurking about?*

"Perhaps those named in the will would like to retire to the study?" Mr. Morgan suggested.

"No," Mrs. Dashwood said, her refusal cutting through the tension in the room. "Not the study."

"I'm more than happy to step out," Mr. Farrows said, and Fanny began to protest.

Elinor caught Marianne's gaze, and her eyes silently pleaded with her.

"Fine," Marianne said, taking the seat on the other side of her mother. "Stay."

Mr. Morgan sat in their father's chair—it was the only empty seat in the drawing room. He withdrew a sheaf of papers from his case, and Marianne thought that they seemed rather thin. Was their entire future to come down to just a handful of papers? Surely that meant Father's will was straightforward . . . but then why was Fanny looking at those documents as if they were a dress box containing the finest gown of the season?

Mr. Morgan cleared his throat. "I've had the honor of working with Mr. Dashwood since we both started in business, and I knew him to be a true gentleman—a bit eccentric at times, I hope you don't mind me saying." He looked to Mrs. Dashwood.

"I'm aware of my husband's eccentricities," she said quietly. "And I loved them dearly."

Rather than look reassured, Mr. Morgan seemed even more nervous. "Well then, I believe that it won't be news to any of you that Mr. Dashwood inherited this house and a small amount of money from his uncle in his youth. He spent it on much-needed improvements, and lived on the fortune of the first Mrs. Dashwood while she was alive."

Marianne knew all of this. When John's mother died, her

money had gone not to her husband but to her son, held in trust until he came of age, which was why Father had to send John to his uncle.

"In recent years, Mr. Dashwood made his living," Mr. Morgan continued with a small cough. "And he even put away a tidy savings."

Marianne felt relief wash over her. She wasn't quite certain what a tidy savings meant in the language of pounds, but surely it would be enough to see them through this period of mourning, and she could sort out where they stood with Norland and Co.'s clients. . . .

"However," Mr. Morgan said severely, "the house is entailed on his male heir."

Hope plummeted into despair. *Of course* their home would go to John, and of course that was why Fanny had been eyeing every detail since the moment she stepped foot inside, as if it were hers for the taking. Because it was. And naturally Fanny didn't possess the tact to hide her eagerness to get her hands on everything they owned, that wench. . . .

Marianne's train of thought was interrupted by Margaret grasping her hand in a viselike grip. Mr. Morgan was saying, "I advised Mr. Dashwood to arrange his affairs for years, just in case. He was always so healthy and strong, and he kept putting it off."

"What is there to put off?" Fanny asked peevishly. "One does not simply break an entail."

Marianne rolled her eyes. Just because the archaic entail dictated that Father's property must go to his male heir didn't mean that Father wouldn't have provided for them monetarily.

"I don't speak of the entail," Mr. Morgan said, casting an apologetic look at the settee upon which the Dashwood sisters and their mother sat. "I speak of the will. Mr. Dashwood had only the one, and it's twenty-two years old."

Silence fell across the room as Marianne's mind raced with calculations. Twenty-two years ago would have been just around the time of John's mother's death. Before Elinor and Marianne and Margaret even existed. Before her parents had married. Which meant . . .

"We aren't named in his will?" Marianne said. "Not at all?"

"But why wouldn't we be in Papa's will?" Margaret asked, and it wasn't clear if she was addressing Mr. Morgan, their mother, or her siblings.

Mr. Morgan took the liberty of answering. "Your papa loved you very much, Miss Margaret. But this will was drawn up before he even married your mother. He simply hadn't gotten around to updating it."

"I don't understand why not," Margaret said, a sharp crease appearing between her brows. The Dashwood ladies knew that it was the only warning of their youngest sister's sass. "He had plenty of time to see to it."

"Even so," Mr. Morgan said kindly, "your papa was not the type to think of dying. He kept busy working, and being a good father, and a good husband. He simply never thought that he would . . . pass."

Marianne hadn't thought it possible, either. She knew, logically, that Father would one day die, and Mother, too. But she had simply chosen to believe that day would be far off, decades away.

"Don't be cross with Father," Elinor said to Margaret. "He never would have left us if given the choice. He was always so *healthy*."

Margaret huffed. "In novels, nothing good ever comes to those who die without an updated will. I shall always have a will, and I will update it every year on my birthday."

"What a thing to say, Margaret!" But the admonishment did not come from her sisters or Mrs. Dashwood—it came from Fanny. "You're a young lady. Young ladies don't need wills."

"It's not illegal, is it?" Margaret challenged Fanny.

Marianne sighed heavily, not wanting her horrid sister-in-law to shatter Margaret's innocence regarding unfair property laws concerning women. "Not if you're unmarried," she told her younger sister, shooting daggers at Fanny.

Margaret looked at her sister. "Why should it matter if I am married or not?"

Fanny was the one to respond. "Because, dear, ladies cannot own anything of value. Our husbands are our stewards, and if one is unlucky enough not to have a husband, then our fathers or sons see to that task."

"And brothers, in a pinch?" was Marianne's sarcastic response. The entire room looked to John, whose whiskey glass was, for the first time all afternoon, empty. "Right, John?"

"Of course," John said, not convincingly. "I mean, Father would have wanted . . . that is to say, no one will be cast out into the streets."

The fact that Marianne had to ask for this reassurance did not put her at ease.

"Of course, we shall see what can be done," Fanny added, and her words only flamed Marianne's anger.

"Whatever do you mean?" she demanded. "Just because our father left us nothing doesn't mean we're inconvenient horses that ought to be put out to pasture. This is *our* home."

The corners of Fanny's mouth turned up in a little smile, but it wasn't she who spoke next. It was Elinor. "No, Marianne. Not any longer. It's John and Fanny's."

"This is why I had Edward stay," Fanny said, smiling brightly and gesturing to her brother, whom Marianne had quite forgotten about. Everyone looked at him, and he grimaced at the attention. "He's an accountant at Hillenbrand and Associates. You've heard of them?"

When no one answered, she continued.

"Anyway, we expect great things from him. He's just the person to handle this, don't you agree, John? He can take a look at the ledgers, and decide what's best for Mrs. Dashwood and her daughters to live on."

"Fanny, I don't think now—" Mr. Farrows began to say, but Fanny continued.

"Is there anything else, Mr. Morgan? All financial arrangements can go through Edward, and we'll of course need full access to the accounts."

Marianne laughed, a sharp and sudden exhale of incredulity. "And what about the business?"

"Well, it's John's now," Fanny said briskly, as if it were no matter.

"That's absurd. John never took a moment's interest in Father's work!"

"Because he doesn't need to, dear." Fanny's condescension was so thick Marianne could have cut through it with her pocketknife.

"Well, pardon me, but I don't think that settling matters you know nothing about should be up to you," Marianne said. She balanced on the edge of the settee, ready to fly to her feet if she needed to. "We have clients who depend on us, and case files that need attending to. If Norland and Company should be anyone's inheritance, it's *mine*."

"My, you Dashwood women have a flair for the unconventional!" Fanny exclaimed. "What's next, do you think women ought to have a seat in Parliament?"

"Why not?" Marianne asked, just to spite her.

"We've discussed this," Fanny said, looking significantly at John, who kept opening his mouth as if to interject, then closing it when Fanny spoke. "John has no need to humble himself by working as a detective, especially not out of his own home."

"Then he has no need for our father's money, which was earned through such *humble* work," Marianne shot back. "Which leaves me to guess the only reason why he's making a grab for it is because someone is encouraging him to do so."

"Marianne!" Mrs. Dashwood and Elinor both exclaimed, but Marianne didn't care. Fanny was horrid, and Marianne saw no use in pretending to engage in niceties.

"I'm so very sorry you see it that way," Fanny said, her voice sweet but deadly as her stare burned into Marianne's flesh. "But I do expect you to keep a civil tongue under *my* roof."

It was a not-so-subtle threat, but Marianne was beyond care. She leapt to her feet. "I *will* carry on the business. And I'll move it out of this house so you can't touch it."

"You can't!" Fanny snapped.

"Who will stop me?"

But her challenge was answered by Elinor. "Legally, you can't." Marianne looked down at her older sister, who gazed back with heartbreak written across her face as she continued, "Everything Father owned, including Norland and Company, goes to John. Therefore, if John wishes to close the business . . ."

"But . . . I want it." Marianne hated the petulance in her voice then. She hated the way Elinor pleaded with her eyes for Marianne to hold her tongue. She hated how John wouldn't meet her gaze and how even Edward Farrows looked down at the carpet, likely shocked at this private family spectacle. Most of all, she hated how Fanny sat back with a satisfied grin.

"Yes, well, we can't always get what we want, can we?" Fanny asked, and that was the final straw for Marianne. She did what she was very good at.

She turned her back on Fanny and her spineless brother, held her head high, and made a dramatic exit.

THREE

*In Which the Dashwood Sisters
Make a Shocking Discovery*

"SHE'S A VIPER! A smug, conniving, money-minded—"

"I think we understand," Elinor cut off Marianne before she could descend into some of the more colorful names she'd picked up while working with their father.

"She's fairly flush in the pockets, and that was *before* she married John. Now together—why, they're richer than Father ever was! Don't try and tell me it isn't true, Elinor. They've got *family* money."

Elinor sighed and removed the old cast-iron pan off the small stove to cool on the scarred wooden table that served as her workbench. After four long, exhausting, grief-stricken days of attending to their mother, instructing the servants, corresponding with all of the appropriate parties to make the arrangements for Father's funeral, then having to endure the event itself and the shocking news of Father's will yesterday, Elinor was wrung out. She felt the vague pulsing behind her left eye that was likely the start of a headache, but she was emotionally exhausted as well. She'd hoped that a morning spent in her makeshift attic laboratory would provide just the sort of comfort and solace she yearned for, but she'd barely lit a flame on her lamp and assembled her equipment before Marianne had barged in to rant about the injustice of the entire Dashwood fortune going to John.

"It doesn't matter that they've plenty of money," Elinor explained for what felt like the hundredth time. "What matters is that legally, they have inherited everything. I don't know what you expect us to do about it."

"We could contest it," Marianne said hotly. "How could Father's will be so old? How could he leave us in such a way? Surely Father didn't mean to—"

"Of course, he didn't mean to die," Elinor interrupted. Then she took a steadying breath and immediately regretted it when the fumes of her experiment hit the back of her throat. "He couldn't leave us the house, anyway. But think about it, Marianne. Father always thought well of John. He likely thought that John would do right by us."

"And he would, if not for *Fanny*," Marianne declared. "I'd like to smack her."

"Well, that certainly wouldn't help things." Secretly, Elinor might have relished this. But being the older sister, she said instead, "Remember what Mother always says—don't let the behavior of others destroy your inner peace."

Marianne sighed and threw herself down on a stool next to Elinor's worktable. "Fat lot of good that does us when Fanny is so awful and our futures are at stake." Her nose wrinkled at the cast-iron pan and its contents. "What on earth are you doing anyway?"

"Making a smoke bomb," Elinor said, and she felt the corners of her lips turn up in a small smile despite the grim mood.

"And you say that I need to rein it in with Fanny."

"It's not for her. It's for Margaret. She read that smoke bombs can be made for diversions, and she wants to write about it in her stories." At Marianne's skeptical look, Elinor added, "It's for *research*."

"You just . . . made that? Out of things you found around the house?"

"Well, I had to ask Father for the saltpeter—that's the main ingredient in gunpowder—but yes, just a bit of sugar and stir it on low heat. . . ." Elinor smiled. She'd been pleased at how well the mixture had come together, just as her research had promised it would. She unfolded a piece of cheesecloth she'd filched from the kitchen.

Marianne peered at the brownish, stinking mess cooling in the pan. "Is it profitable?"

28

"Oh well, I don't know about that. But Margaret assures me it's integral to her writing."

Marianne sighed. "What are we going to *do*, Elinor?"

"Not panic," Elinor said firmly, laying a piece of yarn in the center of the cheesecloth, so a tiny bit hung over the edge. She began to carefully scrape the smoke bomb substance into the cheesecloth. "Mother has a small income from her dowry. It's not enough for all four of us to live on, but if it can secure us a place to live, maybe between the two of us we can make ends meet. Our circumstances will be quite reduced, but . . . if we don't have a house to keep up, then our expenses shall be reduced, too."

Elinor tried to say that last part with a smile, but she feared it came across more like a grimace. She wasn't entirely as optimistic about the future as she tried to project, but what else could be done? Like Marianne, she was upset by the idea of being beholden to Fanny for their future. Fanny was someone who wanted absolute control, and she already disapproved of the Dashwood sisters. Elinor suspected that to Fanny, being John's half sisters wasn't quite enough for her to expend much effort toward them.

"What do you plan on doing to earn money?" Marianne asked, and Elinor chose to ignore her incredulous tone.

"Well, I've been reading up on distillation—it's a method of extracting a plant's essence from the plant matter."

"And is that valuable?"

"Well, not on its own. But it can be used in other things. Medicines, toilet water, perfumes, that sort of thing."

"Perfume?" Marianne perked up. "Those are horribly expensive."

"Don't get too excited," Elinor said. She twisted the cheese-cloth around her substance so it resembled a pouch of curds, then secured it with a piece of string. "Perfumes aren't so easy—or cheap—to make. They require special ingredients, careful lab work, and then there's the matter of formula. I can't just copy someone else's. I need to come up with my own."

"Well, that shouldn't be difficult for you."

Elinor didn't accept the praise. "There are so many compli-cated scents—base, middle, and top notes, and then there's the matter of perfectly proportioning them so that the scents aren't overwhelming. We'll have to buy distilled alcohol, to mix as the base. . . ."

Marianne sighed. "So we're doomed, then."

"Not doomed . . . but now is the time to get serious about our futures."

Elinor carefully stored the smoke bomb in a glass jar, where it wouldn't get wet or be exposed to a stray spark. She then turned to look at her lab equipment and realized all of a sud-den that if they did have to move, she would likely lose this precious space that she'd been building since she was thirteen. The thought took her by the throat and squeezed, but Elinor breathed through the hurt. It was best not to think too closely upon all that they were losing.

"What if . . . Father didn't just die?"

Elinor's gaze shot up. "What do you mean?"

Marianne wouldn't quite meet Elinor's eye, and her fingers twisted in her skirts nervously. "I mean . . . he was healthy. People don't just die out of nowhere. And in his line of work, he was bound to make some enemies. When you stop and think about it, it's awfully convenient that John and Fanny stand to inherit everything."

Elinor saw where her sister was going with this and knew she had to stop her before she could start running with the idea. "Don't be absurd. You just said yourself that they're far richer than Father ever was, so why would they even need to . . . I can't even say it!"

Marianne smiled and leaned in closer, and Elinor realized her error too late—never pose a hypothetical question to Marianne, because she would consider it an invitation. "Perhaps their finances aren't quite as tidy as we assumed. All it takes is one bad business decision, one vice, and fortunes can be ruined. And this house is worth a great deal."

"Look me in the eye and tell me you honestly believe that John could hurt Father," Elinor demanded in a fierce whisper.

Marianne's gray eyes met Elinor's and she shrugged slowly. "Do I think that he did it himself? Unlikely. But, perhaps—"

"No!" Elinor couldn't stand to hear any more. "You're talking nonsense. The doctor said it was a heart attack. And while you may find that difficult to believe, Father *was* unwell—he'd had a cold all week, and he kept working through it, even though we all told him he needed rest. We need to face facts, not conjure up tales."

"But if you would just—"

"*No!*"

It was the first time Elinor had raised her voice in days—weeks, maybe. The force and volume shocked Marianne, who merely blinked back at her. For a fleeting moment, Elinor thought perhaps she'd gotten through to her sister. But then Marianne's expression soured and she said, "Fine. You know best."

But Elinor knew Marianne didn't believe it. And the most worrisome thing was, Elinor wasn't sure she believed it herself.

⚬✂⚬

In the days that followed, Elinor understood why Marianne wanted desperately to believe in some nefarious plot that cast Fanny as a villain. The letters began arriving the day after the funeral—missives that requested certain arrangements and changes be made to the household, in preparation of John and Fanny's arrival. Then came their servants, sent to oversee the movement of furniture and art. And finally, Fanny herself arrived, marching through the house with a keen eye and a nose for where Elinor, Marianne, and Margaret would hide.

"We can't live like this," Marianne complained as the three

sisters huddled with their mother in the spare back bedroom. "This house isn't large enough for us all *and* the gremlin."

The gremlin was their nephew, a spoiled boy of two named Harry, whose temper tantrums could be heard in nearly every room of the house.

"I quite agree, dear," their mother said. "But until we know how much John intends to set aside for us, I don't know what we can afford."

"I think we ought to start looking anyway," Elinor said, wincing at the sound of a distant thud. "Perhaps Mr. Morgan would have some recommendations. . . ."

"Pfft, Mr. Morgan!"

The Dashwood sisters looked at their mother in surprise, and her cheeks pinkened slightly—the first sign of color they'd seen on her face in days. "I don't trust him," Mrs. Dashwood admitted. "He may have been good to your father, but John is his client now."

"Have you heard any more from that awful Mr. Farrows?" Marianne asked.

"He didn't seem awful," Elinor said, the words rising out of her before she quite realized she was about to say them. Marianne and her mother turned to look at her, and Elinor stammered, "I mean . . . he defended us to Fanny, did he not? And he seemed to be well-mannered."

"He was perfectly respectable," Mrs. Dashwood acknowledged. "However, I don't enjoy the idea of him poking through

33

our ledgers, deciding how much money we're to live on. What does he know of us?"

Before the sisters could say anything more, the door to the bedroom swung open and they turned to find Fanny. "There you are! Whatever are you all up to?"

Elinor felt like a child caught in the pantry and grasped for words. Mother was ashen faced again, and Marianne was simmering with barely contained rage.

"We're looking at what needs to be done in this room," Margaret piped up. She really was uncannily quick to come up with a story. "For Harry to move in."

Fanny gave Margaret a puzzled smile and said, "Oh no, dear. This room isn't suitable at all. Harry will move into the nursery."

"But . . ." Margaret squinted at her. "That's *my* room."

"Precisely," Fanny said. "Now, if you're all quite done, I need the key to the formal drawing room."

Everyone stiffened. The formal drawing room, as Fanny had taken to calling it, was Father's study. The sisters looked to their mother, who was already shaking her head. "No."

Fanny looked to Elinor. "Please explain to your mother that we need to clean it out. I intend to restore that room to its true purpose."

"Fanny," Elinor said softly, hoping to appeal to her sister-in-law's humanity—if she even had any. "Please, give us some time."

In the past, relying on social graces, demure manners, and reason was usually enough to get Fanny to back down—at least for a moment. But that was before she had legal claim to all they owned. Now, she simply sucked on her teeth, narrowed her gaze at Elinor, and said, "You've had time—it's been over a week. I've hired a decorator who will be here tomorrow with wallpaper samples, and I can't possibly decide with that room so cluttered."

"You will *not* touch his things." Mrs. Dashwood spit the words at Fanny.

"I'll have Stewart take the door off the hinges if I have to!"

Elinor stepped in between Fanny and her mother, forcing Fanny to take a step back. "Let's all calm down a moment. Fanny, I understand your concerns. I'll take care of it."

"I need everything out, and—"

"I said I will take care of it."

Elinor gave Fanny a firm look, and she was not sure what she would do if Fanny pushed her on this—luckily, neither of them had the chance to find out. Fanny sniffed, and then her face dissolved into a cold, falsely sweet smile. "See that you do."

She swept away, and Elinor turned to her mother and wrapped her arms around her. Mother's tears fell upon the exposed skin where her neck and shoulders met, and Elinor felt Marianne and Margaret encircle them on either side. This was what Elinor had feared, and yet she knew this moment was inevitable. The Dashwoods were the bicarbonate of soda, innocently minding their own business, and Fanny the vinegar that poured over them, causing them all to bubble and spew.

Elinor had done this experiment before, and she knew that all that was left after the reaction simmered out was a giant mess.

Finally, Mother drew back and dabbed at her eyes with a crumpled handkerchief. "I know I should let her, but . . ."

"Hush, she's horrible and she never should have pushed you," Marianne said. "Elinor was brilliant, staring her down like that."

"I won't stay here," Mrs. Dashwood declared. "I cannot sit by and watch that woman disrespect everything that your father and I built."

"But where will we go?" Margaret asked.

"I'll write to my cousin, Sir John Middleton," Mrs. Dashwood said. "No, he's in town now—I'll call on him."

Elinor was surprised by her immediate response. Clearly Mother had been thinking about this. She had met her mother's cousin only once, when she was a child, as he and his family preferred to spend most of their time at his country estate. "Does he know about our circumstances?"

"I'm sure he'll understand," was all her mother said in response, and then she quickly put away her handkerchief. "We should start packing today. Take only what you cannot live without. I'm determined to leave this house by the end of the week."

She withdrew a key from her pocket and placed it in Elinor's hand. Then she swept out of the room without looking back. The sisters watched her go in shock.

"Well, that was an about-face," Marianne said.

"It's probably for the best. I'll see to Father's study, and you two start packing." Elinor always felt calmer when she had a plan.

"I want to help with Father's study," Marianne protested.

Elinor noted her determined expression and decided to not argue. "Fine. Margaret, ring for a footman to bring down your trunk. Pack your clothes before your books, please."

"But you won't make me leave my books behind, will you?" Margaret asked, eyes wide with horror.

"Let's start with the essentials first. Come, we have to move quickly."

Elinor descended to the first floor, Marianne a step behind her. When Elinor caught sight of the young man seated in the hall, she stopped short and Marianne bumped into her. "Elinor!" she exclaimed, but then spotted him as well.

Edward Farrows leapt to his feet and bowed in their direction. "Miss Dashwood, Miss Marianne. I'm sorry to startle you."

Elinor prompted her feet to move and descended the final steps to the hall. She gave him the courtesy of a small curtsy and said, "Mr. Farrows. Have you been waiting long? I'm sorry, no one told us you were here or we'd have received you in the drawing room."

Mr. Farrows shook his head quickly. "Oh no, please don't worry. Your butler let me in, and then Fanny told me to wait here. She said that your mother would open the study and provide me with the household and business ledgers?" He said the last bit with a self-conscious wince, as if he knew just how disrespectful his sister could be.

Behind her, Elinor heard Marianne suck in a hissing breath. She thrust the key into Marianne's hand. "Please fetch the ledgers for Mr. Farrows."

"But Elinor—"

"Just do it, Marianne."

Marianne gave Mr. Farrows one last withering look, then unlocked the study. She entered, then made a big production of turning and slamming the door closed behind her. Elinor heard the key click in the lock as Marianne locked herself in.

"I'm sorry," Elinor said. Mr. Farrows looked at the door with a guilty expression. "We're all a bit . . . well, it's been a difficult time."

"No need to apologize," Mr. Farrows said, turning his gaze back to Elinor. "I'm so sorry you're going through this, and for my part in your troubles."

"Oh, you're not—I mean, it isn't your fault."

"My sister can be . . ." Mr. Farrows trailed off, then concluded with, "Demanding."

That was putting it mildly, but it would be impolite to say otherwise. Elinor decided to neither agree nor disagree. "We do appreciate your assistance. Not knowing how things will be settled hasn't always brought out the best in us."

"I don't know what you're referring to, Miss Dashwood. I've nothing but respect for you and your mother and sisters."

The kindness of this statement brought a smile to Elinor's lips, because how could that be true when Marianne had just been so horribly rude? Yet when she met Mr. Farrows's eyes, which reminded her of warm, dark honey, she saw nothing but sincerity. He'd lost a father, too, and she wondered if the loss affected him more than his sister. That moment of affinity gave her the confidence to ask, "Have you and my brother come to an agreement about the . . . terms of our living situation?"

Elinor had never spoken so boldly about money, and she felt her embarrassment in the warmth of her cheeks. But Mr. Farrows didn't seem taken aback. His gaze softened and he asked, "Has your brother not told you?"

"No, he's hardly said a word to us since he moved in."

"Oh. I'm sorry, I thought it was settled." Mr. Farrows shifted from foot to foot in a manner that Elinor could categorize only as guilty. "Perhaps you ought to ask him."

"Please, Mr. Farrows," she said. "If you know, just tell me. I would be grateful, even if . . ." *Even if it's bad news.* That's what she wanted to say. "I would much rather know now, so we can begin planning."

Mr. Farrows nodded. "I understand completely. And, well, I suppose the matter is decided, although . . . I want you to know that I advocated for waiting until I'd had a chance to inspect your household ledgers before making a final decision. Nevertheless, John and Fanny seem determined. They've decided to allow you five hundred pounds each. Just your sisters, not your mother."

The anxiety and dread that Elinor had been carrying lifted all of a sudden. "Oh! Oh . . . that is, well. That's quite satisfactory. I understand why John might not wish to bestow my mother with anything, as she does have some money of her own, but—"

"No, Miss Dashwood, I'm afraid you misunderstand me," Mr. Farrows rushed to say. "That is not an annuity, unfortunately. My sister detests annuities."

And it all came rushing back—the shock, the cold drench of fear. Elinor had expected that no matter how much money John decided to give them, it would be a yearly payment. "You mean to say that John plans on only giving us five hundred pounds each . . . and nothing more?"

"I'm truly sorry," he whispered, as if he expected her to lash out in anger. "I tried to advocate for more, believe me."

Elinor felt faint. She sank into the chair that Mr. Farrows had occupied just moments earlier. It was still warm, and that fact sent a flush throughout her entire body. "That'll be hardly enough to see Margaret come of age," she whispered.

The dire nature of their situation fully known to her, Elinor felt her mind begin to fail her. She did not normally flinch away from problems—she attacked them one small element at a time. But faced with this news, she was unsure of what to do. They couldn't afford to move out of their home! But Fanny had made it very clear that they were unwelcome. Why was John giving them so little? He wasn't quite reducing them to poverty, but he was stripping them of their social status. They'd scarcely be able to afford food and shelter, let alone participate in the society they'd grown up in. Unless one of them married, and married very well. But no one would marry a girl with no dowry and only five hundred pounds to her name, and besides, Elinor didn't want to marry.

John and Fanny had plenty of money. Why were they so tightfisted?

Unless . . . it was as Marianne suggested. Maybe this was all they could spare.

But that meant there was a chance Marianne was also right about a potential motive for wanting to see Father dead.

The lock to the study clicked, and both Elinor and Mr. Farrows looked up to see Marianne, holding two different ledgers. She dropped them unceremoniously in Mr. Farrows's arms and then looked at Elinor. "Are you ready to begin?"

"Yes," she said, and stood, not looking at Mr. Farrows. "Please excuse us."

Elinor dreaded telling her sister what she had just learned. Marianne was awfully obnoxious when proven right.

"What did he say to you?" Marianne demanded before the

door was quite closed behind her.

Elinor faced her sister. Best to just get on with it. "I'm beginning to wonder if perhaps your theory about Father's death might not be completely absurd."

Marianne's shock would have been amusing if they'd been discussing anything else. "What! Why? Who changed your mind?"

Elinor quickly explained what Mr. Farrows had told her about the money, and predictably Marianne grew incensed. *"That woman—"*

"I know, I don't disagree with you," Elinor rushed to say, hushing her sister. "So what do we do?"

She wasn't often in a position to ask her younger sister for advice. Elinor was the older sister, and the even-tempered one.

But Marianne appeared more than ready to take charge. "We search this room," she declared, turning to survey the study. "And we look for evidence, even the smallest things that might be off."

Elinor followed her sister's gaze and took a step forward, but Marianne's hand reached out and stopped her. "Not yet," she said. "Look around. Tell me what you see. Does anything look out of sorts?"

The drapes were mostly drawn and the fireplace neatly swept. The room was furnished with overflowing bookshelves, its bounty enjoyed by the entire Dashwood family. The cabinets full of their father's files and his tools of the trade looked slightly messy, but that wasn't unusual. Papers were strewn about the desk, and a porcelain teacup sat on top of them. It looked as though their father had merely stepped out for a moment.

"I don't know," Elinor murmured.

Marianne nodded. "All right, go slowly, and be careful not to disturb too much before we've had a chance to inspect it. Look for anything unusual, and of course, anything unfamiliar."

Elinor began inspecting the bookshelves, looking under the furniture, and carefully opening up cabinets. In truth, she didn't know what exactly she was doing, and she kept stealing glances at her sister, who moved throughout the room methodically, intent on her purpose. While she was impressed with Marianne's diligence, she couldn't help but think that this was hopeless. Father died of a *heart attack*. Against her will, the image of her father's body flashed behind her eyelids when she blinked, and she had to stop what she was doing in order to fend off the horrid memory. *No, think,* she told herself. The image flashed again. Had there been anything out of order? But no, it seemed as though Father had simply . . . slumped forward and was gone.

"This is useless," she said to Marianne as she drew closer to Father's desk. They'd started on opposite ends of the room and met in the middle. "How could someone even have gotten in that night without Stewart knowing?"

"Sometimes Father entertained late-night clients." At

Elinor's shocked expression, Marianne smiled and said, "Not everyone wants to be seen asking for Father's help." Then her expression darkened as she said, "Well, not everyone *wanted* to be seen."

The switch to past tense made Elinor's throat tighten. "But if someone killed Father, how did they get back out of the house? If Stewart or any of the servants awoke to find any of the doors unlocked, they'd report it immediately."

"Unless one of the staff was in on it," Marianne said.

"No!" Elinor gasped. She knew everyone on staff, and most had been with the family for years. They hadn't had any troubles since a stable boy had to be let go for drunkenness, but Elinor had been thirteen when that happened.

"I don't want to believe it either," Marianne said. "But we have to consider every angle. Perhaps they were working for John, and he paid this person and paid off a member of the staff—"

"How did they kill him and make it look like a heart attack?"

"Strangulation?" Marianne asked, then shook her head. "No, a doctor would notice that. Perhaps he was smothered?"

"With what?" Elinor asked, and they both looked about the room. A cushion lay on the chaise longue, but before Elinor could point it out, Marianne was shaking her head. "Father would have fought, don't you think? And then he might have woken someone up, or at the very least made a mess . . . but look at his desk. It's—well, not tidy, but nothing looks disturbed."

"Are any of his files stolen?" Elinor asked. "You said he had enemies. Maybe this isn't about John and Fanny, but a disgruntled client?"

"Good thought," Marianne said, and quickly began searching through the papers, opening the filing cabinets. "I don't know. It doesn't look as though anything is missing, but—"

She spun around and looked at the desk.

"What is it?"

"Father's journal!"

Elinor knew instantly what Marianne was referring to. Father carried a brown leather journal everywhere he went. He filled it with notes, and when he got to the end of one, he locked it in his safe and acquired a new identical journal. He was about three-quarters of the way through his current journal, Elinor recalled. But she didn't see it anywhere. The sisters devoted another five minutes to searching for it, not taking as much care now.

"I don't think it's here," Elinor finally said. Marianne swore, and Elinor gasped. "Language!"

"This is maddening!" Marianne exclaimed. "I know something is off here, I just can't figure out what."

"Let's ask Mother about the journal. Maybe she has it. Maybe she came down here one night while we were asleep and took it from his desk."

"Don't be daft. Mother hasn't been going anywhere at night. She takes laudanum and sleeps until her maid wakes her."

Elinor stiffened. "Fine! I'm just trying to help." She turned abruptly and began stacking papers. A bill here, a letter there, a list of household items, a newspaper . . . Marianne's hand rested gently on her shoulder.

"I'm sorry," she said as Elinor turned to face her sister. "I just . . . I'm so frustrated. Father was training me in this line of work and I can't even—I don't even know how . . ."

Elinor pulled her sister close, and the two girls clung to each other. Neither cried, too spent from all the tears they'd already shed. The sense of helplessness was the worst part. Elinor searched for words that would comfort Marianne but found nothing.

Finally, they released each other and hovered awkwardly behind Father's desk.

"The teacup," Marianne said suddenly.

"What?" Elinor asked, turning to look where Marianne was staring.

"When have you ever known Father to take tea in his study?"

"Oh," Elinor said. It was a good question. Father kept spirits in the cabinet behind his desk and would often help himself from the crystal tumblers in the evening. Otherwise, he only drank tea with the family. "But he had a cold, remember. Maybe he wanted something warming."

Even as she said it, a door swung open in the back of her mind and her previous question rose up again. How could someone kill him and make it look like a heart attack?

Poison.

Elinor reached for the teacup and peered inside. At first, she wasn't certain whether Father had drained his cup or the last bit of liquid had evaporated, but what was left looked almost like a dried, sandy substance. There was about a teaspoon's worth, maybe more, and it was the color of, well, dried tea. She made a small *hmm* noise, which made Marianne look closer.

"Father never took sugar in his tea," Marianne murmured.

Elinor dipped her pinky finger into the substance and swirled it about. It felt sandy, but not sticky like sugar left in the bottom of a teacup. "I don't know what this is."

What did it remind her of? Bicarbonate of soda, she realized. After it had been mixed with vinegar and the reaction bubbled and fizzed, and when it finally settled. The result was a wet, dense substance that was finer than sugar. Elinor's mind was running through a list of possibilities. Of course, she could prove it was sugar by tasting it. The simplest solution is often the correct one . . . but what if it wasn't sugar?

"Elinor?"

"I'm thinking!"

"Well, you don't think it could be . . ."

Without saying anything, Elinor turned on her heel and walked out of the study, teacup in hand. The hallway was empty; Mr. Farrows had disappeared with the ledgers. But Elinor wasn't thinking about that right now. She was halfway up the stairs before Marianne caught up with her, hissing, "What are you doing?"

Elinor was not overly excitable by nature, nor was she prone to whims of the imagination. But this teacup, this mysterious substance, their father's sudden death . . . her scientific curiosity was abuzz. The only place she wanted to be was in her laboratory. "Upstairs!" she called back to her sister.

Marianne followed and kept uncharacteristically quiet while Elinor drew out instruments and a clean glass container. The first thing she did was sniff the substance, but she noticed nothing substantial beyond an earthiness that could have been tea. She recorded that in her own notebook of scientific inquiry. Then she scraped the sand-like material into a clean glass jar.

What would be the best test? Taste, obviously. She would be able to tell right away if it was sugar, even if she ran the risk of ingesting a substance that may or may not have killed Father. But how to go about this safely?

She scooped a tiny amount of the substance onto a brass wand and set it in a clean container. Then, she poured a splash of fresh water from a nearby jug into the glass and swirled. She held the liquid up to the light, watching the particles swirl and dissolve. *Water-soluble*, she thought to herself, though she didn't take the time to write that down. Sugar was water-soluble. So was salt.

"Are you going to stare at it forever?" Marianne asked.

"No," Elinor said, and before Marianne could say anything else, she tipped the substance into her mouth. Marianne gave a small squawk of surprise, but Elinor barely registered it. The moment the water hit her tongue, she could taste bitterness and she fought against her instinct to swallow. She held the horrid taste in her mouth for a second more, trying to commit it to memory, and then she spit it back out immediately.

"Elinor!" Marianne shrieked.

Elinor reached for her jug of fresh water and a clean glass and poured herself another cup. She cleansed her mouth, spitting back into the contaminated cup until she could no longer taste the bitterness on her tongue, and then she allowed herself to drink. Finally, she looked at Marianne.

"Whatever is in that teacup, it's not sugar."

"What is it then?" her sister asked, eyes wide with fear, but also a hint of excitement. It was the same excitement that Elinor felt racing in her veins.

"I don't know," she said slowly. "But I think that it's poison. Which means . . ."

They stared at each other, neither of them daring to say it. They were startled when Margaret's voice came from the door.

"Which means Papa was murdered."

FOUR

*In Which the Dashwood Sisters
Begin Asking Questions*

"MARGARET!" ELINOR EXCLAIMED, USING a
tone that Marianne thought of as her mothering voice. "You're
supposed to be packing."

"I was, but I got tired of it. What did the poison taste like?"

Marianne looked to her older sister, because she wanted to
know, too.

"Bitter," Elinor said. "I don't know what it is, but considering how much was in the bottom of that cup . . ." She trailed off,
as she often did when considering the sciences.

Marianne felt a surge of triumph. "Father was poisoned,"
she said. "I was *right*."

Elinor cut her a sharp look. "Is that something you really
want to be right about?"

Marianne scowled, although Elinor had a point. "No, but now we can do something about it." Although what that might be, Marianne wasn't quite certain—yet.

"Are we going to tell Mama?" Margaret asked.

"No," they said in unison. Marianne shifted her gaze to Elinor, surprised to find them in agreement for once.

"I can't know for certain until I run more tests," Elinor said. "Besides, she's been so upset."

Marianne would have liked to take up pacing once more (the movement really did help her think), but alas, Elinor's laboratory was too small and crowded for such an activity. "Besides, we can't reveal what we know too soon," she added. "Not until we know who is responsible."

"Smart," Margaret agreed. "In *The Revenge of the Buccaneer*, Tom reveals that his captain has been poisoned to the first person he comes across, thinking that person is a friend, and it's actually a mutineer. He strands Tom on an island because he knows the truth!"

"Well, none of us shall be stranded on an island," Marianne told her. "What I want to know is how it was completely missed that he was *poisoned*." She looked to Elinor, who had been the only one to see their father's body, aside from the doctor.

"I don't know," Elinor said, and she looked genuinely shocked at Marianne's unspoken accusation. "His death seemed natural. He looked as though he'd merely fallen asleep at his desk, albeit . . . slumped over at an uncomfortable angle."

Marianne tried to picture it, but she just couldn't. She couldn't envision Father ever being that vulnerable. His death still didn't seem real, despite the funeral and everything that had followed. Maybe if she'd been able to see him the day that he'd been discovered, before the doctor showed up. . . . "The doctor didn't notice anything unusual?"

"You know the signs of poisoning as well as me," Elinor said, sounding more and more impatient. "There was no vomiting, or blood in his mouth or throat. His color was pale, but he didn't seem to be in distress in his final moments. It truly looked as though he died in his sleep."

"Could it be laudanum?" Marianne asked, vaguely recalling a case of her father's where a man had given his sickly mother-in-law too much of the stuff, and the woman had died in her sleep. Almost like Father.

"No. Laudanum is brown, almost red. This is . . . well, I don't know what it is. But more analysis is necessary."

Margaret hugged Elinor. "Don't worry. If anyone can figure it out, it's you."

Elinor returned the embrace. "Well, I'm no expert. New chemical discoveries are being made every day, but no one wants to share them with women."

"But can you figure it out?" Marianne asked.

"I'll have to do some reading. It would be best if I could find someone to consult, of course. . . . Why? What are you thinking?"

"I'm serious about continuing Father's work," Marianne told her sisters. No one seemed to have believed her the day of Father's funeral, but Marianne was not one to give up at the first sign of trouble. After all, Father always said, *If someone tells you no, they are likely hiding something.* She had to wonder what was behind Fanny's insistence that she not continue to pursue the investigation. "And I think that discovering who murdered him will be my first solo case."

"Oh, Marianne," Elinor said.

"Don't *oh, Marianne* me," she shot back.

"But how will you—"

"Girls! There you are!"

The Dashwood sisters spun around to find their mother standing in the open door, slightly out of breath, cheeks pink with exertion. It was the most color Marianne had seen in her mother's face since their father had died.

"Good news," she said, smiling brightly, but the expression seemed odd on her, like a dress that didn't quite fit. "I've found us a place to live. We move in the day after tomorrow."

"Where is it?" Elinor asked just as Marianne said:

"How many rooms?"

"Well, it's a bit on the small side," their mother admitted. "It has two bedrooms. One is quite large, and I thought you three could take it. I'll take the smaller room. But it has a lovely drawing room, a dining room, and the kitchen is quite adequate. We'll have to scale back quite a bit, and we shall only be able to keep one servant, but . . ."

Marianne stared at her mother in horror. Only two bedrooms? One servant?

Elinor recovered first. "I'm sure it's quite lovely," she said.

Margaret cast her sisters a knowing look. "This is *just* like *The Mysterious Disappearance of Mrs. H.* But don't worry, it all worked out in the end."

As she ran back downstairs, Mrs. Dashwood said, "Whatever does she mean by that?"

Marianne smiled to hide her unease. "Who can say?"

✂

Marianne supposed that she ought to have been shocked by the confirmation of her suspicions, but instead she got the same feeling when a case began to emerge and the facts all made a terrible sort of sense. The sense that there was something here, something begging to be discovered. But what, exactly? Father had not been wholly accepted in society because of his work, but he was respected. There had even been blackmail attempts in the past—clients who weren't satisfied by the truths that her father had uncovered, those who had been exposed by a client and sought to take revenge, and men who saw her father's success and thought that they might outwit him.

But whoever killed her father hadn't accounted for Marianne.

The first thing Marianne did was pull her mother aside and ask, "Do you have Father's journal? I wanted to make sure it wasn't missed in the mayhem of packing."

Mother's brow creased. "Is it not in the study, with his things?"

"I'm sure it is," Marianne lied smoothly. "We hadn't gotten a chance to pack it up yet, but don't worry—I know all of Father's hiding spots."

Rather than reassure her, Marianne's words clearly distressed Mother. "I thought that's what you and Elinor had been doing. Fanny is having Stewart pack up the study right now."

Marianne spun on her heel and began running downstairs, feeling for the key to the study in her pocket. She hadn't locked it when Elinor rushed upstairs. And Fanny, opportunistic as she was, had seized her chance.

She burst into the study, startling two footmen, a maid, and Stewart, who was overseeing the packing.

"Miss Marianne," he said. "Can I be of assistance?"

"Where are you taking these things?" she asked, slightly out of breath.

"Mrs. Dashwood has asked that your father's things be packed away in storage for now," Stewart said. "And the books be taken to the library."

Mrs. Dashwood? Marianne thought. Then she realized that he meant Fanny.

"I just need to—" Marianne made for her father's desk, intending to grab her father's case files, but Stewart blocked her gently.

"I'm sorry, Miss Marianne. But Mrs. Dashwood was very clear. Everything is to be packed away, and she asked that I see you not remove anything."

Marianne stared at Stewart in shock. "But—the case files. Can I at least take the open ones? I must inform my father's clients of his death, and see to the closing of their cases."

But Stewart would not budge, and the footmen packing books and the maid quickly packing the files would not meet Marianne's eye. For a brief moment, Marianne was filled with an incandescent rage at Fanny, not only for being so horrible but for stymieing this case. She mentally added this to her long list of reasons to suspect her sister-in-law, but she knew from childhood experience that throwing a tantrum would not get Stewart to budge.

"Stewart, did my father ring for tea the night before he died?"

The butler, not easily ruffled, was blindsided by the question. He blinked twice, then said, "I don't believe so . . . but, Mrs. Matthews has informed me that a cup and saucer from the tea service have been missing. I've located the saucer on your father's desk, but not the teacup."

Because it was upstairs, now a vital piece of evidence. But Marianne didn't volunteer that information. If Father didn't ring for tea, then how did it appear in his study? And Stewart raised a very good point, one she should have thought of sooner:

Why was there a single teacup and not an entire tea service?

"Begging your pardon, Miss Marianne, Mr. Stewart," the maid spoke up. She had appeared before them and curtsied nervously. "But Mr. Dashwood asked for tea as he went into his study that night. He didn't ring for it, because he saw me fetching a shawl for Mrs. Dashwood, and he stopped me in the hall."

"Very good, Emily," Mr. Stewart said, his voice stern with the unspoken admonishment for interrupting. But Marianne could have kissed her.

"He asked for tea, just a cup and nothing more?"

"He said not to bother with a full service as he wouldn't drink more, but to bring it with lemon on a tray. He said . . ." Emily trailed off with a quick glance to Stewart.

"It's all right," Marianne said, "but this is terribly important. To my mother. You see, she's been having a difficult time and wants to understand exactly what transpired that night."

The lie felt flimsy, but it was enough for Emily to continue. "Well, he made a joke, miss. He said that what he truly wanted was brandy, but that Mrs. Dashwood would not approve, so please bring him tea with lemon."

"And did you make an entire pot, or . . . ?"

"Well, no," Emily faltered. "We, that is to say, I poured him a cup from the servants' pot. It was fresh, miss, I promise!"

"That sounds sensible," Marianne murmured, but that did

pose an interesting conundrum. The tea had been poisoned, and her father was not in the habit of taking tea in the evening. Which meant that whoever had placed the poison in his tea must have sensed the opportunity to do so. But if the tea had been poured from a pot that multiple people had drunk from, that meant the cup specifically had been poisoned. Which added weight to the deliberate nature of the crime. "And then you brought it up to him?" she prodded.

"I was going to, but Hannah offered. She was going up anyway."

Interesting. Hannah was the Dashwoods' head housemaid. Marianne tried to imagine her poisoning Mr. Dashwood, but it just didn't fit—Hannah was a brisk, strong woman of about thirty, with a pleasant disposition, although Marianne always thought of her as reserved. She was unmarried and she'd been with the Dashwoods since Marianne was young—exactly how long, she couldn't say.

"Will that be all, miss?" Stewart asked, startling Marianne out of her thoughts.

"Oh, yes. Thank you, Emily."

Marianne lingered in the study, watching as her father's things were packed away with brisk efficiency. She tried to imagine what Hannah's motive could possibly be. Money? A better position? Was she in some sort of terrible trouble, the type that Margaret was always going on about in her novels?

A distant bell rang, and Stewart tilted his head. With a nod to Marianne, he swept out of the room. Now, if only it were as simple to get rid of the other servants. . . .

When Stewart's footsteps faded, Emily cleared her throat. "Miss?"

Marianne looked to her and saw that she stood very near the desk, where Father's files had once been stored and were now stashed away in crates. But her hands were on a small stack of papers. "I found these, under the blotter. I don't know if they're important, but . . ."

Marianne looked at the footmen, but they studiously ignored her. Marianne recognized this small opening and crossed the room, taking the files. "Thank you, Emily."

"Just make yourself scarce before Mr. Stewart comes back."

"Consider it done."

She clutched the papers to her chest as she darted back out into the hall, keeping an eye out for Stewart or Fanny. But luck was not on her side—she could hear Fanny's voice on the landing, saying, "No, I don't want to look at it. Store it in the attic, and we'll sell it off after a respectable period of time has passed."

Marianne darted down the hall, mentally mapping out various escape routes. Which room could she hide in until it was all clear? The dining room, she decided—it was hours until the evening meal, and the room would be quite empty. She was about to step foot inside when she heard Stewart's voice from within. "The new Mrs. Dashwood has instructed that this carpet be removed and beaten."

"But we just did the carpets the week before last," Mrs. Matthews protested.

"Nonetheless," Stewart intoned in a weary voice.

Drat! Marianne spun around and darted through the door to the servants' stairs.

She didn't often use the inconspicuous side stairs that led down to the kitchen or upstairs to discreet openings in the hall, but desperate times called for unconventional measures. She began to climb the narrow steps, but she wasn't destined to make an entirely clean getaway.

"Miss Marianne!" a maid exclaimed—but not just any maid. *Hannah.* She was carrying a large basket full of linens and clothing. "Can I help you?"

"Oh, no—I mean . . ." Drat it all, she had hoped to approach Hannah with a strategy, not have Hannah surprise her. Concern creased Hannah's forehead, and her head tilted slightly.

"Were you looking for me?" she asked. "I just spoke with Mrs. Dashwood. I'm to come with you, to your new flat."

Marianne's eyebrows shot up. "Oh?"

"Yes," she confirmed. "I'm a fair hand in the kitchen, and I've been learning from Mrs. Matthews the past eight years. Mrs. Dashwood thought I might be the best fit for your new home."

"Of course," Marianne said, forcing herself to smile. "Well, it will be ever so lovely to have a familiar face."

Before she could think of anything else to say, a door opened below. Marianne willed herself not to turn around. Hannah's eyes dipped and she saw the papers clutched tightly to Marianne's chest. Then she heard, "Miss Marianne? Whatever are you doing?"

Marianne's gaze was fixed on Hannah, so she didn't miss when Hannah's eyes darted down, and she followed her gaze to see Hannah lowering her basket slightly, to let Marianne slip the papers on top. Marianne made a split-second decision. She dropped the papers in Hannah's possession and spun around.

"Stewart! I was looking for Hannah. She's to come with us to our new flat, did you know?"

"Yes," he said. "Mrs. Dashwood had mentioned it. However, if you need help packing anything, you can still ring for any of the servants."

It was a gentle rebuke—Stewart didn't approve of members of the family venturing belowstairs, although he tolerated it. It struck Marianne that this might be the last time she faced the butler, and she softened. "I know, I'm sorry—it's just that everyone is so busy."

"Very well," he said, and stepped aside and gestured for Marianne to come down. "But if you need anything, please do ring. Hannah, where are you taking that basket?"

"They're just my own things, Mr. Stewart. I'm to put them in the wagon to go to the flat ahead of the ladies."

Marianne cast one last glance over her shoulder at Hannah as she stepped back out into the hall. Hannah winked as she went past her, descending into the kitchen.

It wasn't entirely reassuring.

✂

When the Dashwood girls pulled up in front of their new home two days later, Marianne wasn't even sure what she was looking at.

"Is this . . . where are we?" she asked her mother, who'd been completely silent on the drive from their old home.

Mrs. Dashwood startled slightly, as if she hadn't realized the carriage had stopped moving. "Oh yes, this is it."

"But . . ." Marianne stared out the window. They were in Cheapside, the bustling neighborhood where the Dashwood girls had often come to shop—but she hadn't thought about *living* there. The streets were clogged with carts, carriages, and pedestrians. The row of buildings they'd stopped in front of looked to be in good repair, but the houses were narrow and cramped together, and it seemed as though everywhere she looked there were people.

"This looks pleasant," Elinor said, always the do-gooder. "We'll be able to walk to market."

"I like it," Margaret proclaimed. "It has character." She was the first to scramble out of the carriage.

"Margaret, wait!" Elinor called after her, leaving Marianne and her mother inside.

"I know it's not much," Mrs. Dashwood said quietly. "But Sir John was very kind to let it to us."

Marianne felt miserable at the idea of her mother needing to explain herself, so she smiled brightly. "Don't worry, I'm sure it will be . . . very comfortable. And it was kind of Sir John, considering we hardly know him."

"Just because you don't know him doesn't mean I don't," Mrs. Dashwood said, and a hint of her old parental authority came peeking out. "We used to spend summers together when we were children, and we've always kept in touch."

Marianne followed her mother out of the carriage and saw that the man in question stood in the open doorway of their new flat, Elinor and Margaret before him. Marianne felt herself soften a little at the sight of the middle-aged man, his brown hair thinning and his eyes heavily lined, face folded in concentration as he listened carefully to Margaret and nodded at one of her queries.

When they approached, Sir John looked up and said, "Mary! I hope you don't mind the intrusion, but I wanted to welcome you personally."

"Thank you, John," Mrs. Dashwood said, extending her hand for him to shake. "And I see you've met my girls. Elinor, Margaret, and this is Marianne."

Introductions and polite inquiries were made, and Marianne assessed Sir John. He seemed amiable, quick to smile, but then he would dim the expression with a slight wince, as if remembering they were in mourning. Eager to please, Marianne deduced.

"I also took the liberty of bringing a few of my footmen with me," Sir John said, indicating the liveried young men already unpacking their trunks and the wagon full of last-minute items that they hadn't sent ahead earlier. "But you'll want to see inside, I imagine."

"How kind of you," their mother murmured, and the girls followed her inside.

"Oh my," Elinor said, taking in the small space. "Well, it's certainly cozy."

The flat was quite small, but Marianne wouldn't have called it *cozy*. The front door opened to a narrow, dark hall, and the sisters began to explore with a mix of excitement and trepidation. There was a small sitting room with bare floors and no drapes, and the wallpaper was faded but in good condition. It opened into a dining room that was cramped with the table they'd brought from home, one of the smaller ones that seated only eight. At the back of the flat was a cramped kitchen, a small room for Hannah, and an impossibly narrow staircase leading upstairs.

"The steps creak, I'm afraid," Sir John said, "and there is a loose floorboard in one of the bedchambers that I can send a man around to fix."

"I have always wanted a loose floorboard!" Margaret exclaimed, darting up the narrow staircase with excitement. "Please don't fix it."

At Sir John's bewildered look, Marianne explained, "She'll

hide half her things under it by nightfall."

Sir John's delighted laugh was loud. "Well, I would hate to let down Miss Margaret. But if you would like it repaired, Mary, just write to me."

Their mother and Sir John stayed downstairs while Elinor and Marianne followed Margaret up the staircase. Upstairs, there were two bedrooms, just as Mother had described—one large and one small. In the larger of the two rooms sat a single large bed—Marianne and Elinor would be sharing—with a trundle underneath for Margaret. The footmen had brought their trunks up the front staircase and set them haphazardly in the room.

"Well, this is nice, isn't it?"

Marianne turned to find Elinor in the doorway. "Are you serious?"

"The windows are tall, and they get good light."

"There are no curtains. The entire street can look in on us."

"We'll fix that before evening. We can get this place spruced up in no time."

Marianne merely shook her head. This flat was a far cry from what she was used to, but she would dwell on that later. For now, she needed to figure out what Hannah had done with the papers she'd taken from Father's office. The maid had been here a day already, and she hoped that Hannah had left them in their room. She began rummaging about the wardrobe and the chest, patting the bedding.

"What on earth are you doing?" Elinor asked her.

"Looking for . . . Ah-ha!"

The papers had been stashed in a drawer of the washstand, which sat in the corner of the bedroom. Marianne withdrew them and sat on the bed, where the light was good. "Finally!"

Two days of wondering what these papers contained had nearly done her in. Two days of guessing which case file might have been pulled or wondering if this had anything to do with Father's new case that he'd not said a word about but that Marianne had suspected was something dangerous—why else wouldn't he have involved her? But it had also been a long two days of wondering if Hannah could be trusted.

"What do they say?" Elinor asked.

"They're . . . oh." Marianne scanned the first page, then the second. The third and fourth pages were also disappointing. "It's an *old* case file."

Disappointment curdled with resentment in the pit of Marianne's stomach, and she tossed the papers aside and stared at the bare walls. They felt too close, boxing her in. She knew it was too much to hope that on these papers, tucked beneath the blotter that her father had died on, he might have written out the name of the person who poisoned him. But she still hoped that it would be *something* useful.

"What case was this?" Elinor asked, scanning their father's handwriting.

"An old one," she repeated. "Father closed it ages ago.

Wrongful death, or . . . yes, accidental death, I remember now. Father took it on when I was in Bath with the Moores. A Mr. Brandon hired Father to look into the death of a Miss Eliza Williams last year."

Elinor turned over to the next page and read Father's report aloud. "On the thirtieth of March, Mr. Brandon requested that I look into the death of his acquaintance, Miss Eliza Williams. Mr. Brandon and Miss Williams worked together at the apothecary run by Mr. Williams, Miss Williams's uncle, and also attended lectures and demonstrations in the study of medicine together, chaperoned by a Mrs. Jennings. On the twenty-fourth of March, Mr. Brandon discovered Miss Williams on the floor of her uncle's laboratory, unresponsive and lifeless. A doctor was called, but attempts to resuscitate her were unsuccessful. Her death was deemed a laboratory accident, but Mr. Brandon claims that Miss Williams was working on a series of experiments that she thought would be a significant contribution to the medical community, and her notes were missing. On this basis, Mr. Brandon thought that Miss Williams's death was not accidental."

Elinor skipped ahead, scanning Father's summary of those he'd interviewed. "Conclusion: accidental death. He just wrote that after interviewing everyone involved, and hearing Mr. Brandon's own admission that sometimes laboratory experiments could be dangerous, he could find no probable cause of wrongdoing." She looked at Marianne. "So why was this *closed* case on his desk when he died?"

"I don't know."

"Well, it certainly warrants a closer look."

Marianne sat up and swung a withering glare at Elinor, who held the papers before her, studying them with scientific concentration. "Are you serious? It's got nothing to do with Father's death. We have our suspects, remember?"

Elinor finally looked up and did a double take when she met Marianne's stare. "Yes, but I think we should consider all angles and possibilities."

"Except for the one that suggests that John killed Father and paid Hannah to do it?"

"Keep your voice down." Elinor cast a quick glance behind her to ensure they weren't overheard. "I just have a difficult time believing that anyone, especially *Hannah*, could be responsible for something so horrid. And that she would then choose to move with us to Cheapside rather than stay in a fine house with far more comforts."

"Maybe John didn't want her around," Marianne wondered. "Maybe he and Fanny thought the reminder was too much, or maybe they became too suspicious of her, and what she's capable of. . . ."

"What are you saying?"

Marianne knew it would shock her sister, but she said the words anyway. "People tend to kill one of two ways—impulsively, caught up in the moment, or planned. The ones who plan tend to get a taste for it."

"Now you're being absurd." Elinor thrust the papers back into Marianne's hands. "I don't believe for a second that Hannah is a killer."

But Marianne saw a flash of fear in her sister's eyes.

"Fine. But we need to figure out our next move."

"Let's unpack first," Elinor said. "I can't think when everything is in such disarray."

Marianne stashed the papers under the ticking of the mattress and helped her sister drag the trunk across the room and open it. As they began unpacking their things, Marianne whispered, "What do you think of Sir John?"

"He seems nice enough," Elinor replied. "I can't imagine where we'd be right now without him. He's doing us a tremendous favor."

"A favor?" Marianne asked.

"Yes. This flat is a bit beyond what I think our budget can accommodate. But Mother assures me he's giving it to us at a very good rate."

"But I thought we had funds from John?"

"Yes, however we must budget carefully. We need it to last as long as possible, while we figure out how to earn money."

Elinor's last sentence sounded too much like a reprimand to Marianne's ears. "Which is exactly what I'm trying to do, you know. If we solve Father's murder, that will prove to prospective clients that I am worth hiring."

"And if you can't solve it?" Elinor asked.

"You don't think I can?" Marianne asked. Her resentment, a simmer, now began to boil. "What would you have us do instead? Sit and accept Father's murder while looking for rich husbands to rescue us? Doesn't it bother you that John and Fanny have taken everything from us?"

It was the most peculiar and maddening thing about Elinor—the more upset Marianne got, the more patient Elinor appeared. She simply said, "I assure you, a great deal bothers me about our circumstances. But we can't help how Father left things, and we are lucky that Mr. Farrows, at least, is attempting to help us."

"He might have disagreed with Fanny, but that doesn't mean he's on our side."

Elinor's perfect forehead creased. "You might not have noticed since you stormed off during the will reading, but he defended us to her. Not even John can manage to do that."

"Do you have feelings for him?" Marianne asked, incredulous.

Elinor's expression smoothed from frustration to a mask of calm that Marianne didn't trust for a moment. "Don't be silly, I've only just met him."

Marianne might have believed her, if she hadn't then added, "Besides, how could I know if I have feelings for him? Beyond gratitude for his consideration of our circumstances, of course."

"How could you possibly know?" Marianne reiterated. "You would just *know*."

It seemed to her the most obvious thing in the world. Mother spoke of how she'd fallen for Father on the spot, within moments of meeting him and accepting his offer of a dance at a ball. It was Marianne's second most fervent wish, after succeeding as an investigator, to find love just like that.

But when Elinor didn't respond, Marianne shrugged and said, "Well, I suppose it's all right if you felt nothing more. I think he's overall rather uninspiring."

"You require so much, Marianne," Elinor snapped, grabbing the petticoat Marianne had been folding right out of her hands.

"So what if I do?" she asked, watching as her sister fumbled with the garment. "It's not wrong to have standards. Just like it's not wrong to want to know who killed our father."

"Shh," Elinor hushed her, casting a look over her shoulder for their mother.

"I will not hush! I'm going to investigate, and there's nothing you can do to stop me."

"That's what I'm afraid of," Elinor said.

FIVE

*In Which the Dashwood Sisters
Make the Acquaintance of Mr. Brandon*

IN THE LIGHT OF their first morning in their new flat on Barton Street, Elinor wondered if she was mad to entertain Marianne's ideas about investigating their father's death. She could think of half a dozen reasons why they shouldn't: it would only upset their mother; they didn't have a clear path; it could be dangerous; no one would believe them; they could ruin their reputations; and, most important, it wouldn't bring their father back.

But maybe discovering who had killed their father would bring them all some comfort, and comfort was something that the Dashwoods could do with a bit of—especially when Mother refused to leave her bedchamber.

Elinor and her sisters had come downstairs for breakfast to

find only Hannah setting the dining room table. Elinor went back up and knocked on their mother's door, but there was no response. After a minute or two of knocking, she tried the door, but it was locked. That was when she began to grow frantic, knocking and jostling the door until she heard her mother's hoarse voice call out, "Let me sleep!"

"Are you ill?" Elinor called back. "Should I fetch a physician?"

But their mother didn't respond, and finally Marianne intervened. "If she doesn't want to come out, you can't force her. Let Hannah leave a tray outside the door, then come on. We've things to discuss."

Elinor allowed herself to be reluctantly led away, back down to a lukewarm breakfast that she ate without noticing and that sat heavy in her stomach. The second she pushed her fork away, Marianne leaned forward. "We need to formulate a plan," she told Elinor, and even Margaret looked excited. She had a neat stack of paper before her and a quill.

"What're you doing?" Elinor asked her youngest sister.

"Taking notes," she said. "Besides, this might go into one of my novels."

"Well, don't share anything with anyone until we've solved this," Marianne ordered.

"I'm eleven, not stupid."

"All right, girls!" Elinor said loudly, hoping to interrupt an argument before one began. "Marianne, why don't you tell us about what he was working on before he died?"

Marianne rolled her eyes. "Why, what a novel idea, Elinor. Are you sure I'm the investigator here, or would you like to take over?"

Elinor bit her lip. Marianne was clearly in a peevish mood, and it was best to not needle her.

"He'd just closed the Morrison case a week before—it was a truly boring instance of family reunion. Mr. Morrison went to sea and was gone for two years, but when he returned his wife and children were nowhere to be found. Father found his family in Brighton. They moved in with Mrs. Morrison's sister when their landlord raised the rent, and the letter informing her husband went astray. It was touching, a family reunited. All parties were satisfied."

"But you thought he had a new case?"

Marianne grimaced. "Well, that's the thing . . . I don't quite know. We've been trying to close the Palmer suspected infidelity case for weeks, but Mrs. Palmer won't accept that her husband isn't unfaithful. It wasn't something Father was working on much, and it was hardly fodder for murder. I know he was working on something because he let something slip about taking a walk about town to follow a few leads, but he wouldn't tell me anything more. I don't recall seeing a file. If we had his journal, then we might be able to deduce what exactly he was working on."

"What date was that?" Margaret asked.

"What date was what?"

"That he went for his walk about town. It might be important."

Marianne looked at their little sister with grudging respect. "I don't know exactly—he said something about it two days before he died, so it could have been anytime before then and when Elinor found him. I was going to ask him that morning. . . ."

Margaret nodded and went back to writing.

"So, for all we know, this new case might have something to do with his death," Elinor reasoned.

"I don't buy it," Marianne countered quickly. "No, don't give me that look, let me explain. When clients come to us, they have problems they want us to solve. They *need* us. It hardly makes any sense that they would kill Father before he had a chance to get started."

"But we don't know exactly what Father knew, how much he'd investigated, or what he might have uncovered."

"Yes, fine," Marianne agreed. "Are you sure you don't want to investigate this one on your own, because you've clearly gotten it all figured out."

Elinor took a steadying breath and reminded herself that Marianne was hurting. They were all hurting. Arguing among themselves wouldn't solve anything. "I'm not trying to be contrary, I just want to get a sense for where we should focus our attention. Let's make a list of all the potential suspects or avenues of investigation."

This was a strategy she often used when tinkering in her lab—she'd pose a question or experiment and think on it, then write down as many possible hypotheses as she could think of before deciding upon her first course of action. She'd experienced a significant decrease in accidental fires since she'd taken up this method of inquiry.

"I've already got one," Margaret announced, scribbling one last word before looking up. She blew gently on her paper and set down her quill. "All right. John and Fanny are at the top of the list. After that, I have the closed case file Marianne retrieved from Papa's desk. Then, the new mystery case."

She looked to her sisters for approval. Elinor nodded and said, "For the sake of being thorough, put down the Palmer case, just in case."

Marianne huffed her disbelief. "Then add 'random act of violence' while you're at it."

"It doesn't hurt to lay out all our options," Elinor said. "Now, we must discuss how we'll approach each of these theories."

Marianne leaned forward. "We need to discover either a clear motive for the crime, or the means."

"What are means?" Margaret asked.

"Opportunity. Who had access to Father, to his teacup, to poison? Who had the tools and the chance to see that Father could be murdered?"

As if on cue, they heard a knock at the dining room door,

and Hannah entered without waiting for a response. "Begging your pardon, but I thought I'd clear these dishes."

Elinor cast Marianne a warning glance, but her sister didn't heed it. "Of course, come in! We're sorry, Hannah. We didn't mean to keep you."

"It's quite all right, miss. We're all getting used to things."

"How're you settling in?" Elinor asked. It wasn't just the Dashwood women who were experiencing an upheaval, and while it was true there were far fewer rooms here on Barton Street, Hannah's workload would have increased since she was the only servant in the household.

"I'm well, thank you for asking." Hannah began to carefully pile up plates and gather the silver. "Being back in Cheapside reminds me of my first years in London."

"You're from the neighborhood?" Elinor asked.

"Oh, no, I'm just a country lass at heart. I came to London when I was sixteen, and my first position was just a few streets over, cleaning for a very nice lady. She passed, and I was fortunate enough to find a position with your family." Hannah smiled fondly, not at all the picture of a killer.

"You must miss everyone else so much," Marianne remarked, and Elinor thought it sounded too much like a challenge. But Hannah didn't seem to notice.

"It will be different," she acknowledged. "And I'll miss being close to my sister—she had just been hired in the kitchens by the Groffs, you know. First time in a decade that we had

77

lived within walking distance of each other—not that we had ample time to visit, of course!"

"I'm sorry to hear that we took you away from her," Elinor murmured, making a mental note to ask Mother when Hannah's days off were and if they could coordinate them so she could visit her sister.

"Oh, don't worry, miss—we're much closer here in London than when I left to come to town by myself."

She finished stacking the dishes and reached out to pick up Marianne's empty teacup, when Marianne said, "Oh, Hannah—I've not been able to get something off my mind, and I wondered if you could help."

Hannah looked perplexed. "Of course, Miss Marianne."

"It's just that . . . I can't help but think upon Father's last day with us. The worst part about an unexpected death like his is that we never got to say goodbye, or tell him how much we loved him. And I can't help but think about how he died alone in his study, with no one to comfort him in his final hours."

True emotion made Marianne's voice catch, and Elinor suspected that she wasn't playacting her feelings, even if she knew Marianne was manipulating the moment.

"I spoke with Stewart and Emily before we left, trying to understand what that last night would have been like. And Emily said he asked for tea, but that you brought it to him?"

Hannah nodded. "Yes, miss. I was going up to sweep out the fireplace in the dining room, and I saw Emily getting ready to take it up. She hadn't had supper yet, so I offered to take it up when I went."

An awkward pause ensued, while Marianne waited to see if Hannah would say anything more. When she didn't offer any more information, Elinor murmured a banal "How kind."

Hannah seemed a bit puzzled by this question and started to reach for the teacup again, but Marianne said, "I do believe you were the last to see him alive."

If she was hoping for a shocked or guilty reaction, she didn't get one. Hannah's face softened and she nodded sadly. "So it would seem. I'm very sorry, Miss Marianne. He seemed fine to me. He was as concentrated as ever on his work. I offered to build a fire for him, because it was chilly in the room. But he said he didn't plan to work for much longer. I took the liberty of saying I didn't think the open window would be good for his cold, and he assured me the chill was good for his congestion."

Elinor opened her mouth to assure her that she wasn't at fault for not building a fire, but something snagged in her memory. *I offered to build a fire for him, because it was chilly in the room.* It had been chilly in the study when Elinor went to fetch him the next morning. *I didn't think the open window would be good for his cold . . .*

The window had been open. How could Elinor have forgotten? She remembered now, entering the quiet room, seeing the drapes flutter slightly in the draft, crossing the room to latch the window before facing the desk. . . .

The window had been open, and anyone could have come in or gotten back out again.

Marianne thanked Hannah, who took her stash of breakfast dishes and left the dining room. The girls waited until they heard the kitchen door shut behind her, and then Elinor said, "I don't think Hannah did it."

"She could be a very good liar," Marianne argued, but even she sounded uncertain. "Maybe she and her sister needed money."

"She was happy, her sister was nearby, and we paid her more before Father died than we do now," Elinor argued, almost gleefully dismantling her sister's arguments. "But that's not it—Hannah said the window was open. I just remembered, when I went to fetch Father and I found him . . . when I found him. The window was open, just a crack. I closed it before going to Father."

Marianne's eyes narrowed. "Why would you close the window first?"

Elinor didn't know how to explain the sense of wrongness in the room when she opened the door, her instinctive dread and how it was much easier to focus on closing the window first before turning to face the desk. "I don't know, I just did. But don't you understand?"

"Someone could have gotten in through the window," Margaret explained.

Grim triumph flooded through Elinor. "So you see? We shouldn't just focus on John and Fanny."

"But we can't exclude them, either," Marianne said stubbornly. "Margaret, can I see your list?"

Margaret passed over her list of suspects and Elinor and Marianne both took a second look.

"We should write to those involved in the Williams case and ask for a meeting," Elinor said. She was already reaching for the stray papers that made up the flimsy report.

"Fine," Margaret said. "You write the letter. But I'm not going to give up on John and Fanny."

"I would expect nothing less," Elinor said. "I don't know what to do about Father's mysterious new case. I suppose we could ask Mother, but . . ."

She looked to the ceiling, imagining their grief-stricken mother in bed.

"Later," Marianne decided. "We have to do it in such a way that we don't upset her any further." Elinor nodded. They were both in agreement on that, at least.

"As for the Palmers," Elinor murmured, then looked to Marianne. "What do you think?"

But Marianne merely scoffed. "They aren't responsible, trust me. But if you need reassurance, write to your new friend Edward Farrows. He has all of Father's ledgers and case files."

Elinor tried to keep a straight face, but just the thought of writing to Mr. Farrows made her flush. Would he welcome a letter from them, at their new address? Did he even have their new address? Not that he would need it. He could always contact them via John and Fanny. But maybe writing to inquire about the Palmer case would ensure he had their new address. . . .

What was she thinking! She had more important things to worry about.

"I think we should focus first on the Williams case," she said primly, and chose to ignore Marianne's knowing smirk.

✄

Elinor did not have to wait long to hear from Mrs. Jennings. That morning, she sent her a note explaining who she was, conveying the news of Father's death, and requesting a meeting to discuss Father's work on the case. By the late afternoon, Mrs. Jennings sent a response, inviting Elinor and Marianne to call on her at their earliest convenience—but she also took the liberty of sharing that she would be glad to receive them the next day.

"Hmm," was all Marianne said when Elinor showed her the note.

"It has to mean something," Elinor insisted excitedly. "If she thought this case were closed and finished, she wouldn't insist we call on her."

"We shall see," Marianne replied as Elinor picked up her quill to respond.

Margaret was very put out that the invitation did not include her. "It's not fair," she moaned, sitting on the stairs and watching as her older sisters donned bonnets the next day. "I'm helping, aren't I? He was my father, too!"

Her words burned on Elinor's conscience, but it was one thing to let their mystery- and adventure-obsessed youngest sister join in on their discussions. It was quite another to take her investigating outside the house. "Stay and look after Mother," she said. "Make sure she eats. I don't like that she hasn't come down again today."

Margaret groaned, but that was that, and the girls stepped out to hire a carriage to take them to the address Mrs. Jennings had provided. On the way there, Marianne leveled a single serious look at Elinor and said, "I trust that you'll handle all the social graces, but when it comes to asking questions about the case, let me do the talking."

Elinor didn't feel like arguing. "Fine," she said, impatient to get there already.

Mrs. Jennings lived in a slim town house at a respectable address that was just a touch too dated to be considered fashionable. Nonetheless, the sisters were shown all social courtesies as they were led to the drawing room. As Elinor took in the well-kept house and carefully polished furniture, she couldn't help but wonder why Mrs. Jennings would act as a paid chaperone to someone like Miss Williams when she didn't appear to be wanting for material comforts or good society.

Unless she was the sort of woman good society rejected.

"The Misses Dashwood!" she exclaimed when they entered

her drawing room. Mrs. Jennings was a tall woman, with blond hair that had turned mostly gray and sharp blue eyes. She was dressed in very fine but reserved shades of slate blue, perfectly proper—except perfectly proper ladies weren't often involved in cases regarding mysterious deaths of young ladies. Elinor and Marianne dipped into curtsies, but the older woman grasped their hands eagerly. "I was so distraught to hear of your father's passing—my condolences, dears."

"Thank you, Mrs. Jennings," Elinor said. She had the peculiar feeling the other woman would have gathered them into her arms for an embrace if it were at all proper. "And thank you for receiving us on such short notice."

"Absolutely horrid news," Mrs. Jennings continued, almost as if she hadn't heard Elinor. "Your father was the kindest man, and he cared so much for his work. I was absolutely sick to receive your letter, wasn't I, Mr. Brandon?"

Elinor snapped to attention and realized that they weren't the only guests Mrs. Jennings was receiving; and by the subtle intake of breath beside her, she knew Marianne was equally surprised.

Elinor's first impression of this Mr. Brandon was, rather unkindly, of a crow-like man. He stood off to the side, tall with dark hair and gray, watchful eyes. He wore rimmed spectacles and was dressed plainly in a white shirt and cravat, which stood in stark contrast against his black jacket. His expression was grave as he bowed stiffly to the Dashwood sisters. "My condolences," he murmured.

"I hope you don't mind, I invited Mr. Brandon," Mrs. Jennings continued, and Elinor got the impression that even if they had minded, it would not have altered a thing. "When I saw you had questions about poor Eliza, I figured that you would want to speak with Mr. Brandon as well—so here we all are! Please sit down."

Elinor and Marianne sat beside each other on the settee while Mrs. Jennings rang for tea, and Elinor tried to contain the excitement surging within her. If Eliza Williams's death had been entirely accidental, why did Mrs. Jennings seem so eager to hear their questions and call Mr. Brandon? She glanced at her sister, but Marianne was the picture of serene confidence.

"How convenient," she said, eyeing Mr. Brandon. He waited until the ladies were seated before taking a chair nearby. "We do appreciate your willingness to speak with us, and so quickly."

"Of course! I couldn't help but hope that some new information had come to light, even some tidbit. . . ."

Elinor cast a sideways glance at Marianne. Their father might have declared this a closed case, but Mrs. Jennings certainly wasn't acting as though it were.

But Marianne ignored Mrs. Jennings's unspoken question. "What can you tell us about Miss Williams?"

It was as though Mrs. Jennings had been waiting all week for someone to ask this. "Oh, she was the sweetest young lady, Miss Marianne. Just a smidge older than you girls, and very bright, isn't that right, Mr. Brandon? She was determined to pursue the sciences, and she was lucky that her uncle was a chemist. He encouraged her, and she would experiment day and night. Mr. Brandon could tell you all about that. I got to know her when she had the chance to observe some of the doctors at Barts Hospital with the students. It wouldn't have been proper for her to go unchaperoned, so her uncle hired me to accompany her. I've a strong stomach, you understand. My husband was a surgeon in the navy, bless his soul. And I've no children of my own, so I do try and help out young people whenever I can."

Elinor found herself studying Mr. Brandon out of the corner of her eye while Marianne made polite remarks in response. His gray eyes stayed riveted on Marianne while she gently questioned Mrs. Jennings. His serious countenance and plain manner of dressing had made him appear older, but she was surprised to realize that he was probably only about twenty or so. An apprentice and student himself, then.

"Miss Williams sounded awfully clever," Marianne remarked when Mrs. Jennings took a breath.

"She was," Mr. Brandon said, speaking for the first time since their introduction. His voice did not waver in its certainty. "Which is why there is no way she could have died in her own laboratory."

Marianne turned her gaze sharply to Mr. Brandon, who returned her stare. Elinor felt as though she were caught between an unstoppable force and an immovable object.

When no one said anything after a long pause, Elinor decided to break her promise to let Marianne do the questioning. "If it's not too upsetting, can you tell us how it happened?"

She didn't address the question to either Mr. Brandon or Mrs. Jennings, but Mrs. Jennings was the one who answered, her voice soft around the edges. "Her uncle found her, collapsed on the floor in the laboratory one morning when he came down to open the shop. Not a mark on her."

Mr. Brandon took over the telling then. "I came down moments after he discovered her and opened all the windows and doors, then removed Mr. Williams from the room, in case there were any lingering poisonous gases." His voice was stoic, as if he were reading from a script. "A physician was called— I'm only in training—and he was unable to determine a precise cause of death. It was deduced that she must have mixed elements in her experiments that proved to be poisonous, and since she was working late at night, she succumbed to the poison without anyone realizing."

"But clearly you disagreed with that conclusion," Marianne said, her gaze still locked on Mr. Brandon.

"I do," he said, and the use of the present tense left the sisters with no uncertainty as to what Mr. Brandon thought of their father's conclusion. "Miss Williams was entirely too clever to die in a laboratory experiment. There were signs of a slight struggle—substances spilled, some broken glass—but Mr. Williams and the doctor decided that must have been a result of her panic when she realized something was wrong."

A small chill shuddered down Elinor's spine. She had once mixed two chemicals, just to see what might happen, and had been horrified by the immediate chemical stench that caused her to gag. She'd stumbled to the attic window and barely managed to throw open the latch to fresh air before blacking out. Perhaps she wouldn't have died . . . but the memory lingered as a warning of the dangers that chemistry could pose.

"But how did the doctor and Mr. Williams explain the absence of such a poisonous gas when you all found her?" Marianne asked.

"Gas can dissipate," Elinor murmured.

Mr. Brandon's attention snapped to her and she offered a weak smile as Marianne explained, "Elinor dabbles in the sciences."

Dabbles? Before Elinor could come up with a response, Mr. Brandon spoke.

"There was also the matter of her missing notes. She was working on concocting a new substance before she died."

"What was the substance?" Elinor cut in, curious.

"I don't know exactly."

"Don't know, or won't say?" Marianne asked.

"I can't say what I don't know," Mr. Brandon said mildly, unruffled by the trace of hostility in Marianne's tone. "She could be secretive, but she had good reason. In our early days studying at Barts, she hypothesized to an attending surgeon that there might one day be a way to give a patient medicine directly to the blood—perhaps through a needle. She was laughed at, of course. The other students and surgeons bullied her for weeks over that idea, and many wanted her to be banned from observations altogether. I tried to speak up for her, but as a student my position is tenuous. It broke her spirit a bit, having to keep silent."

Elinor was appalled and fascinated in equal measure. To have a life where one could study the sciences openly seemed marvelous, although clearly it had come at a cost.

Mr. Brandon continued, "I think, judging by the equipment she used, that Eliza was attempting to isolate a substance. That means—"

"Distill an active ingredient from a substance," Elinor supplied, then clamped her mouth shut. Marianne's comment about her *dabbling* echoed in her ears.

"Yes," Mr. Brandon said, and Elinor was surprised to find that he didn't appear annoyed that she interrupted. "But beyond that, I couldn't say. We talked about scientific matters, but she didn't confide in me. She wanted to test her theories to see if any had weight before she discussed them with anyone, including me."

"But this was all circumstantial, correct?" Marianne asked, impatience sharpening her tone. "There was no other evidence that suggests foul play?"

Mr. Brandon shook his head, although Elinor was surprised

to find he didn't appear to be upset or offended by Marianne's doubt. "No, nothing. Which was why I approached your father."

They were interrupted then by the maid's arrival with the tea service. While she went about placing the tray, Mrs. Jennings spoke up. "Forgive me, dears, but may I ask why you're so curious about Eliza?"

Elinor looked to Marianne. For all their talk of investigating Father's death, they'd never actually discussed how to explain *what* they were doing.

Marianne merely smiled. "We're settling our father's affairs, and we just wanted to ensure his cases were closed to his clients' satisfaction."

"Well, it wasn't," Mr. Brandon said. When Marianne looked to him, he explained, "Closed to my satisfaction. I don't think the case should have been closed at all."

"I'm so sorry," Elinor murmured.

"Hmm," Mrs. Jennings said, and leaned forward to pour the tea. "Please allow an old lady an impertinent question, but did your father die of entirely natural causes, my dear?"

Elinor drew in a sharp breath, and she felt Marianne tense beside her. She was eager to see how Marianne would talk her way around this one, but she wasn't given the chance.

"Oh, my instincts are correct!" Mrs. Jennings exclaimed, delighted by her own cleverness. "You're asking about your father's old cases because you're suspicious. No, you don't have to say anything, dears. Brandon and I know how to keep a secret, don't we?"

Mr. Brandon didn't respond to her chummy comment, but his head tilted slightly as if he were regarding them in a new light.

"We aren't . . . I mean, our father . . . ," Marianne faltered.

"Marianne wants to take up investigating!" Elinor blurted. "Just like our father."

"It's not easy to be a lady and an entrepreneur," Mrs. Jennings said, "but I had the utmost respect for your father's professionalism and skill. I'm sure you'll manage. And if I can send any referrals your way, I will be delighted to do so."

"Thank you," Marianne said, smiling sweetly. Elinor winced as Marianne's heel came down on her toes. "And do you think that Miss Williams was murdered, Mrs. Jennings?"

Mrs. Jennings dunked her biscuit into her tea and said blithely, "Well, she didn't kill herself, now did she?"

"Right," Marianne said. And then she announced, "We must go."

She stood, yanking Elinor to her feet. Mr. Brandon stood as well, but Marianne was already propelling her away. "Thank you, Mrs. Jennings. Please don't trouble yourself, Mr. Brandon. We shall see ourselves out."

Marianne gripped Elinor's elbow as they took their leave of Mrs. Jennings and Mr. Brandon, but as soon as they were outside she exclaimed, "Well, that was a tremendous waste of time! And I told you to let *me* do the talking."

"You weren't answering!" Elinor protested. "I didn't know what to say."

"You were supposed to sit silently and listen."

"It was *rude*," Elinor insisted. "Just sitting there in silence."

"Silence is telling," Marianne countered. "That's what Father always said. You let suspects stew and their guilty consciences spill out."

"So they're suspects now?" Elinor asked.

"No!" Marianne stopped walking and looked at Elinor. "I just wanted them to talk. It's interesting that Father would close the case when the man who hired him is convinced there is foul play, but not unusual. Clients oftentimes refuse to see reason."

"Mr. Brandon didn't seem to be the unreasonable type to me," Elinor mused.

"Oh, he was positively boorish!" Marianne exclaimed. "Did you listen to him recount the case? He was utterly devoid of feeling. I bet you he's an unambitious lackey looking for a bit of excitement in his life."

Elinor was brought up short by that assessment, and its harshness. "I don't believe that at all. If anything, I think that he cared very much."

"Are we speaking of the same person?"

"Yes," Elinor said simply. "I think that he came across so coolly because of the intensity of his feelings about this case."

Marianne scoffed. "He had no *passion*. Except, did you notice him slip up and call her Eliza? Not at all proper. He seems suspicious, if you ask me. And he likely had the means to kill her himself. I wonder what his motive might have been— professional jealousy? Or perhaps he fancied her, and she didn't care for him. Not that I'd blame her."

"Marianne!" Elinor exclaimed.

"Come, Elinor—you have to admit that their case, while tragic and perhaps a touch suspicious, doesn't have any connection to ours. You need to think more like an investigator. Why would anyone involved with Miss Williams want Father dead? He thought her death was an accident, and if Mr. Brandon is innocent and wanted Father to solve the case, then killing Father certainly wouldn't have helped him any. There are no connections!"

Except, Elinor thought, that wasn't exactly true. Because Father had been poisoned, and before they realized that, it looked as though he'd merely fallen asleep. And although Eliza Williams had been found dead in a laboratory accident and there had been signs of a struggle, hadn't Mrs. Jennings said that there hadn't been a mark upon her?

As the sisters turned in the direction of home, a sickening suspicion rose in Elinor.

Could the two of them have been poisoned . . . by the same substance?

SIX

*In Which a Dashing Young Man
Comes to the Dashwood Sisters' Aid*

WHEN IT CAME TO investigations, Marianne believed, in theory, that it was good to keep an open mind. *Don't set your sights on any one thing too soon,* Father had said to her on more than one occasion. But she also didn't want to neglect what had been obvious from the very beginning—John and Fanny benefited the most from Father's death. And if Elinor wasn't willing to entertain the possibility of patricide, then luckily for Marianne, she had another sister to turn to.

Margaret was in favor of Marianne's plan and all too willing to feed Elinor a story about going on a walk to explore their new neighborhood. For half a moment, they both feared that Elinor would insist on coming along, but then she wrinkled her nose and looked to the skies and said, "Are you certain? It looks like it might rain."

"We won't be long!" Marianne insisted, and escaped the flat with Margaret before Elinor could protest, and the two youngest Dashwoods headed straight back to their family home.

"Do you think it will be awful, seeing Fanny and all her things there?" Margaret asked when they set out.

"Oh yes," Marianne said. "It will probably be horrid. You must prepare yourself."

Margaret was quiet for a moment, and an entire bustling block passed before she said, "I suppose it shall be a good experience."

"Experience for what?" Marianne asked, half-distracted because she was mentally reviewing her plan once they arrived at their former home.

"For my writing. I do my best work when I've actually experienced what I'm writing about. Imagine trying to describe what it must feel like to ride a pony if you've never even sat in a saddle! The best tales always have murder and betrayal in them, and now I know what it feels like, so I can write about it."

This brought Marianne up short, and she reached an arm out to stop Margaret, who was oblivious to her older sister's reaction. She looked up at Marianne and rolled her eyes. "You're not going to go all weepy like Elinor, are you?"

Marianne's smile was shaky, but she managed to hold it.

"No, I promise. But sometimes I wonder if you aren't wiser than Elinor and me combined. What a wonderfully optimistic view of things."

"I still miss him," Margaret mumbled, looking down at the cobblestones.

"As do I. And Elinor, and Mother. And while we can't bring him back, we can bring him justice." That was what Marianne wanted, although for the first time since she suspected that Father's death had not been natural, she wondered not just what justice would look like but what it would *feel* like. Triumphant? Peaceful? Or would she still feel that dull ache in the pit of her stomach when she instinctively thought, *I must ask Father . . .* only to realize that she couldn't ever ask him anything again.

Marianne hated the sadness that crept in when she entertained such thoughts, slowing her gait and needling at her sense of purpose.

When they entered their old neighborhood, Marianne looked sideways at her sister. "Now, you're clear on the plan?"

"Distract Fanny while you search for evidence," Margaret recited.

"Exactly, and don't be afraid to play up the sad, forlorn little girl act."

"I'm not a child," Margaret said, her tone sharp enough to draw blood.

"I know that," Marianne lied, "but Fanny thinks you are, and we must take advantage of her foolishness."

Despite Marianne's focus, she felt an unexpected tightening about her throat when she caught sight of her former home. A lesser young lady might have been deterred by the emotions roiling in Marianne's chest, but Marianne was skilled at funneling all her feelings into determination and action. She strode up to the front door of her house—she refused to think of it as John and Fanny's—and knocked firmly.

But the first stumbling block came when a thin-faced man opened the door. He was dressed as the butler, but he was not Stewart. This man was elderly with a grayish complexion but looked spry enough as he looked them up and down with disdain. "Yes?"

"Who're you?" Margaret blurted out.

"Who are you?" the butler responded with a curt tone that made Marianne seethe.

"We are the Misses Dashwood," she said, her tone polite but icy. "And as of last week, this was our home."

"This is the residence of Mr. and Mrs. John Dashwood," the butler said, unmoved.

Marianne looked him dead in the eye and said, "You may inform them that their sisters have come to call."

The butler relented and showed them in. "Please wait here."

Marianne wasn't about to be made to wait in her own foyer. "Nonsense! We're family—we'll just go on through." She led the way to the sitting room, chin up, and burst into a completely different room from what she had left earlier that week.

The furniture had been completely rearranged and, in most cases, swapped out for upholstered pieces in a garish golden-rod hue that Marianne recognized from John and Fanny's last residence. Their sage-green drapes had been replaced with purple velvet, although Marianne saw that Fanny had kept some of the best pieces of the room for herself—a delicate writing desk her mother had used for her morning correspondence and some of the nicer art. This observation emboldened Marianne to face Fanny, who looked up from said writing desk and made no attempt to hide her disapproval.

"The Misses Dashwood," the butler announced belatedly from behind Marianne and Margaret.

"So I see," Fanny said. "My, to what do I owe the pleasure?"

"You said we can come back to visit anytime," was Margaret's indignant reply.

"Indeed, but you've only been gone for two days," Fanny said, rising from her seat. She made no move to invite the sisters to sit. "I can't imagine that you've had the chance to settle in your new home yet."

"We've settled very well, thank you," Marianne said, her voice practically dripping with civility. "It's such a small flat, we had it set up in no time."

Fanny's left eye twitched. Marianne refused to be the first one to look away. Finally, Fanny caved. "Won't you sit?"

The girls took a seat on a very uncomfortable settee and Fanny sank into an ornate rosewood chair. Margaret wasted no time in asking, "Where's Stewart?"

"Who?"

"The butler," Marianne clarified.

"Oh. He went to . . . Essex, I believe? He had a sister there, or sister-in-law. I don't know."

"You let him go?" Marianne repeated, her shock making it difficult for her to hold the upper hand.

"Well, a house this size hardly needs two butlers. Not like my mother's estate—she has a butler and an underbutler, you know."

"But he'd been with us for *years*."

"And Hayes has been with my family for years," Fanny said. "It's the way of things, Marianne. It's not my fault that your mother is unable to afford a butler."

Isn't it? Marianne thought, but she kept her mouth shut. Instead, her right foot nudged Margaret under their skirts. After a prolonged silence, Margaret said suddenly, "We left some books here."

"Did you?" Fanny asked, turning her gaze on her.

"They're *our* books, not the family's," Marianne said. "Father gave them to us, for birthdays and holidays. We forgot to pack them, so we've come to retrieve them."

"You'll have to speak with John, and he can confer with Mr. Morgan—"

"No need!" Marianne said cheerily, and leapt to her feet. She suspected that Fanny would block her attempts, but Marianne

99

could be quite the immovable force when she put her mind to it. "I'll simply go fetch them—I know precisely which shelf they're on. Margaret, you stay here and entertain Fanny with news of our new home."

"Marianne!" Fanny proclaimed, very nearly raising her voice.

But Marianne dashed out of the room, and when Fanny didn't follow her, she took the stairs two at a time to the second floor, where the family library lived. She pushed the door open and was quite overwhelmed to find the formerly cozy space in disarray. Her father's desk from downstairs had been brought up, and the comfy furniture had vanished. Books and crates were strewn everywhere, and the room held the stale scent of cigars. Apparently, this was John's new study. Marianne's lips curled up in displeasure, but she wasted no time. She grabbed a few beloved titles from random on the shelves as her cover, for it was true that they'd left many books behind, then quickly began picking through the items on John's desk.

There were stacks of letters, bills, and . . . Marianne picked up a half-quarto of paper and squinted at the writing. It read:

My heart beats for you,
Do you feel the same way, too?
You must say the words, my dear—
Your disdain is my greatest fear.

Marianne dropped the paper and had to clap her hand over her mouth to keep from laughing aloud. John, a poet? A rather poor one, but the thought of him laboring over these verses for Fanny . . . even Elinor would have a good laugh at that later.

After carefully sifting through the detritus of John's desk, Marianne finally found something useful—the household ledger. She eased it out from under more attempts at poetry that she didn't want to read too closely and cracked it open to the most recent entries.

Marianne had been taught how to use a household ledger, of course. It was one of the few bits of ladylike training that she hadn't minded because it was useful, and she'd assisted her father on business ledgers a few times. It didn't take her long to deduce that John had been perfectly affluent before Father's death, to the tune of six thousand pounds per year. And Fanny, why, she was splendidly wealthy on her own! She brought in eight thousand pounds per year. That made her father's estate seem quite paltry in comparison.

"You're already living on fourteen thousand pounds per year, and all we rate is a single fifteen-hundred-pound payoff?" she hissed, then slammed the ledger shut and dropped it on the desk, making no attempt to disguise her sleuthing.

So, there were no obvious money troubles for John and Fanny. What had they done to make John so uncharitable toward them? Or was this all Fanny's doing? They certainly didn't need this house or all of the things in it. They could buy their own town house, they could let a grand house in the countryside. *Why?*

Mother would say that money could buy happiness only when there was nothing else left to buy. Perhaps Fanny was just greedy. Unless . . .

Unless it wasn't about the money but about seeing John restored in his family home, his rightful inheritance . . . except John had rarely visited them before, nor had he made much of an attempt to reconnect with their father in his adulthood. Their relationship wasn't contentious, just perfectly polite. Distant.

Frustration welled up in Marianne, and she could imagine Elinor's response: *You have no proof that John and Fanny plotted to kill Father.*

She hated that Elinor was right.

Marianne left the study, three books tucked under her arm, and went back downstairs. This time, she bypassed the formal rooms and slipped down to the kitchen. If she still believed that Fanny and John had paid a member of the household staff to kill their father, perhaps that person had been kept on or promoted.

Marianne's theory began to unravel when she spotted an unfamiliar scullery maid on her way down, and a lanky teenage boy she'd never seen before, dressed in a footman's uniform, openly gawked at her as she entered the servants' hall and stopped short.

Four unfamiliar heads turned to her, surprise giving way to cool civility as they scrambled to their feet. "I beg your pardon," she said. "I'm looking for Mrs. Matthews?"

A tall woman about her mother's age with sharp creases about her mouth answered. "Mrs. Matthews no longer works here."

Marianne felt her eyes widen, but she tried not to appear shocked. "How about Emily?"

The woman shook her head, and Marianne was about to list every single person who had worked for her family when the woman said, "All of the former staff has moved on," she said, and she gestured to lead Marianne back upstairs.

Marianne planted her feet. "Moved on? Or been let go?"

The woman's mouth puckered in disapproval, and Marianne saw the source of her premature wrinkles. "They were *replaced*." She took Marianne firmly by the elbow and said, "Come now, I'll see you back upstairs where you belong."

But Marianne didn't belong there, not anymore.

Marianne was delivered straight to Fanny in the sitting room, like a naughty child. And like a naughty child, she received a scolding from Fanny. "You don't go wandering into servant quarters. It isn't polite!"

"Did you truly dismiss our entire staff?" Marianne asked her, not interested in pretending anymore that this was a mere social call.

"The servants will all find new positions, and I wrote them all recommendations—quite the undertaking, I hope you realize. When you are grown and managing a household of your own, you will discover that a loyal staff is not easy to come by." Then she paused as if to consider her words and added, "Provided you have the opportunity to manage a large household."

The underhanded slight pushed Marianne to her limit, and she took a step forward, ready to let loose some choice words, when she caught sight of Margaret, standing behind Fanny and frantically shaking her head. Instead, Marianne sucked in a deep breath and exhaled with a forced smile. "I'm so sorry to hear you have had such troubles inspiring loyalty in your staff, Fanny. That sounds like a dreadful problem, and one I promise you that my mother and sisters and I know *nothing* about."

Then she held out her hand for Margaret, and she smiled even brighter as she added, "We must be off!"

Leaving behind their former home was both easier and more difficult than it had been three days earlier. Easier because Marianne understood now, on an instinctive level, that this place no longer belonged to her. Even the staff who had helped make it home were gone. But more difficult because this time when she walked out the front door and past the gate, she had little hope of ever returning as more than an unwelcome guest.

She was shaken out of her melancholy when they reached the end of the street and Margaret burst out, "I nicked Fanny's correspondence!"

Marianne stopped short. "You did not!"

"I did too. She told me that I ought to go wait in the nursery with Harry, and I told her I'd rather not, and she got all sniffy and stepped out to go find the housekeeper, and I looked at her desk to see what she was writing, and I nicked a letter from her mother."

Marianne was torn between admiration for Margaret's pluck and annoyance. "Now she'll *know* we stole it."

"You'll want to read it," Margaret said, a smug grin on her freckled face as she pulled the letter out of her sleeve and slipped it to Marianne. Marianne was overcome with curiosity, even as doubt thrummed in her heart. She passed Margaret the books and unfolded the letter as they strolled along the street.

The opening was boring, all standard greetings and gossip about who had come to call. The next paragraph was all about Fanny and John moving into their home, and Marianne's grip on the letter tightened when she read, *How fortunate that John's father's wife and her daughters decided to quit the house—you are under no obligation to provide for them, and if John's father hadn't made provisions for them, then I should think that he didn't mean for John to take up that mantle.*

"You're creasing it," Margaret remarked, pushing a distracted Marianne out of the way of a couple that strolled down the street.

"How fortunate that we decided to quit the house?! As if that vile woman didn't make it abundantly clear that we were no longer welcome in our own home! She would have moved us up into the servants' quarters if she thought she could do so without scandal!"

"Keep reading."

Finally, she got to the interesting bits, at the very bottom of the letter. *You must do everything in your power to see that Edward succeeds and is elevated in society. While having him settle your father-in-law's business matters does help him establish some credibility lost in that horrid Alistair affair, I fear that he is taking too keen an interest in the fate of the other Dashwoods. You must ensure he stays the course, and not allow him to get carried away by his peculiar values. He can do so much more, be so much more. I think the only thing to do is proceed with finding him a good match. . . .*

"The Alistair affair," Marianne repeated, not conscious of how Margaret was tugging on her elbow. "What do you think she means—"

"Look out!" Margaret screeched, and Marianne dropped the letter as she looked up, stunned to find that she'd strolled right into the busy street. To her right, a curricle was bearing down on her quickly, and she leapt back in fright, her foot catching on an uneven cobblestone. Her left ankle twisted and she went down hard, while Margaret screamed her name.

The curricle swooshed past, narrowly missing Marianne's foot, and she felt her heartbeat hammer every inch of her body as she realized that she'd very nearly been run over. Her exhilaration ebbed into a fierce, hot pain that pulsed through her ankle and a dull ache in her bottom, where she'd taken the brunt of her fall.

"Marianne!" Margaret cried. She dropped the books and hurled herself at her sister, hugging her close. By the time Marianne caught her breath, a young gentleman had crouched down before her.

"Don't move!" he advised, and carefully picked up Marianne's injured ankle, feeling it beneath her stocking and shoe. Marianne nearly fainted, not because she had a weak constitution but because a strange young man was *touching her ankle.*

He looked up then. His crystal-blue eyes met hers, and Marianne gasped slightly.

"I'm sorry," the young man said, blond hair falling across his forehead as he bent his head to look at Marianne's foot. "It appears to be a sprain."

But Marianne hadn't gasped due to pain. It was this young man, with a face like sculpted marble—high cheekbones, a strong, square jaw, and heavy brows that made his face so striking, but his mouth was gentle and quick to smile, which he did now as he withdrew his hands from her ankle. "Are you in much pain?"

"No—I don't think so. I mean, it's not terrible," Marianne managed to say.

"Shall I help you to your feet?"

Marianne nodded, and he held out an ungloved hand. His fingers were long and elegant, and she wondered if he played an instrument. Between this beguiling stranger and Margaret's efforts, Marianne managed to rise to her feet and dust off her dirt-streaked skirts, but when she put weight on her ankle, she sucked in a gasp of pain.

"Hold steady, miss," the young man said, wrapping an arm around her waist. "You must allow me to give you a ride home!"

"Perhaps I should just hail a carriage—" Marianne began to say, but before she could finish that thought, the sensation of weightlessness overcame her. The young man had swept her up in his arms and was now carrying her! He was much stronger than he looked, and Marianne threw her arms around his neck.

"Don't worry, my curricle is here. I'll drive you both—it's the least I can do, having caused your injury myself."

"You?" Marianne asked, though there was no contempt in the question. If the price for being rescued by such a dashing young man was near death, she supposed she'd pay it.

"You came quite out of nowhere," he remarked as he set her down in the very vehicle that had nearly run her over. The curricle was a narrow, two-wheeled contraption open to the sunny day, perfect for a gentleman to go zipping along in. Marianne looked down at Margaret, who had retrieved her books and was eyeing this strange young man with distrust, not unlike the feral cats that lurked in the alley behind Barton Street.

"But my sister. Surely we can't all fit?"

"It shall be a tight squeeze, but you must allow me," he said, and Marianne found herself drowning in his piercing blue gaze. It was like falling into the depths of a lake, looking into those eyes. He seemed so repentant, and he clutched her hand. "I could not call myself a gentleman if I left you on the street."

"All right," Marianne said. "You're very kind. Margaret?"

Margaret gave the gentleman a wary look but allowed herself to be helped into the curricle. As the young man checked his horse for injury, she whispered, "Marianne, we don't even know his name!"

"Don't worry, I won't let him ride away without an introduction."

The young man jumped up into the curricle and took the reins. "Where to, ladies?"

"Barton Street, Cheapside," Margaret said, for Marianne was quite unable to speak. Not only was her ankle throbbing quite a bit but she was wedged very tightly between Margaret and her mysterious rescuer, and she could feel the warmth of his thigh next to her own through their many layers of clothing. It was *deliciously* indecent!

"I know it," the young man said, and the horse took off. "Don't worry, I shall have you home before it rains."

Marianne noticed the gathering clouds had moved overhead while she wasn't paying attention—why did Elinor always have to be right about everything, including the weather? Fortunately, they moved at quite a fast clip, covering the ground that Marianne and Margaret walked in nearly a quarter of the time. The streets got busier the closer they got to Barton Street, and Marianne enjoyed how carts and pedestrians made way for their curricle, pulled by a handsome pair of black horses whose coats gleamed with care. They didn't speak as they went along, and Marianne was nearly glad for that. Between the pain in her ankle and the breathlessness she felt every time the young man shifted in his seat or used the reins to guide the horses, she could scarcely think of anything charming to say. Before she was ready for their ride to end, Margaret was pointing out their building, and the man brought the curricle to a halt. Margaret jumped down and ran for the door, no doubt already calling for Mother and Elinor, and Marianne attempted to climb down herself. But before she could manage it, her rescuer was there with an amused smile. "No, no, miss. Allow me."

He picked her up but did not set her down once she was clear of the carriage. Instead, he carried her out of the street and straight to her open front door, where Hannah stood with her mouth agape. He seemed to know just where to go, because he walked straight into the sitting room, where Mother and Elinor stood in shock. He set her down on the settee carefully, making sure that her foot was propped up, then turned abruptly to Mother.

"Forgive me. This young lady fell in the street, and I took the liberty of assisting her home. I'm Mr. John Willoughby, at your service." He gave a curt little bow, but neither Mother nor

Elinor seemed to notice. They came to Marianne's side immediately, Elinor looking truly frightened.

"I'm all right, it's just my ankle," she said. Elinor grabbed a cushion to set beneath it, and Marianne hissed in pain. It would swell, she was sure.

"How very kind of you," Mother said, sounding as if she'd been startled out of a dream, and Marianne registered that this was the first time she'd seen Mother dressed and in the drawing room since the day they'd moved in. "I'm Mrs. Henry Dashwood, and my daughters—Elinor, Marianne, and Margaret. Thank you for bringing Marianne home safely."

"It was no trouble," he said, his gaze lingering on Marianne for a brief moment before returning to Mrs. Dashwood. "If I may, please allow me to call upon you tomorrow to learn how Miss Marianne is faring."

Marianne's gaze was fixed on Mr. Willoughby, and her heart raced. He wanted to see her again! Tomorrow!

"All right," Mother said. "That would be very kind of you."

And with one last look at Marianne and a bow to Mrs. Dashwood, he was gone.

Marianne heaved an enormous sigh and sank back into the cushions. "Oh my goodness."

Mother looked down at her with some amusement. "You seem to have picked up an admirer, my dear."

"He almost killed Marianne," Margaret announced.

Elinor had worked off Marianne's shoe and looked at her with alarm. "What?!"

"It was an *accident*," Marianne proclaimed. "And he was very sorry. He saw us home, did he not?"

"It was the least he could do, considering he nearly *killed* you," Margaret mumbled.

Marianne yelped in pain as Elinor began binding her ankle. "Elinor!"

"Sorry," she said, and went about her work more gently, although her expression was curiously hard when she said, "It seems as though you had an eventful morning."

"I did," Marianne replied crisply. As soon as Mother was out of the room, she was going to tell Elinor everything— about how Fanny had let go of all their servants, how they were exceedingly wealthy, how Fanny's mother implored Fanny to elevate Mr. Farrows at all costs . . .

It was just then that Marianne realized she no longer had Mrs. Farrows's letter.

She patted her pockets, but she couldn't actually remember putting it away. All she could recall was reading the letter, Margaret's cry of alarm, looking up to see a horse bearing down on her, falling, and then Mr. Willoughby's enchanting smile and gentle touch. . . .

The letter, her only piece of evidence, was gone.

SEVEN

*In Which the Dashwood Sisters
Receive Two Gentlemen Callers*

ELINOR COULD THINK OF no task more tedious than watching Marianne be wooed by Mr. Willoughby.

Instead of unpacking her laboratory equipment and experimenting on her mystery substance, Elinor was forced to assemble with her mother and sister in the drawing room the following morning to wait for Mr. Willoughby to call. She supposed it was a small price to pay for seeing Mother dressed and upright, but ever since their visit with Mrs. Jennings, she'd been itching to reinspect the substance that she'd recovered from Father's teacup.

But Mr. Willoughby was true to his word and called with a slender book tucked under one arm and a bunch of flowers in hand. Marianne's ankle was propped on a cushion and she'd very prettily arranged herself on the settee, smoothing out the folds in her skirts just so. She sat up straighter and smiled far too eagerly when Hannah showed him in.

"You came," she burst out. "How kind of you! And you brought such lovely flowers."

"I am delighted that you'll receive me, after our most undignified meeting," he said with a brightness to match Marianne's. "I must assure you that I am not in the habit of being so reckless with my driving. And these flowers are for you, Mrs. Dashwood. An apology for the distress I must have caused your family by barging in yesterday."

He presented the bunch of expensive lilies to a shocked Mrs. Dashwood. Elinor watched as her mother took the flowers, a small, confused smile on her face. "For me?" she asked, looking down at them as if she never in the world expected to receive flowers. "Thank you, Mr. Willoughby. This is very thoughtful of you."

Mr. Willoughby studied Mrs. Dashwood for just a moment too long before saying, "My pleasure, madam." He turned to Marianne and said, "Miss Marianne, do you enjoy poetry?"

"Mr. Willoughby," Marianne said with frightening intensity, "poetry is one of my greatest loves!"

Elinor needed a distraction lest she be caught rolling her eyes in front of company. "Mother, let me go put those in a vase."

Her mother smiled gratefully as Elinor took the flowers

and made a hasty escape to the kitchen, where Hannah was setting out the tea tray. "Just me," she said. "I thought I'd put these in water."

"Very good, miss," Hannah said, hefting the kettle and carefully pouring steaming water in a teapot. "Except, I don't know if we have any vases."

"No vases?"

"I can't say, we left in such a hurry." Hannah looked nervous, as if forgetting to pack a vase were her fault. It wasn't—there was a great deal that had been left behind simply because their new home didn't have adequate space for all of the possessions they once had.

"Quite all right," Elinor assured her. She looked down at the flowers. They really were beautiful, and Mother had looked at them as though she'd never expected to receive such a pretty thing. Then, it occurred to her with a pang, maybe she hadn't. With Father dead, it was unlikely that any man would bring Mother flowers again.

Another unsettling thought rose up in Elinor: Did Mr. Willoughby know about Father's death? Bringing their mother flowers was a kind gesture, but it was almost *too* kind for a total stranger. He clearly was very interested in Marianne, and, well, her sister was lovely. But did that interest stem from a genuine desire to know her better? Surely, he couldn't think that they had money, living where they did. Unless he was laboring under the delusion that the Dashwood fortune was tied to marriage. . . .

Elinor knew her sister. Marianne wouldn't question Mr. Willoughby's motivations. She'd fancy herself in love with him if he could recite well.

Elinor spotted a ceramic water pitcher on the shelf in the kitchen, and inspiration struck. "May I use this?" she asked Hannah.

"Of course, miss," Hannah said, and watched as Elinor filled it with water and arranged the flowers in it. "That's quite lovely, although I'm afraid that pitcher doesn't begin to do them justice."

That is exactly the point, Elinor thought. But she smiled and said, "Oh well, needs must!"

She whisked the flowers back into the drawing room with a cheery smile, ignoring the way Marianne's eyes widened when she noted the pitcher instead of the expected vase. Mother also noticed, but her polite smile didn't waver as Elinor set the pitcher on a nearby table and retook her seat. Mother said, "Thank you, Elinor. Now, Mr. Willoughby, please—tell me about your family."

Ah, the favorite question of mothers everywhere. Judging by Mr. Willoughby's indulgent smile as he sat in the chair next to Marianne, he was expecting it.

"I'm afraid there's not much to tell. My mother died when

I was a child, and my father passed when I was fourteen. I was sent to school by my aunt, who resides at the family estate in Somersetshire. She's elderly and doesn't come to town anymore, but she understands that there is more excitement to be had in London society."

He said that with a small quirk of the lips and a darting glance to Marianne. Mother smiled politely and nodded, but Elinor was less impressed. He was enjoying London society . . . and on the prowl for a wife. She judged him to be about nineteen or twenty, which was a bit young to settle down but not too young to be thinking about the future.

"That's marvelous that you are close with your aunt," Marianne offered. "I'm sure that your company is very much a comfort to her."

"She wants to know that our family legacy is in good hands, and I have a soft spot for her, given that she took me in after my parents were both gone." Mr. Willoughby paused, then added, "Since I have very little family, what members I have left are very important to me."

Marianne seemed to melt in front of Mr. Willoughby, but Elinor had to press her lips into a thin line. He was his aunt's heir, and he wanted the Dashwoods to know it.

Mr. Willoughby and Marianne began speaking of the people he knew, the parties he'd attended, and mutual acquaintances. All people that the Dashwoods would have once socialized with themselves. But given that they'd been at Barton Street for a few days and the only person who'd come to call was Sir John, Elinor suspected that those connections had been severed the moment it was known throughout the ton that the Dashwoods were no longer fashionable or wealthy.

Elinor was surprised to realize that this didn't bother her as much as she would have suspected. Perhaps it was because she'd grown up knowing that Father had built his fortune, so she always knew the goodwill of society hinged on Father's financial success. She had never been ashamed of Norland and Co., and she had the good sense to not let those who thought she ought to be dictate her thoughts and feelings.

But watching Marianne laugh at Mr. Willoughby's jokes and flutter her eyelashes at him made Elinor wonder if Marianne didn't feel quite the same. Perhaps she'd rather marry into money than stay at Barton Street. Certainly the respectability of marriage and the security of a supportive husband would make achieving her goals much easier.

But Elinor couldn't help but wonder where that left the rest of them.

Mr. Willoughby didn't overstay his welcome, careful to keep things very proper, but he did secure a promise to call again soon and to bring more poetry. He left Marianne with the book and bowed at the rest of the Dashwoods before seeing himself out.

The first thing Marianne did was turn on Elinor. "Why

didn't you bring out a vase?"

"It would appear they were all left behind," Elinor said, trying to keep the amusement out of her voice.

Marianne sank back into her seat. "What on earth must Mr. Willoughby have thought of us."

"I'm sure he thought that we were appreciative of his efforts," Mother said, rising to her feet.

"At least the poetry he brought me is perfect," Marianne said with a happy sigh. "I've been wanting this volume, you know. We have mirror tastes."

"How fortunate," Elinor said just a tad too sarcastically.

"It is," Marianne replied, an edge to her voice. "I could never be with a young man whose tastes didn't perfectly coincide with mine—the same books, the same music . . ."

"The same flair for the dramatic?" Elinor asked.

"That's enough," Mother said, and only the weariness in her voice kept Marianne and Elinor from arguing further. "He seems like a nice young man, dear."

She fingered one petal gently and then drifted out of the room and climbed the stairs without another word. The sisters watched her go in confusion, Mr. Willoughby quite forgotten. Then Elinor stated the obvious: "I'm worried about her."

"It's the medicine she takes," Margaret spoke up from the side of the room. "It makes her tired."

Elinor turned to her youngest sister, who had been sitting so quietly that she'd nearly forgotten she was there—which could be useful and annoying in equal measure. "What medicine?"

"The one in the brown bottle."

Laudanum. The doctor had prescribed it after Father's body had been discovered and Mother was so hysterical that Elinor thought her sobs might break her body apart. It did not reassure her to know that Mother was still taking it more than a week later.

"Right," she said, because she was unsure of what to do about that at the moment. "Well, that just means that we must endeavor to solve Father's murder as quickly as possible, hm?"

It was a weak response, because for all Elinor knew, discovering that their father had been murdered might send their mother into an even deeper depression.

"Did you write Mr. Farrows?" Marianne asked, perking up. "We have to know what that letter meant."

"Yes," Elinor said. She'd sent a letter yesterday to his accounting firm, inquiring about Father's case files, but she hadn't asked about his personal life—it would have been rude to do so. "And I promise if I hear anything, you'll be the first to know."

"There's something to it," Marianne insisted for what felt like the tenth time since she'd come home yesterday and whispered the news to Elinor while Mother and Hannah were out of earshot. "And I can hardly be chasing down leads on this ankle, so you have to take charge."

Elinor's idea of taking charge did not involve questioning

Edward Farrows on the contents of a letter that she should not know anything about. Even if she did wonder about the bit where his mother was insistent that he must find a good match—did Mr. Farrows share her urgency? What kind of young lady would he be interested in? Did he already have someone in mind?

But she pushed those thoughts aside. "I don't understand why I must be the one to question Mr. Farrows. We could invite him to tea and you could ask the questions."

Marianne rolled her eyes, but it was Margaret who spoke up. "Because Mother might come down, and besides, he likes you."

Elinor narrowed her gaze at her. "We've barely spoken to each other."

"I think Margaret is right," Marianne said. "When he asked for Father's ledgers, he looked genuinely concerned for you."

"Well, if he fancies me as much as you all claim, then we shall see how long it takes for him to write me back." Elinor said this, knowing full well that it was unlikely that he'd received her note and had the chance to write back in a single day. "He was merely being kind, nothing more."

"Is any young man chivalrous for no reason?" Marianne asked.

Elinor swung a glare in her direction. "So Mr. Willoughby is entirely without motive, then?"

Marianne just sighed. "I should hope *not*."

She and Margaret dissolved into giggles while Elinor shook her head and left them to their nonsense.

⚬

The following day, Elinor begged off sitting with her sisters and Mother in the drawing room, waiting for Mr. Willoughby to come and call once more. "I need to examine the substance I found in Father's teacup, and I can't do that when Mother might walk in," she argued to Marianne. "She'll be distracted by Mr. Willoughby's visit, and you can tell him I have a headache."

Marianne was too excited about the prospect of a second visit in so many days to care that Elinor didn't want to chaperone, and Elinor was relieved . . . although she made a mental note to ask Mother what she really thought of Mr. Willoughby.

The corner of the kitchen that Elinor was allowed for her two crates of laboratory supplies didn't have very good light and had only a single narrow shelf for her to unpack her substances and glassware. As she unwrapped Margaret's forgotten smoke bomb—seeing if it worked would have to wait indefinitely, as they no longer had a garden to test it in—she caught herself thinking of Miss Williams.

What must it be like to have access to a professional laboratory, to have an uncle for a chemist who not only allowed your work but encouraged it? It was probably wrong to envy a young lady who'd died such a sad death. Marianne would probably say Elinor should take what happened to Miss Williams as a warning.

And Elinor did, in a way. If what happened to Miss Williams had been foul play, she intended to be very, very careful.

With her tools carefully unpacked and set out on her shelf, she withdrew the small jar from her apron pocket. This substance was their only true piece of evidence, and the amount inside added up to little more than a teaspoon's worth. Which meant that Elinor needed to be judicious in her experimenting.

First, she took notes. She examined the substance from every angle and shook the jar gently. She wrote down everything she could think of—the brown-yellow tint, how the minuscule granules had dried, what the substance reminded her of. She carefully unscrewed the lid and sniffed the jar, noting the scent seemed faintly earthy. She was forced to acknowledge that she had no idea if this was the substance's true state or if it had been contaminated by the tea it had been mixed into. Perhaps the most active ingredient had evaporated, like the liquid in the tea. But she remembered the bitter taste of the water when she'd mixed just a small amount and knew her instincts were correct. Whatever it was, it wasn't harmless.

She scraped a small bit of the poison (for she'd decided that it was indeed poison) out of its jar and stirred it into water, where it promptly dissolved (*water-soluble*, she officially confirmed in her notes). She tried dissolving it in vinegar (*no visible reaction, results inconclusive*) and in a misguided attempt to see if the substance would melt, she tried heating it over the stove, where it darkened and released a noxious odor. Elinor rushed to open the kitchen window and was careful not to breathe in the smoking mess, but she noted that she didn't seem to suffer from any adverse effects.

She stopped to collect her thoughts. She knew that she could potentially run all sorts of experiments to puzzle out the substance's secrets, but she did not have an unlimited sample size. As it stood, only about half of her original sample remained in the jar. It was possible that she needed a much larger sample in order to run the proper tests. But first she'd have to know what those tests were. . . .

Chemistry. It was Elinor's great love and great frustration.

She was startled by a knock against the kitchen door frame. When she turned, she nearly dropped her glass jar.

Edward Farrows stood in the doorway to the kitchen.

"Oh!" Elinor exclaimed, before her social graces kicked in. "Hello! Are you . . ."

The word *lost* was on the tip of her tongue, but that was absurd. The flat was so small, one would have to be very determined to get lost in it.

"Looking for you?" Mr. Farrows finished with a small smile. "I am."

That was hardly what Elinor had expected. "Whatever for?"

Mr. Farrows seemed to deflate slightly, and Elinor rushed to add, "Not that you are unwelcome. I'm afraid I wasn't expecting visitors, but please . . . come in and have a seat."

He entered the room and pulled out a kitchen chair for her. Elinor removed her apron and sat. "I didn't mean to disturb you," he said as he sat across the table from her. "I could see when I passed the drawing room that you have company. Your housekeeper told me I could come back. . . ."

"You're very welcome," Elinor said. Then, feeling her cheeks warm, she added, "That is, if the prospect of talking in a kitchen doesn't bother you. We can go to the drawing room. . . ."

"It's no bother," he said quickly. "And here is just fine. I was actually hoping to speak with you, as it seems you are the one, ah, handling affairs?"

Elinor looked down at the worn kitchen table. "If by that you mean, am I responsible for my family's finances and keeping accounts, then yes. For the time being, anyway."

"I don't mean to make you uncomfortable," Mr. Farrows said gently, and when she looked up his warm eyes were upon her. Curious, but not probing.

"You haven't," she managed to say, although nothing could be further from the truth. She felt dreadfully uncomfortable around Mr. Farrows, but not in a bad way. She was aware of every movement in her body, and every shift in him, but the last thing she wanted was for him to leave. "I suppose it isn't considered polite, discussing financial matters. But only those who have a great deal of it can afford to *not* speak of money."

"That is very true," Mr. Farrows agreed. "I would take that

observation one step further and say that money is, in many ways, power. To shame people into not discussing it is to limit their power."

"How interesting," Elinor agreed, fascinated not only by his insight but by his unpretentious air. She opened her mouth to ask if he'd come to this conclusion based on firsthand experience but stopped herself just in time.

"You were going to say something else," Mr. Farrows observed, a small smile toying with his lips. The expression transformed his face from plain to something akin to handsome—Elinor could almost see the carefree boy he'd been not too long ago.

"Only that . . . I didn't expect someone such as yourself to hold that opinion."

His jaw clenched. "I'm afraid your acquaintance with my sister has colored your opinion of me."

"Oh no," Elinor insisted, even though it was a lie. "It's just that . . . well. Oh, I don't know what I'm trying to say. We've never been particularly close to Fanny."

"I don't think many people have ever been *particularly close* to my sister," Mr. Farrows said. "She doesn't make it easy."

Elinor bit her lip to hide a smile. "But you didn't come here to talk about your sister, surely?"

It was an attempt to cajole him out of this darker turn in his mood, but it didn't quite work. Instead, he seemed to grow even more serious. "In a way, I did. First, I wanted to apologize.

When she asked me to help sort out your father's financial affairs, I thought it was with your family's full knowledge and blessing. I realized very quickly that wasn't the case. I would have come sooner, but I only just found out that you had moved."

Had he not received her letter? "The house became rather cramped," Elinor said. "And this new flat is quite cozy for the four of us."

Mr. Farrows regarded her with a steady gaze that told her he wasn't fooled, but he simply inclined his head and said, "Of course. I'm glad to have found you well situated. All the same, I am sorry for my part in anything that caused you and your family undue distress during an already difficult time."

Marianne would say Mr. Farrows was being a bore, that he had no passion, but Elinor didn't need grand proclamations and pretty words. She knew that he was speaking from the heart, and that was more than enough for her. She met his gaze to accept his apology and found herself falling into his earnest golden brown eyes.

They stared at one another like that for a long moment, and Elinor was so taken by the sensation that she noted the impropriety of it, but she found it awfully difficult to care in that moment.

Then Mr. Farrows broke their intense look with a small cough. "I did have another reason for calling—my sister wished to extend this invitation to you. She asked that I hand deliver it so you know it's genuine. But please don't feel obligated to say yes."

He handed her a folded note on creamy, expensive paper, with *Dashwood* written in Fanny's precise script. She was so shocked, she asked, "Invitation to what?"

Mr. Farrows grimaced. "A ball my mother is hosting in two days' time."

Elinor let the invitation drop on the kitchen table. "I see."

"There was some debate," Mr. Farrows said after a long pause. "About the . . . appropriateness of such an invitation. But my sister feared that your family would take it as a slight if you weren't invited."

Elinor very nearly lost her composure then. Fanny did not care one whit about what the Dashwood sisters and their mother thought of her—she cared only about what society might think. She didn't really want her husband's relations there, but it couldn't get out that they'd not even received an invitation, so she'd invited them an impossible two days before the event.

But Elinor managed to find some shred of politeness in her. She forced a smile and said, "How kind. I don't think we are quite up to it. It's been two weeks since Father and . . . well, not yet. Perhaps next time."

Those last three words slipped out completely by accident, for Elinor didn't particularly care about attending any ball Fanny or her mother hosted, but she had a flash of fancy—an image of Mr. Farrows seeking her out in a ballroom, of dancing, of his gaze turned to her as they followed the steps of a quadrille . . .

Mr. Farrows nodded. "I would be honored if you saved a dance for me . . . next time."

Elinor felt it was as though they'd shared the same vision of dancing together, and she wished desperately that next time could be two days from now. All she could do was nod.

Mr. Farrows looked away, and Elinor was almost thankful for the reprieve of his gaze upon her, for it was wonderful but intense, and then he said, "I must ask . . . what is it you're working on?"

Elinor felt her cheeks flush. What must he think of her staring at him like that? "Chemistry," she blurted out, flustered into revealing the truth. "I have an interest in the sciences."

Instead of being put off, Mr. Farrows looked fascinated. "Really?"

"I mostly re-create experiments I find in books—the ones I can get my hands on, anyway. The most adventurous I've gotten on my own is distilling plant essences. I'm going to start formulating my own perfumes."

Elinor was afraid she'd made her interest in chemistry sound silly, but Mr. Farrows regarded her seriously. "Do you wish to operate an apothecary?"

"Oh no, that's just to sell, for now." She paused and realized that she was dangerously close to bringing up their perilous financial situation. "My true interests lie in more academic endeavors. I want to . . . I want to study chemistry formally, identify new elements and compounds."

Elinor had never told anyone this, so she was shocked when the words tumbled out of her mouth. She wanted so badly to be seen as someone with expertise, someone who was interesting. And perhaps Marianne's comment about her *dabbling* was still weighing on her.

Mr. Farrows didn't laugh, and for that Elinor was eternally grateful. Instead, he remarked, "That's fascinating! Can you read French?"

Puzzled, Elinor shook her head. "Very poorly, I'm afraid, much to the dismay of my poor governess. I would have rather learned Latin or Greek."

"Pity," he said. "I heard that the French are unfortunately ahead of England when it comes to the study of chemistry. In fact, most countries on the Continent are. The translations of their studies are slow to arrive, and even then— Uh, Miss Dashwood? Is that pan supposed to be smoking?"

"What?" Elinor turned in her chair. "Oh no!"

She leapt up and reached for a rag to pull the pan away from the heat. It was the same one she'd used to boil the dissolved substance, only she had set it right back on the direct heat without realizing, and now the pan was scorched. She looked left and right for a place to set the hot cast iron, coughing against the smoke, when she felt Mr. Farrows gently brush past her.

"Here!" he said. He threw open one of the kitchen windows, letting in a welcome breeze (even if it did reek of the alley), and stepped back so Elinor could set the hot pan on the brick of the window ledge.

"Thank you," she said with an unladylike cough, and began waving her rag to encourage the smoke stink to waft out the window. "I assure you, I'm not usually so careless."

"I distracted you," he replied.

"It was a welcome distraction." The words left Elinor's lips before she could think on the wisdom of uttering them, and she was alarmed to find that she'd adopted a playful lilt that made her sound like Marianne.

"I have to confess, there is one more reason why I'm here." Mr. Farrows looked away from the pan, which was no longer smoking, and straight into Elinor's eyes.

"Oh?" Elinor felt hope swell in her—for what?

"I think it's a shame that John and Fanny chose to close the business—it was quite the successful model. I've spent the last week going through all of the accounting and invoices for the last five years, and I found this."

He withdrew a piece of paper from his coat and presented it to her. Elinor inspected it carefully—it was an invoice for five pounds. She sucked in a quick breath and plopped back down in the kitchen chair.

"It looks like Mrs. Palmer has yet to pay for your father's services," Mr. Farrows said, rejoining her at the table. "It's the only outstanding bill I could find, and well . . . I thought that you could use the five pounds more than Fanny and John."

Elinor fingered the edge of the invoice. Five pounds was no trifling amount to them these days—it could ensure they'd have plenty of heat in winter and keep them in meat for months. "But won't they object?"

"They haven't any clue this invoice exists," Mr. Farrows said, and gave her a conspiratorial wink.

This really was quite kind of him, even if it was a tad dishonest. Elinor was already thinking about how they'd spend it—Margaret would need new shoes for the winter, and their candle supply was low—when she faltered. Marianne was so certain that Mr. Farrows was involved in some plot against them. What if this was a trap, to see if Elinor was willing to steal from her brother?

But just five pounds? When John and Fanny had thousands at their disposal?

Mr. Farrows sensed her hesitation and said, "I promise I won't say anything. If you don't take it, I'll just file this invoice away and never collect."

Elinor didn't want to believe the worst in him, she decided. "Thank you, Mr. Farrows. You don't know what this means to us."

"Please, call me Edward," he said, and Elinor's breath caught. Then he added, "After all, we are quite nearly family."

Elinor laughed, a high-pitched sound that was nothing like her usual laugh. "Indeed. Edward. And you must call me Elinor. Thank you for your kindness."

"Please don't hesitate to call on me if you need anything," he said.

Elinor wasn't sure she realized until that moment just how desperately she wished for someone to offer their help, even if it was just to open a window while she picked up a smoking pan. The money worries, the anxiety around her mother's reclusive behavior, the sick fear that her father had been murdered and the person responsible was going to get away with it. But Mr. Farrows—Edward—couldn't solve any of those problems.

"Thank you," she said, and stood to signal the end of their visit.

Edward stood as well and dipped his head in a low nod to her. "Good luck, Elinor."

She stood in the kitchen long after he left, remembering the sound of his voice as he said her name.

EIGHT

In Which the Dashwood Sisters
Receive an Unexpected Referral

MARIANNE WAS FAIRLY CERTAIN she was falling in love with Mr. Willoughby.

And when he walked into the drawing room for a second visit, Marianne knew that he must feel the same way. Surely no one would call that often, not even if they felt guilty for injuring said person.

"Mr. Willoughby," Marianne said, not rising to greet him. Her ankle was still tender, although she could hobble about the flat without too much pain. But hobbling was so unattractive! "You're so kind to visit us again so soon."

"As long as you'll have me, it's the least I can do to offer you whatever small amusement I can, considering I am the reason for your injury," he said. Marianne wasn't certain what delighted her more: his words, or how his smile seemed to light up when he saw her.

"Please, don't think of it," Marianne insisted. "I was the one who wasn't paying attention."

A tiny snort came from the corner of the room where Margaret sat at the writing desk. "Pardon me," she said, the picture of innocence.

Marianne would have shot her a look, if Mr. Willoughby hadn't been present. "Is your mother well?" he asked Marianne.

"Very well," Marianne lied, for Mother was having one of her dark days. After yesterday, Marianne thought that perhaps the prospect of Mr. Willoughby's interest in her might have shaken her mother out of her strange periods of lethargy, but that did not appear to be the case. "She had other social calls to attend today."

Mr. Willoughby accepted the lie. "And no Miss Dashwood either? I hope my presence hasn't scared your family off."

Marianne raised her chin, feeling bold without Mother or Elinor around. "You could never scare any of us off, I assure you. We Dashwoods are made of sterner stuff than that."

"Oh, I believe it," Mr. Willoughby said, a glint of mischief in his blue eyes. "Why, not even my curricle intimidated you."

It wasn't true—she'd been terrified in the moment—but Marianne laughed nonetheless. "If only I had the power to command street traffic," she mused. "It would make walking everywhere so much easier, especially in this neighborhood."

"You must allow me to take you for a drive when you're properly healed," Mr. Willoughby said, drawing his chair closer to Marianne. "We can go to Hyde Park, or I'll take you anywhere you want in the city."

"I would love that," Marianne said, leaning closer to him. His scent was intoxicating—minty, with an undercurrent of something sharp and earthy.

Margaret cleared her throat, clearly relishing her role as chaperone.

"And Miss Margaret," Mr. Willoughby said, turning to where Margaret was tucked in her corner at the writing desk. "Keeping busy with your writing, I assume?"

Margaret was the picture of innocence as she smiled and raised one shoulder. "I've had a bit of writer's block lately."

"That sounds dreadful," Mr. Willoughby responded, as if Margaret had told him she'd caught pneumonia. "How does one cure writer's block?"

"If I knew, I would already be taking the cure," she said. "But there is none, except to read and think and wait it out."

"Well, maybe this will help." Mr. Willoughby stood up and withdrew a folded piece of paper from his coat, then handed it to her. "I picked it up earlier because it reminded me of you and your interest in stories."

Margaret accepted the gift with curiosity. It was one of the penny broadsides sold on the streets, detailing various crimes of those who stood to be tried or executed at Newgate. They were usually full of lurid and indecent details that Mother would absolutely forbid, but Margaret took it with a cry of excitement. "Oh, I love these! I always get the best inspiration from reading about real cases."

"That's a good one, if you ask me," Mr. Willoughby told her, but his eye was on Marianne, to see if she would disapprove. "It's got fraud, murder, kidnapping—and it was all uncovered by a young lady."

"Really?" Marianne asked, skepticism furrowing her brow.

"Truly," he said.

"Young ladies never uncover crime except in stories," Margaret said with suspicion, but she took the broadside and began reading it, her eyes flitting back and forth over the first lines. "I've found two misspellings already."

She retreated to the corner, and Marianne felt as though she could kiss Mr. Willoughby—if only Margaret weren't in the room. "That was very kind."

"It's not one of the really sordid ones," he promised. "And I'm happy when I can please a Dashwood sister . . . although, Margaret isn't the one that I most hope to charm."

Marianne had to work not to grin as she sat, and Mr. Willoughby chose a seat next to her. "Don't worry. You've charmed this Dashwood sister, too."

"Brilliant," he said, taking her hand. "Only one left to go."

Marianne laughed, although she knew it would take more than a penny broadside to charm Elinor. But she never thought that she might one day find a young man who cared not only about her and her thoughts and feelings but of the good opinion of her family as well. Truly, it was more than she could have ever hoped for.

They spent the visit talking of the best places to go driving, and hearing about the parties that Mr. Willoughby had been invited to, and his favorite places to visit in Somersetshire. Marianne tried not to notice that his social engagements all seemed so much more exciting than the blank slate of her own social calendar. She told herself that it was merely because they were in mourning that the family hadn't received any invitations . . . but they'd received no callers, either. None except Mr. Willoughby.

But he was more than enough, Marianne decided. And besides, once their mourning period had passed, no one would overlook the Dashwoods, especially if she and Mr. Willoughby were to form an attachment . . . but she was getting ahead of herself. It felt very strange to have found happiness after such an immense loss, but Marianne didn't question it. Life was fleeting, as Father's death had proved, so who could blame her for grasping the good when it came along?

When Mr. Willoughby finally took his leave, Margaret looked at her and said, "You aren't going to get married anytime soon, are you?"

"Don't be absurd," Marianne said, although she secretly

thrilled at the thought. "It's much too soon to be talking about marriage."

But maybe she was thinking about it. Was that mad? No, Marianne decided. When you knew, you *knew*.

She hobbled into the kitchen and found Elinor, looking unhappy and distracted as she stared at a complicated bit of glass tubing that seemed to contain water and something else all mashed up in one of its chambers. Wisps of hair were falling onto her face, and she had a far-off look that told Marianne she was likely puzzling about some question of science or mystery of the universe.

"Mr. Willoughby just left," Marianne announced. Then she sniffed. "Is something burning?"

"Hmm, how nice," Elinor murmured, then seemed to come back into herself. "And something was burning, but I took care of it. Mr. Willoughby seems . . . keen."

"He's very nice," Marianne said. "He wants to take me for a drive soon."

Elinor arched a brow. "Just be careful with that one."

"What's *that* supposed to mean?"

"Exactly what I said—be careful."

Marianne scowled. "I knew it. You don't like him."

Elinor looked surprised by the accusation. "I barely know him. And neither do you. Can't I impart a bit of sisterly caution?"

"You can," Marianne allowed. "But your judgment is hardly appreciated when you spent the entire visit hiding away in the kitchen doing . . . whatever it is that you're doing."

"Experimenting," Elinor said, sounding unimpressed by Marianne's outburst. "I was working on the substance that killed Father."

Shame flushed through Marianne. "Right. Have you discovered anything?"

"No," Elinor said with a heavy sigh that sent the hair on her forehead fluttering. "It's beyond my knowledge, I'm afraid."

"So what are you working on now?" Marianne didn't mean for her words to sound like an accusation. Sometimes her tone just came out all wrong.

"Perfumes," Elinor said shortly. "Remember, to sell?"

"I remember. Anything I can sample?"

Her sister pointed at a small glass vial on the table, and Marianne uncapped it eagerly. She well remembered how expensive perfumes could be, and perhaps Elinor could make quite a tidy sum off of her odd experiments. . . .

But when the scent inside the bottle wafted under Marianne's nose, she coughed.

"Is it too strong?" Elinor asked.

Marianne opened her mouth to say *Yes*, but that was worse—the perfume seemed to coat her tongue and crawl down the back of her throat. It was cloying and sweet, with a hardy darker note that made Marianne want to retch. She erupted into a coughing fit and nearly dropped the vial in her haste to get away from the wretched scent.

"All right, so you don't like it!" Elinor said. "But it's not that bad."

"That . . . is the worst . . . scent . . . I've ever " Marianne couldn't finish.

By the time she wiped the tears from her eyes and looked back at Elinor, her mouth was set in a thin line and her eyes flashed, but her face appeared to be completely neutral otherwise. "What was in that?"

"Lily, violet, rose, sandalwood, bergamot, cedar . . . and I think maybe mint."

"I think you might want to consider starting out with simpler concoctions?"

"Simple doesn't sell," Elinor snapped.

Marianne carefully pushed the offensive perfume vial aside. "What has gotten into you?"

Elinor shrugged. "Mr. Farrows was just here."

"*What?*" Marianne screeched. "Did you find out about the Alistair affair?"

"Of course not," Elinor snapped.

"Why not?"

"What was I to say? 'Oh, my sister stole Fanny's correspondence and wants to know the details of your darkest secret'?"

"Don't be absurd! We have no idea if the Alistair affair is his *darkest* secret." Marianne pinched the bridge of her nose and took a moment to collect herself. "There are circuitous ways to get at the truth. You ask him how his work is going, what his favorite parts of the job are, what his aspirations might be. You pay attention to the words he says and the words he doesn't speak, the pauses and little tells . . . and I don't know why I'm explaining this to you."

"I'm sorry I'm not the instinctive interrogator you are."

Elinor's voice was flat, and Marianne knew better than to push. "Never mind—what did you talk about?"

"He apologized for causing us undue distress," she said, watching her glass contraption. "He said that when Fanny asked for his help, he thought we knew and wanted it. He said that Father's business model was good. And then we talked about chemistry, but don't worry—I didn't tell him anything about our investigation. He also invited us to his mother's ball."

She pointed at a folded invitation on the table, and Marianne snatched it up. "*He* invited us?"

"It's a pity invitation," Elinor clarified. "He also brought us this." She handed Marianne a piece of paper, and she recognized it instantly as one of Father's invoices. "He said it was unpaid, and that Fanny and John had no use for five pounds, but he thought we might. He suggested that we collect it ourselves."

Marianne scanned the page and groaned when she read the name. "Mrs. Palmer? We'll be lucky if we can wring sixpence out of her. Remember, she's the one who believes her husband has a mistress. Father shadowed him at least a dozen times, but Mrs. Palmer isn't interested in evidence, she's interested in being right." Marianne tossed the invoice aside. "Mr. Farrows has given us a worthless piece of paper that might as well be burned."

"I'm sure Edward didn't know," Elinor said, snatching back the paper.

"*Edward!*" Marianne screeched, unable to let her sister continue. "Just how familiar are you?"

Two pink spots appeared on Elinor's cheeks. "It's not like that. He told me to call him Edward as he left, as we are *practically family.*"

Marianne studied her sister. It was strange to see Elinor so out of sorts, and over a young man. But she really was quite pretty. She had an air of sophistication that not even her regular day dress and disheveled appearance could mar. "I'm certain he likes you," Marianne said. "And if the sight of you in that old apron bubbling up brews in the kitchen didn't put him off, then it must be more than a passing fancy."

She'd meant to get Elinor to laugh, but instead her older sister scowled. "Well, he didn't come to declare his affections, that's for certain."

"Good," Marianne said without thinking. Elinor glared at her and Marianne sighed. "I meant good, because we still don't know if he's suspicious."

Elinor brushed her hair out of her eyes but wouldn't look

at Marianne. "You still believe that Fanny has something to do with Father's death?"

"I . . ." Suddenly, Marianne didn't know what to say. Beneath the surface of her shimmering hatred for Fanny, there was doubt. *Be careful of working too hard to make the facts come together.* That's what Father had said once. He was the smartest man Marianne had known, and he had a keen sense for investigating. What would he say now, if he could be here, examining his own death?

He would probably say that she wasn't considering all the angles.

"I am not ready to rule it out," she said finally.

"Hmph," Elinor said in that annoying older sister way. "Well, I want to discover who killed Father as much as you do, but we can't pass up a chance at five pounds, Marianne. We must make Mrs. Palmer pay."

"That sounded rather devious of you," Marianne couldn't resist pointing out.

But before Elinor could respond, Margaret came into the kitchen. "Someone is knocking on the front door."

"Well, why didn't you answer it?" Marianne asked, getting to her feet.

"I'm only eleven. Am I allowed to answer the front door?"

"Of course you're allowed," Marianne said, limping toward the hall. "We can't expect Hannah to do everything for us. Just don't invite anyone unfamiliar inside."

Elinor removed her apron and smoothed down her hair before following Marianne. They answered the door together, swinging it open to reveal a very pretty, petite young lady on their doorstep. She had tight blond curls and pale blue eyes. Her pale pink-and-yellow-striped dress made her look just a touch washed out. Her hand was raised to knock once more, but she quickly dropped it and smiled at the sisters.

"Hello! My name is Miss Lucy Steele. Are you the Dashwood sisters who run a private investigation firm?"

Marianne recovered first. "We . . . are."

"Excellent," Miss Steele proclaimed. "I would like to hire you."

Marianne and Elinor exchanged surprised looks and invited Miss Steele in.

They showed their client into the drawing room and offered tea, which she declined, but she seemed overly charmed by everything about her. "What a fine view of the street you have. And such lovely light in this room. My, I do love the upholstery of this settee—you really are so kind to see me unannounced. Mrs. Jennings was going to write me a referral letter, but I was so eager to meet you myself, and as soon as possible."

"It's our pleasure," Elinor said, ever the gracious hostess. "And how kind of Mrs. Jennings to think of us."

Marianne held back a snort. The older woman seemed like

the meddlesome sort to her. "How are you acquainted with Mrs. Jennings?"

"Oh, we go back years," Miss Steele gushed. "But I mean, not that many years. I've known her since I was a child. My father served in the navy with her husband. And now that my parents are gone, she hosts me in London during the season, or whenever she'd like some companionship."

"How nice," Elinor murmured, and Marianne managed a small smile. Mrs. Jennings really did enjoy the company of young people. Although, up close Marianne judged Miss Steele to be slightly older than she initially thought. The youthfulness of her dress suggested a young lady barely out to society, but Miss Steele appeared to be at least twenty-five.

"Anyway, Mrs. Jennings—isn't she just a dear?—told me about these marvelous sisters who were setting up shop as investigators, and I had to know more. I bullied her into a referral, really I did! There are some things that only other young ladies can understand."

Oh dear. Marianne had a feeling that she knew where this was headed. But she kept her composure nonetheless and said, "Why don't you start by telling us about yourself and what you hope we can accomplish. Then we'll discuss what's *realistic*, and our terms."

She left an emphasis on "realistic," but Miss Steele didn't seem to take note. If possible, she beamed even more. "All right, all the details. How far back should I go? No—don't tell me, I'll start from the beginning. My name is Lucy Steele, and I'm originally from Devonshire. I spent a happy childhood there, but my parents died when I was thirteen, and they didn't leave me much in the way of a fortune. . . ."

Marianne's suspicions began to solidify into certainty, and from there it was easy to relax into a persona in order to get Miss Steele to open up. Father had taught her to be the person a client wanted to divulge their secrets to, which was usually easy enough in most cases—all you had to do was take your cue from them.

"We know what that's like, unfortunately, don't we, Elinor?" Marianne made her voice sound good-natured and sympathetic and nudged her sister.

Elinor frowned slightly. "Yes," was all she said.

But it was enough for Miss Steele to begin to see them as potential friends. "Yes, you must know. How dreadful it is to lose a parent, and your way of life. I'm fortunate to have many relations and friends in the countryside and in London, so I never want for a hostess or friendship, but you must understand the toll it takes on a person, not having a permanent home. Being shuffled from relative to relative, always on the lookout for signs that one is becoming a burden rather than a guest . . ." Miss Steele trailed off a bit then, and her lower lip jutted out the slightest.

But before she could say anything, Elinor added, "We also know what it's like to be made to feel like a guest in one's own home."

Miss Steele visibly brightened. "It must be a similar experience, to be sure. Which is why I need your help. I *must* be married. It's the only way I can have my own home. But eligible gentlemen all want the youngest and prettiest ladies. I'm tired of attending ball after ball only to be passed over for a pretty girl with a fortune of five thousand pounds per year."

"So you want us to find you a husband," Marianne stated, making her tone light and playful.

"Oh, I wouldn't want you to find me a husband per se—I just need your help identifying three to five gentlemen of certain standings and fortunes. Maybe do some digging to determine their suitability, and ensure there are no scandalous secrets to uncover after marriage. At most, help secure proper introductions. The rest I can do myself." She gave a high-pitched giggle. "But imagine if you could secure me a marriage proposal—why, I'd give you a thousand pounds if I had it."

"Imagine," Marianne echoed, a little more darkly than she intended. She wasn't entirely surprised to learn that Miss Steele was just as she imagined—a vain and pretty husband seeker who had no mother to help maneuver her into a good marriage, and so she sought out their help. Well, Marianne Dashwood wasn't meant to be a matchmaker, she was an investigator and—

"We'll do it," Elinor stated. "We cannot offer any guarantees on securing you a proposal, but the rest we can handle. Right, Marianne?"

Marianne looked to Elinor, eyes wide in an expression she hoped said, *This is a bad idea.*

But Elinor ignored her as Miss Steele squealed and said, "Really? Oh, I'm so glad!" Then she clapped her hands in delight.

Marianne smiled faintly, trying and failing to match their new client's level of enthusiasm. "We are delighted to help. Of course, there shall be a retaining fee. Five pounds."

To Marianne's shock, Miss Steele opened her reticule right then and there and held out a crisp five-pound banknote. She didn't set it on the table or try to obscure the exchange of money in any way, as politeness dictated. Marianne accepted the note and then quickly tucked it away in her skirts. "Excellent. Now, I'm sorry to do this to you, but can you come back tomorrow? We'll conduct an interview to get a sense of your connections and where to start. It's just that we have another appointment in a half hour."

"Of course," Miss Steele said, rising. "Thank you, ladies! I know I shall be walking to the altar before the year is out."

Elinor saw her to the door, while Miss Steele kept gushing about how kind the Dashwoods were and thanking them. Finally, Marianne heard the click of the door and Elinor came back into the room.

"What were you thinking?" Marianne demanded.

"She's rather silly," Elinor said, which was about as biting as she got. "But I don't think this should be too hard. Besides, I thought you wanted to continue in Father's footsteps."

"I don't care about the level of difficulty of the case. I could find three to five fools who might want to marry her in my sleep. But Elinor, we aren't matchmakers."

Elinor sat across from Marianne and said, "Well, I'm neither a matchmaker nor an investigator, but in case you've forgotten, we have a set income that we are expected to live upon for the rest of our lives, unless either of us marries well. Our choices are to ask John and Fanny for assistance—not now, mind you, but eventually that money will run out—find husbands ourselves, or find a way to earn money. We are not in a position to turn down work."

"*Elinor.*" Marianne expelled her sister's name in a huff, trying not to lose her temper. "There are two types of cases Norland and Company does *not* involve themselves in. Anything that might harm someone else—murder, extortion, physical intimidation—and helping young ladies con husbands."

"In case you've forgotten, Norland and Company no longer exists." Elinor's eyes flashed dangerously. "John dissolved the business. We are starting from nearly nothing. And besides, you can't tell me that Father didn't have to take on silly or menial work when he was starting out. Even Mrs. Palmer's case sounds rather . . . well, silly."

Marianne glared at Elinor, who withdrew the invoice from her pocket and was waving it about. "Norland and Company does sometimes take on infidelity cases, but those are different. Someone is suspected of doing wrong already. Miss Steele wants us to spy on people."

Elinor was unmoved. "We're young unmarried ladies without any prospects, and very little money. Right now we can choose what indignities we suffer because we have some money put aside. But later, we might not have a choice."

Marianne hated everything about what Elinor was saying—her tone, her irrefutable logic, her choice of words. But she knew that her sister was right. She hated that most of all.

"We have more important things to worry about. Like who killed Father."

"Funny," Elinor said dryly, "but you've not brought up Father since you came home in Mr. Willoughby's curricle."

At that, Marianne flared hot. "Funny, but you were the one who didn't want to believe me when I said I thought Father was murdered."

Elinor sagged. "I know. And I haven't forgotten this case. But Marianne, we have nothing more to go on. I've no idea what the substance that killed him is made of, let alone where it could have come from. And you have no proof that John and Fanny are responsible. We don't know what he was working on before he died because his journal has gone missing, and we no longer have access to his files. I'm not saying we ought to forget about this investigation. But perhaps it'll take us longer than we like."

Marianne felt like a scolded child, but she could offer up no argument.

"In the meantime, we need money." Elinor held out her hand for the banknote that Miss Steele had given her. "And we can't be too choosy about how we get it."

Marianne held out the banknote, but she didn't let go of it. Elinor met her eyes. "I'm not giving up," she told her sister.

"I know," Elinor said.

"And if you expect me to take on such menial matchmaking tasks, you better help. You know more about society than me."

"I know," Elinor said again, but the corners of her lips quivered.

"And if you want to sell your perfumes, you're going to have to work on your formulas," she added.

"I *know*," Elinor cried out.

Marianne released the banknote and sank back into the settee. Elinor handed her the Palmer invoice—she was so good at getting in the last dig without saying a single word!—and Marianne sulked. Mrs. Palmer was tiresome to say the least, and she'd be stubborn about paying unless she received the answer she was looking for. She examined the invoice, hoping for something written in her father's hand to give her a clue as to how to persuade the woman, when the last line caught her eye.

The invoice consisted of a dated list of times that Father had followed Mr. Palmer or met with Mrs. Palmer, along with a summary of Father's rate. The last line concluded with a twenty-minute consult with Mrs. Palmer . . . on the day of Father's death.

Marianne's breath caught.

Perhaps Edward Farrows hadn't given them such a useless slip of paper after all.

NINE

*In Which the Dashwood Sisters
Consult an Expert*

THE NEXT DAY, ELINOR rose early, packed a basket with the perfume that Marianne had claimed nearly made her sick, and tucked her notes and what was left of the poison underneath it. She tiptoed to her mother's door and knocked gently. When there was no response, she tried the doorknob. It was open.

Elinor hadn't seen her mother like this since the weeks after Margaret was born when she spent nearly a month in bed, bleary eyed, with her hair unkempt and wild, getting up only to be coaxed into the bath and clean clothes by her maid and to feed baby Margaret before Father hired a wet nurse. But back then, Mother had her own maid, and they'd had a staff and money for a doctor. Elinor still remembered the face of the old physician that Father called after two weeks. She wasn't certain what his recommended treatment had been, but she remembered the fury that had twisted on Father's face and how the doctor had been ordered out and never seen again. Then Father had knelt before Elinor and Marianne and said, "Your mama is going to get well. In the meantime, you must help look after your baby sister."

"When?" Marianne had asked, brave enough at five years to ask the question that seven-year-old Elinor feared.

"I don't know," Father admitted, and it seemed so strange to Elinor that their papa, who had all the answers, couldn't be more specific.

But they'd believed him, and by the time Margaret was smiling and cooing at the sight of her sisters and rolling on the nursery floor, Mother would dress and join them. She was still distant and quiet for many months, but eventually she came back to them.

Now as Elinor stared down at Mother, wrapped in her nightclothes that smelled a bit sour, face turned away from the light pouring into the window, she wondered how Father had known Mother would get well. She wished she remembered more about that time because at the moment she wasn't sure how to help.

"Mother?" she whispered, kneeling down so her face was level with Mother's. "I'm going to the apothecary. Do you need anything?"

Mother's forehead creased, so Elinor knew that she'd heard. But she didn't open her eyes.

"Mother," she said again, gently shaking her shoulder.

"Elinor . . . ," Mother murmured, and sighed wearily. As if Elinor were disturbing her.

"I won't be gone very long," she promised. "Why don't you get up and come down to breakfast? Margaret has been asking about you."

"Hmm," Mother said, turning onto her back.

"Mr. Willoughby might come to call again," Elinor tried, hating that Mr. Willoughby might be a better motivator than herself or her sisters.

"That's nice," Mother said. Then she opened one eye. "You're going to the apothecary?"

"Yes," Elinor breathed. "Do you need anything?"

"More," she said, pointing at something on the small table next to the bed. "Could you get me more?"

Elinor picked up the brown bottle, feeling her stomach drop as she read the label. *Laudanum*. Elinor unstopped the cork and peered inside.

"Please, Elinor," Mother said, squinting up at her. "I need it to sleep. I toss and turn all night without it."

"All right," Elinor said. Laudanum was medicine, after all. And who could blame Mother for sleeplessness? Elinor had experienced more than her fair share of sleepless nights, and not just because she now had to share a bed with Marianne, who kicked. "But why don't you get up while I'm gone? I can ask Hannah to draw you a bath."

But Mother had already turned her back on her and buried her head beneath a pillow.

Elinor had never before set foot in an apothecary. Before Father's death, they'd always called a physician when they or one of the servants were ill or injured. But many people could not afford such, and that was where apothecaries provided an essential service, as well as selling perfumes, toilet water, and other small luxuries. Elinor stepped into the storefront at the address she'd retrieved from the Williams case file. The small shop was pristine, with a small area for customers to stand and wait and a long counter separating them from shelves of glass vials, paper packets, and all sorts of intriguing containers that Elinor would have dearly loved to examine more closely.

A gray-haired man with a stoic but not unkind face looked up from his work at a table behind the counter. "Can I help you, miss?"

"Hello," she said, and when her voice rasped, she cleared her throat. "I am looking for Mr. Brandon?"

He looked her up and down, but not in a way that made Elinor's skin crawl. More as if he were evaluating her. "If you'll wait a moment, miss, I'll fetch him."

"Thank you," she said, and shifted nervously. She tried to calm herself by examining the surgical equipment in the corner—scalpels, linen for bandages, metal bowls whose purposes Elinor could only guess at—until she heard, "Miss Dashwood?"

She looked up to see Mr. Brandon, shrugging on a jacket over his shirt and waistcoat and blinking at her behind his spectacles. "Hello, Mr. Brandon," she said, hoping she didn't sound too nervous.

"Is your family well?" he asked, a small note of urgency in his voice. "Your sister?"

"Oh, they're very well, thank you," she assured him. "No need for worry. I was hoping to consult with you on a matter."

She darted a small glance at the older gentleman who'd fetched Mr. Brandon. Was this Mr. Williams? Father's case notes had said the young woman's uncle hadn't wanted to entertain notions that his niece had been murdered, and Elinor didn't want to say anything that might get Mr. Brandon in trouble. The older man watched her warily, likely suspecting her of being sweet on his apprentice—what other reason would she have for showing up and asking for him? She tried to smile reassuringly at the man, but he just shook his head and reached for a heavy wooden case. "I'm off to check in on Mrs. Fowley, Mr. Brandon. I won't be long."

Those last words hung in the air like a warning, but Elinor was grateful to see him go. As soon as the door closed, she asked, "Was that Mr. Williams?"

Mr. Brandon nodded. "He needs the extra help, especially

now that Eliza is gone. I work here when I'm not at Barts."

"Oh," Elinor said, realizing that they'd asked very little about his life and interests the other day. "Do you aim to become a surgeon?"

"Physician," he said without a trace of ego. "I'm saving up for a course at Guy's, and I need to work on my Latin a bit more before taking the Royal College licensing exam."

"Marvelous," Elinor said, and she truly meant it . . . but also she couldn't wait to tell Marianne that she'd been dead wrong about Mr. Brandon being an unambitious lackey.

"Is it a medical matter that I can help you with?"

"Of a sort," Elinor admitted, and sidled closer to the counter that stood between her and Mr. Brandon. "I know it's an imposition—"

Mr. Brandon shook his head. "Don't think of it. How can I be of assistance?"

Elinor withdrew her small jar of poison and set it on the counter between them. She'd thought long and hard about whether she should do this but ultimately decided that there was no way forward unless she could understand what was in that jar. "Marianne and I weren't completely forthcoming about why we were interested in your case."

Mr. Brandon didn't look surprised. His gaze darted down at the jar and then back up to her. "You never answered Mrs. Jennings's question. Your father didn't die under completely natural circumstances, did he?"

Elinor shook her head, taken aback, but how wonderful it felt to finally acknowledge that. "No, we don't believe he did."

Mr. Brandon picked up the vial and held it up to the light. His eyes looked larger than normal behind his spectacle lenses, but otherwise he didn't appear shocked or scandalized. "And you think this is what killed him?"

"I'm almost positive," she said. "We found it in the teacup on his desk, and Marianne determined it'd been served to him before he died. But no one else in the household took ill, and this was all that remained. We think whoever murdered him poisoned his cup directly. And since we have no idea who that might be, I thought if I could determine what this substance is, we can trace it back to the killer."

"Intriguing," he muttered, shaking the vial slightly.

"It's water-soluble, and I tried to run a few other tests that got me nowhere," she continued. "But I don't *know* enough. I don't want to waste my only bit of evidence."

Mr. Brandon looked at her. "It sounds as if you do a fair bit more than *dabble* at the sciences."

Elinor found herself momentarily speechless. She was shocked that Mr. Brandon had paid such close attention to what Marianne had said, but also uncertain—was his observation good or bad? She decided to be bold. "I want to study chemistry. Like Miss Williams. But . . . I'm afraid I don't know as much as she must have. Or as much as you."

Mr. Brandon nodded again, and she was finding she

liked the way he merely accepted information without feeling the need to comment, protest, or argue everything that was presented to him. He then turned his attention back on the vial as he set it down. "It doesn't resemble any of the popular poisons—arsenic, strychnine . . . but if your father had been dosed with any of them, I suspect you would have known—he would have been violently ill before his death."

Elinor shook her head. "There was none of that. It was as if he simply fell asleep at his desk and never woke up."

Mr. Brandon met her gaze, and she saw the question in his eyes. "I found him," she said. "I promise you, there was no disturbance. The doctor we called said his heart must have given out."

"I'm very sorry. But have you considered the possibility that . . ." He trailed off, but Elinor heard what his silence implied.

"I tasted it," she said. "A tiny bit, diluted with water. The taste is off. I didn't swallow it. I could accept that his death was natural, if we hadn't found this."

Mr. Brandon nodded, and there seemed to be a sheen of respect in his expression. "I know of a few tests I could run, to be absolutely certain."

"What kind of tests? Can you show me?"

Mr. Brandon nodded and motioned for her to step behind the counter. He led her to a back room where a laboratory was set up—beakers and vials and fantastic tubing that she'd never before had the chance to study up close. The walls were lined with more supplies and books, too—books that she would have loved to pore over. On the far wall was a stove, providing heat for the room. It wasn't a hot day, but the full chill of autumn had yet to settle over London, so the room was stuffy.

"Determining whether or not a substance is arsenic is easy," Mr. Brandon told her as she took in the room, and he withdrew a metal spatula from a canister. He opened Elinor's vial and scraped out a small substance. She watched as he carried it over to the stove, then used a small shovel to withdraw three hot coals. "When it burns, it smells like garlic."

"I didn't know that," Elinor said, filing away that information. She almost interrupted him to say that she'd already experimented with the substance, but watched instead as he held the spatula over the coals. It wasn't long before the substance darkened into a deeper brown, then began to burn.

"Inhale," Mr. Brandon instructed, holding the spatula carefully between them. "What do you smell?"

Elinor inhaled deeply, smelling the dried herbs, the crisp scent of alcohol in the room, and the sharp tang of something burning.

"I don't smell garlic," she said.

"I agree." He let it burn for a moment longer, then shoved the coals back into the stove. "Well then, not arsenic."

"But I would love to know what other experiments to try," she added, hoping she didn't sound too eager. She summarized all that she'd done already, omitting the part about leaving the pan on the stove, and it burning . . . but just recollecting the memory of Edward brushing past her to open the window made her flush.

Mr. Brandon looked up from where he was scraping the burned substance off the spatula and into a small bowl as she listed her experiments. "Oh, why didn't you say earlier? It sounds as though you've seen to all of the basic experiments."

Elinor didn't answer right away, partly because she was flustered by his reaction. His question wasn't an impatient demand, nor did it sound belittling. He sounded genuinely curious.

"I suppose . . . well, you're the expert. You've read far more than me, I'm sure. . . ." Her eyes strayed to the books on their shelves.

"Yes, well, all you really need in order to be successful is the power of observation, a meticulous eye to detail, and never-ending patience." He looked up and said, "Don't doubt yourself, Miss Dashwood."

Elinor smiled slowly. It was a rare occurrence when a man spoke to her like a peer. Her father had, on occasion. Edward Farrows had, whenever they'd spoken of money and family and her family's affairs. And now Mr. Brandon. She decided right then that she liked him—not romantically, as Marianne might have assumed, but as a friend. Maybe even someone she could fully trust.

"Do you think the scientific community would be willing

to listen to a woman?" she asked.

He grimaced, and even though it wasn't exactly the response she was hoping for, she appreciated that he didn't try to hide his reaction. "Most of them think that women are utterly incapable of scientific inquiry, unfortunately. I don't hold with ideas of what a person can or cannot do because of the circumstances of their birth. I believe in hard work, pursuing your goals, and proving people wrong if they don't believe in you."

She liked how he said this without affectation or airs. "You remind me of my father," she said.

She forgot until the words were out of her mouth that Mr. Brandon had known Father, had hired him . . . and wasn't satisfied with the work her father had done. But rather than seem offended, Mr. Brandon said, "I liked your father. I disagreed with how he concluded the case, and I wanted him to keep at it. But I understand why he closed it. There were no leads, and I couldn't very well afford to pay him to speculate at what might have happened to Eliza. He said as much to me, you know."

"Father was good like that," Elinor said softly. She wanted to beg Mr. Brandon to tell her every detail about his encounters with Father. One thing she hadn't quite realized until now was that when someone died, you were robbed of new memories of them. But hearing about facets of her father's life she hadn't known about felt like a small reprieve, even if it didn't lessen her hurt.

"He seemed like a true gentleman," Mr. Brandon said. "And one who worked. Unusual, but something that ought to be respected."

"He was proud of the work he did. He built a life for us all through his work. And while the gossipmongers would whisper that he was profiting off of nosing about, he had his own code of honor. Like never charging someone for a job he knew he couldn't deliver on. I can't say what he really thought of Miss Williams's death. He kept his personal notes with him at all times, and when he died . . ."

Elinor trailed off, conscious of revealing too much. She forced herself to redirect, quickly. "Well, his death has forced my sister and me to find our callings."

"Your sister appears to be very passionate," Mr. Brandon ventured.

Elinor smiled. "Passionate is the perfect word to describe Marianne. And so is stubborn."

Mr. Brandon surprised her by laughing then. It was a low, quiet chuckle and it didn't last long. "She reminds me of Eliza."

"Really?" Elinor asked.

"They look nothing alike," Mr. Brandon rushed to say. "But Eliza was passionate about her work and seeing it through no matter what anyone said, and so she could be stubborn. She had to prove to others that she not only understood the science, but she had the stomach for it."

165

"What do you mean by that?" Elinor asked.

"Well . . . in medicine, there's so much we don't know," he said. "And some things we can only deduce by experimentation. But experimentation can be dangerous. . . ."

She thought of her laboratory mishaps. "I agree."

"And it's not always . . . polite to discuss the means by which we determine a poison's potency. . . ."

"Please, Mr. Brandon," she said. "If there are tests to be conducted, or something I haven't tried yet . . . I want to know. I don't suppose it's wise to ingest the poison, but if there's some way . . ."

"I wouldn't ingest it," Mr. Brandon said. "And Eliza certainly wouldn't have ingested a strange substance unless she was absolutely certain it wouldn't kill her, and even then she would have taken copious notes beforehand."

"Then what are we referring to?" Elinor asked.

"Miss Dashwood. Have you ever wondered how we determine just how potent a substance might be?"

Elinor stopped and considered the question, truly considered it. When the answer came to her, she felt foolish for not seeing it first. "Oh."

"I've shocked you," Mr. Brandon stated.

Elinor shook her head, although she was shocked. "To be clear, we're talking about . . . animals?"

"Rats, mostly. I set traps for them in the alley. Partly because they're so plentiful, and because they're small." He picked up the vial containing Elinor's poison. "I could . . . run a few experiments?"

She stared at him and tried to reconcile her queasiness at the thought of killing a living thing, even if it was a disgusting rodent, with her desire to know.

But her hesitation was misconstrued by Mr. Brandon. "I see I've horrified you. I apologize."

"I'm not horrified," Elinor insisted. "I'm intrigued. Maybe a bit queasy."

"It's how chemists test the efficacy of new substances," Mr. Brandon explained. "Otherwise, we wait for poisoning cases, hope we can obtain the body for study, and perform autopsies."

"Autopsies?" Elinor asked. She'd never heard the word before.

"It's from the Greek," he hedged. "It means to bear witness. To see with one's own eyes."

"You examine the body," Elinor reasoned. "But if the effects of poisoning aren't obvious on the outside—"

"We . . . cut people open," he said. "Evidence of poisoning can be seen within."

Elinor waited for her stomach to churn, for the full horror of what he was saying to set into her bones. It didn't come. "Interesting," she said after a pause. "It makes terrible sense, I suppose. If my father hadn't been buried, could you do that? Autopsy him?"

"Perform an autopsy," he corrected, but not rudely. "And

perhaps. It's not an exact science and it wouldn't necessarily provide definitive proof. Nor is it certain that any magistrate or judge would take our word for what might be discovered. I'm afraid our methods of examination are considered rather inhumane, so we're only allowed to examine bodies that are given to us. And most people want to see their dead buried."

"Who gives them to you then?" Elinor asked, unable to ignore her morbid curiosity.

"Ah, well . . . when a person is hanged . . ."

"*Oh.*" This was proving to be quite the educational visit—just not in the way Elinor expected.

"I'm sorry for offending you."

Elinor shook her head no. "You haven't offended me, you've answered my questions, and for that I thank you. But I think it's safe to say I am less interested in what goes on in the body than I am in the substances themselves."

"Eliza would have liked you," he said. "Although her interest was in medicines, not strictly chemistry."

"She was developing a new treatment, is that right?" Elinor recalled what he'd told them in Mrs. Jennings's drawing room, a hypothesis that had gotten her laughed out by the other surgeons.

Brandon nodded. "She wanted to develop a medicine that could dull pain."

"Well, we have those, do we not? Laudanum, for one."

"Ah, but laudanum is . . . imprecise. It may knock one man

out, but it won't do anything for another. And if you have a patient truly in pain, the kind of pain that requires the surgeon to take drastic measures, it takes a great deal of laudanum to be effective."

"All right," she said, thinking of Mother and the different sort of pain she dulled with laudanum. "But why dull pain and not cure it?"

"Because while pain is the enemy of the surgeon, it can be useful to a physician."

"How?"

"It lets us know when there's something the matter," he said. "Think about it—if you seriously injure your leg, pain tells you that something is wrong, to take care, that healing is needed."

"True," Elinor agreed hesitantly. "It's also inconvenient."

"But what happens if you don't listen to that pain, or you push through it?"

"You injure yourself even further," Elinor said.

"Exactly. That is why it's dangerous to think that one can or should cure pain. We ought to respect it. But Eliza thought it could be managed. If a broken bone needs setting, the pain will cause the patient to lash out, prohibiting the surgeon from doing his job. Surgeons can try to manage pain through alcohol, but a man who is used to drink will require much more than a lady who never drinks, and its effects dull over time with constant use. Different patients have different thresholds of pain, you see? And Eliza had a theory that if a patient's pain was minimal, they could heal faster. But first, she had to discover how to control it."

Elinor's mind was racing. "And what did she think was the key to this? Alcohol?"

"No," Mr. Brandon said, his tone clipped. "Opium."

"Ah," Elinor said. "The key ingredient of laudanum. I suppose that makes sense. Why don't surgeons just use pure opium, then?"

"Because it's dangerous. It might not kill you, but have you ever seen someone dependent on opium?"

"Dependent?" Elinor repeated. "As in, dependent on drink? But it's supposed to be medicinal."

"Don't think that just because a doctor or surgeon uses something, it's not dangerous," he said. "And believe me, there are enough charlatans in this city who would dilute laudanum or cut opium with other substances to turn a bigger profit."

"And Miss Williams was hoping to improve upon laudanum?" Elinor asked.

"I believe so, although the precise details have gone with her to the grave."

Mr. Brandon seemed to be staring at a particular corner of the lab, adjacent to the stove. Was that where she'd been found? How awful, to come to work each day and be reminded of her tragic final moment. At least Elinor didn't have to spend her days at the desk where she'd found Father.

"I'm sorry," she said quietly. "Her loss is tragic, to her loved ones, and to the scientific community."

He nodded slightly, acknowledging her implication that he was among Eliza's loved ones. "Thank you."

"Will you take the sample? Run whatever tests you think might be necessary?"

He looked up suddenly. "Are you sure?"

"Yes. We have no other solid leads. If this can lead to something useful . . ."

Mr. Brandon nodded. "It'll be safe there," he promised. "Only Mr. Williams and I have keys to this room anymore, and he never goes digging through my experiments. He can hardly stand to be back here."

Elinor felt a pang for the older man's loss. "Thank you."

"Of course. Now, you must let me walk you home."

"Oh, there's no need for you to bother yourself! Besides, can you even leave the shop?"

"It's no bother," he said, reverting back to his straightforward tone that would almost make her think otherwise, but she was beginning to suspect that Mr. Brandon's habit was to speak plainly. He had impeccable manners, though. "Let me just lock up. Mr. Williams shall be back any moment now, and I think he should be more displeased that I let a young lady walk home than if I close until he's back. Is there anything else you needed?"

Elinor thought of Mother's request for more laudanum and

171

the way her figure seemed so small curled up in bed. She also thought of Mr. Brandon's words. *Don't think that just because a doctor or surgeon uses something, it's not dangerous.*

Mother was in pain, but the Dashwood sisters couldn't lose another parent.

"No," she said. "Nothing else, thank you."

TEN

In Which the Dashwood Sisters
Uncover More Questions

MARIANNE STOOD AT THE window, partially obscured by the drapes, peering out onto Barton Street for the first sign of Mr. Willoughby's curricle. She missed the quiet of her old neighborhood and the space to move about her own home and garden undisturbed, but Cheapside wasn't so bad. Already her street bustled with vendors, carts, and pedestrians cutting through their little slice of London to get to the shops on the next block over, and Marianne could see the usefulness of the anonymity the bustle provided. In her old neighborhood, people stepped out to be seen by others, but here everyone was middle-class, too busy working for a living, to tattle on her to Mother or gossip if she slipped out of her flat at the first glimpse of Mr. Willoughby's curricle turning on their block.

Which was exactly what she did.

He brought his horses to a smooth stop in front of her flat and tipped his hat. "Miss Marianne! To what do I owe this unexpected pleasure?"

"Were you serious about taking me for a drive?" Marianne asked, trying not to sound too coy—although it was satisfying to see Mr. Willoughby watch her, trying to anticipate how to please her.

"Of course," he said, stepping down from the curricle and taking her hand. "But should you really be walking about? How is your ankle?"

She delighted in the warmth of his hand through their respective gloves. "It's only a little tender, I assure you. Besides, I can't spend all of my days sitting about."

She said that last bit with an airy smile, but Marianne had burned to run to Mrs. Palmer's the moment she realized what the dates on the invoice meant. It had been too late to call the day before, and she hadn't wanted to put Mrs. Palmer on the defensive by showing up at an inappropriate hour, demanding answers. She'd spent all evening devising her plan, and she was delighted to see that the first step—convincing Mr. Willoughby to accompany her—required very little effort on her part.

"Where are we headed?" Mr. Willoughby asked as he helped her into her seat, giving her a rakish wink that made Marianne shiver.

"To call upon one Mrs. Palmer," Marianne said, giving him the address.

"And who is Mrs. Palmer?" he asked, his pleasant expression never wavering as he took his own seat and urged his horses into a trot.

"One of my father's former clients," Marianne said, and then she added, "I must wrap up her account."

If he was surprised to hear that Marianne took an active role in her late father's business, he didn't show it. It had come up, of course, in their conversations that her father was recently deceased and that he had been a private investigator. But Marianne hadn't revealed the full extent of her own role in his work, nor had she let on that she aspired to follow in his footsteps. It wasn't that she was embarrassed or ashamed or that she wanted to keep it secret. But . . . young men often had strange reactions to hearing about Marianne's intention to work. And she wanted to discern Mr. Willoughby's feelings on the matter gradually.

Mr. Willoughby didn't appear put off by her plans. He merely remarked, "Not many young ladies are as active in business as you."

Marianne was uncertain if that was a judgment or a compliment, so she decided to offer him a sliver of the truth. "I took an interest, so my father would occasionally bring me along when he made certain calls. He did not think that because I am a young lady I was incapable."

"I admire you for it," Mr. Willoughby said. "And your

father, for not ignoring your potential."

Marianne was unable to hide her smile. "Not every gentleman would agree."

"I know not to underestimate a lady, Miss Marianne. I grew up under my aunt's care, and she is a formidable woman."

Was that a note of bitterness that Marianne detected in his voice? "Are you close?"

"We don't always agree, but we are family."

She glanced at him and noted his tight smile. He hadn't quite answered her question. "How lucky she has you."

"I would love for her to meet you one day," he said.

"Really?"

"Oh yes! She may be elderly, but she's got spirit. Just like you."

Young men didn't introduce you to their elderly female relatives merely for fun. This must mean *something*—ergo, Marianne must mean something to Mr. Willoughby. And he said that they both had spirit. Marianne felt a glow she hadn't experienced in weeks. "I would like that," she said finally.

"This Mrs. Palmer," Mr. Willoughby said suddenly, startling Marianne out of her haze of happiness. "Is she dangerous?"

"Heavens, no!" Marianne said with a laugh. "She's just very obstinate."

But Marianne could be even more obstinate. And she had spirit.

From the moment the butler opened the door at the Palmer residence, they could hear horrible crashing piano music, jarring and stuttering in the distance, and just under that cacophony came a warbling sound that was more the suggestion of a human voice than actual singing.

"Miss Dashwood and Mr. Willoughby of Norland and Company," Marianne said, trying not to cringe at the sounds from within the house. "Is Mrs. Palmer in?"

The butler looked positively relieved for the excuse to interrupt the mistress of the house, and before long they were escorted into the sitting room, where Mrs. Palmer, a woman of about thirty, looked up from her pianoforte with no small measure of impatience.

"Miss Dashwood," she said, completely ignoring Mr. Willoughby. "Have you any news?"

"I'm sorry, Mrs. Palmer," Marianne said, striving for an obsequious tone. "There's been no change since last month."

"I can't see how you would know," she said, gesturing for them to sit. "Your father . . . well, he is, that is to say, no one has been working on my case for weeks."

Marianne bit back a sigh and took a seat next to Mr. Willoughby on the settee. "But even before that, Mrs. Palmer. There was never any evidence of your husband's infidelity."

"Because your father wasn't looking hard enough," Mrs. Palmer snapped back.

Marianne leaned forward and adopted a soothing tone. "I assure you that my father and I both personally followed Mr. Palmer multiple times. We never discovered any evidence of a liaison. I'm sorry you're dissatisfied with our results, but per the terms of our agreement, I'm afraid we require payment for the work performed."

"I paid a retainer," she said, leaning back against the pianoforte so that one ivory key let out a small bleat.

"And my father more than surpassed it," Marianne continued, withdrawing the invoice. It was proof of the accounting that Mrs. Palmer owed them five pounds. "I'm sure he sent a copy for your records, but if you need reminding . . ." Marianne handed it to her, watching the other woman closely.

Father had been able to establish rather quickly that Mr. Palmer didn't have any gambling problems, mistresses, or proclivities to expensive things he could not afford. He just didn't like to be at home, and judging by the sample of Mrs. Palmer's talent—or lack thereof—Marianne suspected she knew why. Of course, she knew Father would never say such a thing to Mrs. Palmer outright. *We don't judge our clients,* he'd told her many times. *We simply try to help them.*

Marianne waited until Mrs. Palmer had read the entire document, then said, "Now, I see that my father did visit you the day he died. Can you tell me how you left things?"

"The day he died? How dreadful." Mrs. Palmer shook her head. "But he seemed perfectly fine. He was even going to follow Mr. Palmer one more time."

"When?" Marianne asked, striving for a gentle and understanding tone but not quite managing to hide her urgency.

"I had asked him to do it that very day, but he said he could not."

"Did he give you a reason why?" Marianne asked, perking up. What she remembered of that day, Father had been out all afternoon, but he'd returned home well ahead of dinner.

But Mrs. Palmer was quick to dash her hopes. "No. I only remember it because he said that his wife would be most displeased if he kept her waiting, and he seemed in quite a hurry."

Marianne saw a flash of hurt, then longing, on Mrs. Palmer's face as she conveyed these words. What would Father do in this situation? Not meddle, but . . . perhaps dispense some advice?

"Mrs. Palmer, you love your husband very much, don't you?"

She looked up from the invoice. "What a silly question."

It wasn't silly, though. Marianne was not so naive as to believe that love was a prerequisite to marriage, at least not within the ton. But Mrs. Palmer didn't strike her as a woman who'd spend good money to prove her husband was unfaithful merely for her own entertainment. "Love is a very special thing. I can understand why the prospect of losing it would terrify you so."

Mrs. Palmer didn't speak, but Marianne felt Mr. Willoughby shift beside her.

"Have you told your husband how much you love him lately?" Marianne pressed. "Perhaps, if you told him how you feel—how much you love him, and how much it hurts you when he doesn't spend time with you—you can talk about where he goes when he's not . . . here."

Mrs. Palmer stared at Marianne for so long, she was afraid she'd offended the woman by speaking so boldly. Then Mr. Willoughby said, "Mrs. Palmer, if I may offer a gentleman's perspective—men are human, emotional creatures as well. We too are plagued with doubt, worry, and fear when it comes to romance."

Marianne glanced at Mr. Willoughby out of the corner of her eye, trying not to let her surprise show. He stared at Mrs. Palmer earnestly, and if the other woman hadn't been married, well . . . Marianne might have been jealous of her. But when she turned her gaze back on her client, she noted a glistening in Mrs. Palmer's eyes. "Fine," she said, but the word had none of the superiority of a few moments ago.

Mrs. Palmer stood and went to a writing desk in the corner and opened a small compartment. After some rustling about, she returned and set the invoice and payment on the tea table between them. She looked squarely at Marianne and said, "Please don't take offense, Miss Dashwood, but I hope I never have to meet with you again."

Marianne picked up the payment with a small smile. "None taken."

Outside, Mr. Willoughby could barely contain his amusement.

"I'm no detective," he began as he helped Marianne into

the curricle, "but have you considered the reason why that man doesn't want to come home is because of his wife's singing?"

"Oh, it's *absolutely* why," Marianne said, her words coming out a touch breathless as Mr. Willoughby's thumb caressed her knuckles. He withdrew, and she forced herself to continue, as if his touch hadn't sent her heart fluttering. "Although perhaps now they can talk about it like adults."

"Why doesn't he just ask her to stop playing?" Mr. Willoughby asked, taking his seat beside her and picking up the reins.

"Who knows? But one thing I've learned in this line of work is that sometimes it's most difficult to talk about important matters with the ones you love the most."

Saying those words made her think of Elinor and her anger with her sister for handling everything after Father's death and not including her. She supposed that the reluctance to have difficult conversations wasn't limited only to husband and wife.

"Things would be far easier if we could all say what we were really thinking," Mr. Willoughby agreed. "I meant what I said inside. How can men not feel the same uncertainty and passion as women when it comes to matters of the heart? It's an utterly human response when we draw close to those that we admire and desire."

Marianne's lips curved into a smile at the word *admire*, but she felt herself grow faint when he uttered the word *desire*. Was he saying he admired and desired *her*?

Then he added, "You were quite good in there. Surely you haven't merely taken an interest in your father's work?"

Very little slipped past Mr. Willoughby, which both delighted and dismayed her. "Would it shock you if I said that I did more than accompany my father on some of his cases—that I was his apprentice?"

She watched his face carefully, but there was no hesitation behind his smile.

"Surprise me, maybe," he said. He guided his horse down a familiar street, and Marianne realized that they were in her old neighborhood. "But shock . . . well, you'll have to do a bit better if you want to shock me, Miss Marianne."

His teasing tone and acceptance warmed her, and his words felt like a dare. For a breathless moment, Marianne was tempted to divulge all she knew. But what would he think if he knew that Father had been murdered? Would he try to warn her off investigating?

"I have been known on occasion to assist Father," she said, testing him out carefully with this revelation. "I even have an alias—Miss Lavinia Stewart. Miss Stewart is oh so silly and loves pink ribbons and gossiping at the modiste and giggling with shopgirls." Marianne's voice took on a breathy quality, and she dissolved into laughter when Mr. Willoughby turned his head to her.

"That was very unnerving," he said, but his lips turned up in a smile. "Do you often have reason to play Miss Stewart?"

Not as often as she'd like, but Marianne didn't say that. "On occasion, when Father needed a female perspective or to question someone without tipping them off."

"You must miss him terribly," he said, voice gone somber.

"I do," she agreed. They were just three blocks away from her old house now, and she longed to see it—but she didn't ask Mr. Willoughby to change course, and soon his curricle slid past the turn it would need to take her by her former home.

"I'm sorry to bring it up," Mr. Willoughby said, interrupting her thoughts.

"No, don't be." Marianne didn't allow herself to look backward. The past was the past. "It would be silly if no one brought it up, because of course I miss him. But one must keep moving forward."

And maybe if she was lucky, Mr. Willoughby would be by her side to help her greet her extraordinary fate.

"Of course," he said, and then fell silent.

Marianne was struck with the overwhelming urge to divulge the secret of Father's death. But the sisters had all agreed they wouldn't tell anyone . . . although at the time they'd made that promise, Marianne had primarily been thinking about keeping the news from Mother and the papers, not from someone like Mr. Willoughby, who kept sneaking sidelong glances at her.

"Would you like to meet Miss Stewart?" she asked suddenly.

"Whatever do you mean?"

Marianne didn't stop to consider whether or not this was reckless. If she was being completely honest, the idea had been lurking in the back of her mind for a few days now. *Take your openings when they arise.* Another tidbit of advice that Father had once given her. Mr. Willoughby seemed accepting of her, so perhaps this was the perfect chance to show him another facet of herself, all while digging up more information.

Marianne directed him to the firm of Hillenbrand and Associates and coached him along the way. "I'll be Miss Lavinia Stewart, and you shall be my brother. We are going to inquire about business advice for an inheritance left to me by our great-aunt. It is my idea to seek an outside opinion, and you're not opposed to the idea, but you want to come along to see that I'm not cheated."

"All right," he said, and Marianne was pleased when he didn't protest. "But why, exactly, are we looking for business advice from this firm?"

"Because I want to see what I can discover about one of the employees, a junior accountant named Edward Farrows."

"And who might that be?"

"You haven't heard of him?" Marianne asked, raising a single brow. "I thought you might be acquainted."

"Farrows," Mr. Willoughby repeated. "Edward Farrows. The name sounds familiar, but I'm not sure I've ever had the pleasure."

"He's the brother of my sister-in-law," Marianne said.

"And why are we curious about him?"

Marianne pressed her lips together and thought carefully about what she wanted to say next. "Because he's involved in settling my father's estate."

That seemed to be good enough for Mr. Willoughby, and Marianne was grateful she didn't have to explain further. She wondered if he'd be quite as game if he knew that she was investigating her father's mysterious death. He'd gone positively white at the thought of Mrs. Palmer being dangerous. No, best to share what she knew slowly.

When they arrived at the firm, they were shown all the courtesy of high-society clients and ushered into a fine, spacious office where a gray-haired gentleman with a rather bushy mustache stood to greet them. They gave their false names and the man introduced himself as Mr. Novak. When they'd taken their seats, he asked, "What can I do for you today, Mr. and Miss Stewart?"

Marianne took the lead. "I have come into a bit of an inheritance," she said with a trilling laugh. "And I would like some *professional* input on how best to utilize the funds."

"Of course," the man said, glancing at Mr. Willoughby. "And your brother is here to oversee the transactions?"

Marianne bristled at the word *oversee*, but Mr. Willoughby drawled, "More like chaperone. My sister has quite a few opinions about the matter."

Inside, Marianne was thrilled at how well he played his

part of disinterested brother. "Yes, I am of the opinion that I want an expert eye on my money, John. Aunt Eloise left it to me for a reason."

"Aunt Eloise left it to you because I got the family heirlooms, Lavinia." While Marianne pretended to huff, Mr. Willoughby stage-whispered to Mr. Novak, "I'll give you three guesses as to who really made out in the will, but you'll only need one."

She could have kissed him. They were really selling this— Mr. Novak cleared his throat and looked down at his folded hands, clearly an uncomfortable audience to this "family" spat. "Yes, well, we have many options for investment and savings, and a special department devoted entirely to investments for ladies' fortunes, Miss Stewart. I'm sure we can find something that we can all agree is a prudent investment. Would you like to hear more?"

"Yes, please!" Marianne said in Lavinia's eager, saccharine tone. Inside, she was wondering, *What on earth is the difference between men's investments and ladies'? Isn't money* money?

She let Mr. Novak rattle on for a while, not really paying attention but trying to look the part. Mr. Willoughby was so distracting—sitting languidly in his chair, acting bored, occasionally letting his elbow brush against her arm, which wasn't all that scandalous considering they were supposed to be brother and sister, but since they were not . . . well.

She struggled back to the present moment when she realized that Mr. Novak was asking how she'd like to proceed.

"Oh, I think I shall go with whatever you recommend. John here is miserable with money and your firm came recommended by a friend of mine. She knows one of your accountants—what was his name again?" She pretended to look at Mr. Willoughby to jog her memory, then turned back to Mr. Novak and said, "Oh, Farrows! That was the name."

Mr. Novak's smile tightened. "May I inquire as to the name of your friend, Miss Stewart?"

"Of course! Mrs. Carpenter."

Marianne beamed at the man, watching closely as he processed the name. He was very good—his expression gave away little, but Marianne could guess that he was mentally searching for the name and a case file to attach it to. Finally, he shook his head and said, "I'm sorry, Miss Stewart. I don't believe I know of a Mrs. Carpenter who has an account with us."

Well, drat. She'd been certain that a firm this size would have at least *one* Carpenter on the books. But no sense dodging about it, she decided. "Oh, my mistake—Mrs. Carpenter is recently married. She has been most recently known as Miss Alistair."

Instantly the man's expression darkened, and Marianne thrilled at the response. The man's Adam's apple bobbed as he swallowed and tried to gain his composure. "Who sent you?"

"I beg your pardon?"

Now he looked to Mr. Willoughby. "Are you with the papers? Which one? *The Times*? *The Morning Chronicle*?

Stooping to using a woman to do your dirty work?" He practically spit out the word *woman*.

"Mr. Novak, I assure you I have no idea what—"

"Save it," he snapped at Marianne, and then he stood. "Mr. Farrows is no longer in the employ of this firm. I will not be speaking anymore on this matter. Don't come back."

He marched to the door and opened it for them. Marianne drew herself up to her full height and focused on maintaining her Miss Stewart disguise to hide her confusion. "Well, I never. I was assured you were professionals, and I am shocked, I tell you, just appalled—"

"Good day, madam," Mr. Novak said rudely, and snapped his fingers at a nearby clerk. "See that these two leave the premises immediately, and never return."

That earned them the scandalized attention of every man working nearby, but Marianne held her head high as they were unceremoniously kicked out of the firm. They didn't speak until they were back in Mr. Willoughby's curricle and pulling away from the firm. Then, Mr. Willoughby turned to her and said, "What on earth did you say to make that man so angry?"

Marianne knew that the name Alistair had set him off, but she didn't divulge that. "Clearly Mr. Farrows has done something to upset him."

"And do you have any idea what that might be?"

"None," Marianne said. But she was dying to know. "It

188

must be quite scandalous if the firm wants to keep it out of the papers, though."

"Or dangerous," Mr. Willoughby added, and Marianne found she couldn't disagree. "How exactly are you entangled with him?"

Marianne weighed her options carefully. Yes, it was true that she'd just met him, but Marianne felt instinctively that she could trust him. Had he not visited her when she was laid up, brought her poetry, and charmed her mother? He agreed to take her wherever she asked today and had assumed an identity for her. He was even hinting at the future. He could see it, too. They were meant to be together.

"I can't talk while you're driving," she said. "Find a place to park."

When the curricle was still, she twisted in her seat to look at him and said, "My father was murdered."

His face was still for a long moment and then his eyes widened. "You can't be serious."

"I'm very serious," she assured him. "Only my sisters and I know. But we can prove it, and we're going to solve it."

"Marianne, you could get yourself killed!"

Marianne gasped at his slip in propriety. Though he'd been calling her Miss Marianne for days, it was shocking to hear him say her name alone, stripped of etiquette.

"I don't think we're truly in danger of being murdered

ourselves," she said, although she didn't tell him about the pocketknife she kept on her person at all times or the basic lessons in self-defense Father had taught all three of his daughters—that was just being prepared. "And we can't sit by."

"I want to help." Mr. Willoughby grasped both of her hands. "Please, tell me what I can do."

Marianne gently squeezed his hands and then spent the next half hour telling him everything. Mr. Willoughby was a good listener, and when she was done, his brow appeared permanently creased.

"I'm worried," he said. "It's not that I doubt you can solve this case, but the poison concerns me. What if someone tries to poison you or your sisters?"

Marianne had never seriously considered that possibility before. "We never eat anything that isn't prepared at home," she said, but then she thought of Hannah. Was she just biding her time until she could poison the Dashwood women, then run off leaving no loose ends? Marianne shook her head. That made no sense.

"If I were you, I would be quite suspicious of this Brandon fellow," Mr. Willoughby continued. "It seems as though he alone had the means to poison someone."

"Maybe you're right," she found herself saying, although she wasn't yet convinced. His case seemed so far removed from Father's recent death. She looked up and found herself rendered immobile by the intensity of Mr. Willoughby's stare, falling into the depths of his blue eyes.

"I hope you won't think this too forward of me," he said, his voice a touch softer than before. "But I find myself completely entranced by you, Marianne Dashwood. And I think I would be perfectly devastated if something terrible were to happen to you."

And in that moment—well, propriety be damned! Marianne found herself perfectly devastated by his words and her overwhelming urge to kiss him. She didn't care who saw or what the judgmental passersby might think. She leaned forward, fluttering her eyes closed, and their lips met. His mouth was warmer than she expected, and for some strange reason that made her shiver. Willoughby wrapped his arms around her and drew her close so she was pressed right up against his lanky frame. His lips parted beneath hers, and Marianne was lost in the sensation as his tongue traced ribbons of heat across her lips. She never knew that kissing someone involved so many different sensations, and they weren't all felt on her lips.

Willoughby pulled away slightly so that he could look down at her, but he still held her close in his arms. "I'm sorry," he whispered, and she could feel his breath on her cheek.

Marianne struggled to come back to herself. "Don't be," she said with a tiny gasp. "I'm not."

"Good." And with a wicked grin, Willoughby pulled her close and kissed her deeply once more.

ELEVEN

*In Which the Dashwood Sisters
Have a Horrible Fight*

ELINOR BALANCED HER TEACUP primly on its saucer and worked to keep a politely attentive expression on her face as she listened to Miss Lucy Steele tell her for a third time about how certain she was that Mr. Bedford had winked at her at Lady Walden's ball last season. The corners of Elinor's mouth felt the strain of her forced expression and she subtly flicked her gaze to the drawing room door.

Where on earth was Marianne?

"I do suppose he could have been winking at Miss Montgomery, but I know she wouldn't give him the time of day, so I can't imagine that he meant to wink at her, but you know gentlemen." Miss Steele shook her head as she leaned forward to whisper to Elinor. "They always want a diamond of the first water, but Miss Montgomery's eyesight is poor, did you know? It's why she always looks so dreamy and far off. Her mama has trained her not to squint, and she can't see a thing."

"Oh really?" Elinor murmured. She'd found that she needed to do very little to encourage Miss Steele—she'd talk enough for three people.

"Yes, and you'll never believe what I heard about her debut! Did you know—"

Elinor tilted her head. Was that—yes! The front door! She smiled quickly at Miss Steele and said, "I'm sorry, but I think that's Marianne."

She rose as gracefully as she could and went out into the hall, where Marianne stood removing her bonnet. She wore a soft, dreamy smile and jumped when she turned and saw Elinor standing behind her.

"Oh, Elinor! You gave me a fright."

"Did you forget we have an appointment?" Elinor asked, unable to keep the sarcasm out of her voice. Marianne's hair was slightly disheveled from her bonnet, and her cheeks were flushed, but she didn't appear out of breath.

"An appointment? Oh, drat!" Marianne peeked past her into the open drawing room. *Miss Steele?* she mouthed.

Elinor nodded, then grasped her sister's arm before she could wiggle her way out of the meeting. Miss Steele lit up when they entered. "Miss Marianne! How marvelous! I've been ever so eager to see you again."

"Miss Steele," Marianne said, audibly more reserved but polite nonetheless. "My apologies for keeping you waiting."

"Not at all. Miss Dashwood and I have been having the loveliest chat." She giggled, then added, "I know I hired you, but I think we're all on our way to becoming close friends."

Elinor smiled faintly. "Indeed," she murmured, although the idea of willingly enduring Miss Steele's company without the promise of payment . . . well, Elinor couldn't decide whether or not she'd rather voluntarily socialize with Fanny first.

"And what progress have you made?" she asked, taking a seat next to Elinor.

"Well, we've discussed my entire social calendar of the last two seasons," Miss Steele said, and Elinor prayed that she wouldn't want to revisit it. She might be in danger of falling asleep if Miss Steele insisted on repeating herself. "And we talked about the eligible gentlemen that I've danced with and had significant conversations with. Would you like to hear—"

"Oh, no," Marianne said, managing to sound gracious. "I think that Elinor can keep me apprised, and I'd hate to waste your time by having you go over it all again. Besides, I think that we can all agree that you are . . . very well connected."

Elinor wondered what word her sister really wanted to fill that pause with, but she merely agreed with her. "Yes, Miss Steele. The benefit of your years in society and your many stays with friends and relations is that you know so many people."

"I do," Miss Steele agreed, but a hint of caution had entered her tone.

"And the goal is to get married, is it not?" Marianne continued. "And to do that, you don't necessarily want to cast a wide net. You want to find that one person who will look deeply into your eyes and make a lifetime commitment."

Miss Steele sighed and nodded, but Elinor glanced sidelong at her sister. She was in a very particular mood. Where had she spent her morning?

"Therefore, you don't need many options," Marianne continued briskly. "You just need one proposal. What social engagements do you have on your calendar this week?"

"Just what I was working up to," Elinor added. How like Marianne to swan in after the tedious work was done.

"Well . . . I'm attending Mrs. Farrows's ball tomorrow night."

"Oh?" Elinor tilted her head in surprise.

"Were you not aware of the ball?" Miss Steele asked as she set down her teacup and looked at her through her eyelashes. The move was so controlled, almost cunning, that Elinor felt knocked off-kilter for a moment.

"No . . . er, yes. We were invited as well, but didn't plan on attending. Forgive me, I was simply unaware that you were acquainted with the Farrowses."

"I'm not," Miss Steele clarified, and her expression shifted back into innocence so quickly that Elinor second-guessed what she thought she'd seen. "Mrs. Jennings was kind enough to secure an invitation for me."

"Oh my," Marianne said, leaning back in her seat. "But that's perfect. I know exactly who we must introduce you to. It's brilliant."

"Do you care to share with Miss Steele?" Elinor asked. *And me?*

"Miss Steele, are you aware that Mr. Edward Farrows is quite eligible?"

The word *no* bubbled up in Elinor's throat, but she swallowed it down hard and fixed a vacant smile on her face. Why was Marianne bringing Edward into this? She knew that she had her suspicions, but he'd been nothing but kind to them all. He was shy, but good-hearted. He didn't deserve to be conned into a relationship with Miss Steele.

"I was not," Miss Steele said, a hint of caution in her tone. "In fact . . . I hadn't considered him at all. He is a few years my junior, after all."

"Really?" Marianne gasped. "Well, no one would know it unless you said."

Miss Steele laughed and clapped her hands in delight at the compliment, which Elinor knew was fake. Marianne launched into her plan for the evening. They'd all attend the ball together and secure an introduction. If needed, they'd encourage Mr. Farrows to ask Miss Steele to dance—yes, Marianne assured her, the Dashwood sisters would definitely be able to manage that—and then Miss Steele would have her opportunity to charm him. Marianne began doling out advice for exactly how to charm a gentleman, and Elinor sat quietly, trying to keep her roiling emotions inside.

How could Marianne? When she knew . . . but no, she didn't know that Elinor liked him because Elinor had never told her. Because Elinor had denied her feelings for him even to herself.

How did Elinor *really* feel about Edward?

She didn't love him. But she liked him. And she thought that perhaps, with some time and a chance to get to know him better, and for him to get to know her, maybe deeper affection and love could blossom.

But now she wouldn't get the chance, because Marianne was turning to her and saying, "Don't you agree, Elinor?"

"Yes," she said automatically. Dutifully. "A splendid idea all around."

"Oh, I'm so glad that I hired you two!" Miss Steele said. "I think that this will certainly be a night to remember. And Edward Farrows is rather handsome, isn't he?"

Miss Steele posed the question to Elinor, and she swallowed her protests once more. "Indeed, he's very fine looking. You will make a lovely couple."

"From your lips to God's ears," Miss Steele proclaimed. She took her leave, satisfied by Marianne's plan. Elinor showed her out, struggling to maintain her composure as she returned to the drawing room.

"Why did you have to bring Edward into this?" she asked, staring down her sister.

Marianne was tidying her blond curls in the mirror above the fireplace, but she turned to look at her sister. "You won't believe what I discovered about him this morning."

That made Elinor stop. "What?"

"I went to Hillenbrand and Associates," Marianne told her. "I pretended that I had received an inheritance and was looking for financial guidance. I told the man I spoke to that a friend who was acquainted with Mr. Farrows had referred me, and he went positively gray. He demanded to know who my friend was, and so I said Miss Alistair—"

"Marianne!"

"—and the man ordered us out! He thought we were newspaper reporters."

Elinor knew this was suspicious, but her mind snagged on something else. "Who is *we*?"

Marianne paused a brief moment, then said, "Willoughby."

Elinor dropped to the settee. "What on earth are you doing involving Mr. Willoughby in all of this?"

"He has a curricle," Marianne said. "My ankle is still sore. He offered to drive me wherever I needed to go."

"So you asked him to take you to Edward's place of business and pretend to be someone you're not?"

"This is what I'm trying to tell you—it's no longer Edward's place of business. The man said he was no longer an employee, and when he heard that name Alistair, he booted us out. So whatever the Alistair affair is, Edward was sacked over it."

"But what does that have to do with us?" Elinor asked, although she couldn't deny the heavy weight of disappointment that settled over her. Edward had always seemed so kind, so earnest. So unlike his sister. To hear that he had been involved in something that had gotten him dismissed from a respected position, despite his family name . . . well, it mustn't have been very good.

"I still think he's suspicious," Marianne said. "Although I am open to exploring other theories of the case."

"Oh, are you?" Elinor asked, unable to keep the sarcasm from her voice. "And setting up Miss Steele with Edward has nothing to do with your suspicions that he and Fanny are involved in Father's murder?"

"Think about it, Elinor. It takes care of two of our problems with one elegant solution. We want to keep an eye on Edward and learn his secrets, and we need to keep Miss Steele happy so she keeps paying. If she finds out anything scandalous about his past, she'll surely report it to us."

"Right," Elinor said. "Because you care very much about taking on additional cases."

"Oh, don't be sour! I also had Willoughby take me to see Mrs. Palmer. She paid up."

Elinor sat up straighter as Marianne withdrew the payment from Mrs. Palmer and deposited it in her lap. It was the full amount that the invoice said they were owed. The invoice Edward had brought them. Marianne continued, "I also asked Mrs. Palmer about the last time she saw Father—he met with her the last day he was alive. She said he seemed utterly fine, normal even, and he was in a rush to go meet Mother. Do you know what they did that afternoon?"

Elinor shook her head. "I wasn't aware that Mother even went anywhere that day."

"Let's ask her."

Marianne twirled on her good ankle and started for the door, but Elinor stopped her with a hand on her arm. "Not now! She'll want to know why we're asking, and besides . . . she's doing poorly. I'm worried about her."

Marianne paused and glanced at the ceiling, as if she could see through plaster to where Mother was curled up in bed. "Well, her husband died. Can you blame her for being devastated?"

"Of course not," Elinor said, irked at the implication that she was unfeeling. "But I'm concerned about the laudanum."

"She takes it for her nerves."

Elinor drew in a steadying breath. This had been on her mind since Mr. Brandon had told her about the dangers of the substance that morning, and she knew she had to find a way to tell Marianne but had hoped she could work up to it. "She's taken the entire bottle the doctor prescribed," Elinor said, then added, "I don't think she ought to be taking any more of it."

"Why not?"

"I went to see Mr. Brandon today," Elinor began.

"Mr. Brandon? Why on earth did you go to him for more laudanum? Surely there are half a dozen apothecaries much closer."

Marianne's tone was sharp and light, and Elinor knew that was a bad sign. "I didn't want to buy laudanum for Mother. I wanted to consult with him about the poison that killed Father."

A dark silence spread between the sisters. Elinor knew even before she had done it that going to see Mr. Brandon about the poison would anger Marianne, but she hadn't expected this stormy look and the challenging tilt to her younger sister's chin as she said, "Why would you do that?"

"Because I don't know what it is." Some small part of Elinor felt like a failure admitting that. "I decided to ask someone who is more knowledgeable than me."

"And what did he say?"

"He's . . . uncertain as well. He said he had to run a few tests."

"And you let him keep our only evidence? Elinor, he may be a suspect!"

Elinor couldn't help the laugh that burst out of her. "When we spoke to him and Mrs. Jennings, you completely dismissed the idea that he could have anything to do with Father's death.

201

And now that I've asked for his help, he must be suspicious?"

"Cases *evolve*. I didn't suspect him at first because I was focused on other leads. But now that those haven't yielded anything, it's time to expand our thinking. Except you just handed our only piece of evidence to someone who might be a killer."

Elinor felt her jaw draw open in shock. "That's rich coming from the girl who took the gentleman she's known barely a week on her investigations. Did you tell Mr. Willoughby why you're so interested in hearing from Mrs. Palmer about Father's last day? Did you reveal why you were looking into Mr. Farrows's employment history?"

"Willoughby and I share a connection," Marianne proclaimed. "He helped me because he cares about me, and about our family."

"Oh, right, well then, that's fine!" Elinor said, laughter bubbling up in her chest. "As long as he cares for you. When is the engagement?"

"Don't be silly!" Marianne shot back, and Elinor was briefly relieved to see that she'd not lost all her sense. Then she added, "It's far too early for that."

Marianne's flippant tone and her obvious hope for an attachment with Willoughby were too much—especially when it came on the heels of her manipulating Edward and Lucy Steele.

"Why do you want my help when we both know you're going to do whatever you want anyway?" Elinor asked, and despite her glib tone, it was a serious question.

But Marianne surprised her by staring at her in obvious shock. "Me? What about you, Elinor? Perfect, sensible Elinor, you're always organized and calm and in charge. Why would you ever need to consult with anyone when you know exactly what to do at all times?"

Elinor merely stared at her. "I don't think that at all."

"You're the one who has to control everything," Marianne continued as if she hadn't even heard. "The budget, how the household is run, how we ought to proceed with the investigation, taking care of the funeral arrangements—you sent for the undertaker before any of us had the chance to say goodbye!"

Elinor was struggling to follow Marianne's anger, her leaps in accusation and logic. Marianne was upset that she'd called an undertaker? "I did that for you, for Mother and Margaret," Elinor whispered, fighting to get the words out through the tightness in her throat. "Finding him . . . seeing him like that . . . it was the worst moment of my life. I wanted to spare you."

"Well, I don't need you to spare me anything anymore!" Marianne's gaze burned through her, and Elinor felt like flinching away. "And if I have to solve Father's case on my own because you're too naive to know that you aren't supposed to *hand off evidence* to potential suspects, then fine! Stick to helping Miss Steele find a husband. She might as well marry Edward Farrows, because you'll both grow old and die before you admit that you like him!"

Her insult landed with the force of a slap, and Elinor found all she could do was gape at her younger sister. She wanted to muster up the words to defend herself, but she also knew if she stayed in this room and kept arguing with Marianne, she would either say or do something that she regretted.

So instead she took a page from Marianne's book: she yanked open the drawing room door, startling Margaret, who'd had her ear pressed against the keyhole, and made her own dramatic exit upstairs to their shared bedroom. She slammed the door behind her and locked it so she was finally at liberty to think and feel wretched in peace.

TWELVE

*In Which One Dashwood Sister Decides
to Break the Law (in Pursuit of Justice)*

MARIANNE WATCHED HER SISTER storm out of the room, annoyed that Elinor had gotten the last word in without saying a single thing—and by pulling off Marianne's signature move! Not that Marianne was up for storming anyway, as her ankle was a bit tender still.

From above, she heard the abrupt clap of a door slamming, and Margaret let out a low whistle. "She's really mad," her little sister remarked.

"Did you hear all of that?" Marianne demanded. Margaret merely shrugged, so Marianne took that to mean yes. "Well, she's wrong."

"About what?" Margaret asked, stepping into the room and flopping down on the settee.

"She was wrong to give away our evidence, for one." Marianne was already at the writing desk in the corner, hunting for a scrap of paper to send a message on. "And about thinking she needs to protect me from everything."

"Who are you writing?"

"Willoughby." Marianne rifled through the contents of the drawer for a quill. "Where are all the quills, Margaret?"

"Why are you writing Mr. Willoughby?"

Marianne spun around. "Not you too."

"I was just asking! No one tells me anything around here." Margaret got to her feet and stomped over to the writing desk and opened up a different compartment and pulled out a quill with a sharpened nub. "Well, whatever you're doing, just be careful."

"You sound an awful lot like Elinor."

It was the worst thing that Marianne could think of saying in the moment, but Margaret was nonplussed. "I do think she's right about Mother."

That made Marianne deflate slightly because even she couldn't deny that. The only times that Marianne had seen glimpses of their old mother since they'd moved to Barton Street was when Willoughby had come to call.

"I know," Marianne said. "But that's why solving this case is important. It could change everything for us."

"And then Mother will get better?" Margaret asked.

"I hope so." Marianne unstopped a bottle of ink and dipped

the quill. But first, they had to get back the evidence that Mr. Brandon had and discover what his involvement might be.

Marianne sent an urgent note to Willoughby, asking him to come to Barton Street the following evening, after Elinor left for the ball. She wasn't quite certain what their strategy might be for approaching Mr. Brandon, but she knew that Willoughby would be by her side.

The next day passed in excruciating boredom. Marianne also did her best to avoid Elinor, which was not so easy in such a small flat but was made simpler by the fact that Elinor seemed to be ignoring her, too. Once evening fell, Mother helped Elinor prepare for the ball, for which Marianne was glad, because it meant that Mother wasn't so bad off that she couldn't still attend to them, and it meant Marianne didn't have to do it. But then they both came downstairs to wait for the carriage that John and Fanny promised to send and Mother said, "Marianne, doesn't your sister look lovely tonight?"

Marianne looked up from the book of poetry that Willoughby had brought her and took in Elinor's appearance. Elinor was fussing over her skirts, which was how Marianne knew that Elinor was avoiding her gaze—Elinor usually didn't care that much about the fold of her skirt. She wore her last new gown from before Father had died, a purple taffeta edged with black lace that made her complexion look clear and bright and emphasized the luster of her dark hair. She did look lovely, but Marianne noted that her coiffure was not quite as nice as it could have been if *she'd* done it. "Yes," she said grudgingly. "I'm sure you'll receive many compliments."

Elinor's eyes flashed in anger for a brief moment, but then she averted her gaze back to her dress. Mother looked between the two of them, clearly puzzled, but before she had the chance to probe, Elinor said, "Mother, I think that's the carriage."

Elinor donned her wrap and stepped out into the evening, and Mother and Margaret followed to see her off. Marianne felt a pang of regret that she wasn't headed to a ball, too. If it were another ball, another life, she could imagine sweeping across the dance floor with Willoughby, who she was certain was a marvelous dancer.

The distant clatter of carriage wheels preceded Mother and Margaret's return inside, and Marianne pretended to be entirely engrossed in her poetry as Mother shooed Margaret upstairs. Then Mother appeared in the doorway, but she didn't say anything. Unable to take the silent scrutiny, Marianne asked, "What is it?"

"Nothing," Mother said softly. "Why didn't you go with your sister tonight?"

"I have a headache," Marianne lied, not quite able to meet her mother's eyes.

Mother reached out and touched the back of her hand to Marianne's forehead, as she used to when Marianne was even smaller than Margaret. Marianne wanted to lean into her touch, overwhelmed with longing. She wanted her mother to wrap her in her arms and her father to tell her she was safe, but most of all, Marianne wished she could go back to a time when she still believed that her parents *could* keep her safe.

But Father was dead and Mother couldn't protect her anymore, so instead she pulled away and said, "I'm not ill, it's just a headache."

She pretended not to notice Mother's face fall. "All right, then. But don't wait up for your sister—try and get some rest."

"I will," Marianne lied, and after a long pause Mother went upstairs—probably to go back to bed.

Only Hannah was still downstairs when the knock came at the door. Marianne leapt to her feet and tried to reach the door before her, but Hannah appeared in the hall, wiping her hands on her apron, a look of concern furrowing her brow. That same look deepened when she saw Marianne pulling on her cloak. "Miss?"

Marianne flashed her a reassuring smile. "I'm just stepping out for a little while—I've a meeting. It's to do with Father's business."

But Hannah didn't relax her concerned expression. "It's late, Miss Marianne."

"I know, but I shan't be long." Marianne said this entirely too cheerfully, but she wondered what on earth she'd do if Hannah put her foot down or, worse, insisted on calling for Mother.

"Be careful," Hannah said sternly, but she didn't move to fetch Mother.

"Don't worry, I know how to defend myself." Father had taught her and Elinor the basics of self-defense and what to do when cornered and, most intriguing, where to hit a man where it hurt the most.

"There are more than a few ways a man can take advantage of a young lady," Hannah warned.

Marianne decided to act oblivious. "I'll be back long before Elinor."

Then she unlocked the front door and slipped out, shutting it behind her. Willoughby had to take a step back to accommodate her abrupt exit. "Hello," he said, his voice husky. Marianne could feel the heat of his body, so close in the cool night. "I take it we're going straight to Williams's apothecary?"

"I am so glad to see you!" Marianne burst out, and then she couldn't help it—she threw her arms around his neck, engulfing him in a hug. His arms came around her to rest on her back and she nearly shivered at how lovely it felt to be held by him, especially after a day spent in anger and frustration.

"Has something happened?" he asked.

"Elinor gave our evidence to Mr. Brandon," she said, her voice slightly muffled in Willoughby's jacket. "We need to get it back."

Willoughby patted her back gently and withdrew slightly so that he could look down at her. Marianne reluctantly let him go, her hands lingering on his shoulders—they felt bonier and more angular than she had expected. "What do you mean she gave your evidence to Mr. Brandon?"

Marianne sighed and pulled him away from their front door as she told him about Elinor's decision to consult with Mr. Brandon about the nature of the poisonous substance and how she'd handed it over without a second thought as to his potential involvement in the case. Willoughby sucked in a sharp breath at that and began to shake his head. "I wondered why the late-night visit," he said.

"I know it's a bit unusual, but I'm beginning to wonder if you're right about Mr. Brandon being more suspicious than he lets on."

Marianne was glad that she didn't need to ask or tell him what she wanted to do. She accepted his offered hand and let him guide her into his waiting curricle. As Willoughby urged his horse forward, anticipation made Marianne shiver as much as the cold breeze. It was late, but she thought that catching Mr. Brandon after hours would be best. He wouldn't be expecting them, and that could work to their advantage. Perhaps he'd even reveal new details if she asked the right questions. . . .

Along the way, she enlightened Willoughby about what she knew of Mr. Brandon and Miss Williams's case. "He claims it was foul play rather than a mere laboratory accident because her notes went missing," Marianne told him. "But the more I think about it, I think it would be rather easy to steal her notes in the flurry of activity surrounding her death, and then later speculate about what their loss could mean."

"But if the doctor concluded it was an accident, why would Mr. Brandon challenge that by claiming that it must be foul play?" Willoughby asked.

Marianne had already thought of an answer to that. "He'd have no way of knowing for certain that the doctor would declare her death an accident, and perhaps he knew her uncle would get curious about her missing notes eventually. It's quite clever, actually, to claim that he is suspicious before anyone else. Because who would hire a private investigator to look into a crime that they committed?"

"Your father truly never found any reason to doubt his intentions?"

"If he did, he either took that knowledge to his grave, or left it in his journal," Marianne said, and then explained how her father kept a journal on his person at all times, full of his case notes, thoughts, theories, and observations.

"Well, this is worrisome," Willoughby proclaimed. "Two deaths, both apparent accidents but not, both scenes missing crucial written evidence. Do you believe in coincidence, Miss Marianne?"

"I do not," she said, tamping down her anger with herself for not seeing the parallels sooner. Of course, Elinor had thought that the Williams case was odd, but then she had turned around and given Mr. Brandon their evidence, so Marianne wasn't putting much stock in her sister's credibility or sense.

Willoughby parked his curricle on a side street and helped

Marianne down so they could approach the apothecary on foot. At this time of night, there were few pedestrians out and the shadows of alleyways and in-between streets stretched long and dark onto Marianne and Willoughby as they walked along. Above them, traces of light peeked out from behind curtains and drapes, but the windows above the apothecary were dark.

"It doesn't look like anyone is at home, and it's fairly early to retire to bed," Marianne whispered, her hand clutching Willoughby's arm. "Drat."

Willoughby halted in the shadows of the building next door. "But . . . were you hoping he would be?"

"Of course," she whispered back, confused by the question. "I want to reclaim what's mine."

"My apologies," Willoughby whispered, and leaned closer so their faces were only inches apart. "But I thought we were . . . well, I didn't think you wanted to *ask* Mr. Brandon for your property back."

"Of course I did, that's the whole purpose of our . . . oh." Marianne found it incredibly hard to think when his breath was tickling her cheek, and she trailed off when she realized what Willoughby was implying. "You mean break in?"

"I thought that's why we came after dark, yes."

Marianne gaped at him. She had asked him to come as soon as Elinor left for the ball because she didn't want Elinor to know what she was doing. But she could see now how Willoughby could have misconstrued her meaning, and it was on the tip of her tongue to set him straight when she stopped and considered. They could ask Mr. Brandon for her evidence . . . but he could refuse to give it back or, worse, destroy it. They could ask him about Miss Williams, but he could lie.

And really, Marianne was not above poking about in someone else's private business. She'd done it with her brother and Fanny without even a twinge of guilt. But she'd been let into their house—her former house—and the consequences, if caught, would not have carried legal implications.

And yet . . . Marianne was sick of feeling as though answers about Father's death were so far out of reach. She glanced up at Willoughby, who offered her a wolfish smile, his teeth gleaming in the scant light. "Can you get us inside?"

"Miss Marianne," he said, his voice caressing her name as his lips wandered to the delicate skin under her ear, "I thought you'd never ask."

He left a fluttering kiss on her ear, and Marianne swayed on her feet before his strong arm tugged her into the rank-smelling alley behind the apothecary. Who knew that kisses upon one's ear could make her feel as if swooning were something one did for real, not just to get attention? Willoughby stopped before an old door and single shuttered window. "Here," he announced. "You keep a lookout in case anyone comes by."

"You're certain this is the one?" She didn't mean to sound doubtful—but it was difficult to tell which door belonged to which storefront from the back.

"Positive." He produced a candle and flint, and with some struggle they got it lit. Marianne cupped her palm around the dancing flame so that Willoughby could get to work picking the lock on the window.

Marianne tried not to notice the shifting shadows beyond the candle's reach—likely rats. She hoped Willoughby would hurry. She was not absolutely opposed to breaking and entering, especially if someone held crucial evidence that would prove they were the murderous sort, but she didn't want to get caught. Her own father had taught her how to pick locks at age ten, but she couldn't help recalling the grave look on his face as he said, *Our tools and knowledge are meant to help people, not cause harm. I'm teaching you how to do this so you don't find yourself helpless in a dangerous situation, but if I find you're misusing your skills . . .*

She remembered the dangerous way his voice trailed off. Father was not a scary man—not to her, at least—but he knew how to use silence to convey a great deal. What would he think of her now?

I'm going to find out who killed you, she promised him silently.

Willoughby had a slender file, what looked to be a small hammer, and an assortment of picklocks and keys on a ring. She watched his technique, willing him to hurry but also to be silent. He slid his file in between the seam of the windows and maneuvered it about, clearly searching for something. When it caught against something—the lock, Marianne guessed—he maneuvered the file at a precise angle and then held the small hammer above the file. To Marianne's surprise, he brought the hammer down on the file in one sharp motion. There was a jarring *clack!* and he quickly pocketed his tools and slid open the window.

Marianne blew out the candle and looked every which way, praying that no one had heard them. She had never had to turn her pocketknife on anyone before, and she didn't want tonight to be the first time she had to wield it. She didn't dare make a single sound as she waited to see if anyone would come running, but she needn't have worried. Willoughby was already opening the window, and then with surprising ease, he hoisted himself through. Marianne heard a small thud and a whispered oath, and she held her breath until she caught sight of shadowy movement inside. Then, there was a click of a lock and the back door opened.

Marianne rushed inside, letting out a deep whoosh of breath, and Willoughby closed the door, then the window. They both listened for movement, any sound that would indicate that someone within had heard their entrance. It was quite dark, wherever they were, and the space smelled sharp and earthy, reminding Marianne of the laboratory space Elinor once occupied in their former attic.

She took tiny, careful steps, but Willoughby groped around in the darkness, moving with a bit more confidence. She followed him through a doorway into a larger space that was even darker and stood immobile, too afraid of knocking anything over and causing a real ruckus that would bring every Runner within a ten-block radius. Then she heard the scratch of a flint and a flame leapt to life before catching on a wick. Marianne saw shelves, the glint of glass bottles, and an open space of a table in the flickering light that Willoughby held.

"How did you learn to pick a window lock like that?" Marianne hissed.

Willoughby's smile was rakish. "Would you believe me if I told you a very enterprising young lady taught me?"

Marianne felt a flare of jealousy rise in her, as bright and sharp as his candle in the sudden darkness, but she stamped it down. "I might. You clearly have many hidden talents."

"We all have secrets, Miss Marianne," Willoughby said, extending his candle to the one she still had clutched in her hand. "Now let's see if we can discover some of Mr. Brandon's."

They appeared to be standing in a workroom of sorts, which was dominated by a larger table in the center. There was a stove in the corner, but three of the four walls were lined with shelves and cabinetry that were absolutely packed with items. There were two doors—the one that they came through from the back and a closed door on the opposite side of the room that Marianne guessed led to the front of the shop. There were no windows, so Marianne wasn't worried about their candlelight being seen from outside, but she did stop suddenly and look to Willoughby's light. "That's their candle," she whispered. "They might notice that someone burned it in the middle of the night, and know that someone was here."

"If we find evidence that Brandon is a murderer, we won't need to worry about that," Willoughby snapped.

Marianne merely blinked. It was such a sharp response for a valid fear, she wasn't certain what to say at first. Willoughby's back was to her, however, and he was already inspecting a shelf full of carefully labeled jars. She decided then that it wasn't worth arguing—especially not if their voices attracted any attention. Besides, she supposed he was right. They might not notice a slightly shorter candle. And if they did find something . . . well, it was best to just get to it.

She moved toward the cabinets on the right side of the room and began opening drawers when Willoughby said, "Start over there, and let's work our way around to one another." He indicated a wall of glass jars on shelves.

"Don't be silly," Marianne hissed back. "It's far more likely that secret notes will be tucked away in drawers or cabinets, not out in plain view. It'll go faster if we both search the cabinets."

Willoughby's face pinched with annoyance, but he didn't protest as she began opening cabinets and peering around. Marianne attributed his reaction to the stress of the moment and focused her attention on the first set of cabinets she came across. They contained laboratory equipment that made her think of Elinor—Elinor would be horrified if she knew what they were doing. But no, Marianne was not thinking about her sister right now. She felt along the underside of shelves and carefully lifted boxes and peered inside. Nothing. Everything was spotlessly clean, not a speck of dust anywhere. If this equipment was used frequently, then Mr. Brandon wouldn't hide anything here. She moved on to the bookshelves and carefully scanned the orderly rows, picking up any book without a title on its spine and flipping through it. But would Mr. Brandon keep such damning evidence in this workroom that he shared with Mr. Williams? Would he really be so confident as to hide in plain sight?

She kept searching, though. She had to set her candle down so she could pull out the books without printing on their spines and crack them open to see if they contained printed text or handwritten notes. She had never seen Miss Williams's handwriting before, of course, so she could only hope that the young lady had written her name at the front. My, wouldn't that be nice.

Marianne had just shoved another book back into place and was ready to turn and ask Willoughby if he'd discovered anything when she heard a sharp intake of breath. She whirled around, fear making her pulse race, but found that he stood before a cabinet that appeared to be full of various boxes and other indistinct instruments. His arm reached into the dark recesses of the cabinet, and when he withdrew his hand, he held what appeared to be a book and a small satchel.

"This was stuffed way back there," he murmured, moving closer to Marianne's candlelight. Excitement made his voice sound overly loud, but she didn't shush him, too eager to inspect his find. He opened the cover of the book and Marianne got the impression of elegant yet cramped handwriting, long Latin-looking words, and tiny drawings. Willoughby flipped through the pages but then found the frontispiece—*Property of Eliza Williams*, it read.

"It really is that easy," Marianne whispered, her calm tone hiding the pounding of her heart. She reached for the small satchel and her fingers snagged on the leather drawstrings.

"Let me," Willoughby said, but Marianne shook her head.

"No, I've got it." She got her grasp on the strings and worked the satchel open. The first thing she drew out was a paper packet of a dry substance. Then, three vials. Two contained liquid, tightly stoppered and sealed with wax. One contained a more granular substance that Marianne held up to the light. There wasn't much there—a teaspoon or two—but it looked exactly like the poison that they'd recovered from her father's cup.

"Is that it?" he asked, delight once again making his voice seem too loud for their secret search.

"I don't think so," Marianne said, because although the substances appeared to be the same, there was more here than she remembered Elinor recovering. "But it's certainly suspicious."

"It's proof that Brandon is a liar," Willoughby insisted. Marianne looked up, and in the dancing candlelight she noted that Willoughby's already lean face looked almost gaunt, but his cheeks were flushed pink with excitement. Marianne had the silliest urge to reach out and touch the back of her palm to his forehead to make sure he was well, as her own mother had done mere hours earlier.

"Yes," Marianne said, but she didn't know why she didn't feel as triumphant as Willoughby seemed. It was nothing to her if Mr. Brandon was actually a killer—in fact, she should be happy to expose a liar and criminal. But it wasn't quite the smoking pistol she'd hoped for.

"Let's take it," he said. "Tomorrow you can go to the authorities."

That was quite the leap, but Marianne's hands tightened around the evidence. She wouldn't be parting with it anytime soon. "I'm taking it all right, but I'm not going to the authorities until we're certain."

She tucked the small satchel deep in her pockets, feeling the small clink of glass, and held tight to the book. Now that they'd discovered something worth breaking in for, Marianne didn't want to linger. She looked up to see Willoughby, his hand inside his jacket, standing before the open cabinet where he'd found Miss Williams's evidence. "What are you doing?" she asked.

He startled but didn't answer her. "What if there's more here?"

Marianne stared at him for a long moment, trying to figure

out why she didn't quite believe him. It was because he wasn't reaching within the cabinet, but more as if he were tucking something away, in the inner pocket of his jacket. Was Willoughby . . . stealing?

"No," she decided, suddenly sick of this whole venture. "Let's not press our luck. We should leave before someone catches us."

Willoughby didn't answer right away, just stared deep inside the cabinet. It was so odd, but what would he be stealing from an apothecary? Dried herbs? Tinctures? He didn't look altogether well, and maybe he was looking for a remedy . . . but Marianne was being ridiculous. It was a trick of the light. Willoughby could afford to hire a physician if he was ill; he wouldn't have to resort to stealing from an apothecary. She shook her head. "Put everything back exactly the way we found it. I don't want Mr. Brandon to come in tomorrow and suspect that we've been here. He might flee London before we have the chance to apprehend him."

"Good thinking," Willoughby said, so agreeably that Marianne thought the stress of breaking into the apothecary was surely going to her head.

In short order they replaced every item they touched and swept the space with their eyes, looking for anything they might have knocked out of place. The only sign that they'd been there was the slightly shorter candle, its wax congealing as they left and swept back out the way they came, Willoughby making sure to lock the window he'd picked open. Marianne clutched Eliza's journal to her chest and thought about how she'd tell Elinor. Her sister would be horrified, but this was one step closer to solving Father's murder.

She just needed to understand how it all fit together.

THIRTEEN

*In Which the Dashwood Sisters
Receive a Warning*

ALL EYES WERE ON Elinor when she arrived at Mrs. Farrows's ball that evening, and Elinor positively detested when all eyes were on her.

Elinor felt a surge of anger toward Marianne for making her come alone with a secret purpose, but she was also certain that if Marianne were present, they'd end up bickering in public and really give society something to talk about—something far more delicious than the fact that Miss Elinor Dashwood, recently fallen in financial status, arrived at a ball sans sister or mama, mere weeks after her father's death.

But she held her head high. Society had always whispered about her family, so why should now be any different? She wore her best gown and she knew for a fact that she looked quite fetching in it. She had a task to complete, no matter how distasteful it might be to her. The quicker it was done, the quicker she could go home.

She spotted Fanny across the room and started making her way to her sister-in-law. A dance had just ended as she made her way around a cluster of ladies, but Elinor wasn't paying attention to the dancers, and she bumped into one of the young ladies stepping away from the dance floor. "I beg your pardon," Elinor murmured, and looked up as the other girl turned around. "Oh! Amelia! Hello."

Elinor and Miss Amelia Holbrook had debuted in the same season, and they'd spent enough time together at society functions that they'd taken to calling each other by their first names. But now Amelia's eyes seemed to be unfocused as she looked at Elinor, her smile uncertain and distant, before she said, "Miss Dashwood."

Ah, so that's how it was.

"It's nice to see you," Elinor said, striving for civility. Amelia merely gazed back blankly, making no move to introduce the young man on her arm.

"You as well," Amelia said, but her wooden tone indicated her words were nothing more than a polite reaction. Then she asked, "Are you here alone?"

"I'm here with my brother and his wife," she said, which was a slight stretch to the truth, but it was bad enough that everyone saw her arrive alone, looking for all the world like a husband hunter. "And how have you been?"

"How nice," Amelia said, but her gaze was already wandering beyond Elinor. The gentleman on her arm looked down and cleared his throat quietly, but it was obvious to Elinor that Amelia's mind was already elsewhere. Perhaps she ought not to have been surprised—after all, neither Amelia nor any of the other girls had reached out to her beyond the initial condolence cards after Father's death. Why did Elinor expect anything more now?

"Well, it was nice to see you," Elinor said, and swept past her former friend, cheeks burning. Of course, half the room had likely seen the snub. Only the knowledge that fleeing would cause even more gossip kept Elinor in the room.

She made her way to Fanny, who caught sight of Elinor when she was about ten paces away. Elinor saw her sister-in-law's vaguely disapproving expression—the one that made her flat face look pinched—before Fanny recovered with a simpering smile. "Elinor, dear. We were surprised you would come on such short notice. Don't think anything of the late invitation—Mother has been planning for weeks, and when the invitations first went out . . . well, it wouldn't have been proper."

Elinor knew that if it were up to Fanny, they'd never see one another ever again. "We were glad to receive the invitation, and I must thank your mother for thinking of us."

Fanny's gaze was already roaming the room. "Thank Mother if you will, but it was Edward who insisted."

Something inside of Elinor tightened. Edward was always thinking of them. Was it really because he was hoping to cheat them in some way? "Well, then I shall thank him as well."

"He's dancing with Miss Avery at the moment," Fanny said, and pointed him out with a subtle nod to the dance floor. "Don't they make a handsome pair?"

Elinor followed Fanny's gaze and spotted Edward, smiling slightly as he danced a cotillion with an auburn-haired young lady that Elinor had met on a handful of occasions. Nicola Avery was the model of gentility at these events, but Elinor and Amelia used to avoid her and her vicious gossip. "Lovely," she pronounced, her throat tightening around the word.

"Indeed. He is much sought after at these balls," Fanny said, and to anyone in proximity it might have sounded as though Fanny were merely making conversation. But Elinor wasn't fooled—Fanny never merely made conversation with her. "My mother and I are hopeful that he will find a good match. We wish to see him settled. I'm sure you can understand that?"

It was less of a question than a warning, and Elinor swallowed hard. What did one say to that? Luckily, she was saved from responding by the sudden appearance of Miss Steele, outfitted in a jarring shade of pink that Elinor would have sworn she could see even with her eyes closed.

"Miss Dashwood!" Miss Steele cried, pushing through the clusters of people. "Oh, I am so glad to see you."

Fanny flicked her eyes toward the newcomer with barely

disguised disapproval. Elinor smiled, relieved to see that at least someone was happy to see her, even if Miss Steele was far from her favorite person in attendance. "Miss Steele, you look lovely tonight. Are you acquainted with my sister-in-law, Mrs. Dashwood?"

Lucy Steele curtsied and Fanny acknowledged her with a barely tolerant smile. "This is quite a to-do," Lucy said, grabbing Elinor's hand as if they were sisters or friends, not acquaintances. "So many gentlemen to dance with."

Elinor couldn't help but feel an ounce of the same disdain reflected on Fanny's face. If this was how Lucy acted in polite company, then it was no wonder she struggled to find a husband. "It is a very fine gathering, and such a pretty room," Elinor said, trying to balance out Lucy's gaffe with excessive politeness.

She needn't have worried, because Fanny's lips thinned and she said, "Forgive me, I see someone I must speak with," and she took her leave.

"Oh dear, I don't think she likes me very well," Lucy whispered, drawing Elinor to the perimeter of the dance floor. "That doesn't bode well for meeting her brother, does it?"

"Fanny often conceals her true feelings," Elinor hedged. "I'm sure that she doesn't know you well enough yet to form a strong opinion either way."

It was the nicest thing she could come up with, which wasn't saying very much. Fortunately, Lucy was either too silly or too distracted to notice.

"How shall we go about this?" she asked. "I was thinking either you could try and catch his eye to lure him over here, or we wait until he's taken a break from dancing and I go position myself somewhat nearby, and then you can pretend to approach me, get his attention, and—"

"No, neither!" Elinor exclaimed, too scandalized to hide her surprise. "Miss Steele, we don't have to resort to trickery. I know Edward. When the timing is right, I'll merely approach and introduce you."

"Oh," she said, sounding almost disappointed. Then she added, "I didn't know you were on such intimate terms with him."

Belatedly, Elinor realized that she'd called him by his first name. Well, there was no backtracking now. "He was very helpful to my family after my father died," she explained. "We are grateful for his friendship."

Lucy absorbed Elinor's emphasis on the word *friendship* and seemed to accept it. "How generous he sounds."

"Yes," Elinor said, her voice faint. She thought of Lucy Steele's five pounds, which were secreted away in the lockbox in her bedroom, and how that money would help see them through the winter. Even though that five pounds was much more dear to her now than a larger sum of money had ever been to her before, it seemed like a paltry amount if the personal cost was denying her feelings. *I will be calm*, she reminded herself. *I will be the mistress of my emotions.*

The music ended and everyone clapped politely, including Elinor and Lucy. Edward and Miss Avery ended up on the same side of the ballroom as them, about thirty paces away. Elinor watched him bow to his partner, and then he looked straight at her. Elinor caught her breath and Lucy whispered, "Oh marvelous, here he comes. He's not the most good-looking young man here, but he does have a fine face, does he not?"

"I think he's very handsome," Elinor admitted quietly.

Lucy giggled. "No need to oversell him, Miss Dashwood. As long as he's pleasant and can provide for a wife, I don't over-care for looks."

But Elinor hadn't been trying to convince Lucy of anything—she really did think him handsome. Not pretty, like Willoughby with his sculpted features and sharp cheekbones. He didn't even have the brooding good looks of Mr. Brandon, who hid the intensity of his gray eyes behind his spectacles. But his face was open and honest and his smile made him look like someone people wanted to know.

"Miss Dashwood," he said, bowing to her. She responded with a curtsy, her heart fluttering. She told herself it was because she was nervous about how he would get along with Lucy, but she knew it was a lie.

"Mr. Farrows, it's lovely to see you again."

"Likewise," he said. "I am so glad that you came—is your sister in attendance?"

"Marianne had a headache," Elinor said. "But I know she's sad to miss everyone."

Edward murmured his wishes for her swift recovery, and Elinor could feel Lucy's eagerness rolling off of her in waves. She would have to introduce them, she knew. But for this one moment, she wanted to relish Edward's attention on her.

Somehow, she managed to pull herself out of the depths of his warm golden brown eyes. "Have you met Miss Steele?"

"Oh, no," he said, turning to greet the other young lady, and Elinor made introductions.

Lucy smiled coquettishly. "What a lovely party, Mr. Farrows. Your mother has wonderful taste."

"She certainly knows how to throw an event," Edward said, and he looked to Elinor as if they were sharing a joke—how she wished.

"Everything's so fashionable," Lucy gushed. "And the dancing is wonderful."

"Well, you won't find a waltz here," Edward said with a slight smile and an almost conspiratorial glance at Elinor. "My mother finds them rather indecent."

"Of course," Lucy rushed to say. "She's quite right."

Elinor was caught between laughing and crying.

"Miss Dashwood, would you do me the honor of granting me the next dance?" Edward asked, and despite Elinor's mission, her heart leapt with excitement. Out of the corner of her eye, she saw Lucy frown slightly.

"Oh, I don't know," she said, because she couldn't bring herself to say no outright.

"Miss Dashwood, you promised," he said, and his smile made her heart stutter. She had promised, when he first delivered the invitation.

"I . . ." She glanced at Lucy, who was staring at her expectantly.

"Of course, I shall not insist if you don't want to," Edward added quickly, sensing her indecision.

And that's what decided it for Elinor. Because even though Marianne was suspicious of him, and her suspicions had made even Elinor doubt his intention, she still didn't want him to believe that she didn't want to dance with him. "I'd be honored," she said. "If Miss Steele doesn't mind?"

"Not at all," Miss Steele said, her tone so cheerful it might as well have been venomous.

Edward held out his hand and led her to the edge of the dance floor, where a handful of other couples stood waiting to join the already crowded floor. Suddenly, Elinor felt tongue-tied. But luckily for her, Edward was more than willing to make conversation.

"Have you seen my sister this evening?"

"Yes," she said. "She sent the carriage so I could come tonight."

"How uncharacteristically thoughtful of her," he remarked,

and Elinor couldn't help the small snort of laughter.

He smiled in a way that spoke to the secret joke they shared, and even though Elinor longed to ignore the awkwardness that stretched between them and her secret mission for the evening, she couldn't dismiss it. If she were Marianne, she would just blurt out the question. But she wasn't her sister.

"Are you well, Elinor?" Edward asked, her name coming out in a hushed tone. "I am sorry if you felt pressured to accept this dance. I understand if you'd rather observe this evening."

"I'm well, I just . . ." Elinor racked her brain for a way to ask the questions that swelled inside her. What came out was, "You never responded to my note."

She hated the words as soon as they came out—they made her sound needy and whiny, all the things that Elinor prided herself on not being. But Edward merely looked confused.

"I'm sorry, I haven't received anything. What note?"

"I sent you a note at your place of business. I wasn't sure of your address, and I didn't want Fanny to see . . ." Elinor trailed off at the blank expression on Edward's face. "You didn't receive it? At work?"

"No," he said, so quietly she almost missed it. "I think I ought to explain some things, but I'm not sure if this is the best setting."

So it was true. Elinor closed her eyes briefly, the roaring in her ears drowning out . . . everything. She felt such a fool in that moment, accusing her sister of being reckless when she herself

233

had been taken in. And underneath that shame, a throbbing hurt that she'd been wrong about the only young man she'd ever wanted to get to know.

"Elinor?" he asked.

Her eyes flew open. "I'm so sorry, I must go."

"Elinor, wait—"

"Please ask Miss Steele to dance," she choked out. "I'm certain that she will be thrilled, and she really is quite a lovely girl."

She fled then, hoping he was enough of a gentleman to do as she asked. She also knew that she should stick close by, and ensure that he did just that, and observe how it went. Lucy was paying her, after all, and Elinor prided herself on being steady in all things. But lately, she felt herself coming apart, like a knitted garment. Slowly unraveling at first, but then faster and looser as more stitches were loosened.

The worst part, she thought as she ducked behind a table laden with refreshments, was that she couldn't truly bring herself to blame Marianne and her manipulations. Marianne had asked her, after all, if she'd liked him. She could practically hear her sister's voice chiding her: *Always resignation and acceptance and duty. Where is your heart, Elinor?*

Her heart was breaking right now. Because she always kept her hopes and desires guarded.

But no, it was more complicated than that. In her sister's mind, liking someone meant romance and roses and visions of the future. Admitting to liking Edward would mean that

Marianne thought she wanted to marry him, but Elinor was only eighteen. She wanted to study chemistry, and when she married, she wanted to be sure it was to the right man. The only thing she had been certain about when she looked at Edward was that she wanted to get to know him better. But now that she had gotten to know him better, she didn't like what she'd seen.

There was cold comfort in that, at least. She hadn't rushed headlong into an attachment only to find out that Edward was dishonest after the fact. Surely that meant she'd saved herself some heartache in the long run?

But catching a glimpse of Lucy Steele clad in her vibrant pink, on Edward's arm, confirmed that her pain now was very real.

"Miss Dashwood?"

Elinor was startled from her wretched thoughts by a soft gloved hand at her elbow and a breathy voice. She turned to find an unfamiliar woman of about her mother's age, with soft brunette curls and an anxious expression. She was dressed very finely in a midnight blue gown that made her look washed out, but her expression seemed generous. "Are you quite all right, dear?"

The kindness in the stranger's voice made tears spring to Elinor's eyes, but she forced a smile. "Oh yes, thank you. I beg your pardon, but I felt so overwhelmed, and I needed to . . ."

Run away. Catch my breath.

"It's quite all right," the woman assured her. Then she said,

"You don't remember me, do you?"

"I'm sorry," Elinor said, racking her brain. The woman didn't look like anyone she could recall ever socializing with in the past. Was she a client of Father's?

"Don't apologize," the woman said, patting her arm. "You were quite young the last time I saw you. I'm Lady Middleton, and my husband is—"

"Sir John!" Elinor blurted out. "I beg your pardon, ma'am."

She dipped into a quick curtsy, but Lady Middleton just clucked her tongue and waved her hand. "I didn't expect to see you here. Is your mother in attendance?"

"No, just me," Elinor said. "I'm here under the supervision of my brother and his wife."

She hated that turn of phrase, but it satisfied Lady Middleton. "How is your mother?"

If Lady Middleton had asked her this question earlier in the evening, she might have provided her with a politely vague answer, but Elinor's defenses were down. "She's . . . struggling."

"Of course," Lady Middleton murmured. "I am sorry to hear that. I apologize for not coming to call earlier. I'm afraid I only just returned to London two nights ago, but I would like to see her."

"I'm sure she would like that," Elinor said, finding her footing once more. "Especially since it's been a good number of years since our last visit."

Lady Middleton's head tilted slightly in confusion. "Oh, no, we've seen each other since then. Quite recently, in fact. Your parents came to call on us, that last day . . . well, the last day of your father's life."

Elinor was shocked for the second time that evening. "Excuse me?"

"Your parents called on us that last afternoon," she whispered, as if talk of death were a scandal. "I returned to our home in the country early the next morning while Sir John remained in London, so I didn't hear the news of your father's passing right away. I would have attended the funeral, but, well . . . we've had family issues of our own."

"Of course," Elinor said. Marianne had learned that Father left a client in a hurry to meet Mother. They had assumed that Father was coming home, but what if he'd been meeting Mother to call on the Middletons? But why would they call on the Middletons together?

"Lady Middleton, may I ask—and please forgive me if this question seems too impertinent—but was there a reason my parents called on you? Beyond merely paying a social call?"

Lady Middleton looked away sharply. "I cannot discuss that here, Miss Dashwood."

"But—"

Before Elinor could formulate an argument, a sharp gasp seemed to sweep through the ballroom, followed by the buzz of many people whispering at once. Elinor knew without having to look that someone had just done something very scandalous indeed, and she couldn't help but turn in the direction of the commotion. At first, the press of partygoers obscured her view, but then someone said, "Let her have some air!" and the crowd shifted.

It was Amelia. She had collapsed in a heap on the dance floor, and the dancers had stopped abruptly, capturing everyone's attention even as the music played on. Elinor assumed she'd fallen into a swoon, even though Amelia wasn't the type. But then she took a few steps closer, her old instincts to see to a friend kicking in. Amelia's face, already pale, was absolutely white. The young man she'd been dancing with had caught her and lowered her gently to the floor, and now Amelia's mother rushed forward, attempting to revive her.

"Poor girl. It is overly hot in this room," Lady Middleton murmured, fluttering her black feathered fan rapidly.

"She looks ill," Elinor whispered back. She recalled Amelia's unfocused, delayed response to Elinor's questions. Perhaps that had been not rudeness but a symptom of Amelia's illness?

Someone said, "Call a doctor!" and Amelia's dance partner swept her up in his arms and began to maneuver her out of the ballroom, Mrs. Holbrook on his heels as Mrs. Farrows herself led them away, presumably to a quiet corner of the house to await the doctor. Elinor watched her go, torn between wanting to follow and fearing her help would be rejected.

Then Lady Middleton sighed so deeply that it seemed to Elinor she was about to swoon herself. Instead, the older lady patted Elinor on the elbow and said, "Tell your mother to call on me," and glided away before Elinor could say a word.

Elinor considered following her for half a moment, demanding answers, but then dismissed the thought just as quickly. Whatever had transpired between the Middletons and her parents wasn't something that Lady Middleton would divulge in the middle of a ball. And besides, Marianne should be by her side for this.

Elinor swept her gaze across the room, looking for the jarring pink of Lucy Steele's gown. She spotted her rather quickly on the dance floor, whispering something to Edward. His head was tilted down so he could hear what she was saying, and they were both looking in the direction of where Amelia had been carried off.

That was the moment that Elinor made the scandalous decision to leave without telling anyone. Let them talk about her if they wished—they would anyway.

The drive home was long and Elinor felt every clatter and bump in her anxious body. Her worries about her former friend slowly faded into the background as she relived the memory of Edward and Lucy whispering together, so she forced herself to think instead of the case. Should she wait until the morning to tell Marianne what she'd discovered or wake her when she got home? It wasn't quite midnight yet—Elinor had never left a ball so early. Perhaps Marianne would be awake still. She should tell her as soon as possible, she decided.

When the driver finally let her out on Barton Street, an anxious combination of nerves, excitement, and worry curled in her stomach. She turned to thank the driver and caught a glimpse of an all-too-familiar figure down the street. The streetlights on Barton Street were not spaced as closely together as they'd been in her old neighborhood, but they still provided enough illumination for Elinor to recognize her sister.

She stepped up to her stoop as the carriage pulled away. When the driver turned a corner, Elinor stepped back out and looked up and down the street for Marianne. She didn't see her right off but said, "You might as well come out, Marianne. I saw you."

A few moments passed, and then her sister appeared from behind the shadows of a neighbor's stoop. "Oh, hello. Did you have a nice time at the ball?"

Marianne was both sarcastic and evasive at the same time, and Elinor didn't bother wasting her time. "Where have you been?"

"Following a lead," Marianne said, her chin raised defiantly.

"At night? Alone?"

Elinor waited for a response and was actually surprised when Marianne said, "I had Willoughby drop me off around the corner when we spotted your carriage."

"Marianne!" Elinor didn't even try to keep her voice down. "It's one thing to invite scandal by going for a drive with Willoughby alone during the day, but at night? You'll be ruined."

"Not if no one sees us," Marianne said with maddening self-satisfaction. "Besides, wait until you hear what we— Elinor? Did you leave the door open?"

"What? No." She turned to see what had made Marianne go rigid.

Their front door stood open to the night.

FOURTEEN

In Which the Dashwood Sisters
Come Clean—for the Most Part

MARIANNE'S FIRST IMPULSE WAS to march up to the front door, but Elinor's hand came down on her shoulder. "Wait," she said in a fierce whisper. "What if—"

"Mother and Margaret are inside!" Marianne pulled away, and Elinor followed close on her heels.

The flat was dark when Marianne pushed open the door, and she paused to listen for . . . well, anything. It was quiet. The front hall and the drawing room didn't seem disturbed, as far as she could tell, but she needed light. Then she heard the scrape of a flint and flickering light illuminated the front hall. Elinor stood with her palm cupped around a candle, her eyes wide in fright. Then they heard a tiny thump from above.

"Mother and Margaret," Elinor whispered, and started up the stairs.

"Wait!" Marianne hissed, following. She dug her pocketknife out of her pocket. Of all the places she'd thought she might use it, Marianne never imagined unsheathing the blade in her own home!

The hallway upstairs also appeared undisturbed, each door closed. Elinor went to Mother's door and knocked softly. "Mother? It's us!" She tried the door handle, but it was locked. After a small pause they heard something move about, and then the lock turned and the door swung open to reveal Mother in her dressing gown, the poker from the fire clutched in one hand. "Girls!" she cried out, and engulfed them both in her arms.

"What happened?" Marianne demanded as she hastily returned the hug. She spotted Margaret across the room, crouched in the corner behind Mother's bed.

"I woke up to a loud crash," Mother said. "And then Margaret ran in and said she thought someone had broken in, and that you weren't in your bed. I didn't know what to do!"

Marianne felt something wet on her cheek and realized that Mother was crying. "I didn't know what to do," she repeated.

"It's all right," Elinor soothed. "We're here now, everyone's safe."

"What about Hannah?" came Margaret's small voice.

Marianne felt a chill shudder through her as she remembered

her suspicions about Hannah—but surely she couldn't be responsible for this. "Stay here," she said, pulling out of Mother's grasp. "I'll search the rest of the house."

"We should call someone," Mother said.

Marianne didn't disagree with her, but she wasn't sure whom exactly they'd call. "Stay here and lock the door behind you," she instructed.

"I'm coming with you," Elinor said, taking the poker from Mother.

Marianne didn't protest, just readjusted her grip on her knife. The truth was, she appreciated that she wouldn't have to search the house alone. Once Mother and Margaret were safe behind the locked door, she and Elinor crept through the upstairs rooms, searching for a sign of a break-in or anything unusual. Then they tiptoed back down the stairs and swept through the drawing room, which Marianne could see now was thoroughly ransacked—papers from the writing desk were strewn about, chairs were overturned, and all of the settee cushions had been slashed to reveal their stuffing. Elinor let out a hissing breath but otherwise kept silent as Marianne led her through the room to the dining room, which revealed thrown-back chairs and the table slightly askew, and finally into the kitchen.

The first thing that Marianne noticed was the broken crockery and glass everywhere. It crunched underneath her slipper, and then Elinor's candlelight fell across a figure on the floor and her sister let out a cry. "Hannah!"

Their maid was splayed out on the floor, her face turned away from Marianne. Elinor set her candle on the table, dropped her poker, and reached out for Hannah's face. Her fingers came back dark with blood as she tried to roll Hannah toward the light.

"Is she . . . ?" Marianne asked, surveying the larder and the rest of the kitchen for any intruders and stepping over broken glass to make sure that Hannah's small room was empty.

Hannah groaned, and Elinor said, "Oh, thank God!"

Marianne crouched down and helped her sister bring Hannah into a sitting position. "Hannah, can you hear us?"

"Caught me off guard," Hannah mumbled.

"Hush, don't worry about that now," Elinor said. "Marianne, hand me that rag."

Marianne pulled a clean cloth from the drying rack near the fireplace and handed it to her sister, who gently began dabbing at Hannah's wound. Then she retrieved Mother and the three of them got her into bed. Mother and Elinor cleaned and bandaged her head wound while Marianne and Margaret ran about the flat to check all the locks. The front-door lock had been broken by brute force and didn't latch properly, but Margaret held the door shut while Marianne slid the dead bolt across, and then she dragged over a chair from the dining room to wedge under the door handle for good measure.

Back in the kitchen, Elinor was sweeping up the shards

littering the floor. "Hannah is groggy, but she appears to be otherwise unhurt."

"Her cut?"

"Mother is dressing it. It's mostly stopped bleeding, and it was smaller than it looked. Hannah was waiting up for us, and she got up to investigate the sound of the door breaking in, but the intruder came charging at her and hit her on the head. She never got a good look at him."

"But she was certain it was a he?"

Elinor raised a single eyebrow. "Do you suspect a woman of creating this mess?"

"No," Marianne said. "Just trying to be thorough."

"She said he," Elinor replied.

"I woke up to a big banging sound," Margaret said. "And I thought about going downstairs to see what it was, but when I stepped out onto the landing, I saw the front door open and I was scared. I ran into Mama's room, and we heard a ruckus, but she said we had to close the door and hide and hope they didn't come upstairs. The noises didn't last long. And then you came home."

Marianne hugged her little sister. "You did the right thing. Who knows what a criminal would have done if they'd seen you?"

"But Hannah got hurt," Margaret said, and her shoulders shook.

"I know, but she's all right. She'll live. There was nothing you could have done to stop them," Elinor murmured, and she looked to Marianne. Marianne thought they were wondering the same thing: *What was the trespasser after?*

"How long before you heard any noises and we came home?" Marianne asked.

"Not a very long time," Margaret said, wiping her tears on the back of her hand. "My leg fell asleep, but it didn't go completely numb."

Marianne nodded, judging that it might have been anywhere between fifteen and thirty minutes. They'd narrowly missed catching him off guard by returning home early. Had their intruder known that the older Dashwood sisters were both out of the flat? Was someone watching them?

Marianne kept her unease to herself as she sat Margaret on the one kitchen chair that wasn't broken and then fetched the dustpan for Elinor, who looked rather absurd sweeping up a mess in a ball gown. Elinor didn't seem to notice that she had streaks of dust on her fine gown. "Whatever they wanted, they made a right mess of the kitchen and drawing room."

"Were they merely looking for valuables?"

"The silver is still here," Elinor said. "But they smashed Mother's crystal. What about the drawing room—is any of the art missing?"

Marianne shook her head. "No, the desk was ransacked, and the cushions destroyed, but . . . it looks as though someone were looking for something specific. There was plenty of value in the drawing room alone if a common thief wanted something to pawn. Why come to the kitchen? Why hit Hannah?"

"They didn't want Hannah interfering with a search."

"But they didn't go upstairs," Marianne continued, looking to Margaret. "Right?"

Margaret shook her head. "The stair the second from the top squeaks. I would have heard, and I was listening very hard."

"Upstairs in the bedroom is where any jewelry or true valuables would have been kept," Marianne reasoned. "But they didn't bother. What did they want in the kitchen, or drawing room?"

"Are you thinking this is related to . . ." Elinor cast a glance at Hannah's closed door and then mouthed, *You know.*

"It seems likely," Marianne said. And then she noticed that the shelf where Elinor kept all of her chemistry supplies was empty. "Oh, Elinor! Your glassware . . ."

Elinor looked over her shoulder at the empty shelf. "I know."

"You don't think . . ."

The sisters were all silent, until Margaret said, "The person who did this was Papa's killer?"

Marianne shivered. "Maybe. But the person who killed Father doesn't seem like the type to go to such lengths. Poison is neat. It's not messy like this."

"Elinor was trying to figure out what the poison was," Margaret said. "Right here."

That made Elinor and Marianne both go still. She was

right. "But we don't even have that anymore," Marianne said bitterly. "You gave it to Mr. Brandon."

But Elinor shocked Marianne by scowling at her and saying, "Do you take me for a complete fool?" She plunged her hand into the pocket of her ball gown and withdrew a small vial. "I didn't give it *all* to Mr. Brandon."

"What! But you said—"

"Well, sometimes you can be very . . . cutting." Elinor looked away from her sister and seemed to collect herself, and then she continued, "I'm sorry I didn't correct you in the moment, but I was angry. I don't care if Mr. Brandon was the most trustworthy person in England. I still wouldn't have given him all of the poison. This is an unknown substance. I went to him for help to discover what it is, but . . ."

Elinor didn't say anything else. She set the vial on the table, and Marianne knew what her sister was thinking. It was their only evidence, but this was also Elinor's mystery. A scientific question to answer.

"I'm sorry I got so angry with you," Marianne finally said. "I shouldn't have assumed."

Elinor gave her a small smile and nodded. "And I suppose I should apologize for getting angry at you for investigating Mr. Farrows."

Marianne felt her eyebrows go up. "Oh, he's Mr. Farrows again, is he?"

"Yes," her sister said simply. "I spoke with him. He

confirmed he's no longer employed at his firm."

"I'm sorry." Even though Marianne had been right, she didn't relish her sister's pain.

"So who broke in?" Margaret asked.

Marianne began to mentally tick off suspects. "Well, it wasn't Mr. Farrows, if you just saw him at the ball."

"He might be involved in something suspicious, but I don't know if I believe that he could have been capable of causing Father's death," Elinor said. "I promise you that's not me being stubborn, either. I truly fail to see it. And . . . well, I know I cast suspicions on Mr. Willoughby, but if you were with him, then he couldn't have done it either."

Marianne accepted this acknowledgment with a small smile. "Thank you. But . . . I'm afraid you're not going to like this. I think it was Mr. Brandon."

"Why?" Elinor asked.

"Because . . . Willoughby and I broke into the Williams apothecary shop tonight."

"You did *what?*" Elinor dropped the broom.

"Daring," Margaret said with admiration.

"Illegal," Elinor corrected. "What if you'd been caught?"

"But I wasn't," Marianne said. "And . . . we found something you ought to see."

She dumped the small satchel on the table and retrieved the journal from her cloak pocket. "It's Eliza Williams's journal. It's got all of her, what do you call them, recipes!"

"Formulas," Elinor corrected.

"*And* her notes. I bet you anything it has her notes about the substance that killed Father. These were hidden in the back of a cabinet, but they weren't missing," Marianne said. "Willoughby found them after not ten minutes of rummaging about—it was almost too easy."

"But why were they hidden there?" Elinor asked. "I've been in that workroom. Mr. Brandon shares it with Mr. Williams. It seems like a rather risky place to hide something that is pivotal in her death." Elinor opened the satchel and spread its contents on the table. There were two vials—one labeled *Ammonia*, one labeled *Acid*—and a paper packet labeled *Poppy*.

"Opium poppy is used as a medicine. It's not a poison," Elinor murmured.

"But what if it is?" Marianne asked. "You're the expert, but what if whatever is here makes poison if it's combined just right, and that's what killed Father?"

Marianne was staring at her older sister, so she had no idea Mother had entered the room until she heard her voice say, "What's this about poison killing your father?"

All three Dashwood sisters turned to see Mother, weary lines framing her face as looked gravely at each of her children. "Well?"

"Mother!" Elinor said. "It's— "

"It's my fault," Marianne said, cutting off her older sister. "I was suspicious, from the very beginning. I made Elinor help me

251

search, and then Margaret joined in, and, well . . ."

"We found out some things," Elinor offered, and when Marianne glanced at her, she saw her older sister had squared her shoulders so that she was standing next to Marianne. With her.

"Right," Mother said, looking between all three Dashwood sisters. "And you didn't think to tell me?"

The sisters remained silent.

"Elinor, put the kettle on. Marianne, Margaret, do we have any teacups left, or did our midnight ruffian smash them all? You girls are going to tell me *everything*."

Marianne had never been so glad to hear Mother sound severe in all her life.

✄

The clock in the hall struck two in the morning before the Dashwood sisters were done telling their mother all the sordid details of their investigation to date. They had to stop multiple times to explain themselves and answer Mother's questions. When they got caught up to that evening, Elinor surprised Marianne with her revelation that Father and Mother had gone to call on the Middletons the day of his death.

"There's something here," she said when Elinor was done speaking. "I just can't see it all. But I was wrong about Mr. Brandon—he is suspicious. I just don't understand why he would kill Father *now*."

"A dead woman's journal and a few scientific substances

can't prove that Mr. Brandon was the one who killed her, or the one that broke in tonight," Elinor argued. "We can't even prove that her substance is the one that killed Father."

Marianne knew she was right. "We need to flush him out. Force his hand so that he shows he's the one."

Mother tsked. "I won't have you three doing anything risky. Hannah is lucky to be alive, and I don't want any one of you to be next."

"But Mother, why did you and Father go see the Middletons that day?"

"I don't see how they have any part of this," Mother insisted. "John and Emily are so rarely in town, but they wrote me and asked if I would come call, and bring your father. They wanted to renew the connection. They quite outrank us, but Emily has never been one for society, so I assumed they were hoping for some advantageous introductions. Sir John wanted your father's recommendation for a club, and a tailor, and asked that we both call on them."

"I met Lady Middleton tonight and I think there's more to it than that," Elinor persisted, her forehead creasing as she recalled the memory. "She asked about Mother, and she apologized for not calling or attending the funeral. She said she left London the morning we discovered Father and didn't hear until later about his death. Which is odd, don't you think? If she'd just arrived to town."

Marianne thought it was more than odd, but she merely

nodded and let Elinor continue.

"It was the way she spoke—she was polite, but a little vague. And she mentioned family troubles of her own. She said that she couldn't speak of it here, and that Mother should call on her."

"If Sir John solicited your father's services, he didn't do it in front of us," Mother murmured. And then a strange look fell across her face. "But he did want to show your father some cigars he procured. They retired to his study."

"But Papa hates cigars," Margaret cut in, as everyone well knew.

"How long were they in there?" Marianne asked.

"A few minutes? We left soon after. I can't imagine what transpired."

"I think we should find out," Elinor said, looking to Marianne.

"But you have to admit that this is something," Marianne said, pointing to Eliza Williams's notes and satchel. The evidence could not be ignored.

"It's something," Elinor agreed, meeting Marianne's eyes. Her sister sounded genuine, even as she added, "I just don't know what."

"Nothing can be solved tonight," Mother proclaimed, and she stood and began collecting their teacups. "We'll go to bed, and try to sleep. I shall go to Lady Middleton tomorrow and ask her what she meant."

"I'll come too," Marianne rushed to say.

"And me," Elinor added, darting a glance at Marianne.

"Then I'm coming too!" Margaret declared.

"Well, we can't all go," Mother said, extinguishing one of the candles. "Hannah shouldn't be left alone, and Margaret, you're too young to stay home unsupervised."

"Then I'll stay," Elinor said. "I'll try and decipher Eliza Williams's notes."

She looked to Marianne as if asking for permission, and Marianne nodded.

"What about me?" Margaret asked.

"You'll stay with Elinor," Mother said sternly. "No one is going off on her own until this killer is caught. Elinor, make sure you bring that poker back upstairs—I don't want to sleep without it."

FIFTEEN

In Which the Dashwood Sisters
Discover Father's Secret Case

THE DASHWOODS SLEPT LATE, despite the excitement that the possibility of answers brought. Marianne chalked it up to the emotional toll of the night before—the terror of finding Hannah injured and coming clean to Mother had leached away all of Marianne's energy, but now that a new day had dawned, she was ready to face it.

The first thing she did after dressing was write a letter to Willoughby. She'd left him in quite a hurry the night before, insisting he drop her off around the corner when she saw John and Fanny's carriage pull onto Barton Street in the distance. He'd said something about coming to call and going to the authorities, and she'd waved him off, far more concerned about how she'd sneak back inside the flat with Elinor home early. Now, she was glad that she hadn't caved to Willoughby's idea that they summon a Runner immediately. Partly because it seemed rather poor form to go to the authorities without all of the information (and with stolen evidence, no less!), but mostly now because if the Middletons were involved in any way, they simply couldn't make an idle accusation against a peer of the realm.

In her note, she laid out what they'd learned the night before and their plan. She was tempted to post it but hesitated. The letter could too easily fall into the wrong hands. She'd leave it on the hall table and instruct her sisters to give it to Willoughby if he called while they were out.

Elinor was gathering up the stuffing of their poor slashed settees when Marianne found her downstairs, dressed in a simple day dress and apron. "Are they salvageable?" she asked.

"Perhaps, although I'm not sure they'll ever look so nice again."

"I have a letter here, should Willoughby call," Marianne said, holding up the folded paper and then setting it on the hall table.

"Will he?" Elinor asked, an arch to her eyebrow that Marianne disliked.

"Perhaps," Marianne hedged, and before Elinor could respond she asked, "How did it go last night? With Miss Steele?"

"Oh." Elinor's expression darkened. "Well, I suppose. I made the introduction and he asked her to dance. She seemed pleased."

The simplicity of the explanation alerted Marianne to Elinor's true feelings about the matter. She could hear the pain in her sister's voice, and what's worse, she knew that she was partly to blame for it. "Elinor," she said softly, "why didn't you say that you liked Edward?"

She thought her sister would deny it, but Elinor's shoulders merely sagged as she looked around the room, at anything and everything but Marianne. "Because, I merely like him. I don't love him. I don't believe he'll propose marriage and save us from our circumstances, and even if he did, I would say no because how can I know if he'll make me happy? Or that I would make him happy?"

"Is that what you think?" Marianne asked. "That I like Willoughby merely because I want him to propose and save me from . . . this?"

Marianne gestured at the ruined settees and the disheveled room and realized with a sharp pang that there was a part of her that did want to be saved from all of this. She missed her old home, not having to worry about money. She missed all their things, and their nice rooms, and who she was before Father died.

"Don't you?" Elinor asked in a tiny voice.

Marianne looked up at her sister, expecting judgment and finding none. Instead, Elinor looked . . . forlorn. Sad. A bit afraid.

"I want . . . well, not this life. But I don't like Willoughby because I want him to save me from all of this. I could never leave you and Margaret and Mother."

"But you want to get married?"

"Of course! I want to get married because I want romance. I want love, and affection, and what Mother and Father had. I'm not a gold digger or social climber."

"I didn't mean to say you were," Elinor said, her tone very serious.

"I know," Marianne relented, and let out a gusty sigh. "But I like Willoughby because he likes me. He likes the same things I do. And he's interested in my work, and he worries about my safety, and he is game for my plots—not many men would be. They want young ladies whose only ploys involve drawing room gossip."

Elinor smiled a little then. "I know. You've never been content to be ordinary. I just want to make sure you have an extraordinary young man by your side. But if you say that's Willoughby, then I'll try to give him a chance."

"Thank you," Marianne said, her relief warring with her uncertainty about how things had gone last night. Willoughby's assumption that Marianne would want to simply break into the apothecary had been . . . odd. But she'd have a talk with him. Explain Father's code of conduct. "And, Edward? You don't love, but you think that perhaps . . . maybe you could be happy with him?"

"Maybe," Elinor said. "But I'm not like you. I'm not certain of things. I need to think about them, test my theories. And maybe I would have had that chance, if Edward had been anyone else but Fanny's brother, and above suspicion, but now I just feel . . . I feel as though . . . I don't know."

But Marianne understood. "That you've suffered all the pangs of unrequited love without any of the hope?"

"Something like that," Elinor agreed, wearing a tiny smile. But it was a sad one.

"I just wish you'd said, is all."

"I know," Elinor responded, and then added, "I wish I'd said, too. But Marianne . . . sometimes I think you believe that you must be madly in love, or absolutely disinterested. You don't allow for anything in between. For possibility."

Marianne remembered what Elinor had said to her a few days earlier—*you require so much*. At the time, Marianne hadn't thought that had been a valid judgment. What was the matter with having standards? But now, she wondered if maybe Elinor had meant that Marianne's standards were impossible for anyone to meet, including her family. The last thing Marianne ever wanted was to cheat her sister out of happiness.

Elinor is always taking care of us, even when we aren't always taking care of her, Marianne realized. And in that moment, she finally believed that Elinor sending for the undertaker before Marianne had gotten the chance to say goodbye to Father wasn't meant to be cruel, and it hadn't been thoughtless. It was exactly as Elinor had said—she was trying to protect them.

"Elinor?" Marianne said, and when Elinor turned she hugged her, squeezing her sister so tightly that a surprised *oof* came out of her. "I love you."

"I love you, too," Elinor said, hugging her back. "Now go and get the answers we need to solve Father's murder."

Marianne was slightly apprehensive when she knocked on the door of the Middletons' grand town house, Mother at her side. They'd faced so many dead ends, she wasn't sure what she'd do if this turned out to be another one.

The butler ushered mother and daughter into the drawing room, where a woman about Mother's age sat on a settee. Marianne caught a glimpse of something on her face in the space between entering the room and the butler's announcement—a blankness that reminded Marianne too much of her mother's face on the days she managed to get out of bed—before it was replaced by a carefully polite, if distant, smile.

"Mrs. Dashwood," she said warmly, standing to greet them. "And this must be Miss Marianne. How wonderful. But where is Miss Dashwood?"

Mother clasped Lady Middleton's hand and said, "Thank you for having us. I'm afraid we had . . . a bit of excitement last night, and Elinor decided to stay home."

"Excitement? Nothing too alarming, I hope? Your family has been through more than enough. My deepest condolences, my dear."

Mother murmured her thanks, and then Marianne and Mother took the proffered seat across from Lady Middleton. Marianne itched to blurt out why they'd come, but she sensed a skittishness in Lady Middleton and didn't want to scare the other woman.

"Unfortunately, someone broke into the flat last night," Mother said, managing to sound matter-of-fact about it. "They knocked our maid unconscious, but Hannah shall recover."

Lady Middleton gasped, apparently at a loss for words.

"Elinor stayed home, to look after things," Marianne added, impatient when no one broke the silence after Mother's announcement. "But she told us that she spoke with you last night?"

"Yes," Lady Middleton said, sounding dazed.

"She led us to believe that you might know something more about Father's last day," Marianne continued carefully. "You see, we don't believe that Father's death was entirely due to natural causes."

Lady Middleton went very still. "You don't?"

"No," Marianne said firmly, glancing at her mother. Mother's expression was tired but set in grim determination. "I'm sorry if this is an impertinent question, but did Sir John hire Father?"

There was another surprised silence, and Marianne half expected Lady Middleton to deny everything, but instead she merely looked at Mother and said, "He didn't tell you?"

"No," Mother said, not sounding surprised in the slightest. "Henry could keep a secret."

"And now your flat has been broken into. . . . Oh, this is dreadful." Lady Middleton rang a bell for the butler. He stepped into the room so promptly, Marianne wondered if he'd been listening at the door. "Fetch Sir John at once," she ordered.

Oh my, Marianne thought, trying not to get too excited.

Lady Middleton refused to say anything while they waited for her husband. Marianne and Mother declined tea, for it seemed that all three women were either too excited or agitated to sip from fine china, and before long Sir John arrived in the room, worry and curiosity drawing his normally jovial face into pinched concern. "What is it, my dear? Ellis said I had to come at once, and oh—Mary! Miss Marianne! Is everything all right?"

"No," Lady Middleton. "Their flat was broken into last night, and they believe that Mr. Dashwood didn't die of natural causes. I think we need to tell them about Vincent."

"Vincent?" Marianne repeated.

"Whatever is the matter with Vincent?" Mother asked, concern sharpening the edges of her tone.

The Middletons exchanged a long glance, and finally Sir John sighed. "Our son has been missing for two months. I wrote to your husband six weeks ago for his help. Vincent is why we've come to London—we have reason to believe he's here somewhere."

It was quite gauche, but Marianne felt her jaw drop as she took in this news. The Middletons had a missing son? Not only that, but a missing son that *no one* had been gossiping about?

"Oh my Lord," Mother said, rising from her seat to join Lady Middleton on the settee. "Oh, you must be completely wrecked with worry."

"He's only seventeen," Lady Middleton said, tears sliding down her cheeks.

Marianne worked to keep her expression sympathetic, not eager. "Can we ask what happened?"

"Just tell them," Lady Middleton said. "Maybe they can help."

"We hired Mr. Dashwood for his discretion, of course," Sir John said, taking a seat on the other side of his wife. "Vincent isn't well. There's no reason we can't get him the help he needs. His reputation shouldn't be ruined over this."

Marianne was even more confused.

"You have to start at the beginning," Lady Middleton said, accepting the handkerchief Mother offered her. "He broke his arm last spring."

"It was a horrid accident." Sir John picked up the telling. "He was riding, and the horse spooked. The fall was bad, and the bone was . . . well, even I shudder to remember it now. We called the best physicians and surgeons up from London, and they were able to set it. But Vincent was in horrific pain."

"They gave him laudanum," Lady Middleton said. "It made

264

him sleep at first, and we were grateful."

"I'm familiar with it," Mother murmured, almost too quietly for Marianne to catch.

Sir John continued, "It was a bad break. He was in so much pain, and it didn't heal in time for him to return to Eton—he hated that. But how could we let him go back?"

"I understand," Mother said soothingly.

"It did heal, but it took months. Vincent resented everyone—us, the tutors we hired, the physicians, even the horse that threw him. I had to sell the animal because . . . well, it's not of any consequence. Suffice to say, Vincent grew surly and unreasonable, and he wanted more laudanum, always more. Then one day, he asked for opium granules. He said the pain was so bad that he'd grown too accustomed to laudanum, and he needed them."

Opium again, Marianne realized. She felt foolish for not seeing it earlier. "Where did you get your laudanum? And the opium?"

"A chemist on Barley Street," Sir John said. "Our family has patronized that shop for years."

Not the Williams's shop, then. Marianne filed that away.

"I did as he asked at first, thinking that a little bit could only help, but I'd never seen anything like Vincent's desire for it before. It wasn't desire. He *needed* it. One day . . ."

He seemed caught up in memory and didn't say anything for a long moment. Lady Middleton continued for him. "The day we knew that something was very wrong was when I forgot to get more opium. Vincent had abandoned taking it in tinctures, and now he simply ate the granules—only two or three at a time, but he ran out. And he realized that there was none to be had in the house, or in the village, and it was far too late to send someone to London. He lost his temper on us, on the servants, and he . . . shoved Sir John down the stairs, then struck Ellis when he tried to help. We raised our son to behave better, but he'd never had a temper before he broke his arm. Even as an infant, he was always the sweetest, kindest, gentlest boy."

Lady Middleton began to cry again in earnest and Sir John put an arm around her as Mother rubbed her back. Marianne felt as though she'd walked uninvited into a private moment. The raw emotion made her own throat clench unexpectedly.

"That opium had taken hold of him, like some demon," Sir John explained. "He wasn't our Vincent anymore. We told him there would be no more. I thought he'd be mad at us, or resigned, but he said hateful things, and threw such a fit that the other children were upset. And then he left in the night. He took valuables from the house, jewelry that belonged to my wife and the girls. We asked in the village, and learned that he'd hired a coach to London."

"But he was never like that before," Lady Middleton declared, adamant.

"We looked everywhere. Ellis and I personally inquired at all the apothecary shops, the workhouses, even at Newgate. I wrote Eton, his friends . . . it's as though he simply vanished into thin air. After a week, I wrote Mr. Dashwood, and he took on our case."

"Henry didn't say," Mother said. "But if I had known I would have come. I'm so sorry that you have gone through this alone."

"It's all right, Mary," Sir John said. "I didn't wish to keep you in the dark, but I asked Dashwood to keep a tight lid on the case. We just want our boy home."

"I knew he had a new case," Marianne murmured. "But he said nothing about it. And he wouldn't answer my questions when I inquired about what he was working on next."

"He was diligent," Sir John said. "On his final day, when you called, I said that I had some cigars I wanted him to sample, but really I was awaiting his update."

Marianne sat forward in her seat. "Did he have new information?"

Sir John hesitated, and Marianne added, "Please. I don't know if your case is related to Father's death, but we are suspicious of another client of his, and opium may have been involved. If there's anything you can share . . ."

"Please," Mother added.

"Tell them everything, John," Lady Middleton said. "I don't care who knows anymore. I just want my son back."

That convinced him. "Dashwood retraced our steps, looking for evidence that we might have missed. He learned of a few private clubs that catered to gentlemen with a taste for opium."

Marianne had never heard of such a thing. "Entire clubs just for opium?"

"Apparently, but it's very secretive. He couldn't just walk into one, and he cautioned that it would take him time to secure an invitation or gain trust. But he did leave me the names of the establishments. Let me fetch the list."

This was more than Marianne had hoped for, and she could barely contain herself as she waited for Sir John to return. Lady Middleton began to pull herself together, and Mother said, "I'm sorry we've upset you."

"I was upset before you arrived," she said. "But you've given me . . . well, not hope exactly. But I do feel better somehow."

"Sharing the burden doesn't always lessen it," Mother said with a sideways glance at Marianne. "But it does sometimes make it easier to bear."

Marianne had the feeling that Mother was obliquely referring to how she and her sisters had kept the nature of Father's death a secret, and she sat quietly with her shame. How much could have been avoided if they'd just trusted that Mother was strong enough to handle the truth from the very beginning?

Sir John returned with a small slip of paper in his hand. He solemnly handed it to Marianne, recognizing that she was the investigator now. Mother stood and came to Marianne's side, and a fist tightened around Marianne's lungs when she recognized Father's handwriting.

On the list were four names written in ink—Roswell Place, Webster's, Groff House, and Grey's. Three checks marked in pencil stood next to the first three names, but that wasn't what made Marianne and Mother gasp. Next to the bottom name, written in Father's hasty hand, was one more name scrawled in charcoal.

"Does that say . . ." Mother leaned in closer but didn't finish her question.

"Yes," Marianne confirmed, blinking rapidly. She suddenly felt as though she couldn't draw enough air into her lungs, and her vision turned hazy as she stared at the slip of paper. Maybe if she looked at it long enough, blinked enough times, drew in a deeper breath, the letters would rearrange themselves to say something else, spell any other name.

"It says Willoughby."

SIXTEEN

In Which the Dashwood Sisters
Face a New Disaster

ELINOR COULDN'T STOP THINKING about Eliza's journal.

The only thing that had stopped Elinor from falling head-first into the secrets of Eliza's brilliant mind the night before had been her exhaustion, which pulled at her like many tiny, insistent fingers. When she woke, there was so much to be done, especially since Mother had insisted that Hannah spend the day in bed. But as soon as Mother and Marianne were out of the house, Elinor nearly ran to the kitchen, where she found Margaret flipping through the pages while she sat eating bread and jam at the table.

"Margaret! Don't touch that while you're eating. You'll smear jam on the pages!"

"Will not!" Margaret said, mouth full. "I'm *very* careful. Besides, there's nothing interesting in here. It's not like any journal I've ever seen."

Elinor snatched up the leather-bound book. "That's because it's full of scientific inquiry."

"It's written in a strange shorthand," Margaret replied. "Are you going to decipher it?"

"I'm going to try." Elinor stared down at the unassuming red cover.

"What are you afraid of?" Margaret asked.

"What? I'm not—"

"You have the same look on your face when you have to go talk to Fanny."

Lord give her strength, Margaret was entirely too wise for her young age. "First of all, I'm not afraid of Fanny. I find her daunting. And I find this journal similarly daunting."

"I thought you liked a challenge."

"No, you're thinking of our other sister," Elinor teased.

"No," Margaret responded very seriously. "I'm not. You used to spend hours in your lab running the same experiment over and over. Why would you be afraid of Eliza Williams's notes?"

"Because I'm afraid I won't be able to understand them."

Elinor spoke the words without thinking. She wasn't a real scientist, just a girl playing at it. No one would take her seriously. Maybe Father would have, if she'd ever gotten up the courage to tell him before he died, but now he was gone and so were Elinor's dreams of ever becoming a scientist and maybe she should just give up.

Margaret didn't look impressed by Elinor's answer. "Well, you certainly won't understand them if you never even look at them."

Elinor picked up the book and opened it to the first page. Then she looked up at her little sister. "When did you get to be so smart?"

"I have always been smart, thank you very much."

That made Elinor laugh, but she turned serious once again as she took a seat and began to read. It took her only a few minutes of scanning the pages and then going back over them much more carefully to realize one thing: Eliza Williams was leaps and bounds beyond Elinor's understanding of chemistry.

She didn't notice when Margaret left the kitchen because she was too engrossed. Elinor *did* struggle to absorb the other young woman's thoughts, theories, and shorthand. Each sentence she wrote contained references to names, experiments, and theories that puzzled Elinor. *It must be all the books that she had at her disposal.* There was nothing so humbling as realizing all the things you didn't know.

But as it turned out, Margaret was right: Elinor was no simpleton herself. And slowly, as she paged through the notes and began paying attention to the dated entries, she figured out that Mr. Brandon had been correct—Eliza wanted to discover what it was that made laudanum . . . no, what had made *opium* so effective.

There must be something, some key ingredient, she wrote in January of the previous year. *I've seen men gulp laudanum and barely feel the effects, but children are dizzy with a few sips. Some women will swear by Uncle's mixture and say it's stronger than Elliston's. Surgeons rail at Uncle if the laudanum isn't strong enough and their patient wakes while they're setting a bone or amputating a limb, while others will sleep for hours after a sip from the same bottle. What secrets does the opium poppy hold?*

From then on, the journal was full of Eliza's notes on the nature of the opium poppy, of her research into the opium suppliers. *Our supplier brings opium from Turkey,* she wrote. *Does the location of origin determine strength? Must procure Indian poppy.*

But fifteen pages later, Eliza deduced that no, where the poppy was grown made no difference. *The strength is in the chemical composition,* she wrote. The sentence was underlined with a heavy hand.

For the last three months of her life, her entries were entirely about her experiments with the opium poppy. She boiled, burned, distilled, to no avail. Elinor found herself flipping pages faster and faster until she came to a page near the end, where Eliza's handwriting was uncharacteristically large and wide. *EUREKA,* she wrote, and Elinor's heartbeat sped up. She knew enough to recognize the Greek word for discovery.

The last experiment was a success! she wrote. *Administered a distilled dose to a stray dog B found in the alley so he could treat the infection in dog's paw. Dog slept for a day before waking. B thought I gave dog laudanum, but this was a substance of my own creation! More experimentation is needed—a very tiny amount diluted in water put the animal to sleep for a day, so my theory that the opium poppy contains a strong alkaloid is correct. But I'm afraid the efficacy is far stronger than I even imagined, and it's unclear what too much could do to a living creature . . . although I could hypothesize.*

Elinor felt her heart beat with the thrill of discovery, as Eliza's must have. But her blood chilled at that last sentence, too. She read the precise measurements, then inspected the contents of the satchel. She had everything she needed here and among her own supplies to re-create this potent mixture that Eliza had discovered. The measurements were very precise, and they involved acid, which Elinor had never handled before. But the result, if successful, was this substance—what had Eliza called it? An alkaloid. This was far more serious than the distillation that Elinor had previously preoccupied herself with or even the smoke bomb she'd made for Margaret.

But if there was a chance that this substance, which Eliza herself declared dangerous, could help her solve her father's murder . . . then Elinor knew what she had to do. She was donning an apron before she could even stop and think about the risks. She didn't look up, not even when Margaret came back into the kitchen.

"I'm going to be handling some dangerous substances, so you best steer clear for a while," she said, not even looking up from where she was assembling her tools.

"Very well," Margaret said, and then she added something more, but Elinor wasn't paying any attention. She murmured, "Mm-hmm, all right then," and rolled up her dress sleeves. By the time she looked up once more, the kitchen was silent and empty, and she was ready to get to work.

In the end, Elinor was surprised at how easy it was to follow Eliza Williams's instructions. Dissolve the opium in acid, neutralize in ammonia, and then just wait. She swirled the glass beaker and watched in awe as the familiar colorless crystals appeared before her eyes, like magic. She could do this a hundred times and never get tired of it.

So far, she'd done it five times. The first two results she wasn't happy about, as they'd produced a murky kind of substance, but Elinor realized she'd gotten the proportions wrong. The third time had proved to work like a charm, and giddy on her success, Elinor conducted the experiment twice more, just to ensure she could. Now, three bottles of morphium, as Eliza had named it in her notes, sat in the center of the kitchen table, labeled neatly in her own hand. When compared with the last bit of poison she'd salvaged from Father's teacup, it appeared to be very similar, if not the same. Elinor's own substance was untested, but she had a good feeling about it.

She heard the distant sound of a door slamming and looked up, rolling the aches out of her back and shoulder from hunching over for so long. What time was it?

"Elinor? Margaret?" Mother's voice called out.

"Back here!" Elinor called, and began tidying up the table quickly. Her mother and Marianne appeared in the kitchen door, and she turned expectantly. "Well?" she asked. "What happened?"

"The Middletons told us they have a missing teenaged son," Marianne announced. "They hired Father to find him."

"How dreadful," Elinor said. "Did Father find him?"

"No," Mother said. "And they kept it secret, even from me."

"But we think Father might have encountered someone we are familiar with," Marianne added, and from the sour twist of her mouth, Elinor knew it was bad news.

"Mr. Brandon?" she asked, already cringing.

But it was Mother who responded. "No. Mr. Willoughby."

Elinor gasped. "Willoughby? But . . . where? How?"

"Marianne will explain," Mother said. "Then we need to discuss our next steps. I see you've been busy. Will it be safe for us to prepare dinner?"

Elinor was still reeling over the news that Father had encountered *Willoughby*. She'd never particularly taken to him, but to think of him as a criminal? He was so . . . gallant.

But his gallantry had been what had bought him an introduction to Marianne. . . .

"Elinor?" Mother asked.

"Yes, sorry—this is just . . . alarming. And I'll clean this up, Mother. But I was able to isolate Miss Williams's substance, and I think it matches the one that killed Father. Which begs the question of how Mr. Brandon ties into all of this. . . ."

"I don't know," Marianne said shortly.

"Where's your sister?" Mother asked.

"Oh, I suppose upstairs if she's not at her writing desk." Elinor turned back to her bottles and began tidying up the mess she'd made, careful not to spill or contaminate the surface where they prepared their food. She was quite shocked to discover that the afternoon light had slid all the way across the kitchen and was sinking low in the alley beyond the kitchen windows. "What time is it?"

"Nearly teatime," Marianne said morosely. "Once the Middletons realized we knew who Willoughby was—his name was written on a scrap of paper that Father had left Sir John—Lady Middleton became hysterical and wanted me to summon him on the spot. We had to tell them all about our own investigation and convince them that we needed to move deliberately, so as not to scare him off. Then the streets getting back were a nightmare. I just can't believe . . ."

Elinor looked up to see her sister shaking her head in disbelief. She didn't say anything at first, too aware of how easily Marianne could be set off. But she noted that Marianne wasn't fiery with indignation. She looked . . . bewildered.

"I thought that maybe he truly did love me," she said, still not looking at Elinor. "Is that so absurd to think? That perhaps after all the bad we went through, I could find some good?"

The practical side of Elinor wanted to say, *Well, it is not completely absurd but maybe a little bit unreasonable to think you could know someone after a week.* That was Marianne's greatest fault—every wish became a hope, and with hope came expectation. But Marianne didn't need a lecture, she needed a sister. "No," she said softly. "It's not absurd."

They were interrupted when the kitchen door flew open. Mother stood in the threshold. "Margaret's not upstairs."

"Are you sure?" Elinor asked.

"It's a small flat," her mother said. "I think I'd know if she were hiding somewhere."

"Maybe she's hiding in her trunk," Marianne said. "I've always told her she's going to get locked in one day and it'll serve her right for all her eavesdropping."

"Marianne, not now!" Mother snapped, sounding so much like the old mother they knew that Elinor and Marianne were both startled to attention.

"We'll help you look for her," Elinor said soothingly. "Come on, let's do another top-to-bottom search."

But Mrs. Dashwood had been correct—Margaret wasn't anywhere upstairs, not under any of the beds or hiding in an empty wardrobe or trunk. Elinor came downstairs and peeked into Hannah's room, but the woman looked up groggily and said that she hadn't seen Miss Margaret since that morning.

The Dashwood women reconvened in the kitchen. "Does this flat have an attic?" Marianne asked. "You just know that she would love to explore something like that."

"I don't know," Elinor said. "Maybe? But it feels as though she's been gone ages. . . ."

"When exactly did you last see her?"

Elinor raked her memories. "I was working in the kitchen. Not long after you left, we talked for a few minutes, then I started reading and she wandered off. . . ."

"Elinor! You let her leave the flat?"

Elinor hated nothing more than to hear Mother angry with her. "No! She didn't leave, she just left the kitchen. And she didn't leave the house, because she came back into the kitchen for something. I told her I was working with dangerous substances, so it was best if she steered clear."

"And did she say anything after that?" Marianne asked.

Elinor closed her eyes and tried to remember. Margaret *had* said something. Why hadn't she paid better attention? Elinor couldn't recall the words, just the tenor of Margaret's voice. She'd responded with a vague *Mm-hmm*, of that she was certain.

What had Margaret asked?

"I'm sorry," she whispered as tears threatened in the corners of her eyes. "I don't remember."

Rather than faint or collapse in grief, Mrs. Dashwood

stood firmly, her features tightening with resolve. "We need to split up, and we need help. Hannah is in no state, and someone clearly wants to harm this family. Marianne, stay near the door, in case she returns on her own. I'll knock on every door on the street and ask if anyone's seen anything. Elinor, fetch your brother. We may need his carriage, and his influence."

Elinor didn't argue. She fetched her cloak and set out immediately, matching her pace with the pounding of her heart. Why hadn't she paid any attention to what Margaret had said? Neither Mother nor Marianne had blamed her, but it *was* Elinor's fault. This knowledge haunted her all the way to her former home, a walk of about three-quarters of an hour under normal circumstances. Elinor arrived at their old address breathless, a little sweaty, and with a stitch in her side barely twenty minutes after she'd set out.

Her former house was a shining beacon of light, so familiar and reassuring that in the time it took Elinor to climb the steps and knock on the front door, she let herself hope that perhaps Margaret had merely grown homesick for their childhood home, their books, the familiar furniture and comfort of old hiding places, and that she had told Elinor she was going home for a visit.

But that fantasy was shattered when an unfamiliar face opened the door and looked down upon her. "Yes?" the new butler asked.

Elinor could hear the disdain dripping from his voice, and

she struggled to find her words. She settled on, "I'm Miss Elinor Dashwood, sister of Mr. Dashwood. Is he in?"

The butler didn't respond, but he did step aside so Elinor could come in. She found herself babbling as she entered. "It's rather urgent, and, well—we couldn't waste time with a messenger. Is he in the study? Oh, well, I gather Fanny's redecorated. I used to live here, you know, but I don't know which room is which anymore, but if you'll just point me in the right direction, I can—"

"Wait here, miss," the butler said, and then turned on his heel. Elinor gaped after him and then followed. If she had to search the house room by room, she would, propriety be damned.

Elinor burst into the newly redecorated drawing room, startling a maid carrying a tea tray. She nearly spilled it but righted herself at the last moment.

"Oh my—Elinor?" Fanny's voice rang out, and the room fell silent.

Elinor blinked at the sight of the full drawing room, so bright and full of chatter that had dimmed the moment she entered. She felt a rush of heat that had nothing to do with the overly warm room as she saw Fanny scowling at her, Mrs. Farrows in the chair by the fire looking rather severe, and her brother looking confused, as if he couldn't place his own sister. Then—her blush deepened. Edward, looking up at her with obvious concern. And next to Edward, Lucy Steele.

She'd interrupted no ordinary quiet evening at home but what appeared to be a dinner party.

Lucy had the most peculiar look of all the assembled people. She was smiling, but not in a welcoming way. More as if this entire scene were a play that existed entirely for Lucy's own amusement and Elinor was the surprise—and unwelcome—twist.

"My apologies," Elinor managed to gasp. She didn't quite know where to look. "It's just—Margaret. Is she here?"

"Margaret?" Fanny repeated, incredulous. "Why on earth would Margaret be here?"

She gestured to the assembled group, which even included Mrs. Jennings. Elinor felt as though she were five years old, trying to explain herself to an adult. "No, I see that she's not present in this room, but she's not . . . here, somewhere in the house?"

"What's the matter?" Edward asked, rising from his seat.

"Margaret is missing." Worry clenched her throat as the words came out. "No one's seen her since this afternoon."

"Are you sure?" John asked. No one else seemed particularly alarmed by Elinor's announcement.

"Yes, we're certain. We've looked everywhere. I thought perhaps she came here."

Fanny gave a very unladylike snort. "Well, she's not been around to call."

The fact that Fanny thought Margaret would ring the

doorbell for a social visit incensed Elinor. She didn't have to like the Dashwood sisters. She didn't even have to invite them to her dinner parties. But if one of them was missing, if the *youngest* Dashwood sister was missing, then the least she could do is care!

"She likes hiding spots," Elinor said, horrified to feel a pressure behind her eyes that foretold tears. "She knows this house better than anyone, and she might be homesick, so perhaps no one saw her come in and she's hiding somewhere. We just need to look for her."

"The very least we can do is send some maids around," Edward said. Elinor didn't have the courage to look at him, not after last night.

"Honestly," Fanny said with an exasperated sigh. "This is absurd. John?"

"Oh, right," John said. "If she's hiding for a lark, I'm sure she'll turn up. When she wants her supper?"

Something came over Elinor just then, a swell of emotion that seemed unfamiliar at first, except that when it overtook her she recognized it as every single bottled-up emotion she'd felt over the past month—no, *years*. Frustration toward Fanny for her dismissive attitude and her selfishness. Grief at her father's death, and betrayal that John had seen them turned out of their home rather than confront his wife about her behavior. Sorrow at the loss of the only home she'd ever known and her financial security, as well as her hopes and dreams. And anger.

Pulse-pounding anger that now, in their moment of greatest need, Fanny was dismissing Elinor and her concerns.

If Margaret hadn't been missing, if their flat hadn't been broken into the night before, Elinor would have swallowed this storm of emotions, and she would have covered the bitter taste with a polite smile. But her panic didn't allow for any social niceties.

"What is the matter with you all?" she demanded. "I come here to tell you my little sister, my *eleven-year-old* sister, is missing. *Your* sister, John. The least you can do is help!"

"Don't be dramatic," Fanny snapped. "You said it yourself, she likes hiding."

"She ought to be punished," Mrs. Farrows agreed. "Bed with no supper, and ten lashes."

Elinor couldn't believe what she was hearing. "John?"

"Oh, er . . . well," John sputtered, looking between Elinor and his wife. "Perhaps we're making a mountain of a molehill here?"

Elinor didn't think he deserved the dignity of a rational response. "Oh, no, I just decided to burst in here unannounced without actually searching our flat. Good idea, I'll just go back now and check under my bed!"

Her sarcasm cut through the room like the sharp unpleasantness of someone who'd passed gas at tea—everyone noted it, but they all looked away, unwilling to address it.

Except Edward. "Now, I don't think that we should be

making light of this situation, not if a little girl has gone missing."

"Sit down, Edward," came his mother's sharp response, but he didn't waver, even as Lucy Steele tugged on his jacket sleeve.

"I'm sure you searched your flat," Fanny said. "But—don't take this the wrong way—you don't exactly live in the nicest part of town, and—"

Her implication was too much.

"We don't live in the nicest part of town, because you drove us out," Elinor said, and she felt strangely calm as she said what everyone knew but would not voice. "You had every right to do so, but do not think that because the law was on your side that it was the *right* thing to do. I suspected you had little regard for us before, but now it's confirmed. If you won't help us now, then rest assured that you will never have to concern yourselves with us again, because from now on we renounce you. We renounce you all."

Elinor pinned John into his seat with the sheer force of her gaze, and he tried to avoid her eyes, but when he looked up and saw her, he froze. "Father would be so ashamed of you, John," she said, which was the cruelest thing she could think of. Then she turned on her heel and left.

Behind her, she heard Edward say, "Elinor, wait—" But he was told to sit down by both his mother and his sister, and she even heard Lucy Steele's voice in the mix, but Elinor didn't stop. She had no time for Fanny, no time for her disappointment of a brother, and no time for Edward and his empty entreaties.

Everyone in that room had let her down, and it was, as always, completely up to her to figure out this mess.

At the front door, she said to the butler, "If the staff finds a girl of eleven with brown curly hair, by the name of Margaret, I'd kindly ask you to send word to Number Thirty-six Barton Street. You might look for her in the library, or the attics."

He blinked slowly and then nodded at her. "I'll send a maid around, quietly," he said.

"Thank you." This small kindness caused the pressure behind Elinor's eyes to burst forth, and tears spilled down her cheeks. But she didn't linger.

She stepped out into the night, feeling more alone than ever.

SEVENTEEN

*In Which the Dashwood Sisters
Track Down a Rat*

MARIANNE FELT AS THOUGH her heart had not
stopped pounding since she saw Willoughby's name written in
Father's hand on the list Sir John had given her.

The memory of his kisses burned her now, and whenever
she pictured his smile she felt sick. There was plenty of time for
her to revisit every look, every word, every hope she ever carried
for Willoughby as she waited for Elinor and Mother to return.
She didn't even have the energy to pace the hall. She just sat on
the stairs and wallowed in her misery, in how easy it had been
for Willoughby to charm her. The most wretched part was how
quickly and easily she believed that he cared for her. No, the
most wretched part was the disappointment.

Marianne had so wanted to find her perfect romance.

Two quick knocks sent her scrambling for the front door, which she opened to find Elinor. "Well?"

"No one's coming," Elinor announced, her voice tight.

"What do you mean, no one's coming?"

"John won't help, Fanny told him not to." Elinor's words were strangely clipped, and Marianne merely stared at her older sister before realizing that Elinor was furious.

"That . . . *bastard*."

And rather than admonishing her sister, Elinor merely said, "I quite agree."

Marianne sank down on the stairs once more. "What are we going to do, Elinor? We don't know if she's been kidnapped, or if she's run off, or if this had anything to do with Willoughby or Father's death, or how any of it is even connected."

"Breathe," Elinor instructed. "Count to three, then release."

Marianne felt her breath come in hitching gasps, and Elinor's voice seemed to grow muffled, as if she were speaking from another room and not right next to Marianne. She was normally so good at storing facts and thoughts and ideas. She rarely felt paralyzed by indecision. But now it seemed that Marianne's hold on everything she knew was unraveling. Was this what it was like to fall into a swoon? She thought only young ladies vying for the attention of young men at balls swooned.

Then, Elinor's voice cut through the fog. "Inhale, count to three, and release." She kept repeating herself, and Marianne thought, *What is the use of breathing when Father is no longer drawing breath? When we don't know if Margaret is hurt or unsafe?*

But no matter how intrusive Marianne's worries, she held on to the soothing rhythm of Elinor's voice until she realized that she was breathing in time to Elinor's voice. She could feel Elinor's hand clutched in her own, the hard wood of the staircase beneath her, the dim hallway light. She took in the hall carpet, the candlelight, the door that had to be dead-bolted shut. The sad little hall table, which held a pair of her mother's gloves but nothing more. Once upon a time, the Dashwoods' hall table was full of calling cards, so many calling cards. Stewart would bring them to Mother to sort through, and . . .

The hall table was empty.

"Elinor," she said, startling her sister out of her litany of breathing exercises. "Did Willoughby call while we were out?"

Elinor raised an eyebrow. "Are you serious right now?"

"Yes! Did he call?"

"No," Elinor said, shaking her head emphatically. "I know you thought he was your knight in shining armor, but I think you really must let go of that idea. If Father was investigating him—"

"I know all of that. But I wrote him a note that I left on the hall table, and I told you and Margaret to give it to him if he called while I was out."

She saw the moment Elinor realized what Marianne was thinking. "You think he came to call and Margaret let him in?"

"She would have," Marianne said. "We told her she was old

enough to answer the door to people she knew. And she must have handed him the note—"

"And he kidnapped her? But wouldn't she have made a ruckus? You know Margaret!"

"I do," Marianne agreed. "Either way, we have a lead. And even if he has nothing to do with Margaret's disappearance, he has some answering to do."

She leapt to her feet and grabbed her cloak. "Well?" Marianne asked. "Are you coming?"

Elinor was already following. "Where are we headed, exactly?"

"He wouldn't take her back to his lodgings—I think we ought to look for him at this private club that Father was investigating." Marianne withdrew the list, which she'd copied word for word from the one Father had left with Sir John.

When Marianne opened the front door, she found Mother coming up the front steps. "Any luck?"

"No," Marianne said briskly, "but we think she might be with Willoughby. You need to fetch Sir John, and tell him to meet us at the last address on his list. Grey's, on Adler Street."

"Grey's, on Adler?" Mrs. Dashwood repeated. "What's that? How on earth did Margaret—"

"Trust us," Elinor added, hugging her mother tightly before releasing her to follow Marianne.

They tried hailing a cab, but it took three tries before someone would stop for them. They climbed in hastily, and

Marianne said, "Adler Street, please."

"Where on Adler?" the driver called back.

Marianne wasn't certain. "Just take us there, and we'll tell you where we want off."

The sisters sat in tense silence as the carriage sped up, the horses taking them where they needed to go far faster than their own two legs could carry them. When the driver pulled onto Adler Street, Marianne peered out, searching for any sign of this Grey's. A private club could look like anything. When nothing stood out, she called out, "You can drop us off here!" and the sisters clambered down. Elinor parted with a few coins to pay the driver, and as he pulled away with a disapproving mutter, they looked up and down the darkened street. It was likely a perfectly respectable street in the daytime, but now, being unfamiliar and dark, it seemed to hold menace in every shadowy corner.

"No street number for Grey's?" Elinor asked Marianne.

"No," she said as she surveyed the street, trying to decide which direction to turn. "We'll have to look about. It'll look respectable, but not too fine. It won't be too close to a residence, either. Look for someplace that has more horse manure out front."

"What?" Elinor asked, startled.

"It's a sign that horses and carriages stop frequently," Marianne said, deciding to head right. "Come on."

Marianne didn't let on, but she was growing more and more discouraged with each step they took. Why hadn't Father written down a street number? Was it because he didn't think it was important? Or had he, as a gentleman, been able to discern the location of this private club more easily than she could? Was it so well-known that he'd merely told his driver where to take him, and—

"Marianne," Elinor whispered. "Could that be it?"

She nodded at a graceful but small stone building ahead, where a man on a horse had just stopped. A young boy ran up and took the horse while the gentleman who'd just dismounted knocked on the door. It was immediately opened by someone that Marianne couldn't make out from this distance, and after a brief exchange the man stepped inside.

"Likely," she said. "Now, we just need to figure out a way in. I doubt they'll simply invite us inside if we knock."

"What if Margaret isn't there?"

"If she's not, then we find Willoughby, or someone who knows where to find him." Marianne felt more determined when she was infused with purpose. *The stable boy,* she thought. She should sneak up on him, try to twist some details out of him. Or better yet, bribe him. "Do you have a shilling I can borrow?"

"What for?"

"Information doesn't come cheap."

"Fine, but this is the last of it," Elinor warned, and dug through her reticule.

She'd just handed over a shilling when they heard a sound

that made them both start. It was a whistle, shrill and breathy and too close to be coincidental. Marianne looked right, then to the shadows in the left. "Who's there?" she asked, making her voice lower and deeper than natural.

A half-hearted whistle came from the gap between two shops, and then an exasperated sigh. The instant that Marianne recognized the whistler, Margaret stepped out of the shadows.

"What are you two doing here?" she asked, her voice accusatory.

"Margaret!" Elinor shrieked, and launched herself at their little sister. Marianne ran after her and pushed her sisters back into the shadows, looking out for unwanted attention.

"You had us worried sick," Elinor scolded, running her hands over their little sister's limbs, checking for injuries. "You could have been hurt out here all alone."

"I took measures," Margaret said, and proudly withdrew a fist-sized object from her pocket.

Marianne's eyes widened as she took in what looked like a clump of old wax. "Is that the smoke bomb that Elinor made for you?"

"I thought if I got into a scrape, I'd light it, and then use it as a diversion to get away."

Marianne couldn't help the snort of laughter that erupted out of her. The idea of her younger sister lobbing a smoke bomb on some nefarious man was too funny. But Elinor glared at them both.

"And how were you going to light that fuse? Do you have a flint in your pocket as well?"

Margaret's devious triumph melted into disappointment, with a hint of embarrassment. "Oh."

"*Oh* is right," Elinor huffed. "Why didn't you tell anyone where you were going?"

"I told you Willoughby was at the door. You said, *Mm-hmm.*"

"Oh," was all Elinor said in reply.

"And I said, *He's acting odd,* and you said, *Mm-hmm, all right then.*"

"Right," Elinor replied. "Well, you knew I was distracted."

Margaret didn't dignify that with a response. "I gave him Marianne's letter and he got very pale and I asked if he was sick, and he said no, but he had to go. So I decided to follow him."

"How could you do that without telling anyone?" Elinor's voice rose in pitch when she became angry. "You could have been hurt! We had no idea where to look for you."

"I left a note," Margaret said, pulling out of her hold with a scowl. "I told him that I might be able to find the address of where you went, and ran upstairs and dashed off a note and hid it under the loose floorboard in our bedroom, with my manuscript. Then I came back down and told Willoughby I couldn't find it. He left in quite a huff, and then I ran after him."

"Oh, excellent," Marianne said. "I definitely didn't think to look *under the loose floorboard,* did you, Elinor?"

"No, that wasn't the first place I would have thought to look either," Elinor responded.

"Well, it should have been." Margaret glared at her older sisters, never happy when they ganged up on her.

"Come along," Elinor said with a quick, sharp clap. "We'll go wait on that corner with the streetlamp until Mother arrives."

"Mother's coming *here*?" Margaret didn't budge when Elinor tried to pull her along.

"She's fetching us in Sir John's carriage."

"But how did you even find me, if you didn't get my note? Even I didn't know where I was going."

Elinor and Marianne exchanged a look. "We'll tell you later," Marianne said.

"But Willoughby is in there!" Margaret pointed at the building that Marianne suspected was Grey's. "He was being very odd, Marianne. He kept asking me about your investigation into Father's death, and where you were. I told him that it was none of his business, and if you wanted him to know, you'd tell him. Then he told me that I was an annoying brat who ought to be sent to finishing school. If you marry him, I'll hate you forever."

"No one is marrying Willoughby," Marianne gritted out, anger bubbling up in her. "That rat!"

Margaret continued, "In my story, Daisy Jones follows Lord Huckleberry when he meets the nefarious kidnappers to exchange the ransom for Lady Cecelia, and I decided that I ought to know what it's like to follow someone, too. I lurked behind a wagon until he climbed up in his curricle, then I grabbed on the back of it and he didn't even notice! I jumped off when he slowed down, except the stable boy saw and he spat on me! I've been here for *hours*, and Willoughby's not come out. Also, I'm hungry."

Marianne's anger had reached its boiling point. If Willoughby had something to do with her father's death, she'd kill him herself. She wasn't quite clear on the particulars at the moment, but one did not pull the wool over Marianne Dashwood's eyes and get away with it.

"Right, well, no one's had any supper because they've been looking for you, so we're hungry too," Elinor said, and Marianne was dimly aware of her herding Margaret toward the well-lit corner she'd pointed out earlier. "We'll get you home, and . . . Marianne?"

Marianne was not going to wait on a corner and go home like a good girl.

"Marianne, don't!" Elinor called out. "Let's go home, and sort this out later."

"No," she said, and her voice sounded strange to her own ears. "We settle this *now*."

And she left her sisters in the shadows and marched straight to the front door of Grey's.

EIGHTEEN

In Which the Dashwood Sisters Rather
Inadvertently Start a Brawl

"WHAT ARE YOU WAITING for?" Margaret asked.
"We have to go after her!"

Elinor felt as though she were made of stone. *Statue of a*
Young Lady Torn was what her inscription would read. All Elinor wanted to do was hold tight to Margaret, drag her home,
and put her safely to bed. But Marianne was her younger sister,
too. Elinor watched her retreating back and wished she could
get ahold of her as easily as she could Margaret.

"Come on," Margaret insisted, tugging Elinor after Marianne.

"Maybe you should . . ." She looked around, wishing that
Sir John would magically appear so she could entrust Margaret
to safety, but of course she had no such luck. She had to choose

between abandoning one sister or putting them all in danger.

Then she thought of Father. *Dashwoods are resourceful*, he would say.

She hoped that if they faced danger inside, they could be resourceful together.

"All right," Elinor agreed, and they both picked up their skirts to run after Marianne.

Elinor saw Marianne knock on the door and a man open it almost immediately, as if he'd seen her coming. There was a brief exchange that she couldn't hear, and then Marianne took a step forward. The man tried to block her entry, but he had no idea who he was dealing with. Marianne feinted left and then ducked right, disappearing inside. At this point, Elinor and Margaret were nearly to the front steps, and the man at the door was so shocked at being rushed by three very determined Dashwood sisters that he all but stepped aside to allow them entry.

Elinor grabbed hold of Margaret's hand, because the only thing worse than taking her youngest sister into a private club would be to lose said sister there. "Marianne!" she hissed in her most irritated and authoritative voice. She could see the back of Marianne's head about ten paces ahead.

The front door opened to a very fine foyer, with dark green wallpaper and heavy oil paintings of what looked like foreign landscapes—desert scenes, lush forests, and beaches that looked nothing like the pictures she'd seen of the English coast. But she barely had a chance to take them in because Marianne kept moving. Elinor and Margaret followed her into what appeared to be a large smoking room. A bar with white-gloved servers stood to the right, and armchairs, card tables, and billiard tables filled the rest of the room, along with the thick scent of tobacco smoke and . . . something else. Elinor's nose wrinkled involuntarily, but she couldn't place it.

"Marianne," Elinor whispered once they caught up with her. "We shouldn't be here."

Because that fact alone was obvious to Elinor. The room was full of gentlemen. Gentlemen of all ages, but *society* gentlemen. She recognized a few faces, some husbands of her mother's acquaintances, but was careful not to let her gaze linger on anyone. Marianne, it seemed, had no such qualms. Her gaze swept the room, searching for Willoughby. Elinor half hoped he would be there, because it was clear Marianne would not budge until she was satisfied he wasn't.

But what would she do if she found him?

A woman appeared at their left, seemingly out of nowhere. She was tall, blond, and stunningly beautiful, albeit in a sharp, pointed way. She wore a smile, but her green eyes were flinty. She was dressed in a beautiful slate-gray ball gown decorated with gauzy lace and dusted with pearls.

"Ladies," the woman said, managing to make the word

sound like a greeting and a reprimand. "I don't know who told you about our establishment, but it's impolite to enter without an invitation."

"We won't be staying long," Marianne said, barely glancing at her.

"Regardless," the woman said, stepping in front of Marianne. "There are other ways for young ladies to find what you're seeking. I can arrange an introduction."

Elinor didn't like this one bit. "Marianne," she tried again. "Let's just go."

"Willoughby?" Marianne called out, getting the attention of a few gentlemen nearby.

Elinor saw the imperious woman make a subtle gesture with her right hand, and she looked behind them. Two muscular men in ill-fitting jackets were approaching them from behind. "Marianne, we need to leave. Now!"

Elinor took her sister by the arm, but she kept calling Willoughby's name. It was as if she were oblivious to everything and everyone around her, she was so solely focused on this blasted man. Elinor would have liked to slap him for all the trouble he'd caused.

Marianne made her move, and since Elinor's grip was tight on both of her sisters, she was pulled along. Marianne tried to shrug her off, but Elinor decided it might be better to follow along, dragging Margaret as well, since those intimidating men had gotten too close. They spun past the gray lady as Marianne made a beeline for an armchair at the back of the room, where a befuddled Willoughby had just stood up.

"Marianne!" he exclaimed. "And . . . Miss Dashwood, Miss Margaret. What in the devil are you doing here?"

"I would like to know the same thing," the lady in gray said, marching after them. Elinor felt her face burn with humiliation—everyone was looking at them now.

"We followed you here," Marianne said, so mad she practically spit the words out. "Or rather, my younger sister followed you."

A few onlookers tittered and Elinor couldn't imagine what they were thinking.

"Oh," Willoughby said. The Dashwoods waited for him to elaborate, but he didn't.

"I have a few questions for you," Marianne said. "I would appreciate it if you came with us."

A man whistled, and Elinor would have liked to sink into the carpet.

"But . . . I haven't finished my . . ." Willoughby waved his hand toward an abandoned pipe on the table near where he'd been sitting.

"Leave it," Marianne hissed.

"I think that it's you ladies who ought to leave," the gray lady said.

Willoughby smiled, looking thoroughly unbothered. "Marianne, don't be upset. Being upset is just so . . . useless."

Elinor looked at Willoughby, properly this time. Had he been drinking? His eyelids were heavy and he smiled at her sister in a dopey, lovesick way. In fact, he looked rather *amused*.

"Don't bloody tell me not to be upset! I've got a lot of questions for you." Marianne made to lunge at him, but Elinor held her back.

"Marianne, my love. You can ask me anything."

"Don't call me that!" Marianne snapped, breaking free of Elinor's grasp. She advanced on Willoughby. "Are you drunk?"

At that, the entire room snickered.

"Drunk? No, Marianne, I'm better than drunk. I'm in the throes of ecstasy."

"What are you on about?"

Elinor looked more closely about the room, trying to push aside her embarrassment. She'd never intruded into the smoking rooms of any of the fine parties she'd attended before, so she had nothing to compare it with, but an awful lot of the men in attendance were sitting languidly in chairs, nursing drinks. A few card games and one round of billiards were underway, but the men were as subdued as if it were the end of the evening, not the beginning of it. The closest man looked up from where he was nursing a short glass tumbler of amber liquid, and it seemed to take a few moments for his gaze to focus on the Dashwood sisters.

"I think he means he's enjoying his laudanum high," Elinor said to Marianne. It all started to fall into place. Their father had come here looking for the Middletons' son, and he'd seen Willoughby because Willoughby took laudanum.

"What?" Marianne asked.

"Have you ever tasted it?" Willoughby said, draping his arm around Marianne. "You must try it sometime."

"How often do you come here?"

"Oh, don't worry—just a few nights per week."

Marianne tried to pull away from Willoughby, but he was leaning heavily on her. "Have you ever met my father?"

The question caught him by surprise. His smile turned into an awkward grimace. "No, I'm afraid not."

"Really?" she asked with mock surprise. "That's so peculiar, because I have it on good authority that he's visited this club before, and he made note of your name."

Laudanum did Willoughby no favors. His expression went from easygoing and relaxed to nervous, fidgety. Even Elinor could tell he was lying.

"Well, I might have seen him here, once," he hedged. "But we never *met*."

"Who's your father?" the lady in gray asked sharply.

Marianne looked to Elinor, and her eyes widened. Elinor glanced over her shoulder and saw that the two men the lady in gray had summoned earlier were now right behind them.

Marianne struggled to wiggle out of Willoughby's grasp. He was in no fit state, that was for certain. "Unhand her!" Elinor ordered, her protective instincts flaring. She tried to peel

Willoughby off of Marianne, but Willoughby clung even tighter. Finally Marianne gave him a great shove on the stomach. Her hand caught the edge of his waistcoat and as Willoughby doubled over, something fell out of his jacket. Something heavy and rectangular.

Margaret darted forward and snatched it off the floor. Elinor pulled Marianne away from Willoughby, already trying to chart a course out of the room. Perhaps it wasn't too late to excuse themselves and just leave this horrid place behind, let Willoughby rot here for all she cared. . . .

"Elinor!" Margaret gasped.

The oldest Dashwoods looked to her at the same time, and Elinor felt Marianne stiffen an instant before she realized what Margaret held.

A brown book. A brown book that looked suspiciously like their father's journal.

"Where did you get this?" Marianne spun around, half shrieking at Willoughby.

Willoughby was patting his coat, confused at what he'd just lost. He looked up and saw what the sisters had.

"Oh, bollocks," he muttered.

And that was when Marianne sent her fist flying into Willoughby's nose.

Elinor knew she should be shocked at her sister's actions—but she also couldn't help but admire the perfect arc Marianne's arm made. Willoughby's face contorted in comic shock as he did absolutely nothing to duck from her blow. Marianne snatched her hand back and shook it once, and then before anyone else could react, she brought her knee up suddenly, connecting right between Willoughby's legs. Just as Father had taught them.

That was the strike that finally felled Willoughby, and he writhed on the floor, moaning in pain. Elinor grabbed Marianne by the elbow, partly to ensure that she wouldn't go after Willoughby with her feet and partly because she saw the menacing men charge forward to intervene. She jumped back, attempting to drag her sister with her, but they got tangled with the gray lady's goons and Elinor lost her hold on both of her sisters. Someone shoved against her right side, sending her careening into an armchair, and she fell to the ground. She got right back up again, rubbing the spot on her thigh where the chair had rammed into her, and surveyed the room in horror.

Marianne was scrapping with Willoughby, the gray lady, and one of her goons. Onlookers had joined in the fray, and Marianne was screaming, "Don't let him go, he's a murderer!" Two men nearby began an argument and one threw a fist, prompting several more onlookers on either side to jump in. Soon it was a mess of brawlers, and Elinor stood frozen just on the edge of it all. No amount of society training or experience had ever prepared her for the moment in which she had to safely extricate her sister *from a fight* at a private club!

Speaking of sisters . . . "Margaret!" Elinor shrieked, drawing undue attention to herself. One of the goons took a step toward her, and Elinor felt like a small creature caught in the crosshairs of a much larger predator. But then she spotted her youngest sister beyond the melee, standing on top of the bar, waving her hand with Father's journal. Good, she was safe.

But that still left the matter of the advancing goon. Elinor held up her hands. "Please, we don't want any more trouble. I'll collect my sisters and leave, and you'll never see us again, I promise."

"Too late for that," he grunted, and lunged toward her.

Luckily, Elinor had the foresight to jump aside at the last possible second. She felt the man's hands brush past her shoulder as she twisted out of his reach. She skirted the roughest of the fighting and elbowed her way through a knot of rowdy men who had no interest in her to reach Margaret at the bar. The bartender was hunched down on the other side of the bar, swilling back a very full glass of port.

"How do we get Marianne out of here?" Margaret asked.

"I don't know, but you need to get out—"

"I'm not leaving either of you!" her little sister declared.

Elinor knew better than to waste time arguing. She could see that the gray lady's perfectly coiffed hair was now down in tangled curls, and her beautiful gown was ripped. Beyond her, Marianne was trying to kick at Willoughby while a goon stood at either side of her, holding her arms tightly in place.

They needed to get out of here. But first, they needed to free Marianne. And the only way she could see that happening was if she created a distraction. Something that allowed them all to leave.

Then she remembered they had just that.

"Give me the—"

Margaret was already thrusting the smoke bomb at Elinor. She found the bit of yarn she'd placed as a fuse and looked around for a candle, an exposed flame . . . anything. She found a lamp and lifted the glass shade so she could dip the wick into the flame.

"You stand right here, and watch for a clear way out when this goes off," she ordered Margaret. "I'm going to go in and grab Marianne, and when you hear my voice, shout until I get to you. Then we run, got it?"

Margaret grinned at the lit end of the smoke bomb. "I can't wait!"

Elinor grimaced, then tossed the smoke bomb into the ruckus—not too close to Marianne, but close enough that her captors would be distracted by it. It landed on a carpet near the closest brawlers, and at first, Elinor was certain that the smoke bomb's flight had snuffed the fuse. A third goon had grabbed Marianne by the ankles, and they appeared to be marching her toward a door on the other side of the room. Panic gripped Elinor as she jumped forward. "Marianne!" she shrieked.

Then the smoke bomb went off.

Flames leapt in the air as it hissed and sizzled, and a thick gray smoke oozed about the room. Nearly everyone stopped what they were doing to look in wonder and shock at the device, but not Elinor. She shoved through the throngs of men and ran toward her sister, who was back on her own feet again after the goon holding her ankles dropped them. The shout of anger turned into cries of alarm as the smoke rose in the room, making people cough and obscuring their vision. Elinor's eyes stung, but she kept her gaze focused on her sister.

Elinor didn't slow down as she reached Marianne—she plowed right into the man holding her right arm. He dropped her in shock as he was knocked off balance, and Marianne stomped on the other man's foot, then jabbed her elbow in his stomach for good measure.

"Willoughby!" Marianne shouted at Elinor, but Elinor didn't care if he died of smoke inhalation or escaped into the night. She grabbed her sister's hand and tugged her back into the smoky mess of the room.

"Head down, we need to move!"

She coughed as she ducked limbs and the more sensible men running back and forth, calling for water. Her smoke bomb flames seemed to be petering out, but the smoke itself was acrid and dense, and the panic of the club lent to the confusion as she tried to pull her sister through the crowd.

"Margaret!" she yelled.

"Over here!" came her little sister's voice. "Keep coming, straight on now, slightly to your left, yes! Another five steps and—"

But Elinor didn't catch whatever she was about to say because suddenly a man stood before her and she recognized Willoughby. "Wait!" he said. "Marianne, you have to understand—"

"Get out of our way!" Elinor snapped, her patience worn thin twenty minutes ago. She shoved past Willoughby, sending him off-kilter. Marianne gasped, and Elinor tightened her grip. "Don't go after him! We need to get out of here."

For once in her life, Marianne didn't argue. Elinor called out for her little sister and then was shocked to find Margaret materialize right beside her.

"That was brilliant!" she proclaimed. "You were brilliant— and the smoke bomb worked even better than I imagined. Only, I think it's started a real fire in here."

Panic leapt in Elinor's chest. The building's exterior was stone, but there was plenty of flammable material inside. Fires had minds of their own and could sweep through a room faster than one could blink. She grabbed Margaret and barked, "Let's go!"

Both of her sisters complied, and Elinor didn't even have to drag them out of the smoking room, which was now literally smoking. They emerged into the hallway and the front door was within sight, finally. They had almost reached it when Elinor heard a voice yell, "Oy!"

She glanced back and saw the gray lady, sooty and back-lit against a light that was burning far too brightly to be safe.

Smoke poured forth, and shouts rang out from behind her. Elinor faltered for a moment, and the gray lady shrieked, *"You set fire to my club!"* And then Elinor caught the shine of a pistol in her hand.

"Run!" Elinor screamed at her sisters.

Elinor heard the crack of a pistol shot, but she didn't pause to see where the bullet had landed. Margaret was ahead of her, running down the steps and into the streets, waving her arms about and shouting at the top of her lungs for help. Elinor thought that she made them look more like a target, but then again, perhaps if they could draw a respectable crowd outside, then that very, very angry woman wouldn't shoot at them again. Elinor and Marianne ran after Margaret, and they were nearly to the street when Elinor heard another pistol crack shatter the night.

And then, Marianne was no longer beside her.

It took Elinor a full five paces to feel her sister's absence at her side. She skidded to a stop and turned back to see Marianne crumpled on the ground, hands clutching her right side. An endless scream pierced the air, and Elinor ran back and pulled Marianne to her feet, but she kept toppling over. Elinor hoisted Marianne up and felt something hot and wet soak through her own dress, and she knew it was blood, but she couldn't look at it. She could only look around for help. She realized the scream was coming from her own mouth, but she couldn't silence it.

Marianne's face flashed pale and scared in front of her.

Margaret stood in the street, widemouthed in shock. Then a carriage slid down the cobblestones, and the driver pulled back the reins in alarm. Margaret was beside her, and there was blood on her hands and the carriage door opened and Sir John leapt out and behind him was Mother, and someone was pulling Marianne away from her and placing her into the carriage, but Elinor couldn't let go. Marianne was her sister, her responsibility. Marianne was . . . no, she couldn't think it. She wouldn't say it. If she didn't think it or say it, then it couldn't be true. But then she realized that she was no longer holding on to her sister, that everyone was in the carriage except her.

"Elinor!" Margaret yelled at her. "Get in! Now!"

Elinor did as she was told, feeling the echo of her scream deep in her bones.

NINETEEN

In Which the Dashwood Sisters
Face Their Darkest Hour

MARIANNE WAS NOT DEAD. Not yet, at least.

The atmosphere inside of Sir John's carriage was frantic. Margaret was crying, Elinor was in shock, and Sir John kept muttering, "Dear God," while their mother barked orders. "Give me your shawl, Elinor! Margaret, hold it tight . . . no, tighter—yes, right there against the wound. Marianne, can you hear me? Marianne, keep your eyes open, love. Talk to me."

"That . . . hag," Marianne gasped. "Shot me."

Hearing her sister's voice jolted Elinor out of her stupor. She added the pressure of her hands against the blood-soaked shawl and said, "It can't be the first time someone has wanted to shoot you."

"Just the first time . . . someone's been . . . successful,"

Marianne responded, her voice weak.

"We need a surgeon," Elinor said to her mother and Sir John. "Where are we headed?"

"Back to my house," Sir John said. "We can call for a surgeon there—"

"Your house is too far," Elinor said, remembering Marianne's complaint about traffic. "We need to take her home. A surgeon will be faster to fetch, too."

Of all the advantages to living on Barton Street, this had to be the most unexpected. Mrs. Dashwood nodded, looking alert for the first time in weeks. "Elinor's right—please, have your driver take us home."

Sir John leaned out and gave the order while Elinor applied more pressure to the wound. Marianne grimaced and then said, "Willoughby . . ."

"I will murder him with my own two hands," Elinor assured her.

"Willoughby!" their mother exclaimed in horror. "Did he do this?"

"I'll explain later," Elinor said, focused on her sister's irregular breathing.

"It's all my fault," Margaret added, a waver in her voice.

"It is not," Elinor said, because Margaret hadn't shot Marianne, and she wasn't about to let the youngest Dashwood claim the blame for this disaster. Truly, if anyone was responsible for putting her sisters in danger, it was Elinor. She was the oldest.

"Willoughby killed . . . Father," Marianne whispered.

"What?" Their mother's voice was high-pitched and sharp.

But Marianne couldn't elaborate. Her eyelashes fluttered shut.

"Marianne!" Elinor said. "Wake up, Marianne!"

She looked to her mother, who had gone white as a sheet. There was nothing more to say, really. Marianne was still breathing, but she was growing weaker. Elinor felt the salt of her sweat stinging her eyes, and hot tears slid down her face as she thought, *We're losing her, too.*

The carriage finally stopped at Barton Street with a shudder, and Sir John leapt out and began shouting to the driver for help. Mother rushed out to coordinate moving Marianne inside.

"Elinor!" came Margaret's gasp.

Elinor looked up from Marianne, certain that she was about to face even more terrible news and uncertain if her heart could take any more.

But instead, she saw a miracle.

Mr. Brandon stood up from where he'd been sitting on their stoop, forehead creased in alarm, his mouth a wide *oh*.

She didn't think about the suspicions surrounding Mr. Brandon and his involvement in Eliza's or her father's death— she only saw someone who could help. The word hadn't even formed on her lips before he leapt into action. He ran forward and picked Marianne up as if she weighed nothing at all and followed Mrs. Dashwood inside. Mrs. Dashwood was rather startled to see a strange young man carrying Marianne, but Elinor blurted out that he was a surgeon, and Mrs. Dashwood merely said, "Whatever you need, we'll provide it."

"Hot water, bandages, a sewing kit, shears, and brandy if you've got it," he said briskly, not even looking at Mrs. Dashwood as he carried Marianne upstairs. "And a pair of hands would be helpful."

Elinor looked at her mother. Mrs. Dashwood was swaying on her feet. "I'll help," she said firmly, feeling her nerves return to her.

Elinor directed Mr. Brandon upstairs and into the sisters' bedroom, where he placed Marianne on the bed. He kept the pressure on her wound while Elinor fetched him a sewing kit and shears from her sewing basket. Margaret ran in with a handful of towels and said, "Mother is boiling water."

"Towels on the bed, and keep the water coming until I tell you to stop," he directed. To Elinor he said, "Wash your hands thoroughly, with soap. Scrub at anything under your nails."

Elinor went to the washbasin and did as she was told, casting worried looks at Marianne. "Will she pull through?"

Mr. Brandon didn't look up, but after a moment he said, "It'll depend on where the wound is, and if the bullet is still inside her."

Elinor supposed that this was not good news, but it assured her to have information, a sense of direction. She rinsed her hands and dried them on one of the clean towels, then switched places with Mr. Brandon so she could hold the blood-soaked shawl to Marianne's wound while he washed his hands and then the shears she laid out. Marianne's face was gray and her eyes shut, but she was still breathing raggedly. If she died . . . if Marianne died . . .

No, Elinor wouldn't think about that.

Mr. Brandon wasted no time getting to work, using the shears to cut open Marianne's dress and her underthings, exposing the angry wound on her side. Elinor felt her empty stomach turn at the sight. The bullet had hit Marianne on her right side, and at first there was so much blood that Elinor thought it had torn up her sister's entire torso between her rib cage and hip. Mr. Brandon got to work, gently cleaning the wound and pouring water over her skin from the pitchers that Mother brought in.

"I think . . . ," he said, and let those words hang in the air between them. He kept wiping away blood and then gently rolled Marianne to her left side to inspect her back. "The bullet went right through. Well, actually the bullet didn't exactly enter as much as it brushed her side and left a nasty gash."

"Is that good or bad?" Elinor asked. Mr. Brandon was studying Marianne's wound, the violent red of her blood, and the puckering of her flesh against the white of her skin.

"It's good that the bullet wasn't left behind," he said, continuing to clean the wound. "But if it was a simple bullet wound,

I'd stitch it shut and we'd hope for the best. A wound this size, we can only dress. It might heal faster, but there's an increased chance of infection."

Infection. Elinor knew that infection could be just as deadly as a bullet to the heart, but it would be a slower, nasty death. She watched Mr. Brandon clean the wound, taking the blood-soaked towels from him and handing him fresh ones. When the wound was cleaned as best as they could manage, Mrs. Dashwood came in bearing the bottle of distilled alcohol that Elinor had purchased for her perfume making.

"Stay," Mr. Brandon implored Mrs. Dashwood. "Hold Marianne's feet."

Mrs. Dashwood nodded and grabbed Marianne's feet while Elinor's eyes widened in horror. "Why does Mother need to hold her feet?"

But Mr. Brandon didn't answer that question. Instead he told her, "I need you to hold her arms. Put your arm across her shoulder, hold her down if necessary."

Elinor did as she was told, looking down at her sister's pale cheek. "I'm so sorry," she whispered.

Mr. Brandon unstopped the bottle and trickled the contents directly on Marianne's open wound. Elinor had thought her sister was asleep, but the moment the alcohol touched her wound, she came awake with a great convulsion and a low, guttural groan that tipped toward a shriek as Mr. Brandon kept pouring. Mrs. Dashwood laid her upper body over Marianne's feet and Elinor struggled to maintain her grasp on Marianne's arms.

Mr. Brandon stayed focused, whispering, "I know, I know, I'm sorry. Almost. Almost there. And . . . done."

He set the alcohol bottle down and immediately began packing the wound with clean bandages, so many bandages. Marianne's body slowly relaxed, and Elinor gradually loosened her hold on her sister. She looked up to see Marianne's eyes, half-open, slide from Mr. Brandon to her, and she smiled encouragingly at her sister before Marianne's eyes fluttered shut once more.

Mr. Brandon finished bandaging the wound, and miracle of miracles, the blood did not soak through—not yet, anyway. "When she wakes, you must keep her as still as possible," he said. "The wound isn't very deep, but we can't risk it bleeding like that again. As it is, you must be very careful. Get honey to pack the wound. The new bandages must be boiled in water and completely dry before you apply them, and you should scrub your hands before and after you change them. We must be vigilant for the first sign of infection."

Mrs. Dashwood stood up, alarm drawing her face into a scowl. "You're not going to bleed her? And do you normally pour alcohol on someone's wound like that? I thought surgeons were supposed to heal, not hurt!"

"I don't have leeches with me, and I prefer not to use them if a patient has bled as much as she has tonight," he said. "As far as the alcohol, it's the most effective way of cleaning the wound. I know it was upsetting to watch, but it was necessary."

Mrs. Dashwood looked ready to protest, but Elinor stood and took her mother's hand. "We should trust him, Mother. Look at Marianne—she's alive still. She's bandaged. She can sleep now. If Mr. Brandon weren't here, she'd still be bleeding while we waited for another surgeon to arrive."

"You're right," she said faintly. "I'm sorry, Mr. Brandon. We are grateful."

He nodded, as if he were used to being interrogated by worried family members. "Brandy would help her with the pain. Or laudanum."

The mention of laudanum caused Elinor to go stiff. "No," she said.

"Trust me, she will need something for the pain," Mr. Brandon said.

"Something like morphium?" Elinor asked, the challenge obvious in her voice.

"Morphium," Mr. Brandon echoed. "But that's . . . that's what Eliza called her substance. But I didn't tell you that."

Marianne had accused Mr. Brandon of killing Eliza to steal her concoction, then killing their father to conceal that crime. But her evidence had come from Willoughby, who had stolen their father's journal and seemed to be quite familiar with laudanum himself. Suddenly, Elinor felt utterly and completely exhausted, as if she would faint if she didn't sit down.

"I think we should talk, Mr. Brandon," she said. "There's something I ought to show you."

Mrs. Dashwood looked between Elinor and Mr. Brandon, then back at Marianne. "Both of you clean up, then I want a thorough explanation of everything."

❦

After scrubbing her hands until they felt raw and setting her bloodstained dress to soak in a bucket of cold water, Elinor dressed once more and entered the kitchen. Mrs. Dashwood and Brandon sat at the kitchen table, his jacket gone to reveal a white shirt beneath that had only a few traces of blood smeared onto the fabric. Margaret sat at the head of the table like a miniature judge, Father's journal before her and Eliza's journal next to it. And Sir John was there, too, next to Mother.

"Who's with Marianne?" she asked, taking a seat next to Brandon.

"Hannah is sitting with her," Mother said. "She insisted she feels well enough, and we need to get to the bottom of this."

But before Elinor could even think of where to begin, Brandon asked, "Where did you get Eliza's journal?"

"Marianne found it," she said. "At the apothecary."

"What? But how—"

"She broke in," Elinor admitted. "With Willoughby."

"Willoughby?" Brandon shouted. "How on earth—"

"The same Willoughby your father took note of?" Sir John asked. "Did you see Vincent there?"

It was too much for Elinor. She rubbed her temple and said, "Hold on, do you know Willoughby, Mr. Brandon?"

"Unfortunately," he said, his tone stormy. "Mr. Willoughby was courting Eliza."

"What?!" Elinor looked up at him. "But you never said. There was no mention of him in Father's report. . . ."

"He was in the country when Eliza died. I mentioned his name to Mr. Dashwood, and I believe your father followed up to confirm he was visiting his aunt, but he was never a suspect."

"All right," Elinor said, reaching for the teapot that sat at the middle of the table. "I think it's best we start this story from the very beginning."

And for the second time, Elinor found herself explaining Marianne's suspicions, how they'd discovered the poison in Father's cup, and Elinor's experiments and Marianne's investigation. How Father's journal had been missing the entire time and how Marianne had met Willoughby. How Elinor had visited Brandon for information about the poison and how Marianne grew suspicious of Brandon, so she and Willoughby had broken into the apothecary . . . only to find Eliza's journal.

"But I didn't have it," Brandon insisted. "I don't understand."

"It never made any sense to me why you would," Elinor said. "And even if you did have it, you're smart and you wouldn't keep it in an obvious place."

"I think Willoughby planted it," Margaret said, causing all

heads to swivel in her direction. "I mean, he had Father's journal, too."

"But how did he get his hands on Eliza's journal if he wasn't even in town when it disappeared? And how did he have Father's journal?" Elinor looked about the table, as if expecting answers.

"Maybe he killed them both," Sir John said.

"But why?" Elinor asked. Her head felt stuffed full of cotton, and she was so frustrated she felt as though she might cry. This whole situation was a dreadful, illogical mess.

"Because he saw Willoughby at Grey's when he was looking for Sir John's son," Margaret said. The entire table turned to look at her. "I read it in his book."

There was a bit of clamoring then, and Margaret passed Father's journal over. Elinor got hold of it and flipped it open to the last page with writing, about three-quarters of the way in. Just the sight of her father's careful slanted handwriting made her want to linger, trace her fingertips over his pencil and ink strokes, but she focused on the words on the page.

Lead on clubs—private, deals in opium. Invitation required. Vincent a member?

Then there was a list of the clubs, exactly like the list that Marianne had showed her, the one that Father had left with Sir John. But next to each name were additional notes.

Roswell Place—est. three months ago

Webster's—no one would admit anything, bribe the
barkeep?

Groff House—informant promises Vincent was never a
patron.

Grey's—wouldn't let me in the door without invite, but
spotted Willoughby entering, related to Williams? Any
acquaintance with Vincent?

"Father saw Willoughby," Eliza murmured. "And he must have remembered him from Miss Williams's case. Officially, he declared her death an accident, but perhaps seeing Willoughby again shook something loose for him?"

"He told me if new evidence were to turn up, he'd take another look," Brandon confirmed.

Elinor wished that Marianne were awake and at the table, to help her test out theories. "What if Willoughby *was* involved in her murder? He knew she was on to something in her work, a new substance that would be even stronger than laudanum—maybe even stronger than eating opium on its own. Perhaps he killed her for the formula, and somehow he escaped detection by making people believe he was in the country. A year passes, and then he sees Father scoping out Grey's. He thinks Father is on to him for Eliza's murder, and so he decides to kill Father, not realizing that Father was investigating a completely different case."

323

Elinor looked about the table. Margaret was wide-eyed in horror, and Mother's lips had set into a hard line. Brandon looked very weary. And Sir John was stricken, shock and horror mingling on his face.

"It explains everything," she added meekly, almost sorry that it all made horrid sense. "He found a way to get to know Marianne, perhaps in an attempt to make sure we weren't suspicious. But when Marianne revealed that she believed Father was murdered, he needed a scapegoat. So he convinced Marianne that Mr. Brandon must be responsible."

"It's my fault, then," Sir John whispered.

"Nonsense," Elinor said. "You hired him to find your son. You had no idea this would be the result."

Mrs. Dashwood nodded in agreement and placed her hand over Sir John's. "You did nothing wrong."

"We should go to the authorities," Elinor added. "Willoughby, wherever he might be, needs to be stopped."

"Leave it to me," Sir John said, standing. "I shall pay the magistrate a visit myself. I'd certainly like to ask Willoughby a few questions and track down the owner of that club. . . ."

"There was a lady," Elinor added. "She was the one who shot Marianne. She said something about how we set fire to her club. Willoughby must have been working for her."

Elinor struggled to remember more, but exhaustion was making her sluggish. Mother stood to see Sir John out, and

Elinor looked to Brandon. He was staring at Eliza's journal.

"I think she did it," Elinor said. "I read her journal, and I followed her experiments. I made the morphium she wrote about."

Elinor nodded at the bottles of the substance she'd concocted, sitting on the shelf next to the table. Brandon followed her gaze and smiled slightly.

"I knew she'd manage it," he said. "I just never imagined that it might get her killed."

"What does it do, though?" Margaret asked. "If it's something that kills people, then why would she want to make it?"

"It's not supposed to kill people," Brandon explained gently. "It's supposed to help them. It's the purest form of opium that we know of, and when you use just a tiny bit, it is supposed to help ease pain. Too much and it makes you sleep. Sometimes forever."

"The sample I gave you," Elinor said, not sure how to frame her question.

Brandon nodded, then looked at Margaret with a small bit of trepidation. "Let's just say that it makes for a very effective rat poison."

"Fascinating," Margaret remarked, surprising Brandon. "So a whole bottle of what Elinor made could kill someone?"

"If they took it all at once," Brandon confirmed. "What are you writing down?"

"Notes," Margaret said, getting up from the table and running off without explanation.

"She's a budding novelist," Elinor explained, too tired to get into it. "She writes mysteries and adventures where someone is always in peril. I'm afraid the events of the last few weeks have given her far too much material."

To her surprise, Brandon laughed at that. "You Dashwood sisters are full of surprises."

Elinor smiled weakly, and Brandon seemed to take this as his cue to leave. "I'll check on Miss Marianne once more before I go, and come back first thing in the morning. But don't be afraid to send for me if her condition changes."

Elinor followed him upstairs. Hannah looked up from her seat next to the bed when she saw them and stood. "She's resting easy, miss. She's a strong one, our Miss Marianne."

"Yes," Elinor said, and for the first time all evening she felt she might really have a good cry. Something about the sight of her sister, lying in bed looking so innocent but poised on the knife edge of life and death, undid her.

She took Hannah's spot and reached for Marianne's hand. When she glanced up to ask Brandon about when she might wake and how soon they ought to change the dressing, the question died on her lips. Brandon was staring down at Marianne with a tenderness she'd never before seen on his serious face. The candlelight glinted against his spectacles, and Elinor tilted her head to try to get a better look at his face; but then it was as though a curtain were drawn on his emotion, and he looked to her, stoic once more. "We have every reason to be hopeful, Miss Dashwood," he pronounced.

"Wait," she said as he turned to go. She wanted to ask him about that strange look on his face, but she didn't quite know how to frame her question without sounding rude. Instead, she asked, "What brought you to our door tonight? I won't complain— your timing saved Marianne's life, I'm sure of it. But . . ."

Brandon nodded. "I'm glad I was there, but don't thank my timing. Thank Mr. Edward Farrows."

Shock made Elinor's mouth fall open. "How do you know Mr. Farrows?"

"I'm afraid I don't," he said. "But I had closed up the apothecary for the evening when I received an urgent message from him that the Dashwood sisters were in need of help, and that our mutual acquaintance Mrs. Jennings believed that I could be of assistance."

And with that, he slipped out of the room, leaving Elinor's head spinning. Mrs. Jennings! She recalled now that the older woman had been seated in the corner of the sitting room when Elinor had burst in on Fanny's dinner party. But she couldn't think on the circumstances and what they meant—she was too weary. She leaned forward in her chair, laid her head on the pillow next to her sister's, and fell into a deep sleep.

TWENTY

In Which the Dashwood Sisters Receive Some Unexpected Callers

ELINOR WOKE TO A gentle hand shaking her shoulder. Her back ached and there was a crick in her neck. Why was she sleeping sitting up? What time was it? What day?

Then she remembered: Marianne!

She sat up with a start and her mother's voice, "Shhhh, it's all right."

"Marianne?" Elinor rasped.

"She's sleeping," Mother whispered. "See?"

Elinor blinked the sleep out of her eyes and saw that it was midmorning—the light bathed the bedroom in a pleasant yellow, an effect somewhat tempered by the metallic smell of old blood. Marianne's head was tilted to the left, her arms laid out carefully at her sides with the coverlet tucked neatly around her. Elinor studied her sister until she saw the gentle rise and fall of her chest and turned to see Mother holding a steaming cup of tea.

Mother pressed the tea into her hands and then tilted her head to the door. "Let Margaret sit with her awhile. We need to talk."

Margaret took Elinor's place, dragging in her writing box. Elinor could only imagine the tales that last night's escapades would inspire. Elinor followed Mother downstairs, where Hannah had laid the table with breakfast, and she gulped her tea so quickly that she burned the roof of her mouth. "Marianne looked well, don't you think?" she asked her mother. "I think she might pull through. She's very stubborn."

"She's not my only stubborn child," Mrs. Dashwood said, "but yes, I think we have every reason to be hopeful."

This reassured Elinor, but it didn't make her feel better. "I'm so sorry, Mother."

"For what, dear?"

"Everything!" Elinor burst out. "Everything just got so out of hand, and I never imagined that anyone would get shot. If Marianne doesn't pull through, I'll never forgive myself. As it is, I don't know how I can. . . ."

"Oh, my Elinor . . ." Her mother sighed and took Elinor's hands in her own. "You take on so much responsibility for us all."

"Of course I do," Elinor said, blinking back tears. Why did

Mother make it sound as though that were a bad thing? "You're my family."

"Yes, and your love for us is one of the reasons why I love you, but my dear, your sisters have minds of their own, and their decisions are not yours. Neither are their consequences."

"So it was Marianne's fault that she was shot?" Elinor asked.

"Heavens, no! The blame for that lies solidly on the woman who shot at you, and I'll let Willoughby share in it as well. All I mean is that you can only look after the ones you love within reason, and you cannot punish yourself for when bad things happen. Why, imagine if you hadn't been with Marianne! I don't think she would be with us right now if not for you, Elinor."

Elinor hadn't thought of it like that, and she remembered her indecision outside of Grey's, as she watched Marianne march in alone. She had thought she made the wrong decision because she put Margaret in danger when she went after Marianne, but Mother was right—it could have been so much worse for Marianne if they hadn't followed her. If it hadn't been for Margaret remembering to grab the smoke bomb, and Elinor creating a diversion, and Margaret directing them out of the fray . . .

Dashwoods really were resourceful. And they worked better together.

"Now, I'm afraid that I must ask you to forgive me," Mother said, her voice wavering and strained. "I have been the worst kind of mother lately."

"What! No, Mother . . . you lost your husband."

"And you girls lost your father. I would hate to think that you felt like you lost me as well." Mrs. Dashwood wiped tears from her eyes, but she managed a small smile. "You've looked after us so well, but I shouldn't have made you feel as though you were responsible for taking care of us all."

Elinor opened her mouth to say . . . well, she wasn't quite sure what, exactly. Not *It's all right* or *Don't worry about it*. No, because the truth was, things were not all right and Elinor was exhausted from worrying about it all. She wanted to share the burden a bit. She wasn't quite sure what would happen to them next—she was already worried about their finances, and she wasn't sure how they would pay for prolonged care for Marianne—but she was grateful to have Mother. Here, upright, dressed, and tidy, looking a bit more clear-eyed and like her old self. Sadder, a bit more haunted maybe. But when Elinor looked at her mother, she was reminded that although she and her sisters carried their father's name, they got their strength from their mother, too.

"Now tell me everything that happened last night when you went after Margaret," Mother said, setting eggs and toast in front of Elinor. "Margaret has told me her side of things, but that girl does love to embellish, and I want a sensible account of events."

Elinor laughed a little at that and began her explanation once more, filling in the gaps from her account last night and Margaret's dramatic telling. Of all the things that Elinor had to tell her, Mother was most amazed at the smoke bomb.

"And you made that?" she asked. "You made it, in the kitchen here?"

"Well, no," Elinor said. "I made it in my laboratory, back . . ." She had been about to say *home*. "Before."

"I knew you liked to experiment," Mother said, "but I always thought it was perfumes and less . . . volatile substances."

"I have been experimenting with perfume," she said. "But Marianne says I'm miserable at it. The last concoction I gave her actually made her retch. I think she was putting me on, though."

"But do you want to be mixing perfumes?" Mother asked. "Or do you want to be mixing substances like Miss Williams, or making explosives for Margaret?"

"I'm hardly making explosives for Margaret," Elinor protested. "And perfumes could be a viable side business for us, actually—"

"Elinor," Mother said sternly.

Elinor opened her mouth, but for some reason it was too difficult for her to simply say what was in her heart. It was impossible. Or nearly impossible. She was needed here, at home. She ought to spend her time on activities that could help her family. And yet . . .

"I think, perhaps, one day . . . if it's possible, that is . . . I'd like to study chemistry."

She said the words while looking down at her plate. Mother reached out and touched her chin, so Elinor had to look at her.

"All right then," Mother said. "I don't know how, or when, but let's see what we can do about making that happen, hm?"

Elinor didn't think that her mother would have ever been so accepting of her unconventional dream, and happiness bloomed inside her. But it was nothing compared with the joy she felt when they heard Margaret thunder down the stairs a moment later, calling out, *"Mother! Elinor! Marianne's awake!"*

They abandoned their breakfasts in an instant and ran upstairs, jostling past one another to get at Marianne's bedside first. Marianne appeared weak and woozy, but she smiled when Elinor and Mother came into the room. "How do you feel?" Elinor and Mother asked at once.

Marianne's face tightened in pain, but she whispered, "Alive. And feeling it."

Elinor laughed and squeezed her sister's hand while Mother felt her forehead. "You don't seem feverish, which is a good sign. How's your pain?"

"Oh . . ." Marianne sighed. "It only feels like someone stuck a hot poker in my side."

"That's not far off," Elinor told her. "The bullet cut right through there."

"Marvelous," Marianne breathed.

"We thought you were going to die," Margaret added.

"Not today," Marianne said, wincing as she attempted to sit up. "I don't think."

"Don't try to move," Elinor ordered. "We'll have to change

the bandages and you should save your strength for that."

"Take some of this," Mother said, already uncapping the laudanum bottle.

Marianne opened her eyes, and when she saw what was in Mother's hand, she looked horrified. "No! I won't."

"There's no glory in pain," Mother admonished, but Marianne was shaking her head.

"That concoction is what made Willoughby so . . . horrid in the end."

"It's medicine," Mother insisted. "Elinor, tell her it's safe."

Elinor pursed her lips, because she wasn't sure what to say. After hearing about Sir John's son, and seeing how despondent it made Mother, she was rethinking just how innocuous laudanum was. Was Willoughby similarly dependent? Had all of the people in attendance at Grey's last night also felt a craving for laudanum that couldn't be denied? If it was so dangerous, why was it sold in every chemist, grocer, and tobacco shop?

If something as dangerous as the poison that had killed Father had been derived from the same substance, surely laudanum ought to be treated with care, if not distrust.

"I don't know," Elinor admitted. "And we can't make her take it if she doesn't want it, Mother. But Marianne, when we clean the wound again, it's going to hurt a lot. You might want a little bit. Last night when Brandon dressed the wound, I thought you were in agony."

"Brandon!" Marianne looked more alert than she had all

morning. "He didn't. But . . . was I even decent?"

Elinor laughed. "Trust you to almost die on us and worry about whether or not Brandon saw anything of you he shouldn't."

"Oh God," Marianne moaned. "I can never look him in the eye ever again."

"Good luck with that, he'll be around today."

Marianne's dramatic moans turned into a small yelp of pain as her movements pulled at her wound.

"All right, that's enough," Mother said, clapping her hands together once. "Margaret, Elinor, let your sister rest. Marianne, I won't make you take any laudanum . . . right now. But you'll take a tiny bit if you're in serious pain, do you understand me?"

Marianne grimaced, but she nodded. "I think I'll sleep now, Mother."

Elinor lingered, wanting to sit by her sister. But Mother shooed her out of the room. "You sat up with her all night long. Let me."

In the hall, Margaret looked up at Elinor and said, "Would you have said that the flames last night were my height? Or closer to Marianne's height?"

"Why?" Elinor asked.

"Well, it would be *much* more dramatic if I could say that they were approximately Marianne's height, as Lady Cecelia is modeled after her."

"Oh, is she?" Elinor asked.

"I'll just say they were *nearly* as tall as Lady Cecelia,"

Margaret decided. "It's dramatic without outright lying."

And with that, she ran downstairs.

Elinor shook her head and followed, but she was stopped by the sound of a knock on the front door. Her first thought was not Brandon, or even Sir John with news about Willoughby, but Edward. Edward, who apparently hadn't merely sat down and done nothing after she had left her former home. He had helped, albeit in an indirect way. But that indirect way had saved Marianne's life, she was sure of it.

She rushed to the front door, not even caring that it was far too early for a social call. She opened it, expecting Brandon but secretly hoping for Edward.

But it was neither.

"Miss Steele!" Elinor exclaimed at the sight of the other woman, dressed in another one of her alarming frocks. This one was lavender and mint green, and with her blond curls pinned up beneath a wide green bonnet, she looked like the picture of a country shepherdess. "Did we . . . have an appointment?"

Elinor remembered no such thing, and she was fairly certain she would recall if Lucy Steele was planning on calling. But the events of the previous two days had quite scrambled her mind.

"Oh, no," Miss Steele said, and stepped inside without being asked. "I simply had to come and see if you were all right." Her voice dipped as she added, unnecessarily, "After last night."

Last night. Elinor sucked in an audible breath, although Lucy had no way of knowing that telling off her sister-in-law was the least dramatic and traumatic event of her evening.

"We are . . . well enough," she said. "How very kind of you to check in."

But she didn't have the feeling that it was kind. Lucy stepped toward the drawing room and Elinor followed her, feeling helpless and baffled as to how to handle her. What was even more baffling was that Edward would like her. Lucy seemed too silly, too vain . . . too much like Fanny.

"Apologies for the mess," Elinor said faintly as Lucy took in the destroyed settee cushions, but she didn't offer any further explanation. She was suddenly grateful for her instinct to guard her heart. She liked Edward, but when it came down to it, she wanted someone who would leap to her aid when she asked, not send a friend along after the fact.

It was disappointing, but Elinor had learned to live with disappointment lately.

"Well," Lucy said, settling into a seat. "Tell me everything. Did you find dear Mary?"

"Margaret," Elinor corrected. "And yes, we did. Thank you."

"Why, that's wonderful news! Why do you look so glum, dear?"

Elinor wavered, not quite sure what she ought to divulge.

The last thing her family needed was for the ton to be whispering that Marianne Dashwood had been shot leaving a disreputable establishment while searching for the youngest missing Dashwood.

"I merely had a long night, that's all," Elinor said, but keeping a polite smile on her face required more effort than usual.

"Understandable. Sit down, you look absolutely wrung out. Have you slept a wink all night? The important thing is that Margaret is home safe." Lucy emphasized Margaret's name as if she expected praise for remembering it. "Wherever did you find her?"

"Oh," Elinor said, sitting and arranging her skirts in an overly fussy manner while her mind raced. "It was as we thought. She had grown homesick and had tried to find her way home—er, rather, to my brother's house. Marianne and I found her wandering the streets, quite lost."

"Oh my!" Lucy gasped. "London streets can be quite dangerous. How fortuitous that you were able to find her. Is she unharmed?"

"Quite," Elinor answered.

"And Marianne, how is she?"

Elinor regarded Lucy Steele. Was she exceptionally tiresome, or was she fishing for something? What had Edward told her? It was possible, Elinor thought, that Brandon had reported back to Edward about Marianne's injury and that Edward had sent Lucy to inquire about them rather than simply come himself. If that was the case, then Edward was certainly not the person she thought he was.

"Marianne was injured over the course of last night's misadventure," Elinor said, watching Lucy for a reaction. The other woman widened her eyes and her mouth formed an exaggerated *oh*.

"Is she going to be all right?"

"We're optimistic that she'll make a full recovery."

"Oh, thank heavens for that!" Lucy said. "I would absolutely hate it if anything happened to you both. You've been so helpful to me, and my life is looking up in so many ways. I don't know how I could ever repay you."

Elinor felt a piece of her heart break off inside of her, but she let it go. Why should she be heartbroken over Edward choosing Lucy Steele, when he proved himself weaker than she'd like? He and Lucy Steele deserved one another.

"I'm so glad to hear that," Elinor said. "Especially considering that I'm not certain when my sister and I will be able to resume work. But I trust that you have no further use of our services?"

Lucy giggled. "No, I think that my days of scouting suitors are over, thanks to you and Marianne. Speaking of, would it be possible for me to look in on her and thank her for her help?"

"Oh, I don't think so," Elinor said, shocked that Lucy would even ask. Even if they would be related (distantly, by marriage) soon enough—and that was quite the daunting thought—it was impudent of her to even ask.

"I promise I won't stay long," Lucy insisted. "I just want to reassure her that she has friends that care about her."

Elinor heard a brisk knock at the front door and looked to the hallway, momentarily distracted. Then she turned back to Lucy. "Your concern is so flattering," she said. "But Marianne is sleeping, and I think it's best if—"

"Sleeping? At this hour? Now, I know she has a penchant for injuries, but don't tell me it's so serious."

The knocking started up again, relentless and urgent. Elinor looked about, as if a servant would answer it, but of course there was only Hannah and she was recovering from her own injury. What if it was Brandon, returned with word about Willoughby?

"Excuse me," she said, "I really must—"

"Don't worry about me. I shall just pop up and look in on Marianne, how about that?"

"Miss Steele, I really don't think—"

The knocking escalated to thundering.

"Fine!" Elinor said, trusting that Mother would see that Lucy didn't overstay her welcome.

Elinor went to answer the door and wrenched it open amid a flurry of knocking. Edward came tumbling toward her and she had to take a giant step backward to avoid being bowled over by him.

"Mr. Farrows!" she exclaimed, her traitor heart stuttering at

340

the sight of him. "Why on earth are you pounding on my door like a madman?"

"Elinor!" he gasped. "Did you find Margaret?"

"Yes," she said, but she was distracted by the dark bags under his eyes that made him appear at least five years older. He looked as though he'd dressed in haste, his cravat limp and his coat misbuttoned. "Are you all right?"

"Thank God," he said, and sagged in relief. "You cannot imagine how worried I've been since last night."

"No," Elinor said, a tiny laugh of disbelief escaping her. "I cannot imagine it. In fact, I would have thought that you were rather ambivalent about our fate."

Elinor expected Edward to look hurt, or defensive, or attempt to charm her—that was what Willoughby or her brother might have done. Instead, Edward nodded, shoulders slumped. "I'm deeply sorry that it's taken me this long to find my courage. I come here with no expectations, and I don't expect that you'll forgive me, but I do owe you an explanation."

Well, that was rather dramatic. And yet her curiosity made her relent. "Come in. You might as well sit down. Lucy is—"

"Lucy Steele is a criminal!" Edward burst out.

"What?" Elinor stepped into the drawing room, Edward on her heels. But Lucy wasn't there. "She was just . . . but what makes you—"

"I've been a fool," Edward said, pacing in the tiny space before the front window. She'd never seen him so animated. "I was never truly interested in her, you must understand. From the moment we met, there was something about you, Elinor. I was . . . *enchanted* feels like such a strong word, but I don't know a better way of putting it." He stopped pacing and looked at her, truly looked at her. "All I knew was that I wanted to help you, and get to know you better. Trust me when I say I normally dislike anyone I meet through my sister, but you are the shining exception."

Elinor merely stared back. There was no response in any etiquette guide she knew of for when the young man you'd secretly been pining after announces that he is secretly pining for you as well.

Edward continued, heedless of Elinor's shock. "I didn't confess my feelings because I worried it would be insensitive. You were in mourning, in the midst of a major life change. I tried to argue on your behalf with my sister, to allow you and your family to stay on in your own home. I admit it was selfish—I hoped to see more of you, and that with time, as the acuteness of your grief eased, you might once more look to the future and maybe . . . maybe I would be in it."

Forget propriety, Elinor's mouth was hanging open now.

"I'm sorry if you felt pressured to dance with me the other night," he continued. "That was not my intention. And when you left, I could have kicked myself for being such a fool."

"But you . . . Miss Steele?" Elinor found herself unable to formulate complete sentences.

"I was merely being polite. I thought I had wasted my one chance with you, and she was your friend, and if I danced with her, then you might . . . well, never mind. Because she tried to *blackmail* me."

Elinor laughed. She didn't think but merely reacted. "Lucy?" she asked. "Lucy Steele? Blackmailed you?" Were they thinking of the same person?

Edward reached out, took Elinor's hands in his own, and guided her to the settee Lucy had occupied minutes earlier. "At the ball, you surprised me by asking about my position at Hillenbrand."

Here it would come—the excuses, the explanations.

But Edward said, "I haven't been entirely transparent, and I let my sister tell your family lies about my employment. I'm sorry."

"But . . ." An apology was not what Elinor had expected. "Why?"

He drew in a slow, deep breath and said on the exhale, "The firm let me go."

"I gathered that," Elinor said, surprised to find that she sounded a bit like Marianne when she was making a sarcastic comment. "Marianne, well . . . she's been investigating various matters. She was the one who dug up the information, and she discovered that you'd been fired. I didn't want to believe it, but when you never returned my letter, and then I confronted you at the ball . . ."

Elinor felt faintly embarrassed to admit that they'd been investigating Edward, but he didn't seem put out. Instead, his face fell. "I'm sorry that you found out that way, Elinor. I knew that if I had any hope of a future with you in it, I would have to tell you the whole story, and I wanted to—I still do, if you'll hear it."

He was looking at their interlinked hands, and Elinor squeezed gently. "Tell me."

"We had a very important client," he began. "Mr. Alistair. His business interests were worldwide. My boss was in charge of his account, and it took months before he'd let me even fetch records on it. Mr. Alistair's business dealings were kept very confidential."

Elinor felt a prickling at the back of her neck. "What happened?"

"I was finally deemed worthy," Edward said with a small ironic smile. "I was eager. I knew he was very important to the firm—so important that if he took his business elsewhere, the firm might not survive the loss. At first, I wasn't privy to everything. But I began to pick up on small details. Goods from foreign shores, establishments of ill repute here in London, and exorbitant profits. I'm not sure how much I ought to say—it's hardly drawing room talk."

"You can't shock me so easily," Elinor assured him. He had no idea what she knew about backroom dealings, poison, and murder!

"Well, the short of it is that I learned that Mr. Alistair makes his money in the trade of opium poppy, and he uses violence to get his product by whatever means necessary," Edward stated.

"Oh," Elinor said faintly. Opium. It all came back to the dreadful opium.

"I read letters about what he did to acquire his fields in Turkey—the dishonesty, the unfair taxation, and the violence. All so he could export it. And not just back to England, but to America and elsewhere, where it is most definitely illegal."

"*Oh,*" Elinor said again. What else was there to say?

"The things I learned—unspeakable. I wanted no part in it, Elinor. And I told my mentor as much. I tried to appeal to his morals, but he merely laughed at me. He said that no one likes to see how the sausage is made, but everyone is all too happy to benefit. And I said that I would not benefit. I gave my notice. And I threatened to go to the papers."

"Did you?"

Edward shook his head, a small, terse gesture. "No. They said that if I did that, they would file a counterclaim that I was caught embezzling funds, and they'd ruin my reputation. The East India Trading Company has been seizing opium in India for decades, and they make a tremendous amount of money off the backs of the poor and those they beat down. And no one in London cares. We all love laudanum too much."

"It always comes back to opium," she murmured.

"What do you mean?"

"Never mind," she said. It would take too long to explain. "So you were let go?"

"I agreed to leave quietly, but I'm being blacklisted by the entire industry," he said with a wry laugh. "Mother is certain that a little bit of time and money can once more open some doors, but Fanny is furious with me for ruining my chance at Hillenbrand. Neither of them cares about what is really happening. They only want to mitigate any potential damage."

"And Lucy Steele?" Elinor prodded, failing to understand how she could know anything about this. The woman was conniving, yes, and she was likely getting on Mother's last nerve upstairs. But Edward wasn't even on her list of eligible bachelors until the Dashwoods brought him to her attention—how on earth did she fit into all of this?

"I don't know how she gets her information," Edward said. "One moment we are dancing and talking about what a pleasant ball it is, and the next she's telling me how terrible it is that I've been sacked. I was too shocked to form words—I hadn't thought the news had gotten out. Then, she claims that she doesn't mind, she's happy to help me keep it quiet, and then she insinuated that an attachment could form between us, and that we ought to let the gossips talk about me asking her for a second dance, unless I wanted people gossiping about my business failings."

Elinor cringed. "I have no idea how she knows. She led me

to believe she had only heard of you in passing."

"How do *you* know her?"

This was the awkward bit. "She, ah . . . hired us?"

"To blackmail me?" Now it was Edward's turn to look betrayed.

"No! Heavens, no. Dashwoods don't do blackmail."

"Then what did she want?"

Elinor knew he wouldn't like her next answer any better. "She wanted help finding a husband. A few discreet inquiries, some introductions."

Understanding dawned on Edward's face, and Elinor wished she could take it all back. "And so you introduced me to her?"

"I didn't want to!"

Elinor's outburst surprised even herself, but Edward just shook his head. "She's good. She didn't have to make demands—she merely told me what she wanted, and then implied that unless I complied, she would tell about my business dealings. She finagled an introduction to my mother, and a dinner invitation from Fanny. When you burst in last night, she whispered into my ear that the only thing more scandalous than me running out on dinner would be the world knowing I'd been caught embezzling, and questioning all of my connections. And Elinor, I truly believed that she would tell those lies. I wanted to come after you, but I'm not the only one that could come to harm if her lies got out—they could potentially hurt you, too.

Your family has been through so much."

"Oh," Elinor said for a third time. It wasn't a nice explanation, but it did make a sad sort of sense.

"That doesn't make what happened right, though. John tried to go after you, but Fanny stopped him. Mrs. Jennings intercepted me and said I ought to get word to a Mr. Brandon. I stepped out to tell my driver to send word to him, and then I went inside and stood up to my mother."

Elinor felt her breath catch in her throat. "You did?"

"I told her that I was never going back to Hillenbrand, nor was I going to continue to look for a position at any of the other firms she has picked out for me. And then I said that I wasn't interested in being a part of a family that cared so little for their members."

"What did they say?" Elinor could imagine Fanny's sour expression—as though she'd been sucking on lemons.

"My mother gave me three days to get my act together before disowning me!" he said with false cheer. "So I am disowned, because I won't be changing my mind. My prospects are grim. I have no hope of providing a home or being able to marry in the near future. All I have is a small inheritance from my father, but it won't last forever. Miss Steele has likely already tipped off the papers and the gossips, like she promised she would, so I might not even have my reputation for much longer."

"Oh, Edward," Elinor murmured, her heart softening to his predicament. Yes, he'd hurt her, even when he tried to do the opposite. But he was a good man, just as she'd thought. Just as she'd hoped.

"I came to beg your forgiveness," Edward said. "I got so caught up in my own worries and problems and last night I acted like a coward, not a gentleman. I'm ashamed of it, and I'm truly sorry."

"I forgive you," she said. "But Lucy—"

"I don't care what she does to me!" Edward proclaimed.

"Oh dear," Elinor said. "Well, I hate to be the bearer of bad news, but Lucy is *here*. She's upstairs, visiting Marianne."

Edward's eyes widened in shock and he stood suddenly. Elinor missed his closeness immediately. "Oh!"

"I'm sorry, too," Elinor said. "I didn't really want to introduce you two. It's just . . . well, it's a long story, and I felt as though I had no choice. But I would like to explain it to you, sometime."

Edward smiled slowly. "I would like that. But I think that perhaps I ought to leave. Matters with Miss Steele might get . . . messy. I need to tell her where we stand, but I don't want you caught in the middle of it."

"Of course," Elinor murmured, but now she was really thinking about Lucy. Hadn't she heard Edward's voice at the door when Elinor let him in? Why had she slipped off? Was she avoiding Edward? Elinor stood quickly, ignoring Edward's quizzical expression, and walked swiftly to the door to the dining room and yanked it open. Margaret tumbled through the doorway with a squeak.

"Margaret!" Elinor gritted out. "What have I told you about eavesdropping?"

"Sorry!" Margaret straightened up. "Only, Miss Steele ran through the dining room and she asked me if there was a back staircase, and I said in the kitchen, and she looked so nervous I decided to listen in on what had frightened her so much, but it was just Edward—hello, Edward! congratulations on being disowned!—and then I got distracted by his apology—"

"All right," Elinor said, falling back into the role of pragmatic problem solver. "But enough listening at doors! It's rude, you know."

"I know," Margaret said without a gram of remorse. Elinor turned to see Edward out, but he still looked nervous as they stepped into the foyer, glancing up the staircase as if he expected Lucy Steele to come flying down.

"Promise me you'll be careful around her," he said, and she didn't have to ask whom he meant.

"I will," she said, and she opened her mouth to ask when he might come to call again when she heard her mother's voice ring out behind her.

"Mr. Farrows! Are you coming, or going?"

"Going, Mrs. Dashwood," he said with a polite bow. "Miss Dashwood has enlightened me about how busy your household has been already this morning, and I don't wish to be a burden."

"Nonsense," Mother said, descending the final steps. "It's quite unusual to have so many visitors so early in the morning, but we are grateful."

"Where's Lucy?" Elinor asked, looking up the stairs for any sign of the other young lady.

"I left her visiting with Marianne," Mrs. Dashwood said. "She brought Marianne up some tea, and I think Marianne might manage it."

"You left Lucy with Marianne?" Elinor asked. "Hannah isn't there, too?"

She wasn't quite sure why she was alarmed at this thought. She only knew that she didn't like it, especially after what Edward had just told her. Dread trickled down her spine, pooling in the pit of her stomach, and her breath came quickly.

"No, I don't know where Hannah is, but I hope she's taking it easy. We've had an eventful few days, Mr. Farrows. Did you hear about our break-in? Our Hannah— Elinor, what's the matter?"

Elinor was already pushing past her mother. "I need to check on Marianne."

Some instinct that Elinor didn't fully understand told her to hurry, and if she had taken a moment to think things through properly, if she had been waylaid a few moments more, she might have talked herself out of her alarm. She felt like Marianne in the moment, overcome with a sense of great urgency, and she didn't

351

stop to think sensibly. She merely took the stairs as quickly and as quietly as she could, making sure to skip the second from the top that squeaked, and swung open the bedroom door.

She arrived just in time to see Lucy standing over Marianne, holding a teacup to Marianne's lips. It might have been a picture of caring and kindness, except that Marianne was pushing ineffectually at Lucy's arm, and her face and pillow were soaked with tea. She coughed and sputtered as Lucy straightened with a small jump.

"Oh dear!" she exclaimed at the sight of Elinor. "How clumsy of me. I'm afraid I'm a horrid nurse."

"Get away from her!" Elinor shouted, and rushed to her sister, shoving Lucy aside in the process.

Lucy stumbled with a cry, but Elinor ignored her. She wiped her sister's face of the lukewarm tea and tried to help her sit up. "Are you all right? Are you hurt?"

"Elinor!" Mrs. Dashwood arrived in the room and took in the scene. "What on earth?"

"I'm so clumsy," Lucy proclaimed.

"What did you give her?" Elinor whirled on Lucy, who looked a little *too* shocked, a little *too* innocent. If Elinor had thought she felt rage last night confronting John and Fanny, then it was nothing compared with the heat searing in her chest. If Lucy had done anything to Marianne . . .

"It was just tea," Lucy protested, and she looked to Mrs. Dashwood. "I was merely trying to help."

"Elinor, you're being rude!" her mother chastised, probably for the first time in years.

Edward lurked in the doorway behind her. His eyes darted to Elinor. "Is she all right?"

Elinor turned back to her sister, not bothering to explain her strange behavior. Marianne's color was the same, and she appeared groggy but no worse than she had earlier. She had finally stopped coughing and gasped for breath, her spare hand flying to her wounded side. "The tea," she managed to say, her eyes finding Elinor's.

"I thought she was thirsty, and it would revive her spirits. Tea is ever so fortifying, as my mother used to say—"

"Bitter," Marianne rasped out before her eyelids fluttered shut.

Elinor's gaze flew to Lucy, who tittered. "It was only a spot of lemon!"

Elinor rose to her feet, but she might as well have been a ghost because she couldn't feel her limbs, she couldn't feel anything but pure panic.

The Dashwoods hadn't been able to afford lemons since before Father died.

"What did you give her?" she shrieked, and suddenly Lucy was right before her, and Elinor was conscious of her shaking and shaking Lucy while the other young lady screamed at her, and her mother shouted in alarm. Then Edward was between them, prying Lucy from her grasp.

Elinor spun around and looked at her sister, who was still coughing intermittently. "She poisoned Marianne," Elinor declared.

Of course. *Of course*, she'd fled from Edward, gone through the dining room and into the kitchen. Into the kitchen, where Elinor had labeled the substances that she'd isolated from Eliza's journal and set them on the shelf *in plain sight*.

"Did you give her the substance?" she demanded, her eyes boring into Lucy.

"What substance?" Lucy asked, but a glimmer of triumph peeked through her innocent facade.

"What's going on?" Mother demanded. "Elinor?"

"Marianne's been given the same poison that killed Father!" She went to Marianne, whose eyes had drifted shut. "Marianne! Wake up! How much did you drink?"

"I don't know. . . ." She sighed. "A lot."

No, no, no. Elinor had thought she'd lived through the worst hours of her life in the last few weeks, but nothing compared with this moment, knowing that Marianne was poisoned and still alive, but that she wouldn't be alive for much longer unless they acted.

"What do we do?" Mrs. Dashwood asked. "Call for a doctor? Brandon?"

"She needs a tartar emetic," Elinor said. It would cause Marianne to become ill and vomit, but only if she took it before the poisoned tea had a chance to take effect.

"Hannah!" her mother bellowed, and ran from the room. Lucy tried to follow, but Edward clamped a hand on her arm without a word, holding her in place.

But all the while Marianne was slipping away, her eyelids sagging once more.

Think, Elinor. Think. How to expel the poison? What could counteract it? Elinor didn't understand how the substance worked, other than it killed if too much was used. She couldn't brew an antidote to something she didn't understand scientifically. Marianne's best hope—no, her only hope—was to rid her body of the poison before it had a chance to take effect.

"Marianne," she said, pulling her sister into a sitting position. "Can you vomit?"

"Why?" she asked sleepily.

"It's important. Try to vomit!"

Marianne coughed, but nothing came out.

"Is she going to die?" came Margaret's voice from the doorway, small and scared.

"No," Elinor said firmly, because she wasn't ready to lose another loved one. "Not if she can vomit up the poison. I need . . ."

Marianne was tilting back toward her bed, sleep overcoming her. A sleep that she might never wake from. Elinor didn't know what to do. She didn't know how to save her sister.

"Oh! Try this!" Margaret exclaimed, and then ran to the corner. She pried a loose floorboard up and reached her hand into the gaping dark hole. She extracted something small—a vial! Elinor stared hard at it.

"Is that mine?" she asked.

"I stole it. You can thank me later!" She uncapped it and waved it under Marianne's nose.

Elinor had been insulted when Marianne declared her attempts at perfume making horrific, but the moment the vial was uncapped, she wrinkled her nose. It really was a most unpleasant scent—what had she been thinking? Margaret waved the vial even more frantically beneath Marianne's nose and finally just upended the contents on her face. Elinor pulled Marianne back up into a sitting position, slinging her sister's arm over her shoulder, and said, "Oh, Margaret, I don't think it will work—"

But then she felt Marianne shudder and cough. Maybe . . .

Her sister began to gag. Her eyes fluttered open, unfocused, and she retched.

"What did you do—" She gasped, and then, in a most miraculous and revolting display, Marianne vomited up everything in her stomach.

TWENTY-ONE

In Which the Dashwood Sisters Serve Tea

❈ ❈ ❈ ❈ ❈

ELINOR WASN'T SATISFIED UNTIL Marianne sagged in exhaustion, dry heaving and whimpering. She rubbed circles on her sister's back as she moaned in pain, noting with worry the red stains that blossomed across her white bandages. Mrs. Dashwood ordered everyone out so they could clean up the mess and change Marianne's bandages.

"Don't let her leave," Elinor told Edward, nodding at Lucy. Edward already had a firm grasp on her elbow, and he nodded before hauling her out.

Marianne's wound looked no better, but Elinor wasn't sure if it was worse, either—the edges had begun to scab, but now they oozed blood and the skin around the wound appeared burned before edging into black and blue. Marianne let them tend to her as she hovered in and out of consciousness, but once they had eased her back down on the bed and coaxed some water down her throat, she closed her eyes and muttered, "Can I sleep?"

"Yes, darling," Mother whispered as she smoothed Marianne's hair back.

But you better wake, Elinor thought as Marianne's breathing turned rhythmic.

A knock at the bedroom door made them turn, and when Elinor opened it, she was relieved to see Margaret, dragging a concerned-looking Mr. Brandon. "Look who came to call!" Margaret announced. "I told him that lady tried to kill Marianne."

Brandon stepped forward, looking as serious as always, but there was an unfurled energy about him. "What happened?" he asked in a voice so tight it nearly broke, and Elinor's eyes widened slightly.

Did Brandon care for Marianne? As more than just another patient?

"Lucy Steele tried to poison her with Eliza's substance," Elinor explained quickly.

"Elinor made her throw up. A *lot*." Margaret managed to sound both disgusted and delighted by this.

"She exaggerates," Elinor said, patting Brandon's shoulder as he took in the sight of Marianne sleeping. "I caught Lucy Steele in the act, and I think we were able to move quickly enough that Marianne wasn't overly affected. She expelled the poisoned tea and we got her to drink some water."

"Why would she poison Marianne?" Brandon asked.

"That's what I'd like to know, too," Mother said, and then three pairs of eyes looked to Elinor, as if she held the answers.

"I don't know exactly," Elinor said, "but I'm going to find out."

In reality, she had no idea what to do next. Elinor longed for Marianne, awake and alert. She would know what to do, what Father would have done. She would come up with a plan, and it would be cleverer than anything Elinor could think of.

Think of the poison, Elinor reminded herself. *You can do this.*

"Lucy Steele knew what Eliza's poison was," she said slowly. "Otherwise, she wouldn't have used it against Marianne. But as to why she decided to poison Marianne now . . ."

Then she thought of all that Edward had told her about Lucy blackmailing him. All along, she and Marianne had been operating under the assumption that the key to solving Father's murder must be singling out one person who had a hand in the events, but really the only unifying element to Father's murder, Eliza's death, and Edward's predicament wasn't a person or a case—it was opium.

Elinor wanted to race downstairs and shake Lucy Steele until the answers fell out of her. She might have been tempted to do just that, except she recalled the flash of cunning in the young lady's expression when she asked about attending Mrs. Farrows's ball.

Lucy Steele was clever. Lucy Steele might have all of the answers, but she wouldn't give them up willingly.

"Elinor?" Margaret asked.

"I'm thinking," she said, closing her eyes as her mind raced through half a dozen scenarios and hypotheses.

"About what?"

Elinor opened her eyes, spotted the tea tray that Lucy had brought up, and was struck with an idea. "About how to get Lucy Steele to confess."

✄

Elinor assembled a tea tray out of the mismatched dishes they had left in their collection, taking her time. She had Margaret listening at the door between the drawing room and dining room for conversation between Edward and Lucy, and when she was finished assembling the tea tray, she crept into the dining room and waved Margaret over.

"Are you clear on the plan?" she whispered.

Margaret nodded, her smile a touch too eager considering the situation.

"All right," Elinor said, and she sucked in a deep breath and let it out slowly. "Time to make Marianne proud."

She retrieved the tea tray and entered the drawing room from the other door in the hall. Lucy and Edward sat side by side on the tattered settee. At first glance, one might assume they were suitors given how close they sat, but Elinor noted Edward's tense expression and Lucy's sour look.

"How's Miss Marianne?" Edward asked, jumping to his feet but keeping hold of Lucy.

"She is no longer sick," Elinor said, not finding it difficult at all to keep her voice terse and worried. "But she's no longer conscious. Mr. Brandon and my mother are attending to her."

"Oh God," Edward said. "Should we call for a physician?"

"Mr. Brandon has already sent for one," Elinor lied, setting the tea tray down between them. "I pray he comes quickly."

"What can I do?" Edward asked.

But Elinor looked to Lucy, who was avoiding direct eye contact. She tried to shrug Edward's hand off her shoulder, but he wasn't so easily deterred. "There's nothing to do but wait," Elinor said, her voice coming out too sharp. *Steady,* she reminded herself. "Tea?"

Lucy looked up, smiled slightly, and shook her head. "Elinor, please—"

"My sister is gravely injured, Miss Steele," Elinor interrupted, pouring the tea anyway. "I wonder why you would insist on giving her tea."

"Well, it's quite fortifying," Lucy said, watching as Elinor set the teapot back down.

"Cream? Sugar?"

"No, thank—"

"Oh, no. You like lemon in your tea, is that right?"

"I . . ." Lucy looked from Elinor to Edward. "I feel as though there's been a terrible misunderstanding."

361

"Hmm," Elinor said, pretending to consider her words. "Perhaps. But it's best to clear up misunderstandings, don't you think?"

"I . . . suppose. I would never hurt Miss Marianne."

It almost sounded convincing, but Elinor was fairly certain she knew better. "Why did you hire us, Miss Steele?"

"What? I . . ." She glanced at Edward, her cheeks turning a soft, becoming shade of pink.

"Please, don't be shy. I don't think you need to worry about what Edward might think of you at the moment—you have more important concerns to attend to."

Elinor noticed the tightening in Lucy's jaw, even as she kept the pleasantly puzzled expression on her face. "I hired you to help me find a husband," she said, then turned to Edward. "I'm sorry if that shocks you, but—"

Edward looked confused, and Elinor realized belatedly that she didn't need him revealing that they'd already spoken and he'd revealed Lucy's blackmail. She interrupted. "Miss Steele, I know why you wanted to hire an investigator—what I meant is why did you hire *us*?"

Lucy watched as Elinor spooned a heap of sugar into her tea. "Well, I thought it would be more comfortable to talk to another young lady."

"Certainly," Elinor said, smiling and reaching for her own tea, which she left black. "And you had a recommendation from Mrs. Jennings?"

"Yes!" she said quickly. "Dear Mrs. Jennings. She is so kind to offer me a place to stay in London, and when she told me of your meeting, I thought you sounded like absolutely the young ladies I needed to hire."

"So you hired us, and when you had an introduction with Edward here, you immediately decided to blackmail him?"

"What? No! I . . ."

Even Edward looked surprised that Elinor would bring this up. He looked directly at her and his brown eyes seemed to ask, *What are you doing?*

Please trust me, she thought.

"I think you've gotten this all wrong," Lucy insisted.

"Oh? Have I gotten this all wrong, Edward? Did Miss Steele not try and blackmail you?"

He looked at Lucy but answered Elinor. "No, I think that is a fair assessment of the situation."

While Lucy sputtered, Elinor pressed her advantage. "You see, Miss Steele, it would appear that you are rather close to some incidents that, when I think upon them, feel rather off. Why would you feel the need to blackmail poor Edward here? Do you not trust our abilities? And if you were in a position to blackmail Edward, why hire us? But the question I really want an answer to is this: Did you know Eliza Williams?"

"I—I don't know . . . Eliza Williams? Why, she was that girl that Mrs. Jennings sometimes accompanied."

"Yes, and she ended up dead," Elinor said. "Did you forget?"

"No. I didn't forget." Lucy scowled. "You're just being rather terse and excuse me for saying so, but mean. I don't know why you're so upset with me!"

Tears glistened in the corners of Lucy's eyes, threatening to spill down her cheeks. *Go ahead*, thought Elinor. *But crying can't get you out of this.*

"I simply want to know how you fit into all of this, that's all. You knew Miss Williams, which makes me wonder if you're acquainted with Mr. Willoughby as well?"

No response or reaction.

"And then you hire us, and I wonder—with what money?"

"I have a small inheritance," she murmured.

"Right," Elinor said, taking in her dress, which was of the latest fashion. Come to think of it, so was her ball gown from the other night and the two morning gowns she'd been wearing when she'd come to call. Elinor should have noted that earlier. "It must not be that small, if you're able to afford such fine dresses?"

Lucy didn't dignify such a gauche question with a response, but Elinor didn't need one. She had hit her stride.

"I know we've spoken about your misfortune as an orphan, but I am much more fascinated by your misfortunate timing. You seem to be at the center of some truly puzzling mysteries."

"Are you implying that I had anything to do with Eliza Williams's death?"

"Did you?"

"That is absurd! How dare you even—can you believe this?" Lucy asked Edward.

"Actually," Edward said, "I can."

Excellent. Elinor had gotten Lucy right where she wanted her—looking rather guilty and defensive. But she knew that Lucy wouldn't admit to anything. Elinor had no proof. So she executed the next part of her plan: she sneezed.

"God bless you," Edward said.

"Thank you." She could just make out the sound of Margaret's footsteps in the hall. "Miss Steele, if you're as innocent as you claim, I think that we can sort out this matter, but you must understand why I am suspicious, especially with my sister as gravely ill as she is. Whatever you gave her made her sicker."

"I didn't give her anything."

"And I don't believe you."

"Well, you're mistaken. You're mistaken and I don't know how many times I have to repeat myself, but you can't hold me hostage—"

An earth-shattering scream split the air, and even though Elinor knew it was coming, the force and volume of Mother's voice made her jump for real. She let the teacup and saucer fall from her hands, where they shattered on the floor, sending splatters of hot tea everywhere. Edward gasped and murmured, "Oh God, no," but Lucy merely went very still.

Elinor's hands flew to her mouth, and it took very little effort to playact the part of a shocked and devastated sister.

She'd unfortunately had too much experience with the role as of late. She held her hands over her mouth, counted to ten, and let the tears fall, thinking of Father.

When she reached ten, she forced herself to her feet, and Edward leapt to her side in an instant. "Oh, Elinor," he said. "Elinor."

He tried to embrace her, and she would have dearly loved that, but she pushed him away, pretending to be too grief-stricken to endure his touch. She heard footsteps on the stairs and turned to the door just as Brandon let himself in, his own grave expression selling the farce just as well as Elinor's dramatic grief. Elinor made to leave the room, but Brandon caught her. "I'm so sorry, Miss Dashwood," he said. "I tried my best. I'm so sorry."

"I have to—my mother," she gasped out.

"She needs a few moments," he said, tilting his head ever so slightly in a question.

Elinor winked once, knowing that Edward and Lucy were unable to see the gesture, then spun around.

"Are you going to tell me again that you didn't poison my sister?"

"I didn't!" Lucy protested. "She was injured, you said—it must have been infection or something of the sort."

"There is no infection," Brandon corrected. "She didn't even have a fever."

"Loss of blood," Lucy continued. "It was a shock to her

body, it must have been, getting shot. . . ."

"Miss Steele," Elinor said, "I didn't tell you that my sister had been shot. I only said she'd been injured trying to find Margaret."

"Oh, no, you must have said, or perhaps your mother . . ."

But Lucy Steele was fluttering too quickly among the three of them, trapped in a web of her own making. Elinor tried not to let her triumph shine through because they weren't there. Not quite yet.

"I'll ask you once more," she said. "Why did you poison my sister? Perhaps if you can explain yourself before the Runners arrive, we can offer the magistrate a decent explanation. Otherwise, I hear the women's prison is no place for a lady."

"I didn't poison her, I swear to you! I've never poisoned anyone in my life. I would never! Why don't you trust me?"

"Because I've noticed that you haven't taken a sip of tea," Elinor said.

This was enough to surprise Lucy out of her tears. She shook her head. "What?"

"Don't you trust me?"

"Don't be absurd. I just don't want any right now. I'm not thirsty."

Elinor saw the moment that Edward caught on to Elinor's maneuver. His face lit with understanding as he turned his attention from Elinor to Lucy.

"But tea is ever so fortifying," Elinor said. "If you didn't poison my sister, then why don't you take a sip?"

Lucy's eyes blazed with defiance. "No."

"Why not?" Elinor stepped forward until she was toe-to-toe with the other woman, not even attempting to mask her fury. "Prove me wrong."

Elinor held her gaze until Lucy was forced to look away. "She's mad!" Lucy shouted at Edward and Brandon.

"No, I think you're the mad one," Edward said. "Mr. Brandon, I think we ought to call for the Runners."

"Straightaway," he agreed. "The courts take poisoning cases rather seriously these days. They hanged Eliza Fenning for attempted poisoning, so I imagine they'll happily do the same for you."

"Wait!" Lucy screamed. Her face was not just pink but a deep, flustered red. "It's not like that."

"There are witnesses," Elinor bit out. "Do you really think that anyone will believe you innocent once they learn you were seen forcing tea down my sister's throat only for her to die of poison so soon after?"

She let her emotion boil and overflow, until she realized that she wasn't merely raising her voice at Lucy but screaming at her. The other woman was crying freely now, shaking her head and sobbing. "It's not like that. It's not! It's only opium. It's not poison, just opium!"

When she said the words, Elinor fell silent. The entire room seemed to go still, except for Lucy's sniffling. She had the audacity to look Elinor in the eye and say, "It's all a mistake. I didn't realize."

"Tell me everything," Elinor said. "And maybe we shall ask for leniency."

She was afraid Lucy would refuse for a moment, but then she pulled herself together and found a handkerchief and cleaned herself up.

"It's not easy," she began, her voice small. "Being an orphan. Being a poor *female* orphan. You may be poor, Miss Dashwood, but at least you have family. This home, although it is rather shabby. Did you know I haven't lived in any one place for longer than six months since I was twelve years old?"

Elinor didn't say anything. Her days of sympathizing with Lucy Steele were over.

"It's dreadful, living out of a trunk. Always worrying about who your next host or hostess will be, never being able to settle in a place. To merely call a bed your own . . . what I wouldn't *give* to have that. A husband would be nice, don't get me wrong. But if I could merely *afford* my own home . . ."

She looked around the room, her eyes hungry. Elinor understood that hunger, though. "You told us you were looking for a husband, but what you really want is to make your own way."

Lucy didn't deny it. "I met Mr. Willoughby at a dinner party two years ago," she continued. "Mrs. Colgate seated us together. The two poor orphans of the table. He was new to London, and he had very few introductions. We got to talking. . . ."

Elinor could picture it—Willoughby being his overly charming self and flattering Lucy, and Lucy thinking that perhaps he liked her.

"It was all him, really!" she exclaimed. "He was the one who knew about the opium and what members of society had an appetite for it. We were merely *gossiping*. He told me that there was a demand for it among the ladies, even. I didn't believe him at first. Eating opium seems so unladylike, but once you knew who partook, and who sent their lady's maid to four different apothecaries searching for more of the stuff . . . well, it was simply a matter of making it *fashionable*."

Elinor recalled suddenly the gray lady at the club the night before. "The woman at the club said if we wanted what she served, there were better ways to get what we were looking for. She said she could arrange an introduction."

Lucy smiled slightly, that cunning look returning. "Willoughby acquired the product, and we put it into colored glass vials and jars, like what you might find for scent water or perfume. I told the ladies it was concocted for the fairer sex. And they paid *triple*."

Elinor recalled the vacant, unfocused eyes of the men in the club, and then another face flashed in her memory. *Amelia Holbrook*. "Miss Holbrook?" Elinor asked. "Is she your client?"

"Yes! I could give you a list—it would shock you, the number of ladies involved! But they tell their friends or their maids, and their maids come find me, and—"

"Is that how Eliza got involved?" Brandon asked, the intensity of his voice startling Elinor.

"Eliza Williams had no clue what we were up to." Lucy clucked her tongue dismissively. "Willoughby bought the laudanum from her uncle's shop, and he would always try to charm her into selling him more. I could barely keep up with the demand at that point. But her uncle placed a limit on how much anyone could buy. Some worry about *suicide*, you understand." She whispered the word *suicide*, as if that were hardly the most scandalous thing they were discussing at the moment. "Willoughby made up a sappy story about his dear aunt suffering from gout, and how he needed it for her."

"But she wouldn't have given it to him," Brandon stated.

"No," Lucy agreed. "She said that it didn't matter if his aunt's pain was really as profound as he said, because no one person should be taking as much as Willoughby tried to buy. Quite annoying, but he couldn't very well tell her that we were diluting it with rose water to make it quite harmless."

Elinor scoffed. "Miss Holbrook would beg to differ. Tell us what happened to Eliza Williams."

Lucy looked as if she might not want to respond, but she must have recognized on some level that she had already told them this much, so there was little use pretending she didn't know. "She told Willoughby that she was experimenting with what gave opium its powers. She said it was possible that she could derive a substance that was even stronger than laudanum, or eating opium. If she could discover such a thing, she could eliminate pain altogether. She felt bad for his aunt, I suppose."

Elinor swallowed hard. Next to her, she heard Brandon curse ever so softly under his breath.

"We *needed* that substance," Lucy added, sounding a touch more frantic. "The ladies always wanted more, and we were having trouble with our supply."

"And she wouldn't give it to you," Brandon said with certainty. Anyone else might have thought that he sounded indifferent, but Elinor felt an undercurrent of dark energy radiating off of him. Brandon was *furious.*

"I waited until Willoughby left town to visit his aunt, and then spoke to her myself, woman to woman. Except she wouldn't sell it, not even to me. I went after business hours, and she was working on it, right in front of me. She was so proud of it, going on about testing and all the possibilities—but she still wouldn't sell. She had so much of it! And she could always make more. I just needed her to understand the power of opium, how important it was."

"And so you made her ingest it?" Elinor asked.

"I slipped a teaspoon of it into her tea," Lucy confessed. "I wanted her to know the power, to convince her."

"But it killed her instead."

"I didn't know! You have to believe me. It was an accident. She began to slur her words, and stumble about, and I thought . . . I thought she needed to sleep it off. I took the rest of her vials, and her journal, too. I was going to hold it ransom. She could have it back if she agreed to sell to me."

"You killed her," Brandon said, his words like daggers. "You murdered her."

"She was sleeping when I left."

"And Willoughby?" Elinor asked.

"He was furious when he heard, but he knew it was an accident. We both agreed he ought to stay in the country for a spell."

And Eliza was buried, and Brandon had hired Mr. Dashwood to look into her death. But he'd not turned up anything and closed the case. Until right before his death, when he wrote Willoughby's name on a slip of paper while searching for Sir John's son.

"What about my father?" Elinor whispered. "Was he an accident, too?"

Lucy went very still. "I didn't . . . I mean, I don't know. . . ."

"Don't lie to me. I know my father was poisoned by Eliza's substance, and you just admitted to taking it."

"I don't know anything!"

"That won't be good enough for the magistrate," Edward said, looking ashen.

"I . . . no! I mean, Willoughby made me! He was mad. You don't know what he's like when he eats the stuff. He saw your father at Grey's, and he panicked. He came to me ranting that an investigator was onto us, and that he would discover what *I* had done. I told him it was ridiculous, there was nothing to connect our business with Eliza. But Willoughby wouldn't be convinced. He had turned careless, and I was afraid."

"Afraid enough to cover your tracks?" Elinor asked, hating how her voice wavered.

"No!"

Elinor wished that Marianne were here, because she wasn't sure if she believed Lucy. On the one hand, Willoughby was the link, the one that Father had seen, the one with the most to lose. On the other hand . . . Willoughby had an alibi for Eliza's death, and Father was never careless when it came to his work.

"You," Edward stated.

Everyone looked to him, and Elinor's heart broke slightly to see that he looked utterly shocked. He was the only one not let in on this plot.

But then Edward continued, "You said last night that Fanny's decor turned out beautifully."

Elinor didn't follow, until Edward said, "How did you know that Fanny had redecorated recently?"

Lucy went pale, but she still tried to salvage the situation. "It was apparent that the room had been decorated to her tastes," she whispered. "Any fool—"

"That's twice now that you've stumbled," Elinor said. "You're getting clumsy. Is it because you've told too many lies to account for them all? You might have killed Eliza Williams by mistake, but even if it was unplanned, it's still murder. And breaking into our home and killing my father . . . well, by then you knew exactly what you were doing. And then you killed my sister in the same way. Did you think that would silence us? Mr. Brandon is correct—women have certainly been hanged for far less."

"No! It was Willoughby, all of this was his idea, you have to just find him and you'll see. I was taken in, and he threatened me! He's a criminal, you can't just punish me, please, Elinor—"

Lucy reached for Elinor, pulling at her arms and skirts in desperation. She was crying even harder as Edward peeled her away from Elinor. Elinor looked at Brandon and raised a single brow. She was satisfied—but had they gotten enough?

"Find Willoughby!" Lucy shouted again. "It will all make sense if you make him answer for what he's done."

"I'm afraid that's impossible," Brandon said, catching Elinor by surprise. "Willoughby is dead."

Lucy hiccuped into the shocked silence that followed, and then her face scrunched up and she broke out into panicked sobs. Brandon looked nearly apologetic as he explained, "I went back to the club last night, after I saw to Miss Marianne. I found Sir John and the fire brigade. They pulled Willoughby's body out of the building." After a brief hesitation, he added, "I'm sorry."

Elinor wasn't entirely certain if the apology was meant for Lucy or if it was an involuntary reaction to delivering the news of someone's death. As for herself, she didn't feel anything regarding the news. Perhaps this whole affair had turned her numb.

"Oh God . . ." Edward exhaled, his features stricken. "So much death. Miss Marianne. Oh *God*."

That gave Elinor the chance to smile just a tiny bit. "Well. Actually . . . that bit was a farce. Please forgive us, Edward. We didn't have time to warn you. But I needed *her* to think that she'd truly killed Marianne, so she'd confess to the rest."

Edward's mouth popped open in shock, and then his hand went to his heart. "I'm sorry, but . . . Miss Marianne is alive?"

"Yes," Brandon confirmed. "Although Mrs. Dashwood's scream was certainly enough to make me question it myself."

Edward sank into the settee, laughing nervously. Elinor studied Lucy, who now looked a wreck—cheeks tearstained and puffy, skirts rumpled, and perfect ringlets now limp. What she saw in Lucy's blue eyes was a coldness so sharp that it put her on edge.

"You horrible cow," Lucy sputtered. "I only tried to kill Marianne because I never thought you'd have the courage to do anything about it!"

The gentlemen gasped, but Elinor just felt empty as she stared down Lucy, every muscle tensed in case Lucy came at her once more.

But when Lucy made her move, it wasn't for Elinor. Instead, her entire body lurched forward as she grasped the teacup she had refused to drink from just minutes earlier. She tilted her head back and gulped down the now lukewarm tea before Edward or Brandon could stop her. Then she threw the cup against the wall, shattering it. Elinor winced—they really did not have any more teacups to spare—but she met Lucy's defiant gaze as the other woman said, "Try to hang me for those murders now!"

Elinor smiled, and felt something like humor for the first time all day. "Oh dear. Did you think that was poisoned?"

Lucy's triumphant smirk slid off her face slowly as Elinor chuckled and shook her head. "I would *never*." She leaned forward and added sugar to her own cup, then took a sip so dainty, Queen Charlotte herself would not be able to find fault with it. Then she met Lucy's eyes as she said, "Poisoning is your area of expertise, not mine."

TWENTY-TWO

In Which the Dashwood Sisters Find Closure—
or Something Like It

MARIANNE FELT AS THOUGH she'd been run over by a carriage, then wrung out like a dishrag. The pain brought her to the surface of consciousness, before she even opened her eyes. Her right side throbbed, and just the involuntary act of breathing sent tendrils of hot agony up and down her side. Her mouth was sour, and her head felt as though it were stuffed with cotton. Aside from that, she was ravenously hungry and so thirsty she whimpered—and realized that her throat was parched.

She opened her eyes slowly, because the lamplight sent spears into her eyes. As she adjusted to the light, she experimentally began moving her limbs. Toes, then feet and ankles. All seemed well, but moving her legs jostled her side, and she gasped with the shock of it.

"You're awake!" a soft male voice exclaimed.

Marianne turned her head to see Mr. Brandon sitting beside her bed—far enough that she hadn't noticed him, but close enough that she could tell he'd been sitting vigil, a book in hand. Her heart did a strange little leap. "Mr. Bra—Brandon," she croaked out. "Water?"

"Here," he said, and lifted a ladle of water to her lips. She sucked it down in a most unladylike fashion, rivulets running out the corner of her mouth and falling down her face, but there was no room left in her for embarrassment—the water tasted so good. How had she never noticed how wonderful clear, cool water tasted before? For the rest of her life she never wanted to take for granted this simple pleasure.

"More?" she whispered hopefully.

"Yes," he said, and even though his mouth didn't shape a smile, Marianne realized at once that his eyes smiled at her. Could eyes even smile? Yes, she decided, because Brandon's eyes were most definitely doing just that—softly crinkled around the edges and so bright as they followed her every movement. "But wait a moment to let that settle. Your stomach is empty, and you'll have to take it easy."

Almost as if on cue, her stomach gurgled loud enough for both of them to hear. "Settle down," Marianne murmured at her gut.

"I'll go fetch your mother and sister," Brandon said.

"Wait!" It came out of Marianne like a whimper. She did

want to see her family, of course, but she also didn't want Brandon and his warm gray eyes to go away just yet. "What time is it? How long have I been asleep?"

"It's evening," he said, glancing at his pocket watch. "You've been asleep half the day. Do you remember what happened?"

"I remember . . . Mother, then . . . Lucy Steele? And then Elinor wanting me to be sick?"

"Yes," Brandon confirmed. "Lucy Steele poisoned you. Your sister saved your life."

Marianne huffed a tiny laugh that made her wince. "She did? Good Lord, she'll never let me forget it now. But why did Lucy Steele poison me?"

"Maybe I should go get your—"

"Mr. Brandon, please," Marianne said, trying to implore him with her eyes. "Can you tell me what happened? The moment my sisters and mother come in, it'll be all dramatics. I know they think *I'm* the dramatic one. . . ." Perhaps the pain had addled her brain, because she rather liked that Mr. Brandon was here.

"Well, all right," he said. "I'll do my best to explain, but Elinor may need to fill in the gaps. She put on quite the charade today."

"Elinor?" Marianne clarified, wondering if he'd gotten her sisters confused.

"Indeed," he confirmed, and began to explain what had happened after she passed out. Marianne couldn't tell if she was still woozy or if this story was as convoluted as he was making it out to be. Lucy Steele was the mastermind behind all these deaths and an elaborate scheme to supply the upper class with "premium" opium? All Marianne could picture was the very silly young lady who'd prattled on about dresses, tea, and eligible bachelors. Marianne felt her eyes fluttering as the facts and details slid into place. Little tidbits that Brandon had revealed to her that, against all logic, seemed to match up. Hadn't Willoughby told her a lady had taught him how to break into houses? But who had broken into their flat? There was more to puzzle out, and if she could just find her way out of this fog of fatigue . . .

"You're tired," Brandon said, stopping his explanation. "I should really—"

"No," Marianne protested. "I mean, yes, I am tired. But I'm also ravenous. But . . . what of Willoughby?"

"Oh," he said in a tone that made Marianne think it wasn't good news. "I'm sorry, Miss Marianne. Willoughby is . . . well, that is, he didn't survive the fire at the club. We think he passed out, and died of smoke inhalation."

The news should have come as a shock, but Marianne just felt empty. The young man who'd rescued her from being trampled, nobly lifted her in his arms, seen her home, brought her poetry, accompanied her on stakeouts, kissed her passionately. He was *gone*. But then again, did that young man ever really exist? The Willoughby she thought she knew was an illusion, and the real man was nothing more than a charming rake. She felt sadness then, like a distant ache, but the more acute pain was the revelation that he had not been her hero. And while a part of Marianne was devastated at this conclusion, she was also grateful to be alive, grateful for the throbbing pain in her side that reminded her of her beating heart, and even grateful for the hot streaks of tears that ran down her cheeks.

"Oh, Miss Marianne," Brandon said with surprising tenderness. "I'm sorry to upset you."

"No, you've not upset me. You've told me the truth." She smiled at him through her tears, to reassure him he didn't need to go running for her mother. "Thank you."

Mr. Brandon fished out his handkerchief, and when he held it up, his eyes asked a question. Marianne nodded, and he very gently wiped away her tears. His soft touch, and the slightly medicinal scent of his handkerchief, took Marianne's breath away.

"I'm sorry," she said when he was finished. "I owe you an apology. I'm afraid I've been a bit rude to you."

He shook his head. "Willoughby surely told you—"

"Willoughby poured poison in my ear, but I was rude before that. I'm truly sorry."

And then wonder of wonders, he smiled with his lips, and Marianne felt herself returning the expression. Brandon really was quite handsome the more she looked at him.

But no . . . Marianne wasn't going to let herself get carried away by a handsome face again.

"I accept your apology," Brandon said. "I know I'm not always . . . well, Eliza told me I was hard to get to know."

"You must miss her."

He looked up to the ceiling. "Yes. I do, every day. She was a great friend, and a brilliant mind. But if anything good has happened since her death, it's meeting the Dashwood sisters. I'm grateful that you've helped discover her murderer."

"Oh, but I didn't—I just made things worse. I broke into your workroom!"

"If you hadn't done that, we might not have ever discovered that Willoughby and Miss Steele were in possession of Eliza's notes. Miss Steele admitted to the authorities that Willoughby planted them, and he was supposed to plant your father's journal there as well. She's trying to throw all the blame on a dead man, but her attempts on your life are more than sufficient to put her behind bars. You can't blame yourself for being taken in."

The words were a tiny bit of comfort. "Will Miss Steele hang for her crimes?"

"Poisoning cases are awfully hard to prove, but you are a key witness to the effects of Eliza's substance. The courts may not be ready to believe in or understand the science behind it . . . but a living victim may implicate her."

"So my poisoning is all that will count? How is that justice?"

"I don't know, but that's not my business. But Mr. Farrows has recommended that you seek advice from a legal firm called

Longbourn. They were in the papers earlier this year, and he thinks quite highly of them. One of the solicitors solved a murder case, so I imagine if anyone can prove that Miss Steele really did set out to kill your father, it's them."

"The one with the lady solicitor?" Marianne asked. "I rather like that."

Just then, Marianne's stomach let out another very alarming growl. Under normal circumstances, Marianne might have been embarrassed, but Brandon merely smiled and stood. "That's a good sign—you're getting your appetite back. Now, shall I go tell your family you're awake?"

"Yes, please," Marianne said. "And Mr. Brandon?"

He turned back to her, and with a twinge of pain in her side, she reached out and took his hand. "Thank you. For everything. Once I've healed up enough, I think I owe you a great deal."

He squeezed her hand. "You owe me nothing, Miss Marianne."

"Still. I feel as though I ought to make it up to you somehow."

"Well," he said, looking suddenly uncertain. His gaze dropped to the floor. "When you're healed and back on your feet, would you like to go for a drive? Perhaps we might stop at Gunter's to sample their ices?" He looked up hopefully.

Marianne very nearly said, *I've been positively* longing *to go to Gunter's!* But she stopped herself at the last moment. She didn't want him to think she was accepting his offer merely for the experience of the outing. So she simply said, "I would like that."

Just then the door burst open and Elinor stepped in, worry etched across her face. It dissolved into joy when she saw that Marianne was awake. Brandon dropped Marianne's hand and straightened quickly, but not fast enough to escape Elinor's notice. She grinned. "Thank heavens! I thought I heard voices. How're you feeling? *Mother!* Marianne's awake!"

Marianne was smothered with attention then, as first Margaret and then Mrs. Dashwood came rushing in. Hannah followed not too long afterward with an ugly bruise on her temple but a relieved smile, bearing a bowl of broth that nearly had Marianne salivating. Marianne even caught a glimpse of Edward lurking in the doorway, almost as if he were afraid to step all the way in. Marianne caught Elinor's eye and raised her eyebrows in his direction, and Elinor flushed.

"Edward, come in here," she said.

"Oh well, all right," he said, and stepped into the room. "Just a moment, though."

He was carrying a large vase of hothouse flowers that must have cost a small fortune. "Oh my," Marianne said. "For me?"

"Yes," Edward said, "although they're not from me. They're from your brother and Fanny. They send their best wishes for your quick recovery."

Elinor handed her the card, and Marianne merely glanced at Fanny's handwriting before tossing it on the bedside table.

"Well, that's the very *least* they could do," she said. "I have no use for pretty words when their actions have spoken so plainly. But I shall enjoy these flowers nonetheless."

Mother insisted on spoon-feeding her like a child while Margaret updated her on the more salacious details of Lucy Steele's interrogation. "And then Mother screamed, and it was so loud I think the crystal shivered!"

"We don't have any crystal," Elinor reminded her, standing like a sentinel at the foot of the bed. But her gaze slid to Edward every now and then and she smiled shyly, and Marianne knew there was a story there.

"Oh, fine," Margaret said. "No crystal was harmed by Mother's scream. But it is a good image, isn't it? I think I shall use it in my manuscript."

"A very good image," Marianne agreed, and contentment settled over her like a warm blanket. Despite her pain, despite the miserable circumstances, despite everything they'd lost in the last few weeks, Marianne knew that everything she needed was right there, within reach.

EPILOGUE

"MARIANNE!" ELINOR CALLED UP the stairs for the third time. "We're going to be late! I'm sure whatever you're wearing, you look lovely."

"I don't just want to look lovely, I want to look professional!"

Elinor smiled but leaned against the banister to wait even longer. Ever since being grazed by a bullet a month earlier, Marianne had undergone a slight shift in perspective. She was still the same obstinate, headstrong, and dramatic person she was before, but she was also a bit more thoughtful. A little less quick to judge. Her biggest change was that she'd accepted Edward and Brandon into their small social circle without blinking an eye, acting as though they were all old friends.

Marianne finally came down the stairs, wearing a new sage-green dress with a dark green jacket and pink trim, to replace the dress that had been destroyed when she'd been shot. Both sisters had to buy new gowns with the income from Marianne's first case. She looked Elinor up and down and said, "Is that what you're wearing?"

So she wasn't entirely changed.

"There is nothing wrong with what I'm wearing," Elinor said, ready to defend her walking dress. It was maroon, with orange undertones, and the color was the boldest thing that Elinor owned.

"I was just going to say I like it," Marianne said, and Elinor braced herself for a follow-up quip that would surely start an argument . . . but one never came.

They called out a goodbye to Mother and Margaret, who were seated at the dining room table. Mother had taken over Margaret's studies, picking up where the governess had left off before Father died, and to say that Margaret was less than thrilled would be an understatement. She still got into plenty of mischief when she wasn't working at her lessons or writing her latest manuscript, and Elinor was glad to see Mother find some purpose in waking up each morning and seeing to Margaret's education first thing.

Elinor followed Marianne out onto Barton Street and drew in her breath at the cold breeze, grateful for how Marianne tucked her arm in Elinor's. "It's a glorious day," her younger sister proclaimed. "I just adore the sound of whistling leaves, don't you? It's a sound I wish I could bottle up and sell."

"Not everyone has your passion for dead leaves," Elinor remarked. "But yes, it's a fine day. Now let's just hope that the place Edward has found is better than the last one."

The sisters were headed to an address four blocks from their home, where they were to meet Edward. Marianne wasn't as quick footed as she had been before her injury, but Elinor could feel the eagerness in her steps. "I hope so. I think I've finally impressed upon him my need for space."

"You'll be spending more time away from a desk than behind it."

"That's not the point, Elinor! We want to look legitimate. It's not enough that I was able to track down Vincent to that dockyard—people won't hire us unless we look the part."

The last month had been very busy for them both. After seeing Lucy Steele in a prison cell, and once Marianne had been nursed back to health, the sisters had spent hours piecing together every detail. Two questions emerged—who had broken into their flat the night of the ball, and where was Sir John's son? But one visit to Lucy in prison and they'd gotten their answers in exchange for some decent food and a change of clothing—Lucy had hired a pair of criminals to scare the Dashwoods, and she'd no idea where Vincent was, but she gave up nearly every bit of info she had. It was enough so that Marianne, Elinor, and Brandon were able to track down Sir John's wayward son, who was currently recuperating in the country—and Sir John paid them handsomely for their efforts.

Now they'd have to wait and see what the justice system would do with Lucy Steele. There were rumors that she was attempting to sell her story to some of the more lurid papers to curry favor with the public, but the Dashwoods had no control over what Lucy Steele did next—they were just glad she was out of their lives, and eager to focus on matters they could control.

They turned onto the appointed street corner and spotted Edward in front of what appeared to be an empty storefront. He grinned and waved at them from afar, and Elinor's heart thudded in anticipation as they closed the space between them.

"Hello," she said. "Have you been waiting long?"

"Not at all!" Edward had the excitement of a small child on Christmas morning—he couldn't stop smiling, and he kept fidgeting. "Well, this is it! First impressions?"

He gestured toward the flaking paint in the windows announcing that the space they had come to inspect had once been a barbershop. It was narrow and inconspicuous, tucked in between a tailor's shop and a coffeehouse. It looked as though it'd been empty for a while, judging by the cobwebs inside, but that was nothing a good afternoon of work couldn't fix.

"I like the location," Elinor said. "It's convenient."

"The window is a good size," Marianne said, not quite approvingly but with more optimism than Elinor expected.

"Let's go in," he said, and produced a key to unlock the front door. It opened with a slight squeak and revealed an interior that smelled faintly of hair pomade and dust. A few broken crates lay splintered in the corner, but the walls were unscuffed and the floors would shine again with a good polish.

"A little on the small side," Marianne said, walking wide circles around the main room.

"Honestly, Marianne—"

"But, I can fit two desks and a cabinet in here, so I suppose it shall work."

Elinor looked to where Edward watched them in the door. He was grinning in a way that immediately made her suspicious. "What is that look about?" she asked.

"Look? What look? I'm merely pleased you like it."

"No, you look as though you've got another trick up your sleeve," Elinor countered.

"No tricks. Although, I'm glad to hear it will suit your needs. Here."

Then, Edward produced two more keys, identical to the one he'd used to open the door. He handed one to Marianne and then presented the other to Elinor.

"You leased it?" Elinor asked, her voice quiet. Edward looked so delighted with himself, but Elinor felt her spirits sink. When he had proposed a week after Lucy had been taken into custody that he invest his small trust into the Dashwoods' new investigative agency, Elinor had been flattered—and then worried. She hadn't wanted Edward to invest in their business merely because he felt sorry for them, but a tiny part of her was scared, too. What if they weren't successful and Edward was throwing away his inheritance? Their father had taken years to build up his clientele, and he was a gentleman! They were just two young ladies—two young ladies who'd been lauded as heroines in all the papers for catching their father's killer and an illegal opium dealer, but still two young ladies nonetheless.

And then there was Elinor's secret fear, which was unfounded but haunted her nonetheless: What if Edward invested but then refused to stay the silent partner he'd promised to be?

Signing a lease on an office space without consulting them was *not* the type of partnership that Elinor had agreed to.

When he saw her frown, Edward's face fell. "I know that you wanted to consult on the space, but I learned of it just yesterday, and I came to see it myself before telling you about it—I didn't want a repeat of the last tour."

Elinor winced at recalling the first place they'd inspected—a dank office near the docks, spotted with mold. "Well, this is certainly an improvement. . . ."

"When I saw this place, I knew it was perfect. But there was another offer on it, so I simply acted. I didn't want someone else to have it."

"How awfully opportunistic of you," Marianne declared, holding her skirts in one hand and spinning gracefully into the open space in her own odd way of measuring it. "I can do four turns, Elinor! And it's within the budget."

"How do you know that?" Elinor asked, but she was

distracted by Edward's hands on her shoulders.

"Elinor, you haven't even seen the best part yet."

Marianne skipped to a door leading to the back of the shop and swung it inward to reveal another room. "Oh! Brandon! Whatever are you doing here?"

Something in Marianne's voice alerted Elinor that this might be a setup. She turned to Edward. "What's going on?"

But Edward didn't even try to stifle his grin. "Go take a look!"

Elinor followed Marianne, Edward trailing behind her. When she entered the second room, she gasped.

It was the same size as the front, but at the center was a large worktable. A stove sat in the corner, and shelves lined one wall completely. A bank of windows high against the ceiling on the right side let in slanted light, but that wasn't the best part—the best part was the tangle of glass beakers, tubing, and other assorted laboratory equipment on the table.

"What is this?" she breathed.

"This," Edward said, "is to be your new laboratory. You need your own space, or else Hannah will put in her notice as protest. The front used to be a barbershop, but the owner used to make his own hair tonics back here. He was quite awful at it, apparently—his concoctions used to make his customers' hair fall out—but he agreed to leave some of his equipment here, and—"

"We asked Brandon to help set you up with your own

393

laboratory!" Marianne burst out.

"You were in on this?" Elinor asked, whirling on her sister.

"Come on, Elinor—do you really think that Edward would have leased an office space without our consent? He sent me a note last night explaining everything. I told him to snatch it up! This is everything I've ever wanted for us."

"But . . ." Elinor was still reeling from the fact that she'd been tricked. "I thought I was going to keep records for you."

"We can both keep records," Marianne said. "We'll develop an absolutely splendid filing system."

"How exactly do you propose I make money at chemistry?"

"If I may?" Brandon asked, cutting in between the sisters. "Continue with your studies. Experiment. Find your passion. You'll discover a way."

"But—"

"I think that you could be called upon as an expert witness every now and then," Edward said. "The secretary at Longbourn mentioned that the solicitors might have use for someone who can offer a scientific opinion on various chemicals and substances."

"And your last perfume wasn't *nearly* as bad as that first attempt," Marianne added.

"That first attempt saved your life," Elinor reminded her.

"As if I could ever forget!"

"And I'd be happy to assist in any way I can," Brandon said. "I've taken the liberty of bringing you some books."

Elinor itched to inspect them, but still she protested. "Perfumes will hardly bring in enough income to justify this space. I'm sorry, I just don't think this is very sensible."

Edward and Brandon looked to Marianne.

"Elinor," she said, grasping her sister by the shoulders. "You are the most sensible person I know. You plan for everything! You keep the books, and keep me in line, and tell me when I'm spending too much or charging too little, and I know I'll grit my teeth and endure it because I know you're right and I trust you. But I also know that you will sacrifice all of yourself if I let you, and I don't want that. Norland and Company was Father's project, and now mine, and you helped because I needed you, but if we are going into business together—the three of us—then something ought to be in it for you."

"Seeing my family happy and successful is all I want out of this," Elinor said, which was true—mostly. But looking around at this space, which could be hers, she found it was harder to deny that she wanted it.

"Is this because I once called your interest in chemistry dabbling?" Marianne asked. "Because if so, I am a wretched sister for ever saying that, and I command you to dream bigger."

"I don't—"

Edward, Marianne, and even Brandon were all looking at her very expectantly. Brandon smiled at her and nodded. Edward looked hopeful. And Marianne was . . . well, very bossy.

"Do you need to go over the business plan again?" she asked, and then turned to Edward. "She'll become convinced once she can figure out a way for it to make *sense*."

"If you refuse, I'll have to lug all of this equipment back ten blocks," Brandon added. "And I am not a packhorse."

"Mr. Brandon! Was that a joke?" Marianne asked, delight breaking across her face.

"Perhaps," he said. "But truly, that was a very heavy crate."

For a brief moment, Elinor was overwhelmed by the memory of Lucy Steele in those final moments of their confrontation, when Lucy revealed that she believed Elinor was too much of a coward to be a threat to her. Although Elinor didn't like to admit it, those words still needled her. She didn't want to be a coward. And besides, Marianne was so happy to arrange this surprise for her. But making her sister happy wasn't the only reason why Elinor was inclined to give in. Perhaps the bravest thing they could do was to pursue happiness in their own right. "All right!" she declared. "You all have already outwitted me, and I wouldn't want to put Mr. Brandon out."

"Yes!" Marianne grabbed Elinor and twirled her around in excitement, causing Elinor to laugh.

"Who ever heard of an investigator and chemist going into business?" she asked when they finally stopped spinning.

"Not I," said Edward, who took her arm as soon as Marianne released her. He stroked her knuckles and added, "But I think it sounds like a success in the making."

"Do you now?"

"I ran the numbers for you," he said. "I promise you'll be pleased with the margins."

Elinor bit her lip and bade her beating heart to calm itself, lest she start to feel faint. Who knew that Edward could be so attractive when speaking of numbers? "I trust you."

"Excellent!" Marianne said, and Elinor turned to see that she had taken Brandon's arm, causing him to give in to a rare smile. "Now, I was promised ices!"

And so the Dashwood sisters said goodbye to their new office space—just for now—and stepped out into the autumn sun, happier than they ever dared to imagine. Elinor wanted for nothing more in that moment, except for perhaps a bit of patience for their eventual success. But she decided to give it a prettier name and call it hope.

FINIS.

AUTHOR'S NOTE

Sense and Second-Degree Murder, like *Pride and Premeditation*, is set during the Regency era but takes some liberties with what may and may not have been proper for young ladies of the time. My version of Elinor and Marianne Dashwood as two young women interested in business beyond the drawing room allowed me to explore tensions that weren't exactly the topic of polite conversation.

Opium is at the center of this mystery, and while we understand its dangers now, not that many people were particularly concerned about the potential side effects of opium in the early nineteenth century. Most of Britain's opium supply came from Turkey or India (procured forcibly and violently by the East India Trading Company and the British government), although domestic efforts to produce opium were certainly underway. Opium was sold in a variety of different forms: tinctures, laudanum, and other proprietary mixes. It was also sold pure—or as pure as anyone claimed. In fact, many suppliers cut opium with poppy leaves and stalks, sand and gravel, egg whites, water, and other mixtures to increase profit. It was sold at chemists and pharmacies as well as stationery shops, general stores, and open-air markets. Even the poorest of the poor could afford it, and it sold well—there was no health care system in place, and for most of the population, opium was good for what ailed you and far more accessible than a doctor or surgeon.

Because it was seen as a part of everyday life, it took some time before the public began to realize that opium not only was highly addictive but could cause death. Thomas De Quincey's *Confessions of an English Opium-Eater* was published serially in *The London Magazine* in 1821, and it was a sensational piece of writing that exposed the public to the dangers of addiction and in part spurred more study and record keeping, eventually leading to reform that controlled production, sale, and use of dangerous substances.

Of course, all of that happened after the events of *Sense and Second-Degree Murder*. My story imagines the characters discovering an even more powerful substance—morphine. Morphine is an opium alkaloid, and it was actually discovered around 1804 in Germany by Friedrich Sertürner, but it would be some years before his work was acknowledged by the medical community. Therefore, I didn't think it was such a stretch to imagine that a young lady, curious about chemistry and the effects of certain chemicals on the body, would experiment with opium and discover that if you dissolve it in acid and neutralize it with ammonia, you get one of the most lethal (and at that time undetectable!) natural substances of the day.

Which leads me to another fascinating aspect of my

research: forensic science and the law. Death by poisoning was common in the nineteenth century, largely because the British government did nothing to regulate dangerous substances, and those substances were sold in varying qualities by people who had different educational backgrounds and weren't always aware of the dangers or simply did not care when a profit was to be made. Public health wasn't a priority either, so many poisonings were in fact accidental. (I've often marveled that humanity has survived at all, given what substances were once deemed safe for human consumption.) During this time period, the only way to determine if a person died by poisoning, and catch the poisoner, was for a doctor to examine the body for clues and learn as much as possible about the victim's last hours. Certain physical evidence could point doctors toward heavy-metal poisons such as arsenic, but organic-based poisons (from plants) were much subtler. Opium doesn't make a person violently ill, bloody the esophageal tract before death, or turn the skin and eyes different shades—it simply lulls people to sleep, and they stop breathing.

Many people got away with poisoning, and those who did get caught were often exceptionally stupid or were suspected only when they killed one too many times. Even then, there was the small matter of convincing the justice system that what the doctors observed was actually poisoning—courts were reluctant to believe the evidence given by doctors and scientists. A famous French poisoning case was tried in 1823 and the prosecutor, Jacques-Nicolas de Broë, passionately declared, "Bunglers that you are, don't use arsenic or any mineral poison; they leave traces; you will be found out. Use vegetable poisons; poison your fathers, poison your mothers, poison all your families, and their inheritance will be yours—fear nothing; you will go unpunished!"

While Sertürner was aware that a tiny amount had a great effect on the human body, it wouldn't be until after the invention and wider use of the hypodermic needle and syringe in the 1850s that morphine was used in medicine. Therefore, I thought that it might be the perfect drug for Lucy Steele to use against Eliza Williams and Mr. Dashwood. I fudged the timelines of actual historical discovery just a little bit in order for the mystery to come together, but all inaccuracies, intentional and otherwise, are completely my own.

ACKNOWLEDGMENTS

I drafted and revised *Sense and Second-Degree Murder* while sheltering in place during the COVID-19 pandemic, which was a unique challenge that I never could have foreseen. Therefore, it's only fitting that I thank my partner Tab London first, for being so supportive and patient while I wrote this book during so much uncertainty, and for not minding that I turned our dining room into my workspace.

Many thanks to my agent, Taylor Martindale Kean, for being such an enthusiastic reader and supporter of this series! Thanks also to the team at Full Circle Literary. I am eternally grateful to my editor, Claudia Gabel, for her keen editorial eye and for being willing to brainstorm wild plot ideas. Many thanks to Stephanie Guerdan, whose early feedback on the outline was so valuable, and to Louisa Currigan for her help in revisions.

The entire team at Harper has been so supportive and wonderful. Thank you to Anna Bernard, Sabrina Aballe, Shae McDaniel, Sona Vogel, Jessica Berg, Corina Lupp, and the many other people who work hard to bring books to shelves that

I don't have direct contact with. I am also in awe of Jess Phoenix and Filip Hodas, who outdid themselves in creating yet another gorgeous cover for this series. Thank you.

I am not sure I would have survived writing this book in the midst of a pandemic if not for my wonderful writer friends. Thank you to Monica Roe, Anna Drury Secino, Nora Shalaway Carpenter, Emma Kress, Melissa Baumgart, and my entire VCFA writing community. Thank you also to the wonderful 21ders for being a great debut support network for my first *and* second books—here's to many more novels from us all!

I am so thankful to all the readers, librarians, booksellers, and teachers who picked up *Pride and Premeditation*, shared photos and videos, and recommended it. I am so lucky that I get to keep writing books, and it's because of your support!

Finally, thank you to my family for cheering me on and believing in my work.